Trade Secret

Chris Cairns

1

SKYE NEWS 12/8. 11.35
news@skyenews.co.uk

Union Jacks and cheering crowds were the order of the day as Prince Charles and the Duchess of Cornwall visited The Isle of Skye Museum earlier today.

Despite disappointing weather, which made raincoats and umbrellas the order of the day, the royal couple delighted their fans with a walkabout.

Curator Brian Wilson was on hand to greet the royal couple and show them round the popular museum at Staffin, which has just benefited from a £1 million refurbishment.

In a surprise development, the prince wore a kilt. Indeed, kilts were the order of the day as Mr Wilson was similarly attired.

The royal couple were introduced to museum workers including guides, for whom dressing in period costume was the order of the day.

As the duchess made small talk about the weather to distressed-looking reception staff, the prince met guide Tom Scullion who was dressed as an 19th century blacksmith complete with mutton chop whiskers, leather apron, hammer and anvil.

'And what are you supposed to be?' asked the prince.

'Spiderman,' said Mr Scullion. 'What did you come as?'

Crowds, estimated by police to be in excess of 12, happily waited a little longer in the rain as her Royalness took the opportunity at the end of the visit to have a dump in the staff toilet.

Eventually the prince and duchess emerged and mingled with the devoted fans of the Royal Family and their carers.

Becky Lindhurst and her daughter Frittata from Beaconsfield are holidaying in Fort William and came especially to meet the royals.

'We got here last night and camped out down the road there,' said Mrs Lindhurst. 'But I wouldn't have missed it for the world. Charles shook my hand and said: 'Pleased to meet you'.'

Worth any 250-mile round trip and a night in a sleeping bag in the pissing rain, I'm sure we'd all agree.

Sue MacKenzie from Armadale said: 'They were absolutely wonderful. And the Duchess does not look like a horse at all.'

Tim Holdesworth and his wife Samantha from Newcastle were just passing when they saw the 'crowd' and stopped to see what was going on. Was he disappointed when he saw who it was?

'Aye. I was hoping it was going to be an accident or at least somebody off the telly,' he said. 'Can't stand that jug-eared bastard.'

Doyle hit 'send' and downed the rest of his pint.

The Isles Inn was still a bit cold, still had a faint whiff of all-purpose cleaner about it, but at least it was beginning to fill up. He'd been the only one in for elevenses. Now the lunchtime regulars were arriving, every blast of cool, breezy air from the open door doing nothing for the temperature in the pub as they pushed inside, flapping the drizzle from their jackets. At any other time of the year the big, open fire would have been lit but no-one was going to admit it was that cold. Not while there were tourists out there walking around in shorts and flip flops – tourists, presumably, from parts of the world where August was a month in summer.

Fat Murdo was his usual unwelcoming self. One of those barmen who is always too busy to actually serve drink, he was, an hour after opening, still engaged in vital logistical matters behind the bar and treating every order like an annoying interruption to his real work. Apart from stacking glasses and moving boxes of crisps from a to b, one of his first tasks had been to switch on the TV, tune it to BBC News 24 and put the sound on mute. In this way the Isles Inn, like a million other businesses across the country, believed itself to be plugged into the world beyond its doors – tuned to the pulsating beat of the information age. To a journalist the damn things were hypnotic and so Doyle sat with his back to it. Better to have the rest of the bar occasionally looking at the wall a few inches above his head than be glued to it himself.

He stretched his arm out on the table and stared at the empty pint glass in his hand. In his head the usual crowd of miseries began elbowing themselves into a bad tempered queue, but he hadn't had nearly enough drink to face them yet. He looked up, ready to test Murdo's patience with an outrageous request for another pint of 80/-, when Alex walked in and offered to get in a round. Scooby wasn't far behind and before long they were seated with their drinks and the bar menus Alex had brought for them to peruse – even though they each knew its contents off by heart.

'Well, here's to the end of another long day at the office,' said Doyle, raising his fresh pint.

'Cheers!' said Alex and Scooby as one.

The Isles Inn did it's best to attract the tourist trade. It had rooms to let, threw the occasional ceilidh and even had its bar done up like a Disney version of one of the island's old black houses with a stone base and thatch 'roof'. But it was the local trade it attracted which, in turn, attracted Doyle. There were bar restaurants in town where, if the decor didn't offend an islander's sensibilities, the prices certainly would. And there were pubs so spit and sawdust you felt out of place if you didn't own your own tractor. Somehow the Isles Inn managed to create an easy bridge between the working life of the island and its daily throng of visitors. Doyle was a visitor. Because that's what he told himself every morning.

Alex and Scooby, on the other hand, were definitely locals. Alex looked like Homer Simpson and sounded like Barry White but gave the impression she had long since stopped caring about either. She was a strange old bird who worked at a local travel agents – mostly, in Doyle's experience, remotely through her Blackberry. Scooby was a wiry young guy with the beginnings of an alky's shake. He was dressed either by his mother or the Salvation Army and nipped outside for a cigarette so often he had a permanent chill about him. Although obviously regulars, neither had ever spoken to each other before Doyle had dropped in. A week later (and Doyle took no little pleasure in appreciating his role in this) the three unlikely amigos were almost a daily fixture, sharing absolutely nothing in common but an appreciation of daytime drinking, good craic and the thought of being anywhere but Portree.

'Busy morning?' asked Alex in her usual deep rumble as Doyle closed his laptop and slipped it into the bag at his feet.

'Story about a couple living it large off the state,' he said dismissively. 'Nothing too taxing.'

'Sponging bastards,' said Scooby.

Scooby said this sort of thing a lot. He wasn't really Mr Angry but he was always ready to take someone else's point of view and give it the cab driver treatment. He liked things black and white though obviously not necessarily consistent; he didn't work and was undoubtedly no stranger to the tax payer's munificence himself.

Thus they settled into the first major topic of the day, taking time out from discussing the idle rich – and poor – to order lunch from the bar. Doyle's mobile went off as he started in on his pie, chips and beans and he was mildly surprised to see the number wasn't Bob's before he switched it off and put it in the bag next to his laptop.

The tide of lunchers washed in and then out an hour or so later, leaving the rock of Doyle and his two faithful companions behind. From a starting point of the welfare state their conversation ranged easily far and wide, with every round of drinks its passion growing in inverse relation to its rationality. By the time the Croatians walked into the bar, benefit cheats had led by a series of steps (which had seemed logical at the time) to whether or not another moon landing was a sensible use of NASA's resources. Doyle was half way through an impassioned pitch on behalf of a laser-guided shield to protect the planet against meteors and Romulans when he noticed he'd lost half his audience. Scooby was still gripped by the whole Bruce Willis-ness of it all but Alex had the unmistakable expression of someone not listening to the person they're looking at.

Doyle glanced up and saw a couple of newcomers at the bar. They were dressed in matching navy blue Hilfiger wind cheaters, matching pristine white Reebok trainers and had matching Olympus cameras slung over their shoulders. But it still took an effort to think of them as a pair. The angry-looking tall one had a pudding bowl haircut last seen on Moe from the Three Stooges and the face of a man just about to lose at arm wrestling. Curly, by comparison, was small, fat and bald with swimmy eyes and a mouth way too big for his head. They broke off from a low conversation in their own language as Murdo finally got round to delivering the coffees they had ordered. The wee guy thanked him in a distinctly Slavic accent.

'Croats,' whispered Alex. At least, that's what she meant to do, but she wasn't very good at whispers and the entire bar heard her. Moe stared in their direction, his brow, previously low enough, now down around his knees. Once they had moved to a small table a safe distance away, Doyle, ignoring Scooby's enquiry about life on other planets, asked Alex how she knew.

'I studied the language when I worked in Opatija before the Balkan wars,' she said. 'I might even know the dialect - Stovakian would be my guess. Anyway, they're definitely not Serbs. You would hear the word 'da' in between the conjugated verb and the infinitive if they were Serbs. But what they did, for example in the phrase … '

It was Scooby's fault really. As Alex continued her discourse on the nuances of Serbo-Croat, Doyle noticed him nodding in scholarly agreement. The guy wouldn't know the Balkans from a serious foot complaint and there he was looking like Melvyn Bragg agreeing with a particularly apposite observation on Strindberg. Doyle burst out laughing. Unfortunately laughter at that juncture could easily have been misinterpreted. And it was. Before

Doyle could explain to his friends what had gotten into him, Moe was walking purposefully towards their table.

'You are finding funny?' he demanded.

To which the answer should have been something along the lines of, 'Just a private joke … no offence intended … welcome to Scotland, by the way.' But Alex and Scooby had now caught the giggles and there was no way back for any of them.

Moe was struggling with control of another sort. 'You … not laugh!' he growled.

At which point Scooby leapt to his feet. 'Haw! We'll laugh at whatever we want,' he said. 'This is a free country, pal. You're no' in Croteland noo.'

Moe smiled and showed his teeth. It was like tarpaulin being dragged from a mass grave. He took a step closer to Scooby.

'Drazan!'

It came from Curly still seated across the pub. Moe – that is, Drazan – froze and his eyes narrowed, darting from Scooby to Alex and Doyle. The tarpaulin was slid back.

'You laugh,' he said. 'Go. You laugh.' And he turned back to his table.

'He was lucky,' said Scooby with a straight face as he re-took his seat. 'Ah'd a had the big ugly bastard.'

Doyle and Alex managed to hide their amusement. From being the group's dunce, Scooby clearly saw himself now as it's undoubted expert in the business of seeing off unwanted foreigners. He took centre stage and began regaling them with unlikely tales of previous acts of vaguely racist 'heroism'. Ten, maybe 15 minutes later, with Scooby still milking it, Doyle had a quick look to see if the Croats were paying them any attention but his eye was immediately drawn to another new arrival at the bar.

Flaming red hair in long, loose curls, ivory skin flushed a little pink at the cheeks and green eyes the highlights of a face the pre-Raphaelites could sue over for breach of copyright. Doyle had only been in town a little more than a week yet he was instantly convinced she must be an even more recent visitor. Surely, he told himself as he took in the slim figure, he would have noticed, even heard tell of her, before now. Yet tourists, he failed to reason, rarely arrive in Portree in tailored navy linen trouser suits – nor make a bee-line for Murdo at the bar, greet him as an old acquaintance and begin an earnest conversation.

Doyle drained almost half a pint in one and asked, through a stifled belch, if either of the other two wanted a refill. With no takers he moved to the side of the bar and began trying to sober himself up through sheer willpower. It was a demanding enough job for him to fail to notice Scooby heading off for a piss. Or, for that matter, Moe following him.

Two things happened in quick succession. First, Murdo turned and pointed to Doyle with a 'perhaps he can help you gesture' (for which Doyle instantly vowed he would owe him a lifetime of love and devotion) followed shortly by what sounded like a small family car hitting the back of the door to the Gents. Doyle hoped no-one else had heard it as he beamed and strode towards the redhead. But, even as she was opening her mouth to speak, Alex shouted at his back, 'It's Scooby!' It was a sign of just how drunk Doyle was that he paid more attention to Alex. One of the three amigos was in peril. Duty called.

'Hold that thought,' he said to the girl and turned towards the Gents.

The small family car had indeed been Scooby. He was gamely trying to get to his feet as Doyle managed to squeeze into the cramped toilet. The Croat was standing by the sink and the moment Doyle saw him he knew they had made an awful mistake. He had no weapon and was not poised, hands in fists or karate style, ready to strike. That was the problem.

Ordinary blokes like Doyle and Scooby who get into fights about as often as they have sex with lingerie models tend to go overboard on the angry alpha male routine. They roar a fair bit and wave their arms about in big, hopefully menacing gestures. And they talk – big, tough talk. All of it, as with its parallels in the animal kingdom, designed to avert an actual fight. Cats arch their backs, gorillas pound their chests and men walk around in circles trying to remember lines from *Lock Stock and Two Smoking Barrels*.

But not this guy. He had two opponents to face now (Scooby, encouraged enough by the reinforcements to be promising all manner of amputations and subsequent insertions) and he looked like he was waiting in the check out queue at Waitrose. He wasn't even making the mistake of being deliberately casual; he wasn't inspecting his nails or whistling. He just stood completely and utterly at ease, his scowl gone, a man in his element. Doyle almost wet himself there and then.

Suddenly, Scooby lunged at Moe and immediately doubled up in gasping pain. So tight was the space in there and so fast did the guy move that Doyle had no idea whether he'd used fist or foot. In the next instant Scooby was wheeled round and, like a battering ram, hurled at Doyle. Scooby's head caught Doyle in the midriff and he slammed into the back of the door. They slid to the floor and Doyle felt a shudder as Scooby was hit again. He looked up in time to see the light bulb over the sink quickly disappear behind the heel of a pristine white Reebok trainer.

Doyle came to as water rushed over his face and neck. He spluttered and shook his head only to crack it against the side of the toilet bowl he'd been rammed into. There was movement behind, angry words and then someone grabbed him. Doyle struggled until he recognised Murdo's voice.

'You're a' right, son,' he said. 'He's gone.'

Doyle tried to stand up on what felt like the rolling deck of a ship. Murdo moved in to help then promptly backed off as Doyle threw up over the floor. He made it to the sink and mirror, took a look – through his one functioning eye – of a nose probably broken and everything else covered in blood, snot and vomit. He threw up again, sank to his knees and hugged the sink, willing the world to stop spinning. Murdo moved aside and Doyle heard different footsteps carefully picking their way over the floor. A pair of navy linen trouser legs over smart tan court shoes moved into view and he felt a hand gently touch his shoulder.

'Dan? Dan Doyle?'

He raised his head and saw those gorgeous green eyes now filled with concern.

'Yeth,' he said. 'Hoo …?'

'Holly Thompson. I'm your boss. You're fired.'

2

'You're fired.'

'See? I told you,' said Doyle.

Pete Simpson, assistant editor of *The Sunday News*, was breathing heavily and, for once in his disingenuous life, not actually smiling. It was perhaps the first time in two years Doyle had been able to look at the smarmy bastard and not see his teeth. He'd certainly been giving him the full Tony Blair since Doyle had walked into the room five minutes earlier.

It was a Friday – these things always happen on a Friday – and Doyle had been working like crazy. Not his normal M.O. but then the previous few months had been far from normal. Hard work, he'd found, achieved two things: it limited the amount of spare time he had to think about what a twat he'd been and it offered, perhaps, maybe, stranger things have happened, you never know … a faint chance of keeping his job. So he was chasing up long shots, re-working agency copy, writing cheesy picture captions; he was the newsdesk's bitch. And they knew it. Just after 11am, his phone rang. An internal call from an extension number he didn't recognise.

'Come in Dan, take a seat,' said Pete after Doyle had finally found his way to an office on a floor of the building he'd never been on before. Pete sat at the far end of a long conference table and behind him a huge picture window afforded a view down river to London and Tower bridges, in between them HMS Belfast and the teetering stack of coins that is City Hall glinting in the sun. In the newsroom they had a graffiti level view of the main line into and out of Cannon Street station.

Pete was flanked by Doug somebody or other, one of the company lawyers Doyle had met a couple of times before, and a secretary who was studiously scribbling away at her note-taking – even though all anyone had said so far was, 'Come in Dan, take a seat.' A chair was already pulled out for him near the door. Doyle pushed it back in, walked the length of the table to where the other three were and sat next to Doug.

'By all means, of course,' said Pete with one of his warmest smiles in a 'now why didn't I think of that?' kind of way. Doug made an odd little noise and gave Doyle a chicken-like bob of the head.

'Dan. There's no easy way to say this,' began Pete. 'You know we've been fighting this thing for you. But I'm afraid we've gone as far as we can.'

'I think what you meant to say there Pete was 'You're fired'.'

'That's … ah, now Dan,' Pete's smile flickered and dimmed like it had a bad electrical connection. 'This is not easy for anyone here.'

'Samantha couldn't make it?'

'No, no. She's still in the States, as you know. At that conference. Of course, as editor, she would want to be able to talk to you personally at this time.'

'Why? She hasn't talked to me personally, as you tautologically put it, for months. She didn't talk to me personally when this thing went tits up – she didn't even personally order me to do it in the first place, as you well know.'

Doug cleared his throat and looked between Pete and the secretary. This was veering towards his territory and he was clearly uneasy. The secretary was there because she had to be – this was a dismissal and as such under employment law needed to be minuted. But he was obviously there to ensure the reason for the dismissal – as far as the record was concerned – remained as vague and non-actionable as possible.

'We have already covered this, Mr Doyle,' he said. 'The exact details of what may or may not have happened remain subject to a confidentiality agreement signed by all parties – including you.'

'Yes, thank you. I remember,' Doyle said tartly.

Actually, he had forgotten. Not that he'd signed the thing (that was just one of many occasions in the whole shameful saga he'd meekly allowed his arm to be twisted up his back), but that its terms were so strict as to exclude anyone else in the company not already in the small, exclusive loop who knew exactly what happened. So, what they should have done was take him aside before this and make sure he would play ball. But they hadn't and now he was sitting there, confidentiality agreement notwithstanding, a potential loose cannon in the company of a secretary making notes. No wonder they were queuing up outside, waiting to put the boot into this bunch of wankers.

'They' were the Press Complaints Commission, the House of Commons culture select committee and, quite possibly, the Crown Prosecution Service and the Met. Their beef was with illegal phone tapping and their strong suspicion was that *The Sunday News* had been party to rather a lot of it. For reasons he was fast forgetting, Doyle knew from first hand experience that it had.

'So Dan,' Pete cut in quickly. 'Like I said, I'm afraid we've come to the end of the road.'

'You mean I'm fired.'

He managed to sigh and smile at the same time. 'I mean the company, as you well know, have been looking at any way we could possibly find a solution that would involve you retaining your post. We are a good employer, Dan – our staff are not just any other resource.'

'We? Our? Since when were you in management, Pete? Or have I missed something? I know we don't see you down in the newsroom much these days. Is this your new office? You must be very proud.'

Pete smiled again – this one his remedial teacher trained to handle the tantrums of difficult children smile. 'I understand how you … must be … feeling …'

Doyle had raised his hand. 'Pete,' he said once he'd stopped. 'I can say with absolute confidence that, in so many ways, you understand fuck all.'

Since they were clearly going to take his job from him he saw no reason to continue with the niceties. But he wasn't daft enough to deliberately breach the terms of the confidentiality agreement. To do so would have been to kiss goodbye to their guilt money and ensure he ended up facing Doug here at some point in court.

'Last year,' he continued, 'the Wicked Witch of the North let it be known through another of her flying monkeys – not you obviously, Pete – that I was just about the luckiest hack in the world. Not only was I about to be handed a job that would make me the envy of my colleagues, but I was being given a heads up on what could have been a career-ending mistake should I make it – to wit, not accepting the job.'

'Funny, this didn't appear to be your recollection in our earlier discussions,' said Doug airily.

Doyle turned slowly and leaned into him. 'I was being a good boy, Dougie,' he said with some heat as the lawyer backed off as far as his chair would allow him. 'I was saying what you wanted me to say because I needed the paper's protection and I wanted to save my job. You haven't protected me and now you're taking my job. In the circumstances I think you should count yourself lucky I'm not dangling you by the ankles from that window.'

'Dan, Dan,' said Pete, himself now desperately glancing at the secretary who was having difficulty both keeping up and stopping herself from laughing. 'Let's calm down here. I think we all agree mistakes were made last year. But it's water under the bridge.' He paused … 'What's done is done,' … he continued his search for just the right phrase … 'We are where we are.'

Not really worth the wait. 'When you're quite finished stating the bleedin' obvious,' said Doyle. 'You don't need to worry. Your sordid little secret is safe with me. But tell me this, what's the deal?'

'Deal?'

'With the slavering media watchdogs outside. Come on, Pete, you don't expect me to believe this hasn't been cooked up in advance.'

More nervous glances at the secretary. Pete began another waffle – Doyle heard a 'you may think that, I couldn't possibly comment,' before Doug cut in.

'I think it would be in everyone's interests if Mr Doyle was assured that this course of action has been given, um, widespread approval.'

'In other words, don't look for allies elsewhere,' said Doyle. 'Or, as Pete here would probably put it, you're all singing from the same hymn sheet now.'

Doug nodded.

'But why?'

'Perhaps we can help you with that later,' said Doug. 'But you might begin by considering the electoral calendar.'

Doyle instantly felt even more of a twat. It was April and it was an election year. The government needed all the friends in the media it could get and this paper and its daily sister had been sitting on the fence for too long now.

'Can I at least take it I won't be jumped on by Plod the moment I walk out the front door with my sad little box of personal possessions under my arm?'

Doug quickly nodded as the secretary finished her note of the question, but said nothing. Doyle was the fall guy but he wasn't to fall that far. It made sense; the last thing *The Sunday News* would want was one of their reporters standing in a witness box with his hand on a Bible. It was, he knew, the only way the whole thing could have ended. Deniability had been at the heart of the paper's strategy right from the start. One of Doyle's many mistakes was that as he busied himself with maintaining the – ultimately fatal – distance between them and their phone hacker, the paper was carefully managing its distance from him. When the shit hit the fan he discovered he was the only one in the room.

'So, a good old 'by mutual consent' won't cut it – wouldn't constitute the required pound of flesh,' he said. 'I'm fired.'

'I don't think we need to get bogged down in the terminology here,' said Pete. 'What's important is that you understand we have run out of options.'

'OK,' said Doyle turning directly to the secretary. 'Let the record show that I resign. My choice. I've had enough and would like to leave the company for personal reasons. I'll even write the press release for you, should I merit one.'

'You can't resign,' said Doug. 'That option has already been removed. It's just a timing thing.'

'So I am fired. Effective some time in the last five minutes presumably.'

Pete said, 'Dan. We really don't have to – ,'

'Oh, go on, say it. You know you want to.'

Doyle stood in the fresh air, a few personal possessions under his arm. It was four months later and the air was considerably more fresh than before. His nose was also considerably more broken than before. But he was just as fired. The redhead was indeed his (ex) boss. His first hope – that it was a freak case of mistaken identity and that she was firing him from, say, a job in a bank he'd never had, proved as unfounded as it was desperate. She was from Skye News and he, it seems, no longer.

The wind pulled at the tops of the Scots pines looming over the tight little car park of the Portree Community Hospital as Doyle heaved his laptop bag over his shoulder with a wince and began limping up the access road. Moe had made the most of his time with him and Scooby before help had finally arrived – Murdo having decided calling the cops was his first priority. Scooby was still back there in A&E with a broken jaw while Doyle, apart from the nose which had been excruciatingly re-set, had 'escaped with severe bruising and minor lacerations' as the patently unsympathetic doctor had put it.

As he neared the top of the hill Doyle passed the angled glass front door to a medical centre and caught his reflection. This he had to see. He took a step closer and peered at it with his one good eye. A white plaster covered his nose and those minor lacerations were to his cheek and forehead. The sandy hair was matted over a swollen cut above one of the trendy pointy sideburns he thought went with his trendy pointy goatee. At first he thought it was a trick of the glass that he looked shorter than his usual 5' 11" but then he realised he was actually hunched up in discomfort. He pulled his shoulders back, stood tall, felt a rib crack and went back to the hunch.

A little further on he stopped by the railings overlooking the harbour. Just after 8pm and a dull, overcast highland evening was busy draining the life from everything it touched with its flat, grey light. Portree's douce little town centre had rarely looked less like the Las Vegas Strip. Doyle drew a deep breath and caught a heady mix of old chip fat from the harbour front and stale vomit from his ruined Hugo Boss suit. What he needed was to get back to his digs, have a shower, a fistful of ibuprofen and go to bed. What he wanted was a drink.

Half way down the hill he passed some cars parked on the corner outside the RBS. Muffled voices suddenly became louder as the passenger side door of a Subaru 4x4 opened. A guy he recognised from the A&E waiting room got out and stood on the pavement.

'But the doctor told you,' he heard a woman complain from inside the car before the guy simply closed the door and fell into step about 50 yards in front of Doyle. A minute later and they were both standing at the bar of MacNab's Inn.

Lit like an airport café with some tables and chairs to match, MacNab's also tried for the clubby feel with leather sofas in the corners. There was bare floor and also carpet, ye olde prints and flashing arcade games, posters for upcoming summer events and forgotton Christmas decorations above the bar. It even offered TV and music at the same time – both competing at full volume. This was a pub that was hedging its bets. Apart from the walking wounded at the bar, there was a bloke rhythmically donating money to a fruit machine by the door and a couple of tourists at a table putting a brave face on their choice of holiday.

As the other guy ordered, Doyle noticed he had a lot more than an injured arm. There were blood stains on his shirt collar from a nasty triple scratch to his cheek and his left hand was also gashed and covered in sticking plasters.

Doyle heaved himself onto a barstool with a grimace and the barmaid looked from him to the other guy and back again.

'He took my last Rollo,' said Doyle.

The man began fishing about in the pocket of his battered Barbour jacket, eventually bringing out a packet of antibiotics which he tried to read with his arm at full stretch.

'Here, allow me,' said Doyle. He took the packet, removed the leaflet inside and read. 'You're OK. Nothing about avoiding alcohol.'

'Too late anyway.' And with that the guy drained almost his entire pint.

He was big. The hands were like a goalie's with his gloves on and he had a kind of woody, outdoor scent about him. Doyle's guess was an estate worker, a forester perhaps. He must have been in a fair few scrapes and injured himself before but this was clearly different.

'Hard day at the office?' asked Doyle.

'Aye,' he said staring ahead.

'I got beaten up by a Croatian. You?'

He turned and glared at Doyle. 'It was a pine marten, OK?'

It was obviously the umpteenth time he'd said this in the last hour. It was also obviously a lie.

'No, I just meant – ,'

'You're from Glasgow, eh?' he said, looking Doyle up and down. 'Are all Weegie's this nosey?'

Doyle suddenly became even more aware of the man's bulk. He'd had enough grief in pubs for one day and he couldn't care less if the horny big teuchter had been trying to shag his sheep dog. He waved an apology at him and took his pint to the far side of the bar.

Skye. Back of beyond and still thick with lunatics. What the hell was he doing here?

With no immediate answer to hand, he lifted his drink and beckoned oblivion take him away.

3

Ron Nutt read the final page, closed the file and looked up, a mixture of dismay and hope in his eyes.

'You're sure?'

For five minutes she'd been looking at the shiny white bald patch on the top of his head, 'pensive yet confident' at all times with occasional moments of 'understanding sympathy'. Now Chloe Carew switched to 'mummy knows best' – but she'd keep it at about 60 per cent; this guy was old school, he would only take so much.

'I'm sure, Ron,' she said softly. 'You've got to focus and you've got to prioritise. The survival of Nutts is all you have to think about just now. And that means making some hard decisions.'

'But this ...' Ron picked up the file and put it down. 'This is not how we've ever done things here. We've always taken people with us. We're a family business, and our staff – ,'

' – are our family. Yes, Ron, you've said. But even families change from time to time. People need to be allowed to grow, Ron, spread their wings. Mothers must sometimes let chicks fly the nest.'

Ron looked at the ceiling, obviously trying to work out the parallels between the life cycle of a sparrow and making two thirds of his workforce redundant at a stroke. She needed to get in quick.

'Look, you remember the five golden rules,' said Chloe briskly. 'You've got to identify your winners and losers,' she began counting off on her fingers, 'get onto your front foot, play to your strengths, keep it lean and sell for all your worth.'

'Yes,' he said unhappily. 'Yes, I do.'

'Your grandfather and father created this marvellous company in a completely different era, Ron. Times have changed and, well, you know what I say …'

'Go with the flow or off you go,' mumbled Ron by rote.

Chloe smiled her 'my work here is done' smile. 'That's it,' she said standing up. 'Be a winner, Ron. Make Nutts a winner!'

He stood and they shook hands.

'Cut! Thanks guys.' Marcus, the director walked out from behind the camera. 'Excellent Chloe, really good. Now all we need are a few noddies from you both and, Ron, then we'll be out of your hair.'

Ron sat down again on his 1970s black leather chair behind his 1990s beech veneer desk. Damp patches began to show under each arm of his 1980s grey and white, two-tone shirt. 'Misha, darling. Could you?' said Marcus waving at them. One of the production assistants bustled over, lifted Ron's arms and began drying him off with towels and a small hand-held fan.

'Continuity,' she said to an alarmed looking Ron. A consideration that did not extend to Chloe's appearance. When you're approaching the wrong end of your fifties, 5ft 2in in heels and only thrust into the media spotlight after a lifetime of resigned comfort eating, getting the most out of your appearance was almost a full time job in itself. By the time she was asked for a few moments of nodding, smiling and placing her head in positions of 'you have my undivided attention', Chloe had applied another coat of everything to everything from the neck up.

They left a dazed Ron Nutt in his office overlooking the factory floor and made their way down the free-standing staircase with the cacophony from more than a dozen lathes, drills and pressing machines filling the air.

'You think he'll go with it?' yelled Marcus.

'Not a chance,' shouted Chloe, ignoring the signs all around her and sparking up a cigarette. 'He'll bottle it and this place'll go tits up.'

'Problem?'

Chloe stopped and took a drag. 'No ... no, I don't think so. We can't keep having success stories can we? It'll be good to show the consequences of not doing what I say from time to time. Now if he took the prescription and the business still folded – that would be a problem. But he won't. I know the type.'

They walked on between the huge machines. Operators swung articulated gibbets back and forth, turned wheels, pulled levers and generally did their best to look like a time and motion man's wet dream – just as they'd done every time she'd walked by over the last two months. Morons. Some of them, she'd been told, were making things called self-tapping screws, others countersunk nib bolts, flange nuts, dome nuts, blind rivets, cold rivets, groove pins and a million other arcane bits of junk that no doubt had DIY pervs beating off over copies of the Screwfix catalogue in their garden sheds. That, she reflected on not for the first time, was the calibre of the enterprising, free-thinking DNA running through the Nutt family ... 'Hey, I know. We're called Nutt – let's make nuts!' Presumably so they'd have to spend less energy remembering who they were or what they did.

'OK, Chloe. Just a quick wrap up, if you will,' said Marcus as the crew stepped out into bright sunlight. 'Usual drill.'

A few minutes (mostly spent in front of her compact) later, Chloe was walking slowly towards a retreating cameraman with a stabilised hand held camera down somewhere around his knees.

'Ron's situation is no different to a thousand other CEOs of small businesses up and down the country,' she said, moving her arms in best Fiona Bruce fashion. 'The British manufacturing base is growing once more but that doesn't mean it's a free for all. Only the leanest, fittest companies will survive and grow. Nutts is a fine old company making vital components the rest of industry depend upon. But they're not the only ones. It's not called a competitive market for nothing; there will be winners and losers.'

Close up.

'We'll be back in six months to see if Ron – and Nutts – have got what it takes to be among the winners.'

Step into car. Drive off.

Marcus waved a thumbs up and the driver stopped, backed up a few yards. Chloe got out, snatched her lit cigarette from a runner and took a final, long drag.

'Triffic, Chloe,' said Marcus. 'Next week at the studio?'

'OK, see you then.' Chloe twisted the cigarette into the road and disappeared once more into the back of the Bentley which sped off. In here it was all cool cream and burr walnut. The air conditioning smelled of apple blossom and the only sounds were the hum of the engine and two or three clinks as Adam poured a flute of Paul Goerg from the freshly opened bottle.

'Thank you, Adam. You are a darling.' She took the glass by the stem, gave the Northfleet Industrial Estate in Dartford a final glance through the window and drank deeply. Then she burped loud and long. 'Christ, what a tosser! Honestly, I sometimes think this lark can't be doing my reputation any good at all. Ron Nutt a winner? Who the hell am I kidding? He's over priced, over staffed and leveraged up to his eyeballs. His product line is out of date, he … '

Chloe continued in like vein for a full minute. It had been a long summer filming schedule and her frustration at having to deal with so many imbeciles had been building steadily. Adam scrolled up and down the iPad and allowed her to vent. He was patient and understanding and neither of those were among the reasons she'd hired him. When she'd run out of steam, he refreshed her glass.

'We have a problem,' he said matter of factly. His confidence was one of the reasons she'd hired him; he never looked concerned about the chances of Chloe confusing the message with the messenger. She suspected the moment she did, he would be off.

'Oh good, just what I need.'

'We've been contacted by a private investigator, one Dick Collins.'

'A nut maker called Nutt and now a private dick called Dick? Brilliant.' Chloe kicked off her heels and settled back in the traditionally tanned, hand stitched leather seat. 'And what did Dick want.'

'He wanted to tell us that those rumours of phone hacking by *The Sunday News* a few months ago were in fact on the money. He also wanted to tell us that the operations were not, as speculation would have it, restricted to soap stars, England's left back and the Chairman of the 1922 Committee. He wanted to tell us that he knows this because he's the hacker.'

Chloe was slowly pushing herself back up the seat.

'And he also wanted to tell us that he is willing to sell us the tapes of messages left on your phone.'

4

Doyle lay on his back and wished he was dead. Not in a 'the world's out to get me, what's the point in carrying on', kind of way. It was just that he was clearly dying anyway and he'd rather he got on with it. The complaints coming in from every inch of his body were loud and demanding. He felt like a general in charge of a calamitous campaign hearing reports from all fronts to the effect that they were more or less fucked. He would've gone back to sleep – or whatever state of unconsciousness he'd just emerged from – but it had been his swollen bladder that had dragged him out of it and it was not about to let him return. For a moment, he seriously considered simply wetting himself. How, he wondered, could that have made his situation any worse? He was going to die soon anyway and the moment he breathed his last sour breath that sphincter was going to blow like a Texan gusher. May as well do it now and at least pass from this life in something less than total agony. But he didn't. Instead he just lay there and waited for death. And waited. And waited … Nope. Looks like he was going to have to get up and piss after all.

But moving, every fibre of his being told him, would be a bad idea. His insides felt like they were busy quashing rebellion, his brain was dangling by a single thread inside his head and his limbs felt numb and lifeless. One other problem – he hadn't a clue were he was.

Shifting only his one good eye – and even that hurt – he could see the ceiling was white wood chip, the walls blue. The Chinese lampshade above his head was almost brown with age and nicotine and daylight was slanting in through filthy curtains off to the right. There was an airless, sickly sweet mustiness to the room but Doyle had to admit he was probably partly responsible for that. The bed he lay on (fully clothed, thank God) was so soft the mattress was almost enveloping him, like he was being held in a large mitten. It would've been hard work getting out of there even fully fit. But the howl of nature was getting ever louder and he could postpone the effort no longer. Slowly does it, he told himself. No sudden moves – let's take this nice and easy. After a quick final check he decided on the safest preliminary move. He wiggled his big toe.

And all hell broke loose.

Doyle wailed as a noise like a riot in a Tibetan monastery crashed over and through his head. He squirmed on the bed and the noise grew in intensity.

'Ah-aaahh!'

A door somewhere clattered open and a pair of monstrously enlarged eyes appeared over the horizon of the mattress. They stared, dark and intense from behind a pair of thick, greasy spectacles, a mixture of fear, confusion and latent violence in their expression. Doyle writhed helplessly like a fly in a carnivorous plant, caught in the warm, sticky embrace of its death bed. Slowly, a lean, muscular frame moved over Doyle as the cacophony grew but he was hypnotised by the eyes, the unblinking, magnified eyes. And then the expression changed; the clouds of confusion lifted and a calmness eased itself into place. But it was the calmness of resolution; the eyes had decided upon a course of action. In that instant, a large machete came into view.

Doyle screamed again and the eyes darkened once more. They caught the direction of Doyle's frantic stare and followed it to the rusty blade. They blinked, a large, slow motion blink and then the man straightened up.

'Sorry, man.' He moved to the foot of the bed, Doyle felt a tug on his foot and the clamouring immediately ceased. 'Just making sure you were alive.'

Doyle was panting and a cold sweat prickled his body and made him cling to the inside of his shirt. He heaved himself onto one elbow and looked down the bed. His right shoe and sock were off and a length of string was tied to his big toe. This, until recently, had run over the propped open edge of a wardrobe door, hanging from which was the biggest set of wind chimes he'd ever seen. You could've called in the five thousand for lunch with them.

'Where am I, who are you and what's with the fucking wind chimes,' is what Doyle meant to say. But his mouth felt like he'd been eating cat litter all night and what came out was, 'Whey ah … hoo ah, oooh a' whathaa fa' in win' cha?'

'My place, Norrie and, like I said, I needed to know if you were a' right,' he said, displaying unbelievable powers of comprehension. 'You weren't movin', hardly breathin'. I figured …' he tailed off and frowned for a bit then broke into a yellow, gap-toothed grin. 'Not sure what I figured, to be honest. 'Spose I was pretty out of it an' a'.' And he laughed a high-pitched laugh like it was the funniest thing he'd ever heard in his life.

Now that he'd started, Doyle saw the need to just keep moving. Getting out of the bed was like getting out of a swimming pool without using the ladders but eventually he stood unsteadily on the floor, one shoe on, one foot bare.

'Bog,' he rasped. Norrie led him into the hall and, even as he pointed to a door opposite, Doyle was through it.

Ten minutes later, he was following rustling and clinking sounds down the hall. He found Norrie in a neat enough but threadbare kitchen diner clearing up from one hell of a party. With a black bin liner in one hand, he was moving from table to counter top to carpet, emptying ashtrays (being careful to salvage the usable remnants of many spliffs) and chucking in empty cans and bottles. Doyle found a stained beer glass upside down on the draining board pretending it had been washed. He rinsed it out, filled it with cold water and drank deeply. It was like the first rains of the season landing on a dry river bed. Doyle stood for a long moment feeling his internal organs rehydrate. Then he turned back to Norrie.

'Looks like it was some do. Many folk?'

Norrie laughed. 'Naw. Just you.'

Doyle would've argued but since he felt exactly like a person would who had consumed that amount of beer and smoked that number of joints, and since he couldn't remember a damn thing about the previous night he decided not to bother. He stood in a rumpled and stained suit with one bare foot, looking like he'd lost an argument with a threshing machine and realised he didn't actually know what to say or do next. Apart from being this guy

Norrie's guest, he didn't know where – the curtains were still drawn. For want of anything better to do, he checked his watch. 1.20. He remembered the earlier part of the day before so he knew he wasn't late for work. Not any more.

'Um … eh, thanks.'

'What for?' Norrie didn't look up from his labours.

'You know, the, eh, drink … the bed … the dope.'

Norrie straightened up, amusement again in those bug eyes. 'That was yours, man. And good shit it was too. I should be thanking you.'

'What?' asked Doyle.

'What?' asked Norrie.

'Wha – , I mean … ' Doyle ran a hand through his hair. 'Mine?'

'Aye. Lebanese hashish. That's rare stuff.'

'I, eh … ' Doyle closed his eyes and, ignoring the grinding noise it was making in his head, concentrated as hard as he could. It was one thing having a black out – this wasn't his first in the last few months – but the worst he ever found out the next morning was that he'd made an arse of himself with some girl or been barred from a nightclub. Not that he'd turned into a minor drugs baron. He had scored dope years before – but only once and only by accident; he thought the guy on the corner outside the White Hart in Fulham had copies of the Big Issue inside his coat, not one ounce bags.

'So, did I get it at the pub?'

'Man, you really were out of it, weren't you?' Norrie grinned. 'Naw, you had it already. Still do – check it out.' And he looked meaningfully at Doyle's jacket. Doyle put his hand in his pocket and brought out a rolled up freezer bag. Inside was a still considerable lump of yellowish resin and on the side a white label. In blue biro and an uncertain hand it said: 200g Lebanese blond (Zahret el Kolch).

'You sure?' he said, turning it over in his hand. 'I'm not really that much into this.'

'Well, you must've spent the thick end of 300 quid on that lot, man. I'd hate to see what you are into,' and Norrie was off on another high laugh.

'You want it?' asked Doyle.

'Cannae afford it,' said Norrie returning to the clear up. 'Haven't got 30 quid never mind 300.'

'For the bed and the beer,' and Doyle placed it on the kitchen table.

It took some time to bat away Norrie's protestations and claims of unworthiness but eventually he managed it, securing a cup of tea in the process. As he sat nursing the cup, Norrie filled him in as best he could on the night before. There wasn't much to say (when is there ever about a drug-fuelled piss up?). Norrie had been the guy at the fruit machine when Doyle had walked into MacNab's. They fell into each other's company, saw eye to blood-shot eye almost immediately and, not in a romantic way, Norrie unnecessarily pointed out, one thing led to another. He was adamant Doyle had struck no deals with shifty young men in leisure wear and jewellery at any stage of the evening.

The curtains were pulled back to reveal a neat little cul de sac of bungalows, most of them run as B&Bs. They were north of Portree, somewhere off the Staffin Road, he was told. Even from the inside, Doyle could tell Norrie's place was letting the neighbourhood down badly.

'I should be going,' he said, creaking back onto his feet.

'Me too,' said Norrie, picking up the machete. 'Got to make it look like I've been at the roddies all day.'

'Roddies?'

'Rhododendrons.' Norrie pointed at the Wildlife Conservation Trust logo on his sweatshirt. 'Alien scum. Worse than the English.'

It took half an hour to get back to his flat in Portree, another hour to shower, and the rest of that day to doze on the couch in front of the TV. By the next morning, the sweats were over, he'd managed to hold down a bowl of Crunchy Nut Clusters and he no longer believed everyone on BBC News 24 was out to get him. He could also see out of both eyes again, although the right one was black, swollen and shiny, like a fake keeker from a joke shop.

He stepped out into another wet day in August, but at least a little warmer. His flat was in York Drive, just behind what passes for Portree's beating heart, Somerled Square – home to the Isles Inn, among other bars and cafés. By London standards, the commute from his flat in Clapham to *The Sunday News* had been an envious one – half a mile to the tube, Northern Line to Monument, Circle or District to Cannon St and then he was only a block away from the office. On a good day, maybe under an hour. Today, Doyle turned right, away from the square, and took Stormy Hill a few paces down onto Sraid a' Bhanca. This he crossed and climbed the stairs between Cuillin Crafts and the Carmina Gadelica bookshop to the offices of Skye News. A two-minute walk. At least now he was free from the need to invent an excuse for being late every day.

There was no receptionist and that was only partly because there was no reception area. The budget didn't stretch to either luxury. And so Doyle walked through the cheap laminate door straight into what Bob insisted on calling the news room. It had two desks straining under the weight of second hand computers so big they made the room darker. On a table by the window was a kettle and the fixings for tea and coffee. Between those, a couch, two filing cabinets and a sloping ceiling, it would have been snug for a dwarf. Bob Miller, however, was an old prop forward from Bath who'd seen no reason why retiring from the game should affect his consumption of pies. He sat wedged in behind his desk in the corner like a beach ball in a shoe box.

'Marnin',' said Doyle in the comedy yokel accent he knew annoyed Bob. 'What's a' doin' moi lovely?'

Bob, who'd looked up as Doyle came in, returned to scanning the copy of *The West Highland Free Press* on his desk. 'You're either the cheekiest bugger on the planet or you've blacked out again and forgotten what happened on Monday.'

Doyle peered round the other computer monitor. 'The enforcer not in today? Now I know what they mean about fiery red heads. Fire-y, geddit?'

'Ever the wordsmith, Dan. No, Holly is not in. She's up in Staffin at the Isle of Skye Museum. She's spending several hours there trying to find enough material for a feature we've promised the curator we will have in at least three publications north of the Highland line before the month's out, thus dissuading him from leading a local tourist industry boycott of Skye News – an agency so inept it lost the report it had on a visit by the heir to the throne. I decided on the technological cock-up version, Dan, rather than the one about the reporter who couldn't be arsed taking the job seriously. It wasn't an easy decision but just another one of those things we grown ups have to do every now and then to get through the working day.'

Bob looked back at his paper for a few seconds and then back at Doyle. 'And yes, I appreciate you coming in here to allow me to say all that. You look like shit, by the way.'

'Compared to how I felt yesterday I'm the bionic man,' said Doyle, sitting at the free desk. He waited an appropriate amount of time before saying, 'Sorry, Bob.'

'I know you are. Your heart's usually in the right place, Dan. The problem these days is working out where the hell your head is.'

'Well, I think we know it's not doing royal visits and fish prices.'

'We won't go over all that again. It was a gamble. It didn't work – let's leave it at that. I take it you're off back to London.'

'Probably.' Doyle ruffled through some papers on the desk. After a moment or two, he said, 'Well, since you're not volunteering the info, can I ask the obvious question? Who the hell is Holly Thompson?'

Bob shook his jowly head. 'I read an article once about how everything – every last piece of information you hear, see, smell or feel is stored in your memory somewhere, whether you were consciously aware of it at the time or not. Our brains are like powerful recording devices that store every single experience of our entire lives. The trick is being able to access it.'

'Don't tell me I've missed the start of Cake and Bun Magazine''s cognitive science series. Damn.'

'Point is I told you who Holly was, when she would be coming back and what she would be doing. You just weren't listening, but the information is all inside that thick head of yours somewhere.'

'No, you told me about someone you had to run the office. Some girl that organised the diary, dealt with the accounts, got the … ah, got the place … ' He tailed off. 'Ah.'

'Exactly. I never took you for a sexist Dan. Thought it was some secretary, didn't you?'

'OK, I got the wrong end of the stick. But you talk that much Bob, a person can't be expected to listen all the time. So, at the risk of repeating myself, who is she?'

'She is – was – your boss. Editor of Skye News.'

'And?'

'And why should you care? You've been here all of one week – less time than she's been on leave.' Bob sighed. 'She's a journalist, Dan. A fully qualified journalist with six years' experience in local and regional news. She has everything she needs to run this place properly, may be even take it forward, grow the business.'

Doyle detected more than a little defensiveness there.

'I'm sure she's Pulitzer material, Bob, but you know what I'm asking. This is your agency. You bought it out, what, seven years ago? Last time I looked you were the managing editor, chief reporter and pie monitor. You let me help you out – ,' Bob arched his eyebrows. 'OK, well that was the idea. But surely that's all you need. Somebody just a teensy bit more reliable than me.'

'It's not as simple as that.' Bob looked back at the paper on his desk.

Doyle waited just a few seconds. 'Look, we both know you're going to tell me sooner or later. You're too much of a blether.'

'She's my daughter.'

Doyle was flabbergasted, and he looked it.

'Did I not mention I had one before?' asked Bob, awkwardly.

'You said you'd sown a wild oat or two but of course I didn't believe you,' Doyle now broke into a huge grin. 'Bloody hell, Bob!' he said, getting up to shake his hand.

'What's all this?'

'You, you sly old dog. You must have hit the jackpot.'

'What?'

'Come on, Bob. Even with half her gene pool coming from you she still looks like that? Her mother must have been a total shag.'

Bob screwed his eyes shut. 'Have you any idea of how inappropriate and hurtful that is – on so many levels?'

Doyle grinned some more. 'So, you're starting you're very own media dynasty. Good for you. But tell me – she's running the office, paying the bills, doing the leg work. What's up with you?'

'Funny you should ask.'

5

At 6am on 19 April 1882, William Ivory, Sheriff of Inverness, approached The Braes crofting township at the foot of Ben Lee on horseback. In his saddle bag he carried warrants for the arrest of five ringleaders of an attack on his officer, Angus Martin, two weeks earlier. Martin had come armed with eviction summonses for the same five men. Not only did Martin fail in evicting the men, but the summonses had been burned in front of him by the crowd of angry crofters who'd gathered to defend them. The men's 'crime' had been to organise a boycott of rents due to Lord MacDonald and agitate for the return of common ownership of grazing land – something The Braes and hundreds of other communities across the Highlands had lost during the Clearances.

Ivory was not about to make the same mistake as his underling, however, and he did not approach with just a handful of men. He came with 50 Glasgow police officers armed with truncheons. The five were taken but as word of the action spread, 300 Braes men and women descended on the sheriff's party and a pitch battle ensued. A volley of rocks was launched at the police who replied with baton charges and beatings. The casualties mounted and horrific injuries were suffered on both sides though, miraculously, no-one was killed.

Eventually, with one concentrated charge, the police broke free and escorted Ivory and his prisoners north to Portree.

The men were tried without a jury and, to no-one's great surprise, found guilty and imprisoned. But word of 'The Battle of the Braes' spread and sympathy grew for the men and their struggle. Similar actions took place across Skye and the north west of Scotland – at one point necessitating the sending of a government emissary on board a Royal Navy gunboat to the island to sue for peace. Slowly, the tide began to turn the crofters' way. The Battle of the Braes may have been lost but the war was eventually won when, in 1886, Gladstone passed The Crofters Act, giving every crofter in the country security of tenure.

Lands of myth and legend do not have a cut-off point. Just as history unrolls relentlessly, so the stories used to explain and embellish events in places like Skye never cease to be spun and re-spun. The so-called Battle of the Braes was named by the press, not military historians, and the boast, often heard in island pubs to this day, is that it was the last ever true battle on British soil.

This is, of course, total nonsense, as anyone who's seen footage of the 1980 Old Firm Cup Final (coincidentally also involving Glasgow cops and truncheons) will testify.

There aren't many obvious similarities between London and Skye but the criteria for choosing a car would have to be one of them. Nothing to do with the familiarly high proportion of 4x4s, albeit that folk up here had the strange habit of taking the things off road occasionally. No, it was all about risk. Why have a new car with paintwork to worry about on bumper to bumper streets where on-coming traffic is treated like the opponent in a medieval joust? Equally, thought Doyle as he ducked and weaved his way round last winter's still unrepaired pot holes on what purported to be the main road from Portree, why own a car on Skye with wheels you were particularly fond of? His ten-year-old Saab 900 carried the scars of a thousand tournaments in South London and had never been washed by anything but rain since he'd bought it. But its tatty exterior hid another reason for owning a 900. Not knowing a dipstick from a pre-dinner nibble, Doyle appreciated a car that considered its first 180,000 miles as little more than a run-in for an engine he would never have to locate, let alone fix.

Less than two miles from town, he took a hard left down a track that crossed a river, took another left through a scattering of crofts and eventually parked up off the side of the road in a place called Penifiler. He locked the car and took the path over Vriskaig Point and down towards the black sands of Camas Ban. The rain had stopped but the fern he pushed through was still dripping and he was soaked by the time he reached the shore. Following the sheep tracks at the far end of the bay, he climbed behind the crags and up onto the slopes of Ben Tianavaig, a strengthening westerly tugging at his wet trouser legs. Close to the edge of the cliffs, he concentrated on every step as he skirted round old ruins and eventually reached the summit.

As the day's weather continued to improve, shafts of sunlight split the clouds like searchlights, here picking out a small freighter heading north up the Sound of Sleat, there a flank of hillside above Applecross over on the mainland. The crags he stood on could now be seen as part of a massive geological feature running up the eastern seaboard of the island, north over Loch Portree and the Sound of Raasay all the way to distant Trotternish. Doyle untied the arms of the waterproof he had wrapped around his waist, laid it on a flattish rock and sat looking out across the sound.

Introspection was not one of Doyle's strengths, as more than one old girlfriend had opined. Yet it seemed to him he'd done a fair amount of it recently – albeit usually through the bottom of a pint glass or over the rim of a toilet. So he wasn't there to stare at the scenery and ask himself where it had all gone wrong. Been there, done that. But he did think about Bob.

Things had been getting out of hand in London. The lack of prosecution only fuelled the media frenzy surrounding the hacking allegations and Doyle found himself at bay – suddenly a fox being hunted by his erstwhile colleagues in the pack. He needed to get out of town and Bob Miller took his call when many others wouldn't have. As it happened, at least for a short time, Bob needed an extra pair of hands and Doyle, virtually unemployable anywhere else, agreed to fill in.

They'd met and worked together at the daily *County Post* in Bristol, Doyle's first job after graduating. Bob was the old hand, the paper's chief reporter with an encyclopaedic knowledge of the region and 14 years' experience under his already expanding belt. Doyle was a brash young know-it-all with qualifications he thought made him an expert. He arrived like a signing coup from the continent, swearing allegiance to the world famous Breestole Roveurs while already planning his next transfer to a Premiership club. Doyle's destiny was the nationals in London and if an apprenticeship in the provinces was absolutely necessary then he was determined it would be as short as possible.

Surprisingly for both men, they hit it off. Doyle, who knew his best chance of making a quick getaway was to be hard-working and willing, found in Bob a man who shared his idea of what constituted a news story. Bob, surrounded for so long by jaded has-beens and functioning illiterates from the local sixth form colleges, was caught up in the younger man's enthusiasm for the job. Doyle gave Bob a professional second wind. Bob gave Doyle the benefit of his experience and, after much nagging, introductions to all the local stringers and staffers for the London nationals. Their paths inevitably diverged soon afterwards but they'd remained in touch – a bottle of Talisker the usual casualty of their occasional reunions.

Doyle stood and walked a little closer to the edge of the crags. Waves crashed onto the rocks 1,000ft below but even this high up he could taste the tang of salt in the air. He put his hands in his pockets and lifted his gaze again to the mainland.

A day earlier he'd have put this thought down to his marijuana hangover, but it did seem to him now that events were, if not exactly conspiring, certainly following a definite pattern. The screw up in London and his need to escape, the gig at Skye News, everything that had happened to him (or he'd let happen) since he'd arrived on the island and now Bob's news; colon cancer with a fighting chance but months of chemotherapy the price to be paid. Doyle didn't ponder the possibility of his friend not surviving – that was an indulgence for another day, hopefully many months from now, if at all. But he knew that what would have been his natural response – crack an unsuitable joke, wish Bob a breezy 'all the best' and then bugger off to pretend it wasn't happening – wouldn't cut it this time. Why?

Despite it smelling awfully like introspection after all, Doyle knew the answer was in himself as much as the events and coincidences that had led him to this point. He was no longer the young guy who'd walked into the offices of the *County Post* all those years ago, sparky with enthusiasm and ambition. The ambition had long since hijacked his enthusiasm and claimed it for itself, eventually leading him to ruin. And, at 36, he was beginning to stretch the definition of 'young' to an embarrassing degree. He would have dearly wished this point of self-awareness to have happened somewhere other than on Skye, but he wasn't given the choice.

He picked up his jacket and turned west to take a different route back off the hill. As he did so he caught sight of the landscape below and a series of connections went off in his head. There was the hamlet of Camastianavaig nestling at the head of tiny Tianavaig Bay and, just beyond, The Braes below Ben Lee. Somewhere down there, he'd been told, was a cairn marking the spot where 300 men and women who'd lost a wee bit more than a flash job and an expense account, who'd actually nothing left to lose but their liberty, made a stand against what hippies would later call The Man. It was a lesson in reality, in responsibility, courage and defiance. And Doyle shook his head, irked at the world for taking another opportunity to lay it on thick.

Fat Murdo's jowly face wore an expression of unenthusiastic anticipation, like a food poisoning victim trying to decide between a shit and a boak. He was, in fact, trying to remember something, but taxing his mental capacities to this extent was clearly taking him well beyond his comfort zone.

'Ah … eh … Naw,' he said eventually.

'Is that 'Naw, I hadn't seen them before' or 'Naw, I don't know where they're staying'?'

'Eh … baith.'

Doyle sighed. 'OK, thanks.'

'Anyway, did you not get enough from that big guy in the bog? I mean, look at you.'

'Don't worry, I'm not after round two.'

The door to the Isles Inn opened behind Doyle and he turned to find Alex coming in for a later than usual afternoon snifter. 'Area manager in town,' she said wearily. 'Had to keep up appearances.'

After fussing over Doyle's injuries (Scooby hadn't been seen for the last couple of days) she too confessed to not having seen the Croats before, but she did remember something from that afternoon.

'The smaller of the two looked really angry … ' she paused to take a draw from her large white wine and soda. 'Angry and I thought pretty worried. After Murdo here called the police, he was almost beside himself. He kept screaming at the other one.'

'You didn't see either of them stick something in my pocket, by any chance?'

'What? No, I didn't see anything that went on in there - thank God. But I did see them leave. Why, what did they put in your pocket?'

Doyle waved the question away. 'Did you see where they went?'

'No. Well not beyond the far side of the square. They got into a car in the car park and drove off.'

Without meaning to, Doyle made an anxious face, the kind that goes with men asking women if they knew what make and model of car. But before he could even form the question Alex said, 'Silver VW Lupo. British plates,' and grinned.

Doyle smiled back in apology and thanks.

'I'm not sure that's going to help you much, though,' she added. 'Not if you're trying to track them down.'

'Why?'

'The tourist trade on Skye is pretty diverse – we get all sorts from all over the world. But a lot of it can be split between the outdoors types – the climbers, sailors, hunters etc - and the coach parties who do castles and cafés and only look at the mountains as they're passing.'

'So?'

'So, normally anyone from as far afield as Croatia would come in a coach party and then there would be only so many hotels on the island they would be staying at. But if they've hired a car then they're on their own. They didn't strike me as the huntin', shootin', fishin' types so I'd be surprised if they're in one of the posh country house hotels. My guess is they're self-catering.'

'And that means they could be anywhere from Kyleakin to Glendale.'

'Correct.'

'Great.'

Doyle left the pub a few minutes later and, notwithstanding Alex's pessimism, began a trawl of Portree's shops, pubs and cafés.

To his astonishment, he struck lucky almost immediately. At the Co-op, one of the girls at the cash registers knew exactly who Doyle was talking about from his description. She said they'd been coming into the store off and on over much of the summer – and she had a pretty comprehensive memory of their average shop, from which it was clear they were indeed feeding themselves … when they weren't drinking vodka and smoking.

Making a note to buy his hard core porn and Preparation H elsewhere, Doyle thanked her and continued his search. By now it was almost closing time and patience with his requests was getting a little thin on the ground. His cover story that they'd won a prize draw with the West Highland Free Press but filled in their address incorrectly had only limited success. Too often, he spent more time explaining the black eye and plaster on his nose. But he did get two more confirmed sightings – at a restaurant on the harbour and in the petrol station on the road to Sligachan.

Skye is a big island. But only the wildlife can truly lose itself in it. Sooner or later everyone else has to pop up in one of only a few locations connected by fewer still roads. As he made his way back to his flat that night, Doyle knew it was only a matter of time before he'd find Moe and Curly. Or they found him.

6

The next morning, Doyle set off across Somerled Square, turned right onto Rathad Drochaid and followed the road round the rocky southern inlet of Loch Portree. After less than half a mile, he turned right through the gates of what looked like a low security prison, a large, blue and white three storey building dominating the southern approaches to the town. It was in fact the high school, though he was sure there would be kids in there for whom the prison analogy would work pretty well. Up against it, like a slightly smaller building being shouldered out of the way, was the library.

With no Wi-Fi at his flat and no internet café in the town, this was Doyle's best option for getting online. He filled in a form and showed his press pass to the librarian as proof of ID before taking his seat at a free screen. After half an hour's trawl through the archives of Skye News and every other paper and agency operating in the north west highlands, Doyle was heading back into town armed with three names.

'Davy Scanlon, Hussein Mahmoud and Vic Robertson,' he said to Bob, as he took a seat in the Skye News office and put his feet up on a desk. 'What can you tell me?'

Bob pushed back from his work irritably. 'Inverness Caley's new midfield? I don't know, Dan, give me a clue. No, better still, just spell it out.'

'They're the only people convicted for drug offences on the island in the last ten years. You covered Mahmoud and Robertson's arrests and prosecutions, do you remember?'

Bob exhaled and stared at the ceiling for a bit. 'Yes, that's right. Mahmoud worked at a hotel in Dunvegan, I think. Possession with intent to supply. Robertson was caught in a police trap on the bridge on his way back from Glasgow with a door cavity stuffed with coke. What was it, ah … two years ago?'

'Three. And Scanlon was done for flogging dope to the young and adventurous behind the bike sheds seven years ago.'

'OK. And, indeed – so?'

'So, where are they now?'

'I don't bloody know. This is a news agency, Dan, not a social network for ex cons.'

'No word of any of them in the last few years? No rumours of continued nefariousness – or even conversions to upright citizenship?'

'Nothing that's been newsworthy and, despite your low opinion of us, that's still our business here. Why don't you ask the cops?'

'Mmm. Bit delicate. Anyone at the local nick I can trust not to ask too many questions in return?'

Bob threw his hands up in preparation for a more theatrical display of exasperation when his phone rang. He contented himself with a glare at Doyle as he picked up. The call lasted no more than 30 seconds during which Bob's contribution was a 'when', two 'where's and a 'thank you'. He replaced the handset and checked the clock on the wall.

'Lobster boat missing. Two-man crew,' he said. 'Should've been back last night but there's no sign of them.'

'Coastguard?'

'No, that was a local contact. There's a search underway. I'll call the coastguard but they're probably checking the crew didn't just get pissed in Mallaig last night. That happened a couple of months ago. Boy, those guys got it in the neck.'

'OK. So, coming back – ,'

'This doesn't sound like one of those, though,' said Bob, ignoring him.

' – do you know any such trustworthy cop?'

'Still, we should be up there.'

'You know, someone who is prepared to see the big picture. Not get all picky about the details.'

'Holly's at the Sheriff Court. Won't get out for at least an hour – ,'

'Hoi!'

'What?'

'Police. Drugs. Hard news – all that stuff.'

'Dan, stop being such an arse and just tell me what the hell you're on about, will you?'

Doyle told Bob what he knew and what he'd been told about his (mostly drunken) movements over the relevant 24 hours – culminating in him being the surprised owner of a large amount of high quality Lebanese hash. Doyle's meaningful raise of the eyebrows at that point was met with only a blank stare.

He sighed and explained: 'This was a wholesale amount of dope, Bob. And it wasn't mine. It was planted on me. Who had an opportunity to do that? George Clooney from Croatia that's who. Sandy made a big deal about calling the police, remember. According to Alex, at least one of the pair was panicking. I think they stuck it in my pocket while I was head first down the lavvy.'

Bob rubbed his face with his hands, clasped them together and slowly dropped them to the table.

'Why the Croats and not anyone else you were in contact with during this day-long binge? Is it perhaps because one of them beat the crap out of you? I think the police might suspect you had an ulterior motive for fingering him, Dan. And what has any of this to do with three locals who were done for drug offences years ago?'

'No-one else I was anywhere near would have a reason for gifting me 300 quid's worth of marijuana and I certainly didn't pay for it. Plus this Norrie character swears blind it wasn't anyone at MacNabs. But you're missing the point, Bob. They were from Croatia.'

'Sorry. You're right – all Croatians are drug dealers. I'd forgotten there for a moment.'

'No, not all of them, but more than you obviously think. Look, western Europe gets most of its drugs through what they call the Balkan Route. I did a story on it once. All those recently war-torn states with hopeless police forces, mountainous borders and squiggly coastlines – it's a Godsend for smugglers. Now then – long stretches of lonely, inaccessible coastline. Ring a bell?'

Bob's expression became positively condescending but before he could say anything Doyle carried on.

'Do you know exactly how long Skye's coastline is?'

Bob opened his mouth but Doyle ploughed on.

'350 miles. 350 miles, Bob. So let's assume that pair weren't tourists – my information is they've been around here for longer than your average holiday – and they're carting about serious quantities of rare hash – it's at least a working theory that someone might be investigating opening up a little branch economy. And who better to give them a helping hand than locals with a known relaxed attitude to imports and exports?'

'If the Croatians aren't tourists, if the drugs came from them, if they're not just a couple of dope heads, if any of the locals are still involved in supplying, and if there's a reason for choosing Skye over, say, Norway, then yes, there is an outside chance your story might stack up. Tell me, Dan – don't you have something better to be doing? Like packing?'

'I've decided to hang about for a bit.'

'Why?'

Doyle shifted in his seat. 'No reason.'

Bob looked at him levelly for a long time. Doyle tried to hold his gaze but it was he who blinked first. Literally.

'I appreciate it, Dan. I do,' said Bob. 'But I don't need a long shot.'

'I'm telling you, it's not as long as you think.'

'I bet you don't say that to all the girls.'

Their laughter served its purpose; potentially awkward moment avoided, blokeyness restored.

'Seriously,' said Doyle. 'I know it's all circumstance and guesswork at the moment, but what if I'm right? That would be a hell of a story for Skye News. With the right contact at the cops you'd have it to yourselves. You'd make a fortune.'

'Like I said, Dan, I appreciate it. But even assuming the whole thing pans out, it would only be at the end of a long police investigation; stake outs, informants, possibly an undercover operation. You'd be lucky to get anything to print before Christmas. And you'll be long gone by then.'

'But – ,'

'And you will be. I'll make sure of that. Relax. You owe me nothing.'

'Owe, schmowe. I'm a journalist. It's a story.'

'It's a theory.'

'It's an earner.'

'It's a luxury.'

'What – you're so busy you can't spare the time for some old fashioned investigative reporting?'

'Correct.'

'With what?'

Bob looked back at the clock on the wall. 'With missing lobstermen for a start.'

Doyle felt the ground shift beneath him. 'But you'll be covered for that, right?'

'Not really.'

'Ah, now. Wait a minute – ,'

'Come on, Dan,' said Bob with a smile. 'You want to help out. Here's your chance.'

'Well, I'd love to, of course. But I've been sacked, remember?'

Bob puffed out his chest and adopted a solemn expression. 'I hereby revoke said sacking. Welcome back, Mr Doyle. We trust you had a pleasant sabbatical.'

'And you'll be …?'

'Off to hospital, I'm afraid,' said Bob, his grin returned. 'My first session's this afternoon.'

Doyle growled. 'But you said they could be sleeping it off in Mallaig or something. Should we not wait to hear from the coastguard?'

Bob gave him a 'you know better than that' look. 'The sooner we get started – ,'

'All right, all right. Jeez.' Doyle slumped in his chair. 'I walked into that, didn't I?'

'You're an idiot.'

'I know.'

The rain was back on with a vengeance as Doyle raced from the flat's door to the car. He fired it up and headed back along the streets he'd walked an hour earlier. Just short of the high school and library he took a right and headed north out of town on the Dunvegan road. Without knowing exactly why, Doyle reached over and switched on the CD player (MP3 capability was not one of this old car's virtues). The last time he'd had it on was during the drive up from London and he wondered what he'd been listening to. Half a bar in and he had it. Eric Dolphy, best known for his alto sax or bass clarinet, could also play a mean flute and his haunting phrases backed by the spare chords of Jaki Byard on piano were unmistakable. *Outward Bound* was the album and *Glad to be Unhappy* the name of the track. Though he liked it, of course, he remembered why, not being in the slightest bit glad, he'd switched it off somewhere half way up the A9. Doyle listened to it now, slightly uneasy that, less than a fortnight later, he heard it like the soundtrack to a previous life.

He drove for mile after mile through nothing much more than heather moorland, although even that was often obscured as the land rose quickly from the roadside to about level with his roof. It mattered little as he only had eyes for the road where every puddle on the pot-holed road threatened an axle-breaking abyss beneath its surface. He reached the head of Loch Snizort Beag at Kensaleyre with its big, boxy white kirk before the road rose gradually to a summit near Cuidrich. Here, stacks of spruce logs formed walls either side of the road, their circular cut ends turned bright orange by the rain. Shortly afterwards, he was rounding a high headland and looking down on the CalMac ferry from Lochmaddy as it approached the pier at Uig.

There's a lot less to Uig than meets the eye. At first glance its cliff top roads and nestling harbour may make it look like some picturesque Greek Island port, only in worse weather. But Uig is a place most people go through, not to. Apart from a pub, a store and the statutory pottery shop, it offers little to persuade anyone from delaying their visit to the Outer Hebrides. From the high road to the south, Doyle could see the queue of cars and lorries outside the big barn of a ferry terminal on the other side of the bay, and also a small knot of people gathered by what looked like a café at the landward end of the long, concrete pier.

With the ferry still disembarking, Doyle had to park by the terminal and walk the length of the pier down to a small collection of low buildings at the end. In one of these he found the harbour master's office. The latest news was that they'd found the boat earlier in the morning. She was on rocks at the southern end of the Shiant Islands off the Lewis coast and already breaking up. She was also quite deserted. Although indeed a creeler, the skipper had been 'working for', as the local phrase had it, prawns and crabs rather than lobsters. He'd headed out first thing the day before and not returned. Since it had been the first time the weather had let him get out to service his creels that week, he hadn't been expected back until very late at night; with anything up to 1,500 pots that would normally be checked every two or three days he would've been pushing it – getting the very most he could out of the long summer evening. The assistant harbour master concluded with a few straight answers. There had been no mayday, no sightings since around lunchtime and, no, he couldn't remember any similar scenarios when the crew had eventually turned up alive and well.

Doyle walked back up the pier, this time dodging traffic now being herded on board the ferry by guys in high visibility vests, and headed towards what a sign told him was the Pier Restaurant. As he approached the dozen or so people standing by the picnic tables outside, he knew what they also knew – but would not be admitting any time soon; that they were not there to await news of a rescue. He kept his notepad and pen in his hands and clearly visible. On such occasions, it didn't do to be coy, diffident or sneaky.

'Hi,' he said to the only person who'd met and held his steady gaze as he approached. The small, stocky woman merely jerked her head up in response.

'Dan Doyle from Skye News. I've got some details from the harbour master I'd like to double check.'

The representative of the fourth estate, doing his duty.

'Aye, OK.'

'It's the Morven II, yes? … And we're waiting on George Macleod - small 'l'? … OK, and Kevin Patterson - two 't's? Good … And you are …?'

Mary Walker, a neighbour of Kevin Patterson, didn't pause to ask herself why her name was necessary – nor, indeed, to wonder why names, ages and addresses of the missing men should need to be so rigorously verified at this time or, indeed, by her. She just kept going, answering questions, dropping in a detail here, agreeing with a banality there. Within a minute, Doyle had achieved his aim of turning a largely sham Q&A exercise (the harbour master had confirmed the details he'd already gotten from the coastguard by phone) into a free flowing conversation. And it wasn't long after that he'd managed to bring in some of the others.

Although it was clear he was the first reporter on the scene – Bob's contact had been quick off the mark – he knew that wouldn't last long. Yet he couldn't come straight out and ask for the usual tributes and recollections family and friends provide on the occasions of unexpected or particularly tragic death for the simple reason that death, in this instance, was not yet confirmed. And, not only was he out of practice – the national press tend to leave such menial journalistic tasks to, well, agencies like Skye News – he was also having to deal with the natural reserve of the islanders. You don't see many people from Skye on The Jeremy Kyle Show.

But he was getting there. Twenty minutes or so after arriving, he was sitting at one of the picnic benches chatting to an appropriately ruddy-faced old lobsterman. The displacement activity of an explanation for Doyle's black eye then a long exchange about the scale of the search and rescue operation – the lifeboat and coastguard helicopter from Stornoway plus the Portree lifeboat and, of course, every other available creel boat – was at last leading to some quotable material on the life and times of George

Macleod. Just then, he heard someone else join the group and start asking questions. The pack, he guessed, had caught up with him.

'Well, you lot are not short of staff, are you?' he heard someone say. 'Why don't you two just compare notes?'

The group of people in front of Doyle parted and he saw Holly standing there, notepad at the ready. He'd seen her only once before, but he'd been pissed and then almost comatose. He'd wondered once or twice since if his memory of a flame-haired beauty was a trick of the 80/- or the kick in the head. It wasn't.

'I, ah – Dan. I didn't see you there,' she said. 'Yes, of course. Shall we …?' And she gestured for Doyle to join her as she took a few steps out onto the road. Her almost instant recovery of poise was certainly impressive. But not impressive enough to have him walk to heel like a border collie. Doyle waved an 'in a minute' gesture before returning to his lobsterman. By the time he stood to join her, she'd been left reading her notes and talking on her mobile – or, at least, pretending to – for ten minutes.

'Hello darling,' he said under his breath. 'Fancy meeting you here.'

Holly clicked her phone off so forcefully she nearly dropped it. 'What the hell are you playing at?' she hissed.

'Smile sweetheart. Mustn't let everyone know we're having a domestic.'

'I – ,' she stopped herself, took a deep breath and managed to at least take the scowl from her face.

'I thought you were in court,' said Doyle.

'Case adjourned for legal arguments. Look, this is an important story for us, for these people. I'm not going to let you ruin it.'

'So you came here to take over from the drunken screw up. Fine by me,' said Doyle. 'I'll be on my way.'

'That's it?' Scowl back on.

'Of course. What did you expect?'

She settled her weight on her right hip and looked at him oddly. 'An argument, perhaps. Some professional pride, at least.'

Doyle had to control himself. Smiling was one thing but it wouldn't do to burst out laughing next to a gathering of the shortly to be bereaved. 'Don't flatter yourself or your job, Holly. I'll do my best to help out Bob as long as I'm wanted. But I don't need the gig or the grief.'

'Helping out. Is that what you call your effort on the royal visit?'

Doyle glanced again at the relatives and friends a few paces away, thankfully busy with another round of teas and coffees. He slowly turned his back on them and faced Holly.

'I've apologised to Bob for that and, I suppose, I owe you one too. I'm sorry for your trouble,' he said mildly. Once again, she looked wrong-footed. 'But don't get any ideas about taking up permanent residence on the moral high ground. You don't know me. You don't get to judge me. And you sure as hell don't get to tell me how to do my job.'

He put the smile back on, turned back again and nodded at her notepad. 'Now then. What've you got?'

Her lips pursed. Had they been on their own Doyle was sure he'd have been in for another broadside and he delighted all the more in her frustration. Eventually she looked at her notepad and flicked a mostly empty page back and forth. 'Nothing yet.'

'OK. Look,' he said, reluctantly. 'Any other hack on the island will be onto this by now and they could be here any minute. As a favour to Bob I'll ignore your latest effort to relieve me of my duties. I'll carry on with these people but there's no family of George Macleod here. You should go and doorstep his house, check out his neighbours.'

'Where?'

'Halistra. It's in Waternish.'

Holly shook her head. 'I'm afraid you'll need to do that. I caught a pot hole on the way up here and my tyre's gone. I only just made it.'

'Bugger.'

'No big deal. I'll take over here, you do Halistra.'

'Eh, no. I'll fix your car. You've a spare I take it.'

'Yes, I've a spare and no, I don't need you to change it for me. I'll do it once I'm done here. Off you go to Halistra. You said it, we don't have all day.'

Doyle looked around, clicking his tongue. 'Burdz are always better at that sort of thing. You really should do it. Here, take my car.'

Holly's expression went from offended to bemused as she looked down at the proffered keys. But before she could speak, a white Transit van with 'BBC Scotland' in purple on the side pulled up behind them. The sliding door opened and a camera crew stepped out, the presenter immediately putting up a big white BBC Scotland umbrella to protect his suit and ridiculous comb over from the drizzle. Without so much as a glance at Holly and Doyle, he waded straight into the gathering like a doctor arriving at the scene of an accident. It's all right, you can relax. I'm here now.

'Well that's that,' said Holly. 'We won't get a look in.'

'I can still pick up some scraps by listening in.'

'It's not worth it, Dan. Come on, let's get to Halistra.'

Doyle hesitated. 'I should at least write this lot up and file it.'

'You can write while I'm driving. We'll be able to cover more ground when we get there if there's two of us.'

Doyle really wanted to argue with that. But he couldn't.

'What the hell is that?'

'What?'

'That ... that racket.'

Doyle tutted and turned the volume down as Holly took his car back out of Uig. By now, Dolphy on bass clarinet and Freddie Hubbard on trumpet were riffing joyously on Miss Toni.

'An important bridge between the recognizable motifs of bebop and the free playing improv that was to come with the music of Ornette Coleman and, of course, the later work of John Coltrane,' Doyle looked at Holly. 'Since you ask.'

'Christ! A jazzhead. I should've guessed.'

At that Doyle turned the volume back up and began transcribing his notes onto the laptop balanced on his knees.

Waternish is the middle of the three large peninsulas that make up northern Skye, the others being Duirnish to the west and Trotternish, where they were now. Holly, therefore, had to drive almost three quarters of the road back to Portree before being able to make a right at Borve and head north again, this time on the opposite shore of Loch Snizort Beag. Doyle complained that the twisting road and Holly's evasive manoeuvres round pot holes wasn't doing much for his typing. By the time they'd left the main road to Dunvegan at the Fairy Bridge and headed towards the head of Loch Bay on a single track road, he had made little progress. Despite – or perhaps because of – Holly's injunctions to get on with it, he soon gave up the effort altogether and took to looking dolefully out the window. After about three miles along a high road above the northern shore of the loch and through scatterings of mostly crofts-turned-holiday homes, they swung by a tannery and, of course, pottery shop and carried on another few miles through Hallin to the hamlet of Halistra. Doyle directed Holly to a parking space by a small church, a telephone box at its back.

Either side of the road, meek little bungalows and old stone cottages stood inside strips of fenced off ground, some by the roadside, others at the end of long drives up or down the hillside. Crofting townships do not provide the viewer with aspects of bucolic charm. Not unless the viewer has a soft spot for early '70's lower middle class suburban architecture. There is nothing indigenous or even appropriate about a lot of rural housing in the Highlands – a basic design that in Neasden or Bishopbriggs is merely dull, here at least adds the excitement of being almost useless at keeping their inhabitants warm and dry. For those that can afford them, therefore, new roofs and pvc doors and windows are a must.

'That's it there,' said Doyle, pointing. 'The jobbie brown pebble dash one with the phoney stain glass front door. Off you go, I'll finish this.'

Holly gave him a withering look before stepping from the car. Two minutes later the door opened again and she leaned in. 'No-one at home. Come on, let's do the neighbours. You take that side of the road.'

'I'm still writing this up. You'll be done in no time – it's not exactly Beijing .'

'Dan, for crying out loud,' said Holly. 'If we get some joy here you'll need to re-write that anyway. Come on!'

Doyle sat for a long time then slipped the lap top onto the driver's seat and slowly got out of the car. He looked around with little enthusiasm. 'OK, but I'll take this side, you take the other one.'

'Whatever!'

Twenty minutes later, Doyle was already back in the car waiting for Holly.

'Any luck?' she asked, climbing inside.

Doyle shook his head. 'You?'

'Not much. Macleod lives with his elderly sister apparently but that's all I know. The guy that lives in that dump next door should know them pretty well. He wasn't in, though.'

'Shame. OK, let's go,' said Doyle nodding at the ignition.

Holly looked at him, a question clearly forming in her mind. But she just sighed and switched on the engine. She spun the car around and made to head back up the road when they saw a beat up old Astra estate come bombing down the road from Hallin straight towards them. Holly indicated her intent to duck back beside the church hall but it swung right just yards before them and headed up the driveway of Macleod's neighbour's house.

'That's him!' said Holly.

'But … you can't just – ,'

Holly put her foot down and followed the Astra through the gate. She kept a respectful enough distance and, after parking on the driveway, got out and walked up to meet an old man now standing warily by the rear of his vehicle. Doyle still had the laptop open and he stared at the keyboard, his hands hovering. A minute later, he hadn't typed a word.

'Ah, fuck it,' he said, closed the lid and stepped from the car. He walked towards Holly and the old man who now stopped in mid sentence and stared.

'Hello Dad,' said Doyle.

7

The most efficient and humane method for killing rabbit is with a high powered air rifle. Use the telescopic sight and aim between the eye and the ear. Death is instantaneous and, if the rifle is of good enough quality, the shot will be almost noiseless and shouldn't scare the rest of the population back into their burrows.

Chloe Carew stood square to her line of target, feet slightly less than shoulder width apart, left foot forward a little. She pressed the Holland & Holland, hand-carved, double-triggered Royal Side by Side shotgun to her cheek and then lifted her shoulder up to meet the stock. Keeping both eyes open and staring down the 32-inch barrels, she gave the triggers a quick 'slap'. Bugs disappeared in a pink mist shortly before every other rabbit in a quarter mile radius flew underground, bobtail arse last.

'Can you tell me why I'm even bothering to carry a gun?' asked Robin French.

'Because it looks better and because I pay you,' said Chloe walking ahead and ejecting the spent cartridges in small pops of smoke. 'Stop being such a moaning minnie.'

The rabbit was missing most of everything between its head and its hind quarters but whatever the lead shot hadn't blown into the neighbouring field was doing its best to keep the thing alive. There was twitching, certainly, but also signs of respiratory function, the odd voluntary pull in the direction of the nearest burrow. Chloe stood over the stricken creature and watched. At these times she didn't think, didn't analyse. It would be wrong to say she gloried in it; she simply couldn't take her eyes from it. Death.

Less than a minute later and it was over. She crooked the shotgun over her arm and Robin fell into step as they headed back to the house. He was a friend as well as the finance director of her holding company and personal accountant – a status which explained both his sufferance of her peculiar sporting persuasions and relative freedom to speak.

'Now that you've used both barrels I feel a bit safer telling you we've had a heads up on that environmental impact study for Beckton. It's not good, Chloe.' She gave him a sideways glance as they walked. 'Basically, the old gas works were a lot bigger than anyone thought. And we're right on top of a spoil heap.'

Chloe stopped. 'How the blazes did that happen? We had the place surveyed!'

'It's a very old part of the site – goes back hundreds of years – and, well, our guys didn't have the equipment the EPA have. It's not stopping us from suing them, of course.'

Chloe shook her head and walked on. She knew that was as good as irrelevant. By the time the lawyers had had their fun and games the economics of this deal – good or bad – would be history.

'How much?'

'To clean up? One mill. To walk away … two.'

She rammed her hands further into the pockets of her Barbour. More expense. Perhaps Robin read her thoughts.

'Chloe, I know you think me an old woman but you must be able to see it yourself.' They'd been walking through an old plantation wood. Now they stopped by a stile over a wire fence at its edge. Robin turned to face her. 'Your cash flow is … well, put it this way – it's not flowing in the right direction. You've been wealthier on paper than in reality for some time, as you know, but it's getting serious now.'

'I'm doing my bloody best, Robin. The book's out in the autumn and I've been tarting myself all over the nation's television screens for two years – in between trying to run the companies. What more can I do?'

Robin gave her a look.

'Don't, Robin. Just Don't'

'As a businesswoman, you have one weakness,' he said, waving down her complaints. 'And it's that.' Robin nodded left over the fence and across easily 400 yards of open pasture to the limestone and redbrick neo-Jacobean pile of Thuxton Hall. 'There's a reason why the landed gentry are all now landed in Kensington and Chelsea, Chloe. It's because even the most expensive town house is cheaper than trying to keep one of these places up and running.'

He was right: she did have one weakness – and a lack of self-awareness wasn't it. She knew the place was sucking her dry and she knew why she continued to let it do so. It was the reason she'd moved out to the country ten years ago and thrown herself into the life here with her usual 110 per cent commitment. It was about freedom, about principle, the things the country stood for and the nation used to. It was about taking on the suffocating forces of interfering do-gooders, the cretinous PC brigade and their campaign to turn Britain into some kind of lobotomised, dribbling shadow of its former self. She wanted to live her life with the same independence she used in running her businesses – and the life of a landowner gave her that. Yes, it was expensive – damned expensive – but she would rather die in poverty out here than go back to the city and subjugate herself once more to the dead hand of regulation and control.

Chloe knew Robin knew all that so she didn't bother explaining herself again. She just let him help her over the stile then she linked her arm through his and set off for the house. 'You're right, Robin.'

'I am?'

'Yes. I do think you're an old woman.'

She stood on the top step and received a peck on each cheek. 'Are you sure you won't stay for lunch?'

'Sorry, Chloe,' said Robin. 'I've a pile to get done before the weekend. We've got to put Beckton to bed now and I've a Danbury Healthcare finance committee meeting this afternoon. But dinner last night was delightful. Sometimes, Chloe, just sometimes I see what you see in this place.'

Chloe smiled generously and waved him off. In truth she wasn't sorry he was gone. She had her own business to conclude.

Half an hour later, her Range Rover weaved it's way into the woods. After less than a mile, the old mixed plantation of sweet chestnut, hazel and willow ran up against a wall of dense Sitka spruce. From dappled light, soft shapes and forms she now drove into a dark, looming cathedral of towering columns of greys and blacks. Ten minutes later, the ruin came into view. An 18th century chapel, it had been abandoned ever since the French Wars and Corn Laws had combined to change the local agricultural map. What was left of it after 200 years of neglect now cowered in a clearing only as big as itself, menaced on all sides by the Sitka giants.

Chloe sounded her horn and lights were switched on behind the chapel. Even in the middle of a summer's day they were enough, in this coniferous gloom, to throw it's crumbling walls into sharp silhouette. They were the headlamps of another Range Rover, this one parked such that it could illuminate the inside of the building's one intact corner. They were needed because two photographers' lamps with umbrella reflectors on tripods that stood just inside the ruin were switched off. Chloe knew, however, they would still be warm.

Adam walked round from the driver's side of the other car as Chloe parked up and made her way into the cramped space. It was like the set from some provincial stage production. He carried a camera and was wearing just a white t-shirt over his perfectly toned and muscular torso. He'd clearly been working up a sweat. This, thought Chloe, was definitely another reason she'd hired him.

'Anything more at his place?' she asked, trying keep her eyes on his face.

'No. I think that's the lot. Then again ...' he gave Chloe a glance of the LCD screen at the back the camera, ' ... we do now have our insurance.'

Chloe nodded and they both walked over to the pool of light cast by the headlamps. Sitting on the ground like a drunk against a broken, moss-covered sarcophagus was Dick Collins. He was blinking hard and trying to focus on the hand he held in front of him. At first glance, he was the same cocksure, oily operator who'd strutted up to their meeting the night before: no obvious injuries or trauma. But a closer look would reveal hair slicked down with sweat, not gell, a redness in the eyes, some fresh dirt on his hands. He also looked liked someone else had put his clothes on for him. Someone else had.

Collins began flexing his fingers and then slowly became aware of his immediate surroundings. After inspecting the ground around him and the trees above, his gaze fell on Chloe and Adam. The blank, stupefyed expression was immediately clouded.

'How are we doing, Mr Collins?' asked Chloe sweetly. 'I do hope you found everything to your satisfaction. A man with such diverse tastes as yours can be difficult to accommodate but we do try our best.'

Collins said nothing but he seemed suddenly troubled by a recent memory.

Chloe turned to Adam. 'Recap?'

Adam fished a few folded typed sheets of A4 from his back pocket and handed them to her. 'We went back to his office and he was most co-operative. I listened to the tapes and that is, as he said, an accurate transcript of all the messages and their numbers. The tapes are now in hand.'

'Good. So, what was the scam?

'*The Sunday News* hired Collins to tap the phones of Mandy Chalmers, Susan Colletti – ,'

'Is that one in Eastenders?'

'Holby City, I'm told.'

'Oh.'

'Sir George Oberon and Terry Johnson.'

Chloe raised an eyebrow.

'Tottenham Hotspur and England,' said Adam. 'Anyway, this he did for several weeks. But his handler from the paper began to get nervous, said he thought the operation wouldn't have long to run. One day he asked Collins if he could target you. He got your number and then used his tried and tested method to trick the automated server at Hotmail into thinking he was you and you'd forgotten your password. Once that was sent to him, it was plain sailing.'

Chloe felt her mobile in her pocket. It was a new one – bought the day she'd heard about the hacking – it was a different make and used a different network but she would still never trust it.

'He only got a week's worth of messages before the reporter, one Dan Doyle, told him he'd been ordered to pull the plug. Handing over a copy of this transcript was the last transaction they had. He has no idea what, if anything, the paper then did with it.'

Chloe looked again at the list of messages. There were 24 in all. It was clearly just an ordinary working week back in the Spring before they'd set off filming the new season of Chloe Carew, Business Angel. Most were in connection with new contracts being signed by Danbury Healthcare, a lot of the others were from Robin and her general counsel regarding that property deal on Teesside, plus a few innocuous odds and sods. Only Chloe and Adam could possibly know which one was not quite as innocent as it sounded. And yet ...

'He clearly thought he had an angle,' said Chloe, watching Collins watching them, regaining all the time more and more of his faculties. 'What was it?'

Adam grunted – the nearest she ever saw him come to a laugh. 'He didn't know.'

'What?'

'He didn't know. He just figured someone like you was bound to be up to something. He didn't understand a lot of what was being said but, and I quote, 'it sounded well dodgy'.'

Chloe bent down. 'Just assumed everyone's as crooked as you, eh?'

Collins smacked the lips of a gummed up mouth. 'What do you call this?' he asked, thickly.

'This is due diligence, dear boy. I never enter into any kind of deal without making sure I know exactly what I'm getting. Turns out you have nothing.'

A knowing look came across his face. He tried for confidence and swagger but he was still sprawled on the ground and not entirely in control of his mouth. 'Must've thomthing,' he said. ''Else you wouldn't be threatnin' me.'

'Threaten? No, no, no, you misunderstand. I don't threaten, Mr Collins. I do.' She straightened up. 'While you were enjoying yourself this afternoon – or, at least appearing to – my associate here was careful to make a full and, from the little I've seen, perfectly focussed and artistically composed record of your activities.'

Collins unconsciously began to fidget with this shirt and trousers. 'What ... what activities? I haven't – ,'

He was interrupted by a snuffling and a small grunt from off to his right. Collins didn't even bother to look. He stared ahead in horror for a moment before closing his eyes and burying his face in his hands.

'Tsk, tsk,' said Chloe as Collins began to sob. 'Man up, for God's sake. It's not as if you did anything nearly as naughty as the poor unfortunates featured in the extensive library of downloaded material now buried in your hard drive at home.'

Collins' tear stained face shot out from behind his hands.

'Oh yes. It seems your illegal tastes stretch well beyond the farmyard.' Her tone hardened. 'We will be watching you very closely, Mr Collins. Any attempt to approach anyone over these messages, any attempt to contact the authorities – not, of course, that you are in any position to – and, indeed, any attempt to dispose of your computer and we will act. I urge you to believe me.'

She turned her back on the now catatonic Collins. 'Right,' she said to Adam. 'Get that filth off my land. And find Doyle.'

8

It was hard to tell who was more surprised. The old man, for that's who it was, stood blank faced with shock while Holly looked from one to the other, her expression changing from annoyance to dawning realisation that Doyle was not just making a prick of himself again.

'Love what you've done to the place,' said Doyle, breaking the silence and surveying a front yard strewn with rusting engine parts, sun-bleached marker buoys and ropes, even an actual kitchen sink. 'You must let me know your designer.'

'Dan?' His father stared, eyes narrowing. 'What … what are you doing here?'

'I'm working. I believe my lovely assistant has been asking you some questions. It would be tickety if you could answer any of them.'

'But I don't understand …'

'Yes you do. You're just stalling for time. Trying to work out an angle. Well, there isn't one.'

The shock was gone. The old boy's face clouded over and Doyle could see the scheming truculence return, as he knew it would.

'I see you haven't lost your lip,' he pointed at Doyle's black eye and plastered nose. 'No wonder somebody smacked you.'

Doyle opened his mouth to speak but stopped. His hackles were rising, pulse quickening – just the sound of the old bastard's voice had propelled him back through a worm hole 20 years. This was precisely why he hadn't wanted to come here – to come to Skye at all. He let the air from his lungs out in a soft whistle and smiled.

'And you're still quite the old charmer. Like I said, if you could see your way to answering our questions, we'll be on our way.'

Just then, there was the sound of a car on the road behind. Doyle saw Holly glance at it and he turned in time to see a Nissan Micra pass by his father's gate and pull up in front of Macleod's house next door. Doyle didn't wait to debate the matter with either Holly or his father. Quickly, he turned on his heel and ran down the driveway, pausing only to grab his notepad from inside the car.

Moira Macleod was just back from a shopping trip to Dunvegan. She was the type who did things like that in times of stress. Doyle introduced himself and helped her carry her bags into the kitchen. She was a game old dear and he liked her immediately. By now, the lack of news on her missing brother and his crewman spoke for itself and she seemed already resigned to their deaths. But she was holding it together and Doyle guessed she welcomed his presence as a reason for doing that just a little bit longer. Over a cup of tea, she told him more than he would ever need to write about a missing creel boat skipper. But he sat and listened and took notes. And, at the end, he was offered not one, but a selection of photographs to choose from. As Doyle was shown out through the front door, he noticed Holly had brought the car around.

'Thank you, Miss Macleod,' he said. 'And remember, the press operate a pool system in these cases so everything you've told me will be made available to everyone else. If any other journalists come around, you just refer them to Skye News, OK? You take it easy now.'

She nodded and closed the door. Doyle jumped into the passenger seat and Holly drove off. 'You lying sod,' she said.

It was already after midday and they had to file quickly if they were to maximise their income from the morning's work. Doyle typed furiously on the laptop, ignoring Holly's tart comments about suddenly being able to do so in a moving car. By the time they got back to Portree, he had finished. 1,000 words for a 'Fears are growing …' piece was way more than a missing fishing crew would merit in a news item, even in a local paper. But news agencies have the luxury of not having to pare copy down too much – they leave that to their clients. After a quick check with the coastguard (no change), Holly uploaded the story, scanned the photograph of George Macleod and immediately fired them off via email and a news wire service to every newsdesk in the country.

There followed a few moments of strangely awkward silence between them. Holly fussed with nothing in particular on her desk and Doyle simply lounged on Bob's – extra large – office chair.

'We should get more on the other guy, Kevin Patterson,' said Holly eventually. 'A picture at least.'

Doyle shook his head. 'Not worth it. I spoke to his brother at the pier and that quote I've got in there is all anyone will get. The family have closed ranks. If and when the bodies are found, it might change.'

Holly accepted that and went back to shuffling papers and clicking on her email.

'I can man the fort, if you'd like,' he said.

'What? Why?'

'You know, if you want to go somewhere.'

Holly looked puzzled. Then her face cleared.

'Shit!' she wheeled round and looked at the clock, grabbed her jacket and left.

That evening, Doyle walked once more towards the school and library. This time he passed them by and kept going until he came to what, if it didn't sound ridiculous for a place the size of Portree, might be considered a suburb. He took a right turn up a cul-de-sac of more bungalows – these a bit more manicured than those in Halistra – and walked through the gate of a whitewashed house near the end. It was a surprise when Holly came to the door.

'Hi,' she said, unsmilingly. 'He's in the living room.'

The heat and smell of egg fried rice hit Doyle like a wall. He found Bob wearing a scarf and woolly hat, a shawl on his lap and sitting beside an electric fire, all four bars lit. Holly stepped in and began clearing a half-eaten Chinese take away from a card table next to Bob's chair.

'Eh, I can come back another time. Like, when you've thawed out,' said Doyle, flapping the sides of his jacket back and forth.

'Shut up. I'm cold. Take a seat.' Bob's voice was croaky.

Holly folded up the table. 'At least he can talk now,' she said. 'He was almost speechless when we got out this afternoon.'

Although clearly an effort to do so, Bob gave Doyle an account of his first session down at the McKinnon Memorial Hospital's chemotherapy unit in Broadford. Weird and unsettling, it had nevertheless been painless enough. As warned, however, the moment he stepped into the fresh air, his throat seized up and the shakes set in. These symptoms, he was assured, should pass, but there were other treats on the way – everything from nausea to blisters and constipation. Some people were lucky on chemo – they didn't suffer many side effects and certainly not to any great extent. Bob, it was clear from his first dose, was not going to be one of those.

'OK,' he said in conclusion. 'Here's the deal. I should be fit enough for the office again come Monday. But I've obviously got more of these sessions to go and no-one can be sure how long it will be before I'm having to take time off, days – maybe even weeks at a time.'

'I can handle it,' said Holly, now sitting by the window. 'I'm not a bloody trainee.'

'I know you can, Holly. I know. But look at today. If you'd been on your own with that court case to cover you'd never have even heard about the missing boat until it was too late. The case got adjourned – no pay – and you'd also have missed out on the income we're in line to get from Dan's piece. How many takers did we get?'

'We won't know for sure until tomorrow, but it looks like more or less across the board,' said Holly unhappily. 'But look, the business model for Skye News says a payroll of precisely two. Whether or not you can make it in, I'm assuming you'll still want paid. We can't afford him.'

'We can. I've got income protection in my health insurance.'

'They'll never pay out. You know what these insurance companies are like.'

'I've checked. All I need – ,'

Doyle cleared his throat and stood up. 'If you don't mind. I have socks to wash.'

'Sit down,' said Bob. 'Just answer me this. Are you staying on Skye or not?'

'This morning you were desperate to get rid of me. Didn't want any grand gestures or hand outs.'

'And that's still the case. Forget what Holly says. We'd be paying you. Remember, Dan, you're the one who called me. No-one forced you to come to Skye. And the job's still there if you want it.'

Bob was being matter of fact about it and talking like this was simply a business proposition. But Doyle knew he wouldn't be saying any of it at all if he wasn't worried. If he hadn't before, he now knew Bob was in for a rough time of it. Before he could answer, however, Holly spoke up.

'If I'm going to have to work with this joker, I'd like a few things cleared up.'

'I must say, this is all delightful,' said Doyle, sitting back and putting his hands behind his head. 'I'm having such a lovely time.'

She turned to him. 'Did you or did you not conduct illegal phone hacking? I mean, *The Sunday News* continue to deny it yet here you are all washed up and out of work.'

'Thank you for that. Yes, I'd tell you, of course. But sadly I am bound by a confidentiality agreement.'

'And the only reason you'd sign one of them was if it was true. So,' she folded her arms. 'We know what you are

– unethical. Now we come to who you are. Why is your father on Skye? Did you follow him – is that why you're here?'

'Holly!' Bob croaked. 'That's enough.'

Doyle was content to let the silence that followed linger for a long time. Eventually, he said, 'You've a high opinion of yourself, haven't you? Even the prospect of sharing an office with me gives you the right to my life story, does it?'

She opened her arms and looked at Bob, 'We'd just like to know if we're in for any more surprises.'

'It's no surprise, Holly,' said Bob, wearily. 'Of course I've always known he's from Skye.'

Holly gawped. 'You … you're *from* Skye?

'Remind me again why MI6 turned you down, Bob,' said Doyle.

'But you're a Glaswegian,' said Holly. 'You look like a Glaswegian, you sound like a Glaswegian, you drink like a Glaswegian, you even throw up like a Glaswegian.'

'Then I must be a Glaswegian. Or maybe I'm from Burkina Faso. What difference does it make?'

She ignored that, too curious now to care why. 'So what gives? Why are you not what you appear to be, Dan Doyle? I mean, is that even your real name? Just how deep does this identity crisis run?'

Doyle smiled. 'Ah, identity – the specialist subject of Holly Thompson, the girl who's spent a lifetime looking for one.'

She scoffed. 'Don't try and turn this around. What do you know?'

'I know you grew up in South Wales. State education, I'd guess – a public school would've eradicated any last trace of an accent. But it's still in there, even though you've moved around the country since then. Maybe a long spell on Merseyside? Yes, thought so. You obviously didn't have much, if any contact, with your father but things don't seem to have worked out so well with your mother either. Why else are you here now with a man I know for a fact she hasn't had anything to do with for a very long time. Why else, in fact, would you go into the same profession as him? Was it deliberately to spite her? And it is a profession to you, Holly, not a trade, not an industry. Ordinary workers, tradesmen, they don't wear made to measure linen trouser suits – linen's always a dead give away; only hand cut linen suits will still sit right at the end of the day. Most journalists in London aren't turned out as well as you, Holly – and you cover a few hundred square miles of rock and sheep shit in the Inner Hebrides. And why is that? You've worked hard at your job, yet after six years' experience and being as bright and talented as you are (Bob's not too soft that he'd put Skye News into the hands of an eejit) you still haven't gone anywhere near the nationals or, more surprisingly given the looks, television. It's because you like local news, isn't it? I've seen the passion. You really care about this stuff. You want it to matter … to you. You need roots, Holly, an identity. The one you never felt you've had, the one you hope your father's life can give you. The one even your marriage didn't deliver.'

Holly eventually closed her mouth and turned angrily to Bob. 'Did you leave anything out?'

Bob had slumped further into his blanket, the evening clearly going nowhere near as well as he'd hoped. 'I didn't tell him any of that, Holly. It's a thing he does. Bloody annoying.'

'Rubbish! What, he's Sherlock sodding Holmes now?' She turned her glare on Doyle who merely nodded at her hands. She looked down and noticed that she was unconsciously twirling nothing around the faint groove left on her wedding ring finger.

Doyle stood and made for the door. 'See you Monday,' he said over his shoulder. 'Milk and two sugars if you're in first.'

At the end of Bob's street the main road back into Portree was busy with cars and pedestrians and Doyle remembered hearing something about a concert that night at the Aros Centre further out of town. He turned left into the tide of people heading in the opposite direction. Several minutes of weaving and 'excuse me's and 'sorry's later he reached the turn to cross Somerled Square and head for his flat. But the rain had stayed off for the rest of the day, it was now a warm and pleasant evening and he was in no hurry to get back to his tiny TV set and stack of ready meals in the fridge. He walked on towards the harbour, his mind idling between the events of the day and what he'd just let himself in for.

The prospect of a prolonged stay on Skye was not a happy one. But then, as Bob had said, it was his idea to come here in the first place. Besides, what was waiting for him back in London? Perhaps only an old friend like Bob – and one in his predicament – could be in a position to offer him employment. His pay-off from *The Sunday News* wouldn't last for ever and, be it ever so humble, at least working for Skye News for a time would prevent a large hole appearing in his CV …

The foot traffic having thinned out, Doyle walked on at a decent pace. It wasn't long before he reached another junction and, deciding against heading past the Skye News offices again, he turned right up the hill that led eventually to the hospital. At the railings he'd stopped at before, he once again paused to look out over the town with the harbour below.

'You have light?'

Doyle turned to the question and immediately felt something hard in the small of his back.

The wee guy held an unlit cigarette and looked up at him unsmilingly, the slope of the road down the hill exaggerating his lack of inches.

Doyle swallowed, resisting the initial bolt of panic. 'You shouldn't smoke,' he said. 'It stunts your growth.'

Curly's English was clearly no better than his friend's. He remained even tempered, just nodded for Doyle to walk on up the hill. Doyle felt the pressure on his back ease and he turned to see Moe falling into step beside him while placing something back in his pocket. They were still in their navy windcheater and white Reebok combos and Doyle could only guess what an odd threesome they would've looked like … had there been anyone there to see them. He glanced resentfully at the suddenly deserted streets.

After a few yards they reached the half castle, half church oddity that is the Skye Gathering Hall. Moe grabbed Doyle by the elbow and steered him towards the right side of the dark sandstone edifice where, between it and a steep slope buttressed with a stone wall, there was a narrow passageway that ran the length of the building. To accommodate the hall's irregular flanks, the path turned right and left, growing darker and more dank with every step. Water from the rain earlier in the day still streamed down the wall and dripped onto the fern and moss that sprouted in the crevices.

After one more turn the passageway came to an abrupt halt at a chainlink fence with padlocked gate, empty stainless steel beer kegs stacked behind it. The wall to the right and the bank above it were now almost as high as the castellated top of the hall and it was, Doyle dolefully admitted to himself, a perfect spot for ... whatever it was Moe and Curly had in mind. He turned to face them.

'So,' he said brightly. 'Who wants to know what you won in the prize dr – ?' Moe didn't break stride, just kept going and struck Doyle so fast and hard in the gut that no amount of time to brace himself would have made the slightest difference.

It wasn't the pain that worried Doyle so much as having every last gasp of air blown from his lungs – that and the feeling it could be weeks before he'd be able to breathe in again. His legs buckled and he fell to the ground where he flapped like a landed trout, his mouth working noiselessly and pointlessly. And then he did feel pain, but not in his gut. Moe had grabbed hold of his left arm, had twisted it and now held it easily in one hand with his foot rammed into Doyle's shoulder. The slightest pressure and Doyle would suffer excruciating pain.

Moe exerted the slightest pressure.

In order to scream, however, Doyle would need some air. The body clearly has a way of working out its priorities and from somewhere Doyle suddenly reacquired the knack of breathing. He sucked in with the rasp of a drowning man breaking the surface before howling in agony.

Moe took the pressure down from searing to merely unendurable and Curly began a thorough search of Doyle's pockets. He didn't find the dope – but he did turn up his wallet with his NUJ press card. The slightest twitch at the edges of his wide, wet lips betrayed something. Relief? He leaned into Doyle's face.

'You look for us. Why?'

'Wh … ,' from being unable to breathe only seconds before, Doyle was now panting like a race horse. 'Wha … what can I say? I think you're swell.'

'Sw – ,' he nodded at Moe who turned the screw.

By the time Doyle had stopped screaming, stars were popping and fizzing in front of his eyes and he was breathing even harder.

'Again. Why?'

'I wanted … some more hash. That … that was good stuff.'

Curly straightened slowly. He looked for a long time at Doyle then muttered something in Serbo Croat. Doyle could see Moe wasn't buying it. He tightened his grip on Doyle's arm and was about to push when laughter rang out and footsteps clattered up the passageway towards them. Through Moe's legs, Doyle looked down to the last corner and saw a pair of black lace-up shoes, white knee-length socks and chubby pink knees above them. He sagged.

'Haw!' was followed by the sound of gum being loudly chewed. ' 'you up tae?'

The girl's legs were joined by those of another. 'Wassup, Na'lie?'

'Dunno, Kaylee,' chomp chomp.

Curly took a step towards them and began talking. But he barely got a word out.

'Ugly wee bastard urn't ye?'

The legs did not move. In fact, Doyle would guess one of them was now leaning – insolently, no doubt – against the wall.

Curly stopped then turned back and forth between the girls and his unfinished business with Doyle.

'Say cheese,' said one of the girls and then Doyle heard one of the most beautiful sounds he'd ever heard in his life: the sshh-chick of a mobile taking a picture.

'Hey!' shouted Curly.

'Ha ha!' laughed the girls and then they ran. Despite Moe's protestations, Curly did the same and Doyle heard the chase echo back down the passageway and beyond. Moe's final, spiteful shove on Doyle's arm all but dislocated his shoulder. As he lay on the ground fighting to remain conscious, he saw Moe stomp unhappily down the path, pausing only to pick up and pocket the discarded wallet.

***

The range of a creeler out of Uig is anything up to 15 miles and takes in many of the sea lochs in the north of Skye as well as further out into The Minch. A serious bit of ocean, The Minch can reach depths in excess of 300 metres and throws in some of the strongest and most treacherous currents in British territorial waters.

Creel boats have 'strings' or 'fleets' of roped together pots which can be upwards of a quarter of a mile long. These are worked on the starboard side of the boats. A common cause of accidents is the freak combination of the string snagging on the sea bed as it's being winched up at the same time as a big enough wave hits on the port side.

Once overboard, a factor in determining the fisherman's chances of survival is what he's wearing. Despite advice from the Marine Accident Investigation Branch among others, creel fishers and trawlermen tend not to wear life jackets. They believe the bulk actually adds to the dangers aboard rolling, pitching vessels with ropes and winch gear all capable of tripping and entangling the luckless crewman. What they do wear are things like heavy woollen sweaters and rubberised chest waders.

The traditional Aran knit jumper is water resistant up to a point. Good ones can absorb up to 30 per cent of their weight in water before they feel wet. And, of course, they're damn cosy. Good reasons for fishermen to wear them. Yet, there is also the old (fish?) wives tale that trawlermen wear them so that, if lost overboard in cold waters with no hope of rescue, the sheer weight of the saturated sweater will quickly drag them down and drown them, thereby saving many minutes of traumatic, instinctive but hopeless struggle.

The humble big rubber dungarees are no less contentious. Many health and safety experts contend they are potentially lethal since they can readily fill with sea water and drag the wearer down or, worse, trap air at the bottom and turn the wearer head down in water thereby making drowning all the more likely. This is disputed by others who say the water in the waders is no more 'heavy' than the surrounding sea and cannot therefore act as a drag.

All sides in the various fishermen's clothing debates agree, however, that having your waders stuffed with lead weights is never a good idea. Nor is having your Aran knit punctured with bullet holes.

9

Summer gave way to Autumn early and without a fight. The weather improved accordingly and, as the tourists and midges thinned, the warmish, wettish westerly that had plagued the island since July finally abated and blue skies returned.

First with pillar box red rowan berries, then with the blues and purples of scabious, knapweed and thistle, Skye slowly began to experiment with its new season's colours. It wouldn't be long before the hill grass and fern turned from lush and green to a patchwork of ochre, umber and bronze. Imperceptibly, the island was beginning to turn its thoughts to winter – it pays to be well prepared in this part of the world. Nature stuffed her face, grew thicker coats and programmed the sat nav for anywhere nearer the equator while the human population, though still technically engaged in summer activities, began laying plans for the autumn, Christmas and New Year. Skye is no longer a place where the changing seasons can be easily seen in its agriculture. Not for more than 40 years has the island boasted an arable production worth talking about. The hay stacks, corn stooks and died back potato fields ripe for harvesting that once created a varied, checker board landscape at this time of year in areas such as Trotternish and Bracadale are now a thing of memory and Old Skye photograph collections in gift shops. Now crofters in tractors trail big bale silage machines and crop the grass earlier in the summer, wrap it in black plastic and leave it stacked where it will be needed during the winter. And everywhere else the sheep graze. And graze.

After an initial recovery to his first chemotherapy session, Bob's side effects became ever more deleterious. The pain in his feet made it difficult for him to walk some days and, even when he could make it into the office, similar sensitivity in his fingers made it impossible for him to type. It was also Doyle's guess that, despite ladylike dismissals of any such problems, Bob's previously fearsome digestive system was not quite operating at its peak. Trips to the toilet were more frequent and lasted longer. More worrying – startling even – was that food was sometimes being left on the plate.

Concern for the old boy was, of course, invisible, unspoken. But it was also the air that both Doyle and Holly breathed. They shared it and, in doing so, allowed each other a latitude perhaps no other context would have. Because if Doyle had entertained the hope that the circumstances of their initial contact were no more than unfortunate, that given a 'normal' working environment they could learn to appreciate each other's skills and contribution, he was to be disappointed. Nothing in Holly's behaviour suggested his methods were going down well – not unless passive aggression was the latest thing in affirmative man management. As for him, he'd never reacted well to control freaks and pernickety editing. He didn't need her approval for his work but nor did he need the feeling that everything he so much as looked at had to be given an immediate health check like he was some sort of journalistic virus.

When a local councillor stood down from the Western Isles Health Board, Doyle's request for contacts was her cue for leading him by the nose through the 'intricacies' of a story she seemed to think as big as Watergate. The alleged sighting of a 'really big cat' near the 5th green of the Skeabost golf course had to be covered like the golfers who reported it weren't pished (which they were). A threat of closure hanging over one of the island's post offices led to a warning about getting too political, while the opportune theft of groceries from the back of the Co-op in Broadford, including fast food and runner beans was apparently a serious incident and definitely not a chance to try breaking the world pun record.

The only consolation was that Holly seemed genuinely interested in the more enervating aspects of local news. She loved nothing more than a day in court listening to the same policemen give the same evidence about the same fights involving the same drunks outside the same bars that happened every Saturday night. Council committee and health board meetings, CalMac ferry timetable changes and anything the Wee Frees or Church of Scotland got up to? She was in there in a flash. Doyle knew she wasn't daft enough to think he'd actually be interested in the stories and had to conclude she was merely making sure she kept him a safe distance from who she would presumably call 'important stakeholders' or some such tosh.

It left him with something of a 'roving reporter' remit and that suited him fine, even if his copy was going to be butchered at the end of it. The freedom from the newsroom diary also meant he had time to sort out his accommodation. His holiday let flat was too expensive to keep on for more than a fortnight so, reluctantly, he moved into the cheapest B&B he could find – a chintzy house set in a Teletubby garden off Home Farm Road. It helped control the nausea if he came and went during the hours of darkness. Also for his own sanity, Doyle made sure he had time to pursue, even if only on a part time basis, what he considered to be real news.

Because he couldn't think of a good enough reason not to, Doyle had reported his mugging at the hands of the Croats to the police. Nothing came of it. Certainly, there were no reports of traumatised schoolgirls nor did the photograph they took ever surface. It appears Natalie and Kaylee's good citizenship only stretched so far. Moe and Curly hadn't been seen since and Doyle had to conclude they'd left the island, at least for the moment. It did not mean he was going to leave the story alone.

***

It is a matter of historical fact that all kings of Norway – indeed, all Vikings – were enormous men with big beards who shouted a lot. King Haakon IV, according to the Skye tourist industry at least, was no exception. In paintings, cartoons, even sculptures, Haakon grins or scowls out from beneath a thicket of ginger/fair hair and, of course, a horned helmet. Several Haakons have associations with the island; like the rest of the Hebrides it was for centuries part of a Viking empire. But No. 4 is particularly remembered for mooring his fleet of warships in 1263 at the place now named in his honour – the Kyle of Haakon (Kyleakin) – before heading down for a must win match against the Scots under Alexander III. A score draw, on the other hand, would be good enough for the Jocks and, having crapped out of a full-scale battle and secured just that at Largs, they no doubt blew raspberries and waved their arses at the retreating Haakon and his ships as they headed home to avoid the winter at sea. After a brief stop over once more at Kyleakin where, if history is as accurate about Viking tempers as it is about the beards and pointy hats he will have done a fair amount of cat kicking and table thumping, he set off again.

Unfortnately, he only got as far as Orkney, where he fell ill and died . . .

. . . Making it all the more surprising that the big fella should be sitting in a pub on a Friday night. And not just any pub – the King Haakon Bar in Kyleakin. Yet there he was, a great big ginger teddy bear of a man, supping a pint and tapping his foot to the pulse of what is nowadays called contemporary Celtic fusion. Something between a rave and a ceildih was going on all around him but he sat at a table – like a grown man at an infant's school desk – and seemed almost calmed by the frenzy of it all. Doyle pushed his way through the dancers.

'Sandy.' It was a statement, not a question; Doyle was in no doubt whatsoever.

The man stood and came close to nutting a light fitting. He looked down on Doyle and said, 'Dan.' Another statement. For a long moment they just stood and looked at each other.

'Well, are you going to ask me to dance or what?' said Doyle at last.

'Christ. It is you!' And the big guy broke into a frankly enormous grin. The hand he stuck out was equally huge. Doyle felt his own like a baby's as he tried to grapple with it.

'You get cheap beer in here?' asked Doyle, nodding at a painting on the wall, a spitting image of his companion in full Viking regalia.

'No, but I wouldn't need it if I had a fiver for every time someone's asked me that.'

'Sorry. But I bet the tourists love you.'

Sandy groaned. 'Aye. Every summer at least one yank thinks I'm some guy called Haakon with a high opinion of myself and a pub. What can I say? I'm just the big growing laddie I always was. You, on the other hand,' he looked Doyle up and down and felt the collar of his suit. 'We don't see many … ?'

'Paul Smith.'

Sandy raised an appreciative eyebrow, ' … Paul Smith suits round here. You're clearly doing all right for yourself.'

'Ah, well. Let's just say I'm not sure where my next suit's coming from. Long story. I'll bore you with it later.' Doyle stood back and grinned. 'So – the cops, eh?'

'Aye. Man and boy. Love it.'

Doyle bought Sgt Sandy McNair another pint and a coke for himself. He'd always hated the drive from here back up to Portree and didn't think being half cut would improve it any. Besides, he was drinking with the polis. It wasn't the easiest of venues for a reunion but of course that was not the purpose of the meeting. Plenty of ambient noise was exactly what was needed to keep sensitive conversations from being overheard. After only a few minutes reminiscing about their school days together (tricky – he'd wiped most of his youth from his mind the moment he'd docked at Kyle of Lochalsh that day 18 years before), Doyle felt it was time to broach the subject.

'Sandy, what sort of drug scene do we have on Skye at the moment?'

He shrugged. 'The usual, I suspect. Plenty of weed, as always, plus maybe one or two idiots experimenting with something harder.'

'There's been no recent, em … increase in activity? No signs of more gear on the market?'

'Not that I know of. I can check, if you'd like.'

'Please. And can I give you some names? Davy Scanlon, Hussein Mahmoud and Vic Robertson. Ring any bells?'

'Well, I once beat the shit out of Scanlon. But he was 14 at the time.'

'That's right!' exclaimed Doyle. 'I knew that name was familiar.' He sat back and laughed. 'Aye, he was 14 – and you were nine!'

Sandy laughed too and the floor shook more than it had during the Canadian barn dance. 'I liked Frankie Goes to Hollywood and he made sure he told me they were gay. I didn't know what that was but I guessed he was taking the piss. So I hit him.'

'And he stayed hit,' said Doyle. 'Anyway, it seems not to have been enough to deflect him from a life of the ne'er-do-well. Along with those other two, he's among the latest names to feature in minor drugs busts on Skye. I just wondered if the police have had any recent dealings with them, any suspicions that any of them are back in business.'

Sandy nodded. 'I know a man I can ask.'

'Also, you haven't by any chance come across a pair of Croatians? No oil paintings … fondness for Tommy Hilfiger and Reebok?'

Sandy made a blank face. 'Nope. But, again, I can ask.'

'Thanks.'

They drank in silence again for a minute.

'You don't seem interested in why I'm interested,' said Doyle.

'Not really my scene. But I'm guessing you think there's some big drugs smuggling operation going on – boats from Columbia moored in The Minch, that sort of thing.'

Doyle looked at his drink. 'Well, I think the boat might be from the Balkans but otherwise, yes.'

Sandy grinned. 'What is it with journalists? You're convinced the north west coast of Scotland is a major highway for drug smugglers. We get this – usually from some London paper – at least once a year. It's all boats on a lonely shore stuff, desperate men holing up in caves, signalling with torches and all that. I think you lot read too many Enid Blyton books when you were wee.'

'Yes, well … '

'Ach, don't worry, Dan. I'm sure it'll be spot on one of these times. Who knows – you could be the lucky one.'

'And you're not interested in knowing why I have my suspicions?'

'Like I said, Dan – not my scene.'

Doyle frowned. 'You're a cop. I thought all crime would be your scene.'

'Bob Miller didn't tell you did he?'

'Tell me what?'

'I'm the wildlife liaison officer for Skye and Lochalsh.'

Doyle lowered his coke to the table and stared. 'What? You mean birds eggs, badger baiting – that sort of thing?'

'That's me,' said Sandy with a grin.

Doyle shook his head. 'And that – with all due respect, Sandy – is the best contact in the police Skye News has?'

Sandy laughed. 'Aye well, the rest of them are all pigs.'

Later, they stepped out into crisp evening air, the enveloping quiet like a cool shower on a hot, sticky day. Sandy breathed in deeply. Doyle got the feeling he did that sort of thing a lot; indoors was not really Sandy McNair's natural habitat. His own indoors was a cottage close to the old harbour but he walked Doyle to his car, one of only a handful in a vast car park the village once needed as an overflow for the ferry before the bridge was built.

'You're not here to stay,' said Sandy simply.

'Correct. Just helping out.'

Sandy nodded and waited awhile before asking, 'Have you seen him?'

'Unfortunately, yes.'

'Who won?'

Doyle shrugged. 'Him, probably. He always won.'

Sandy put a large paw on Doyle's shoulder. 'Not always, Dan. You remember that. Not always.'

Doyle gave him a tight smile, got into his car and drove off.

At 5 o'clock the following morning, the sun still had a way to go before clearing the mountains of Lochalsh to the east. But its herald, a strengthening wash of grey blue light, was still enough to add definition to the Heidi cup trees and gingham curtains of the B&B's kitsch kitchen. Doyle stood in the semi-darkness and bolted his cereal. He poured coffee into a flask and headed for his car. Once more, he took the road north west from the town. Less than an hour later, he was slowing down outside his father's croft in Halistra. There wasn't much cover; like most crofting villages it was all wide open spaces and not much else. But just across the road from the old church hall was a house for sale. It's driveway gate was open and, by the road, the property was edged by a drystane wall, gnarled old Atlantic oaks, holly and hazel bushes getting what shelter they could in behind it. Doyle reversed into the driveway and made sure his bonnet was a good few feet back from the road's edge.

On the way over, Billy Strayhorn and Johnny Hodges had been doing their damndest to lighten the mood but when even Don't Get Around Much Anymore can't get the job done, Doyle knew it was a lost cause. He switched off the CD player as he cut the engine and, because he'd always known he was going to have to do it one of these days, he let his mind wander where it would.

Gerry Doyle was a chancer, likely lad, a bit of a rogue. Unfortunately for him, enough dour Scottish blood had watered down his fifth generation Irish ancestry to have removed all the charm and wit that usually makes such a personality acceptable, attractive even. What Gerry (and everyone who came into contact with him) was left with was a sharp tongue and a belligerent conviction that the world owed him a living. His own world was a part of Glasgow's north east so deprived it didn't even have its name any more. Royston is what the city had been determined to call it since the Second World War. The Garngad was the original, medieval name and what its increasingly unemployed, isolated and eventually displaced population still chose to call it. Add in the city's own particular 'cultural' dimension (The Garngad was essentially a Catholic ghetto) and a siege mentality was inevitable. It takes a particularly subterranean rank of lowlife to subvert the kind of community spirit a place like that engenders. But that was Gerry. No job was so easy or well paid that it couldn't be dodged or pockled. No friend or relative was so close that they couldn't be used or betrayed in the Cause of Gerry. By his mid 20s he'd managed to alienate anyone who could ever have mattered to him and he was looking for options. A chance encounter with a homesick teuchter in a city centre bar and big talk of an easy life made rich by cash-in-hand jobs and other working skives made his mind up and one day, unannounced to anyone, he bought a one way ticket to Mallaig at Queen Street Station and was never seen in Glasgow again.

Maggie MacDonald, despite a sweet and generous nature, was cursed by an inability to make the right choice. In anything. She quit school when she needn't have, took a job behind a bar in Dunvegan when better prospects lay elsewhere, got pally with the wrong people and eventually decided, to general astonishment, that the Weegie incomer with a growing reputation for fecklessness and unreliability, was her perfect mate. There weren't many who believed Maggie's attraction for Gerry had nothing to do with her sudden inheritance of the family croft on the death of her father. By the time their son was born, what little glow there had ever been in their relationship had flickered and died. Maggie doted on her boy while Gerry – as ever – doted on himself. Soon the only physicality to their relationship was when he beat her.

Crofting, or rather what it had become for some – a miscellany of odd jobs and seasonal work – suited Gerry down to the ground. He kept his best earners sweet and short-changed everyone else. He worked his scams everywhere from fish farms to garages then grew some spuds and called himself a farmer. Through the years, Gerry kept himself in reasonable shape and proved it as often as he could with any barmaid or pig-tailed backpacker stupid enough to let him.

Dan Doyle grew up convinced he was the milkman's. Neither his mother's cowering submission to her ever more violent husband nor this guy's self-serving laziness and sheer dishonesty chimed with anything he felt inside. And then there was the whole Skye thing. His old man was a cameleon – a gallus Glaswegian when it suited him and a crofting radical the rest of the time, the accent changing accordingly. But while his father would struggle to name so much as a Cuillin, his mother knew the English and Gaelic names for practically every rock and green thing hardy enough to grow on it. She knew some of the old stories and Doyle grew up with images of giants, fairies and improbable battles peopling his imagination just as much as his favourite TV shows. But more and more she spoke about Skye as if it was lost to her – a thousand miles away instead of just outside her front door. Had she given up entirely? Was she suffering an illness that would soon take her away? One day, shortly before his 18th birthday, Doyle found out what she'd been waiting for.

The old man was not happy. Neither of them knew why or cared – it was just another one of those evenings to keep your head down and your mouth shut. Doyle busied himself in his room with his studies but his concentration was soon broken by the unmistakable noises of a fight brewing next door. She had answered back. God knows why but it had been enough to send his father into a fury.

Every six months or so for as long as he could remember, Doyle had stood up to his father and received a beating for his trouble. When he'd been just a boy, as young as ten, the blows were carefully delivered to anywhere his school uniform would cover up. But Doyle never gave up. Time after time he put himself between his father's fists and his mother because not to do so, not to even try, was unthinkable. It had not escaped his notice that, in recent years, it had taken more and more out of his father to eventually best him. When he heard his mother being hit yet again this evening, his heart began to pound and his mouth went dry. He knew it was time for another crack at it.

Doyle walked into the room and found his father holding both his mother's wrists in one hand while punching her unprotected face with his other.

'You fuck off,' he snarled over his shoulder. 'You'll know soon enough when it's your turn.' He made to deliver another blow.

Only he didn't. Not then and not ever again.

Doyle moved forward and grabbed the swinging arm at the wrist with his left hand. And he held it firm. Like all bullies, Gerry Doyle was of course a coward. For a second or two his anger was intense as he tried to shake off his son and then – and Doyle will remember this split second for the rest of his life – the anger in his eyes turned to fear. Doyle was not left handed yet the power of the grip that held his father's arm tight was easy. Perhaps Doyle's expression also changed. After all, he was seeing, as if for the first time, that he was now inches taller than his father – and well built (years of forcing his son to do labouring jobs he had been hired to do himself were about to backfire spectacularly on the old man). The scales had been tipped and both of them knew it. Gerry Doyle was momentarily lost for words or action. Not so his son.

'It's all right, Mum,' he said still looking levelly at his father. 'You go and clean yourself up.'

She prised herself free and did exactly as she was asked. No words of defiance, not even caution to her son. The sound of the kitchen door closing behind her was like the snap of a hypnotist's fingers to his father and he swung a haymaker with his free left hand. Doyle ducked beneath it, came back up fist first and caught his father in the gut. Every last gasp of beery breath was blown from his lungs as he doubled up. Doyle took one step back and swung his boot with the force of a lifetime's hatred behind it. It broke his father's jaw and shattered half his teeth shortly before lifting his entire body clean off the floor and slamming him against the wall. He slid to the floor and sat half conscious and gurgling through the mass of blood and bone where his mouth had been.

Doyle was combusting with anger. Angry that it had come to this. Angry that he'd only beaten his father on his own, barbaric terms. But also angry that it was over – that he was not his father and could not – no matter how much he dearly, dearly wanted to – kick a man when he was down. It took a full minute of simply standing over him, fists clenched and breathing hard before his own battle was won and he stepped away.

'No more,' was all he managed to say without crying. They were to be the last words spoken between them until 'Hello Dad' 18 years later.

The following afternoon, Doyle returned from school on the bus as usual and climbed the path to the house. His father was still in hospital being fed through a tube and his mother … well, she was leaving. Her suitcases filled the hall when he opened the front door. Now she knew her son would be safe in her absence, she could go with her mind at rest. She had a sister in Aberdeen and would write.

He could go there when he'd done his highers. They had a university as well, you know.

But he didn't go to Aberdeen. He finished his exams less than a month later, gave the Scottish Qualifications Authority the address of a friend in Glasgow, packed his own bags, stole his father's car and left the island, he thought, for ever. He'd seen his father only once since – years ago at his mother's funeral in some dingy church in a blank Aberdeen suburb. They were the only two there, her sister having died before her. But they arrived, attended and left entirely separately.

The croft as it was then, Halistra as it was, began to fade and overlap with what Doyle found himself looking at now as he pulled himself from his reverie. The old place hadn't changed, and that was the problem. No repairs, no new paint, nothing by the looks of it in almost 20 years. While all around him newcomers and new generation locals were embracing the tourist industry, smartening up their homes, building new ones, the old bastard was stuck in his own, warped time. The sun finally topped Beinn Bhreac to the south west and sent a laser of light bouncing off Doyle's wing mirror, making him wince. He was glad of the excuse to close his eyes.

By 6.30, Halistra was beginning to stir, even on a Saturday morning. Doyle heard a diesel engine and ducked from the reflected light in time to see a vehicle coming over the high road from Geary on the other side of the peninsula. It paused at a junction just a few yards to his left, turned towards him and then pulled in to the space beside the old church hall he and Holly had parked in weeks before. Doyle took the last slug of coffee in the mug, screwed the flask shut and slid down in his seat, peering through the spokes of his steering wheel. It was an old pale blue LandRover of Born Free vintage and had been much reparied and patched up over the years; one of its doors was dark green. Leaving the engine running, an old man got out and went into the phone box. Doyle checked his watch and timed the length of the call. The old man emerged and, without as much as a glance in his or any other direction, drove off.

A light came on in his father's house. Doyle pushed up in his seat, fired up the Saab and slowly eased onto the road behind the tail lights moving east towards the morning.

10

By the time Holly and Bob got into the office the following Monday Doyle was already there wrestling with several Ordnance Survey 1:25 000 scale maps and scanning an old island gazetteer. He mumbled a 'good morning' and continued cross checking. As he folded up one of the maps a minute or so later he was in time to see Holly put a fresh cup of coffee on his desk. If Tom had offered Jerry a drink of his milk it couldn't have been more surprising.

'Oh, eh … thanks.'

Holly gave the briefest of nods and sat herself at her own desk. Bob, as he increasingly did nowadays, took the small couch against the back wall and settled down to read the newspapers. He gave a cheery enough smile but, though he'd needed to lose weight for as long as Doyle had known him, the growing gap between his clothes and the man inside was still unnerving to see. But they had a rule in the office: no asking about Bob's health – at least, not when he was there.

Doyle sat back and sipped on his coffee. It was good, just the way he liked it. 'What do we know about Knott House?' he asked. Holly shook her head and looked at Bob.

'Where is that, again?'

'Off the 850 between Bernisdale and Flashader.'

'Oh yeah,' said Bob. 'The one set back in the woods. Never seen it myself. It's Geoffrey Lytton's place, part of the Suladale Estate – in fact it's the estate's 'big house', although they're never very big on Skye.'

'Is that the teapot guy?' asked Holly.

'That's him.'

Doyle did the obligatory puzzled look.

'Biggest collection of novelty teapots north of Crianlarich,' said Holly with a smile. 'Or so he says. He donates a few for exhibitions at craft fares. Completely missing the point, of course. These things are supposed to showcase local products and he's sticking in pots that are not only from around the world, they're not even for sale.'

'Anything else?'

'Nope, don't think so,' said Bob. 'He's your typical old money landlord. The estate's been in the family since, eh …'

'Just after the First World War,' said Doyle, lifting the gazetteer. 'Assuming it's the same Lyttons mentioned in here.'

'Yes, that's them. I don't know how many acres but he makes his money from fish farms.'

'Interesting,' said Doyle, teasing the tip of his goatee with his fingers. 'Have you ever done anything on him – features, profiles?'

'Nope. We only do that sort of thing if we're commissioned.'

Doyle bounced his eyebrows up and down, fished out his mobile and scrolled down his contacts list. He got through to the publishing company's main switchboard and asked for editorial at *Swanky* magazine.

'Felix, it's Dan. How are you, you old poof?'

Ten minutes and a conversation with more double entendres than Kenneth Williams reading from a copy of Viz later, Doyle hung up in triumph.

'Sorted. Consider ourselves commissioned.'

The other two looked at each other for a long moment before Holly said to Bob, 'Allow me.' She turned to Doyle. 'This, eh, Felix … not a deep and meaningful relationship, I take it. Just the perverted sex, was it?'

'Hey, we all have our personal journeys to make.' Doyle laughed. 'The man's outrageous – and, as far as I know, still a virgin and living with his mother. But he talks a good game.'

He told them of the über camp former features editor of *The Sunday News*, Felix Goodwood (with a name like that he couldn't have turned out any other way), who inherited a fortune when his father died, quit the paper and fulfilled a lifelong dream of starting up his own publication. Then he doubled his money by selling it to a major publisher while retaining editorial control. A style magazine with a difference, it was aimed at the tasteless and the tacky, the gaudy and the gimcrack – all, hopefully, seen to be done in an ironic sense. No amount of pleading from his friends could dissuade him from calling it *Swanky*.

'As you can appreciate, some toff with a Highland estate and a thing for teapots would be right up his alley.'

'Oo-er,' said Holly.

'Quite. Moreover, a contributer has just let him down and he's got a big hole in his next edition with a deadline looming. He'll pay a premium if we can get this to him inside 48hrs.'

Bob said, 'I appreciate you generating the income, Dan. But something tells me it's not this man's teapots you're interested in. This wouldn't by any chance have anything to do with your drugs smuggling theory, would it?'

'No, no no. Then again … maybe.'

'I see your enquiries are at an advanced stage.'

'Look, I'm going to do a proper job on this – for Felix's sake as well as yours. But I just want to have a look round the place. As soon as I know anything worth telling you, I'll tell you. Trust me.'

'How much will this Felix pay?' asked Bob.

'Three grand, words and pictures.'

'Of course I trust you young man,' he said brightly.

Shortly afterwards, Holly went to the usual Monday morning briefing from the police (at which the world's waiting media would be told how many lawnmowers had been nicked from garden sheds that weekend). She left with another smile and a general 'cheerio' – not one directed exclusively at Bob.

As her footsteps faded down the stairs, Doyle said, 'I appreciate I'm asking her father this but did she get lucky this weekend?'

'Da-an!'

'Well, it's either that or you've been spiking her tea.'

Bob tried indignation, then ignorance before finally waving in submission. 'OK, OK. But don't get angry, Dan. I did it for your sake.'

'You did what?'

'I told her about you and your mum and your old man.'

Doyle scowled. 'Why?'

'Because I was getting sick and tired of her bitching about you all day every day. You thought it was bad enough in here? You should've heard what she said about you behind your back!'

'So I push her buttons, big deal. I can live with that. Besides, what the hell has ancient history got to do with it?'

Bob was clearly uncomfortable. After a fair amount of sighing and shrugging, he said, 'You were right – well, partly right – that night at my place. Holly has a thing about families and roots and all that.'

'Yeah, well, that's your fault,' said Doyle.

'So, apart from all the other obvious reasons you're an annoying sod, I think – I know – she really resented the fact that, as far as she could see, you had everything she didn't – a family, a settled home life and a place like Skye to call your own. Yet you gave it up, stayed away for years and, now you're back, you walk about like the entire island is something unpleasant you've stood on. It really bugged her.'

Doyle said nothing, so Bob carried on, 'I know why that is, Dan. In fact, I know a lot more about it than you've ever told me over a Talisker. There are plenty of people here who remember what your father was like and they remember you.'

Just what he was afraid of. The sooner he got away from here and back to the loving embrace of a city big enough to not give a damn about him the better.

The following day, Doyle sat parked on the single yellow outside the Co-op and across the road from Skye News at just after ten in the morning waiting for Alan MacLeod, one of the local freelance photographers they regularly used. He was checking the battery on his digital dictaphone (he'd found that people who want to be interviewed actually quite like the things) when he heard and felt the camera case being dumped in his boot. It was no little surprise then when Holly jumped in beside him.

'Alan called in sick and we weren't able to get Steve or Rory at such short notice. I'm afraid you're stuck with me.'

'Delighted I'm sure,' said Doyle. 'But this is glossy magazine stuff. It's the pictures that will sell it. We need a professional.'

'You've got one,' said Holly, oddly sheepish.

'Eh?'

'I'm a photo journalist. That's my qualification.' She stared defiantly straight ahead.

What a strange girl, thought Doyle. The things she gets hung up about…

'Cool,' he said, and started the engine.

Holly had ditched the trouser suit look in favour of something a little more 'snapper' like. Underneath a yellow waterproof, she wore a shirt and jumper – both smart/casual affairs – and agreeably snug jeans over a pair of light weight Karrimor boots. The loose red ringlets were also tied back and held by a single scrunchy. After having the whole photography set up prised from her (she would do most of the picture-taking in future once the existing contracts Bob had with certain freelancers had run their course) Holly took the first opportunity to change the subject.

'So, you think Knott House is the centre of an international drugs ring, eh? Maybe he's getting the stuff in disguised as tea for his pots.'

'You've never seen Beverly Hills Cop, have you?'

'What?'

'It's coffee they use to throw off the sniffer dogs. Not PG Tips.'

After an harrumph and a pause, she was back. 'Seriously. What is it you're really after from this?'

Doyle was about to bat the question out of the ground when he stopped himself and thought for a bit. 'OK,' he said at length. 'I'll do you a deal. Let's just do this job and afterwards I'll ask you what, if anything, might be wrong about Mr Lytton and Knott House. We'll compare notes.'

To his surprise, she agreed.

Knott House didn't present it's best side to the visitor by road. In fact, it showed you its backside. And that was after you'd made an unmarked turn off the main carriageway, driven for half a mile through thick birch woods on little better than a dirt track and convinced yourself three times you were heading up the wrong lum. Your reward for perseverance was first, a glimpse of dirty white washed gable ends, then a sudden emergence into a back yard of outhouses and garages with the rear of the house, all downpipes and fire escapes, looming over you. Even before Doyle swung round to park beside an old pale blue LandRover with a dark green door they could hear the dogs. As they got out of the car, the noise intensified but, fortunately, remained distant. Doyle listened and surveyed the scene as Holly went to the boot to fetch her bag. It was obviously a working house; various trailers, cages and pallets lay around but none looked they'd been there for very long. Tracks swept and zig-zagged across the muddy yard and one corner was completely taken up by a stack of huge cradles filled with scaffolding. Something bothered him, something about the dogs. But his efforts to pin it down were interrupted as he was hailed from the back door.

'Mr Doyle!'

An old gent stood inside the incongruously grand doorway, one with a large stone surround which, Doyle guessed, echoed whatever was round the front door of the house. They walked over and shook hands.

'Do come in. Yes, that's right ... excuse the slight disarray. We're having a little work done.'

Geoffrey Lytton was tall, if a little bent with age, thin and vaguely vulture-like in appearance. Two beady, though not unfriendly, eyes twinkled either side of quite a snozzle while a thin whisp of grey curls around his ears did its best to compensate for a boiled egg of a pate above. He was, of course, in hunting tweeds complete with mustard yellow waistcoat and plum Paisley pattern cravat – though that was possibly just for the camera.

After a minute or so of weather related small talk he turned to Holly. 'Shall we see the collection, mmm? Yes, I think so. This way, my dear.'

Holly followed Lytton through a cold scullery, past a large kitchen with appliances old and new and down a flagstone floored passageway, Doyle dawdling at the rear. They emerged into a reasonably tight sun-lit hall with an old rug on the floor and an oak staircase squared against the walls. The drawing room he led them into was of a proportionate size and reasonably comfortable. As with what Doyle could see of the rest of the house, however, it clearly hadn't been decorated in some time. But this observation he only made after finally dragging his eyes from the most hideous waste of money he'd seen in a long time – several hundred teapots. He fought to keep his expression bright as he inwardly groaned, realising for the first time the horror of the next hour or so he had condemned himself to spend learning much more about teapots than he would ever be able to later forget, no matter how hard he tried. They were, of course, in display cabinets – massive mahogany ones that filled three walls and rose to picture rail level. But there were others sitting out on a dining table set in the middle of the room and more half in and out of packing cases on chairs and on the floor.

'Gosh, what a lot of pots, Mr Lytton,' said Doyle. 'This, I take it, is the complete collection; you don't have more elsewhere in the house?'

If Lytton was hurt by the question ('What, this isn't enough?') he didn't show it. No, this was indeed, the full compliment – save for two which, he proudly assured them, were currently the star attractions of an exhibition at Northampton Borough Council's Abingdon Park Museum. Lytton and Holly seemed intent on getting on with taking photographs but Doyle had his reasons for wanting to conduct the interview first. As he and Lytton sat around a corner of the table, Holly contended herself with a wander round the display cabinets.

'So, *Country Homes & Interiors* magazine is interested in my collection? How wonderful,' said Lytton.

'Among others, among others,' said Doyle hastily as Holly gave him one of her looks from over Lytton's shoulder. 'We're aiming for syndication, you see. It could appear in a number of quality magazines.'

'Splendid.'

And so, taking a deep breath, Doyle dived into the world of antique and collectable teapots with as much phoney enthusiasm as he could muster. Lytton began by explaining the collection had started life under his grandmother and succeeding generations had taken it upon themselves to add to it over the years. Some lame anecdotes about pots almost breaking and guests actually making tea in them – oh, how we laughed – followed before Lytton, with entirely predictable reverence, took Doyle in minute and excruciating detail through the last 150 years or so of novelty teapots. There was the Measham teapot with itself in miniature as the handle of its lid, the gaudy Welsh 'Buckle' pattern and the fine example of Sevres hand painting. There was the Victorian Staffordshire Majolica fish-shaped pot and the Copeland Spode Chinese Rose. There were big pots and small pots, porcelain pots and silver pots, Bakelite pots and earthenware pots. There were pots shaped like clocks, handbags and other everyday objects. There were birds, fruit & veg, maps of Guernsey and, of course, all the major historical figures from Bismarck to Bob the Builder.

By the time they'd finished Doyle's attempt at an expression of perpetual pleasant surprise had calcified into something closer to the Joker from Batman. But he'd done what he'd needed to – and widened the subject matter from time to time sufficiently to make the whole exercise not entirely worthless. Holly had by now rejoined them and had contributed her own oohs and aahs to Lytton's conveyor belt of tat while taking close-up shots of each pot it featured. Once she had Lytton to herself she began constructing a series of man-and-pot compositions.

'I wonder if I could use your bathroom?' asked Doyle.

'Of course,' said Lytton absent-mindedly as he tugged his waistcoat into place for another shot. 'Second door on the right beyond the stairs.'

Doyle went out into the hall and walked to the far side. He found the bathroom, opened the door and then closed it again with a thump, doubled back and took the stairs two at a time, sticking close to the wall to lessen the chance of any creaking. At the top was not an open balcony but a wall and closed fire door on an hydraulic return spring. He opened it barely wide enough to let him squeeze through and still didn't like the sigh of the piston as it released and closed again.

The upper hallway beyond was dimly lit; since the stairwell and its cupola above had been blocked off by the wall at the top of the stairs, it was receiving little natural light. It was obvious, however, that it was floored by old and sagging boards running its length under a balding carpet. The slight rises of the supporting cross beams could be seen every few yards. Doyle paused, checked his watch and kept his breathing as shallow as a sprint upstairs and the sudden rush of adrenaline through his body would allow. He listened intently for a few seconds and, hearing nothing, set off, again keeping close to the wall. Two slightly damp and musty guest bedrooms later he saw what he was looking for on the other side of the hall. He found the contours of the nearest cross beam and stepped along it and into the room beyond.

Something about the man meant Doyle was not surprised to find Lytton's office a mess. Half a dozen ancient filing cabinets, most with drawers left open, lined the right hand wall of what was little more than a short, broad corridor. To the left was a motley collection of shelving units and bookcases, an equally miss-matching row of framed photographs on the wall above them. Beyond that a table piled high with papers sat under a window and against the back wall was an old oak roll-top writing desk. This too had files stacked on top and each little drawer was open and crammed with tippex bottles, elastic bands, paper clips and every other office accessory from a bygone age. Lytton did, however, have a computer … still in its box and sitting on the floor.

Doyle eased through the room and diligently registered everything he saw, conscious that one man's chaos is another's perfectly logical system. He found a desk diary and flicked through recent months and those to come. Lytton noted what looked like the usual business reminders for an estate, also references to his infernal teapots and meetings, some with names appended, a few rather pointlessly annoymous. He turned his attention to the paperwork.

His guess – that Lytton's clutter hid a method of sorts – proved correct. Quickly scanning the teetering piles of papers and correspondence on the desk and floor, he could see the split between business and personal. He sussed the chronology and, working back from the estate's looming deadline, soon tracked down Lytton's tax return and supporting material. The pink manila file it was in matched one sitting out on the open drawer of the nearest filing cabinet and Doyle was suddenly looking at copies of accounts from the last 15 years. He took a bundle of the most recent files to the table by the window, pulled out his mobile phone and began photographing. Reading as much as he could as he went along, he could see the Suladale estate, as Bob had suggested, relied heavily on its fish farms. There appeared to be two – one doing considerably better than the other – and just a smattering of forestry and around a dozen crofts, of which four seemed to be unoccupied. The others, as was the lament of crofting landlords all over the country, earned the estate little more than peppercorn rents.

Doyle checked his watch again, replaced the files exactly where he'd found them and, giving the room a final check, headed back to the door. Where he froze.

The hydraulic sigh was unmistakable; someone had opened the fire door at the top of the stairs. Someone already upstairs going down? Lytton lived alone – but a cleaner perhaps?

The creak of a floorboard in the hall.

Shit! He had five, maybe six seconds. It wasn't orginal, it probably wouldn't work, but he had no option; he ducked behind the office door. If it had opened left to right, he would be safely in behind a filing cabinet. But it didn't and he could see right down the left hand wall of framed photos, the shelves and bookcases below them. He'd just manoeuvred a coat hanging behind the door around his shoulder when footsteps strode purposefully into the room and stopped.

'Right. I know you're in here somewhere.'

It was Lytton.

'Come on. Where the hell are you?'

Doyle's heartbeat was pounding through the arteries in his neck and so loudly he was sure Lytton could hear it – after all, the man was only the thickness of the door away from him. Hobson's choice time, thought Doyle: do I stand here and shout 'Ta da!' when he pulls back the door, or walk out and 'fess up to being a nosey bastard with no sense of propriety let alone professional ethics? He'd just plumped for the latter and had taken hold of the handle when Lytton moved on into the room and began rummaging through letters on the table by the window. 'Gibsons, Gibsons, Gibsons ...' he muttered to himself as he flicked through a pile of invoices. 'Come on, now – where did I see that?'

Doyle's relief was so great his legs sagged and he nearly fell against the door. He recovered just in time, steadied himself and pressed as far back behind the coat as he could. Lytton was on his side of the room and a glance to his left would be all it would take. As the old man continued muttering and rustling through the mail, Doyle could only stand to attention, keep his head back and stare at the wall and its photographs only inches in front of him.

'Ah-ha!' exclaimed Lytton eventually. 'Georgian lustreware, silver jubilee 1935 – I knew it!'

Doyle remained stock still as Lytton hastily rearranged whatever pile of letters he'd been going through, turned on his heel and stomped from the room. As his footsteps creaked their way along the hall and back down the stairs, Doyle stayed where he was. The silence that descended was broken some seconds later by the soft clunk of the return spring finally closing over the fire door. And still Doyle did not move. Doyle, in fact, had barely blinked.

He was staring into the laughing eyes of Chloe Carew.

11

Chloe had the laugh of a three-year-old at the business end of This Little Piggy. Almost a squeal of uninhibited delight, it made those who heard it go all gooey and was known to bring out the indulgent streak in otherwise hard-headed executives – known, that is, by Chloe.

The quarterly board meeting of Carew Holdings Ltd had gone as well as she could have expected. Of course she should be relaxed, confident. If she had been putting on a show, it would've been a convincing one. But she wasn't; she knew the figures would be right. Now everyone else round the table knew as well, they could all relax. Fraser Morton, managing director of Thuxton Developments, was certainly on form: ' … and then the guy said "Could you check my balance?" So I pushed him over!'

Ha, they all dutifully laughed, ha.

His own balance sheet had been one of the better ones reported to the board. Still in the red (the continuing slump in the commercial property market made sure of that) but, thanks in part to those old Olympic site deals in Stratford, it was once more heading in the right direction. He was one of five senior management representatives from Chloe's various business interests present. Property being her original game – buying and developing slum flats in London had made her her first million – she was particularly pleased by this upturn. Would that she could say the same for all the others. But Danbury had come good and that's all that mattered.

Indeed, even Guy Latchford from Assured Equity seemed relaxed. Chloe looked from his happy, smiling face to Robin French who gave her a wink as he stacked his papers in front of him.

'Moving on to any other business,' said Bill Sutton, the chairman, once the merriment had died down. 'We've got a request here from Haringey Council for our esteemed majority shareholder to support their Immigrant Innovators Scheme. Basically, what they do – ,'

'I know what they do,' said Chloe sharply. 'They've approached me before.'

Sutton looked less than happy at being interrupted. 'Yes they mentioned that in their letter. They got a photocopy of a form letter in reply. They thought it might not have reached you.'

'It did.'

Smiles around the table were becoming a little fixed. The temperature was taking a dip.

'And?'

'And I'm sorry Bill but I've got too much on my hands in here and with Business Angel to be spending time helping Sri Lankan asylum seekers and Iranian draft-dodgers take work away from local businesses.'

Sutton looked like he was swallowing hard on his indignation and offence. When he spoke it was with deliberate measure. 'I think the point they would make, Chloe, is that it's all wealth creation. The businesses wouldn't exist if these entrepreneurs hadn't come here and started them up.'

'Wouldn't they? If Haringey Council and every other loony London borough wasn't so keen on helping attract these entrepreneurs, as you call them, from every economic basket case in the world, don't you think there might be more council tax payers' money around to help English businesses get started?'

From warm, back-slapping bonhomie to chilly stand off, both sides wondering how far to risk ruining the occasion. Well, Sutton probably was. Not Chloe. This was one of her specialities, one of the traits that made her a figure of fear as well as affection in the business world – a total disregard for mood and ambience. She would speak her mind at any time in any place, to hell with the feel-good factor. If those who knew her better suspected there was more to it than just independence of mind and principle they would be right. Chloe liked to be the centre of attention. What kind of attention was neither here nor there. And she had an almost allergic reaction to satisfaction (or smugness as she saw it) in others. Perhaps someone else might have paused to consider that the general mood of optimism and conviviality in the room was to their advantage – why piss on the party? Not Chloe. She'd been unusually quiet, uninvolved during the meeting. The upturn in profits, the subsequent securing, for the moment at least, of Carew Holdings' funding from Assured Equity and the sense of a corner having been turned – none of that was seen to be Chloe's doing, just sound fiscal management by her lieutenants. The fact that she knew it was nothing of the sort was no comfort. It was time, in the words of Francis Urquhart, to keep the troops in line, put a bit of stick about, make 'em jump.

'I think we could debate this at some length,' said Sutton after a pointless scan of the paperwork from Haringey. 'But this is obviously not the time or place. It's clear you will not be lending your name to this venture.'

The old coward had backed down, as she knew he would. Insincere smiles were exchanged and the room let out its collective breath. There being no other items on the agenda, the meeting broke up, everyone relieved to have the cover of movement, papers, briefcases and chairs to get the cheerful small talk back on line. Chloe remained seated. It was another thing she did. Anyone who wanted to shake hands or bid a personal farewell just had to do so with her in her seat. In truth, she wouldn't be that much higher up if she stood. But everyone knew that wasn't why she did it.

The boardroom cleared except for Chloe and Robin, who re-took his own seat. 'You're not a fan,' he said.

'Oh, the man's insufferable,' said Chloe.

Robin laughed. 'Maybe so, maybe so. But he's Assured Equity's appointment – just part of the price we have to pay.'

'It's one thing being a snoop for the bean counters, Robin, but must he really foist his PC crap on us at every turn?'

'Once a Labour minister, always a Labour minister I suppose. Anyway, don't let him wind you up. We kept your 'bean counters' happy for another three months. Carew Holdings Ltd survives to fight another day!'

'As I knew it would. I told you you were an old woman.'

'Perhaps, but I still think – ,'

There was a knock on the door and Adam entered. 'Sorry. I can come back ...'

Chloe knew he didn't mean it. He wanted a word now. To Robin's obvious irritation, she waved Adam in and said they were just finishing up. Deciding his point could wait, Robin contented himself with a reminder about their lunch date the next week and left.

Unbidden, Adam took a seat opposite Chloe. That confidence again. 'It's Doyle,' he said.

'At last! Where is he?'

'We don't know for sure. Yet.'

Chloe wound herself up for an outburst but caught it in time. She eyed him closely as she exhaled softly and lay her hands palm down on the table. The internal wall of the boardroom was one big window. Soundproofed of course, but the lobby of the executive suite was out there – secretaries at their desks, PAs and others passing by, glancing in. Now she knew why Adam hadn't waited until she was back inside her own office.

'You say 'yet' as if that's supposed to be encouraging. Perhaps it would've been a month ago, Adam. Not now. Now it's just more incompetence.'

Adam gave her his contrite butler just informed that the morning egg was too runny look. It was the nearest he ever came to admission of failure. 'As you know, Doyle hasn't been at his flat for over a month,' he said. 'No-one at the paper has heard from him, neither has any friend we've been able to find. We put a bug on his phone and he has called to check his messages, but he used his mobile. We couldn't trace it.'

Adam's reluctance to get to the point – even now – was worrying.

'And yet you have news,' she said levelly.

'We couldn't find his family. All anyone knew was that he was from Glasgow. We now know they were wrong. He's from Skye.'

'I thought that was supposed to be soundproof,' said Tracy walking past the boardroom two seconds later.

***

She was at the front of the group (naturally) and laughing with the rest of them at whatever shared joke had just been made. The scene was rural – some nondescript bit of woodland, an expanse of hill seen through the trees – and hunting tweeds and quilted jackets were much in evidence. There were a dozen of them squeezed into the shot, one or two, apart from Carew and Lytton, vaguely familiar. Looking along the row of photographs, each was a variation on the same theme. Some were taken in exactly the same spot, a distinctive stretch of deer fence in the background, while earlier ones – identified as such more by their frames than any great difference in composition – were taken in a different, though equally anonymous location. Records of friends out enjoying days of huntin', shootin' and/or fishin'? That, at least, is what they appeared to be ... Doyle reached the end of the row of photographs and was jolted out of his thoughts back to the here and now. He did not have all day to stand there and ponder.

He retraced his steps across and back down the upper hallway to the fire door. Easing it open, he could hear

Lytton and Holly still down in the drawing room. Half way down the stairs, however, their voices grew suddenly louder.

' … much more attractive prospect, I think you'll find.' Lytton led Holly out into the hall and Doyle ducked below the level of the banister. 'Perhaps I should go and check on your colleague first, he's maybe unwell?'

Doyle took a peek and saw Lytton had his back to him. He stood up. Holly saw him immediately. In an instant, she turned her involuntary glance into a thoughtful stare at the ceiling. 'Well now, well now … I suppose I should tell you he did complain earlier of a particularly vicious hangover. He drinks a lot you see.'

'Oh? Oh, my.'

Taking Lytton by the elbow and leading him to the front door, she went on, 'Yes, I'm afraid so. He'll surface eventually and I'd be grateful if you didn't say anything. He's still pretty much in denial and will just come up with some old story about food poisoning or some such. Classic symptoms, obviously. Very sad.'

Doyle was tip-toeing down the stairs as she spoke.

'How unfortunate,' said Lytton. 'Still, part of the culture up here, we're told. After you my dear.'

They reached the porch just as Doyle ducked inside the bathroom and eased the door closed. He splashed some water around the sink, flushed the toilet and went out to join them as they took the steps down from the front door.

'Ah, Mr Doyle,' said Lytton, obviously a little ill at ease. 'I was just saying how the road access doesn't do our place justice. You see, even as late as the turn of the 18th century when this house was built, the easiest way of getting about was by boat …' As Lytton continued burying what he obviously saw as an awkward situation in a history of Highland estate architecture, Doyle managed a quick exchange of looks with Holly. He could read nothing in her expression.

They walked down a gravel path to the end of the garden where there was a stretch of heavily sheep-grazed foreshore leading down to an old stone jetty, the expanse of Loch Snizort and The Minch beyond. At the water's edge they turned back to face Knott House which now, as Lytton said, did indeed present a far more impressive countenance to the world. A typical Georgian period grand Highland lodge affair, it was all white harled stone, sash windows and a bit of castellation at the top. Doyle could see the patchwork repairs on the roof Lytton had mentioned in the course of their interview and the need for the major restoration that was about to take place.

Holly took another ten minutes of shots of the house, some with Lytton in 'master of all he surveys' pose in the foreground, before there was just no longer any good reason for them not to leave. Passing through the house again, Doyle glanced in as many rooms as he could. At the back door Holly gushed some more to Lytton about the house and his collection while Doyle tried to look suitably honoured to have been given so much of his time. Lytton beamed in response and offered a more in depth follow up whenever they liked, perhaps for a specialist collectors magazine, before shaking Doyle's hand and telling him to take care of himself with almost paternal intensity.

Doyle reversed in an arc before taking the track again through the trees, Lytton still waving in his rear view mirror. Neither he nor Holly spoke until he had swung back onto the main carriageway and headed south east back towards Portree.

'Thanks,' he said.

'For what?'

'In the hallway. I must say that was pretty quick thinking.'

'Well, I didn't have time to think up a lie.'

Doyle glanced over and thought he saw her fighting a smile.

Holly sipped on a soda water and lime. Doyle, reasoning he had a reputation as a lush to uphold, took a deep draw on his pint.

'So. What did you think?', he asked, wiping the froth from his lips.

He had spent the drive back to town deep in thought and, since he'd dealt with little in the way of conversation from Holly, had to assume the same went for her. Now they were at a window seat in the faintly Art Deco bar of the Bosville Hotel waiting for their lunch orders to arrive.

'I think it's a fascinating house and certainly an impressive collection of tea pots,' said Holly. 'I think Geoffrey is a sweet and kindly old man with charming manners who looks as if he wouldn't hurt a fly … '

Doyle's eyelids drooped.

' … And I think he's a total fraud and we should nail him.'

He jerked up as if from an involuntary nap.

'Interesting,' he said, trying not to grin. 'And why do you say that?'

'No-one is like that. It was an act – had to be. All that 'Oh, I say, my dear … splendid, what? ' stuff – honestly, he was like some old country gent from central casting. Dick Van Dyke does Lord of the Manor.'

She leaned forward on the table and warmed to her theme. 'And not once did he say anything even remotely interesting. Yeah, I know tea pots are not the most fascinating of subjects. But we both talked to him about loads of stuff; the house, his family, the estate, the island … and the man managed to say not a single word that was even mildly thought provoking never mind controversial. Did he have any opinions about anything? If he did they were so wishy washy I never even registered them. I'm telling you, no-one is that bland.'

'You can't suspect someone just because they're boring.'

'He's not boring, Dan. He's a phoney.'

'Woman's intuition?' As soon as he asked, he knew he shouldn't have.

'Yes, that's exactly what it was. 'Cos, you know, it's all we've got, isn't it? Can't expect our fluffy little brains, already so full of cake recipes, to have room for anything else, any other instincts or – I know, you'll laugh – to actually use deductive reasoning.'

Doyle was spared further sarcasm by the arrival of their lunches – penne with a mushroom sauce for her, the sirloin steak for him.

'Sorry. Just playing devil's advocate,' he said as the waitress left the table.

She glanced up from her food, not entirely placated. 'All right then, Raffles. What did your snooping about get you? And don't think for a minute I'm suddenly all in favour of your methods.'

No, he was sure she wasn't. And yet here she was more concerned about evidence against Lytton than how he had gotten hold of it. This was not predicted. This was not the woman who had given him so much grief over the last month – who would've probably fired him for correcting Lytton's grammar in a quote let alone trespassing on his property. Bob's heart-rending tales of childhood in a croft weren't responsible for this. Did she have her own agenda or had he just misread her?

'Well?' she pressed.

OK, he thought. We'll take it a bit at a time.

'You will agree,' he said, making a start on his steak, 'that he's recently come into a fair amount of money.'

'You mean the new stuff he had in the kitchen? I spotted that. But it's a few hundred quid here and there, nothing significant surely.'

'Not just the kitchen, Holly. But since you mention it, let's start there. That place was like something out of Upstairs Downstairs – the huge Belfast sink, the food mixer that could've come from a Clyde shipyard. And yet there's a brand new microwave oven, a Miele coffee machine – and those things cost thousands – blenders and the like. That's decades of nothing followed by the sudden arrival of state of the art appliances. It's as if the last hundred years never happened for that kitchen. And take the tea pot collection itself; new pots everywhere – on tables, in their packing cases – and nowhere to put them.'

Holly waved a forkful of pasta at him. 'He's a tea pot collector, Dan. You don't think he regularly buys tea pots?'

'I think he would've liked to but until recently he hadn't. Look, the collection is and always has been in that room, as he said. The display cabinets held so many – probably the same amount for years. Now, all of a sudden, he's buying again – I've seen the receipts – and he's got more pots than he knows what to do with.'

'You've seen the receipts, have you? Would that have been when you were supposed to be powdering your nose? What else did you see?'

'I'll come back to that. Let's stick to the obvious stuff. What about the state of the house itself? The interiors are all clean and tidy enough but that place hasn't been redecorated, hasn't seen a lick of paint, I'd guess, for at least 20 years – but now he's undertaking a huge re-roofing operation.'

'It's obviously a priority, Dan. No point in tarting up the inside of a house if the roof's about to cave in.'

'Who's playing devil's advocate now? Yes a priority, but one he's only now able to take care of. Why wasn't it done years ago? Because he was broke, that's why. He's not broke now.'

'Come on, we both know these places don't make huge amounts of money. Maybe he was just saving up.'

Doyle shook his head. 'The roof's been a problem for many years. You saw all the patchwork repairs on it from the shore. That was all he could afford. And I've been upstairs, it stinks of damp up there. He's tried everything to keep Knott House in one piece – he's even hired it out in the past.'

'I don't remembering him saying that.'

'He didn't. You were right about him being deliberate in what he said, almost like he was working off a script. That's not the sort of thing that would sit well with his image of the successful landed gentry.'

'Yes, but how do you know he hired it out?'

'The fire escapes crawling all over the house's back side? The fire doors and extinguishers everywhere? You don't see them in *Horse & Hound*'s mansion of the month slot – that's health and safety conditions for a public licence from the local authority. I bet if we check we'll see it was used as some sort of corporate team bonding centre – all raft-building and shagging. Or an outward bound place for wee shoplifters from Castlemilk and Pilton.'

'OK, say you're right. Surely he'd know we could work that sort of stuff out or just look it up?'

'Not if we're only there to do what we were supposed to be doing – bumming up him and his bloody tea pots. And, with all due respect to Skye News, it is … well, Skye News. He doesn't know why we were there.'

'Mmm. Good point,' said Holly, putting down her fork. 'Why were we there?'

'Ah, now … ' Doyle took on board a mouthful of steak.

'Come on, Dan. What gives? You obviously have your suspicions about the guy.'

Doyle swallowed. 'I do and I've just had most of them confirmed.'

'But you're not going to tell me what they are.' She looked at him hard. 'You don't trust me, do you?'

'It's not about trust, Holly. Honestly.'

'OK, tell me what you found upstairs.'

'His office – again like something from 30-40 years ago but with a new computer, one I don't think he actually knows how to work.'

'And?'

Doyle told her about photographing the accounts. He would let her see them in due course but he would bet on them confirming his suspicion of an estate bumping along against its overdraft limit for years only to suddenly find itself cash rich.

'OK,' she said. 'But that just brings us back to the $64,000 question – or, rather – both of them. Where do you think all this new money has come from? And why are you interested in the first place?'

'I don't know the answer to the first one. And, trust me Holly, you don't want to know the answer to the second.'

12

It was, of course, the wrong thing to say. Once, on a date with a girl and enjoying a pleasant enough dinner, Doyle had said something indistinctly at the end of an exchange. To this day, he couldn't remember the triviality under discussion (it was a second date so he guessed they hadn't got as far as the Middle East peace process or assisted suicide just yet) – nor his mumbled contribution, just that it was some throw away, not that funny remark.

'What was that?' his date had asked.

'Nothing.'

'Come on, Dan – ' (naughty grin). 'What did you say?'

'It was just … look, it was nothing. Seriously. So! How's your starter?'

'Fine.' (Pause). 'It must've been something otherwise you wouldn't have said it.'

The smile was becoming a bit of an effort. The quip, if it even qualified as such, was now out of context and even more lame as a result. 'Honestly, _____ (insert name –

he'd forgotten that as well) it really was nothing at all. Just a ... you know, a remark.'

'Saying?'

'Saying nothing of any importance, trust me.' (Final big grin and a gesture he hoped said 'drop it – but please still have sex with me tonight'). He looked around in some desperation. 'It's nice in here, isn't it? Could do with a few more waiters, though.' And he began waving like a drowning man.

'If it wasn't that important, why won't you tell me?'

It had clearly become a point of principle. For them both. To repeat it now would be to add capitulation to the shame felt at his lack of wit.

'Because it was just a daft, nothing sort of comment, a throw away line of absolutely no consequence whatsoever.'

'That can't be repeated?'

'That doesn't deserve to be.'

'And yet it must remain a secret.'

'Secret? No. Just forgotten – left to wither on the vine of unheard, unremarkable banalities. Another victim of my shocking lack of diction and poor acoustics.'

She returned his generous smile with a tight little one of her own and played some more with her dressed crab.

'But I don't see why – ,'

'OK. I said you're a precious, insecure pain in the arse and that yours, by the way, looks huge in that skirt.'

There was no third date.

Likewise, as Doyle was about to find out, Holly was not untypical of her sex and placed circumspection in conversation somewhere between a vice and a challenge. When it came with a dollop of condescension ('trust me, you don't want to know ...') it had all the calming qualities of a slap in the face with a chainmail glove. Throughout the rest of their lunch, no matter what road Doyle took the chat down Holly always seemed to find a route back to his interest in Lytton and from where it stemmed. By the time they'd finished up, paid the bill and stepped out onto the street, it was if their recent rapprochement had never happened. He'd have loved to have waved a cheery goodbye and buggered off. But, of course, he had that sodding feature on sodding tea pots to write. They walked the short distance to the office in a tense silence. Bob was at his desk writing out a note as they entered.

'You've just missed a call, Dan. Moira Macleod.'

Doyle took a while to place the name. 'Eh … oh, aye – the sister of the missing creel boat skipper?'

'The same. She'd like a word when you've got the time.'

'Have they found the bodies?'

'No. Leastways I don't think so. It didn't sound like that. She kept saying it wasn't urgent, probably nothing, in fact, and you needn't bother if you didn't want to etc. etc.'

No matter how unappealing another drive out to Halistra was – with, of course, the attendant risk of running into his old man again – it was still better than spending the afternoon with a sulky Holly and he decided to call and tell her he would come over. As it happened, Moira Macleod had something she wanted to show Doyle.

Just under an hour later, he pulled up outside her brown, pebble-dashed bungalow and, consciously ignoring his father's unkempt croft next door, rang the doorbell. He remembered now he'd been in this house many times when he was younger. Old Iain Black, a proper crofter (not a charlatan like his father), had lived there, the range of his agricultural activities slowly but surely closing in on him. Once, he'd had more than 100 black face split between his own land and the common grazing over the hill – that and his allotment near the cottage, even a few chickens scurrying about. By the time Doyle had left, the old boy was all but housebound, his grazing overgrown, the fruit and veg restricted to a row or two of neeps and a bush of some summer fruit by his back door. There can be fewer lifetime journeys as poignant as the one from self-sufficiency to getting your dinners from meals-on-wheels.

Moira welcomed him into her cosy, immaculate front room. Doyle noticed only two differences from his visit a month earlier; a framed photograph of her brother George on the tiled mantlepiece above the fire and a tattered red notebook on the coffee table. He accepted the offer of tea and spent the time she was in the kitchen trying to remember what the house had been like when he'd been in for either a cuff round the ear for kicking his football into Iain's highland raspberries, or a conciliatory glass of cordial and some bun.

'I understand you used to live next door,' she said coming into the room with a tray. She glanced up and saw the concern in his face. 'Oh, don't worry. It wasn't your father who told me. But you must remember what it's like living round here – news travels fast in places where nothing much ever happens.'

'Yes, I do remember. I hope for your sake you don't have many dealings with the old bugger.' It could've been a risky sentiment to express; Moira was of generation that usually put great store by the ties of kith and kin. But he guessed she'd been there long enough to work out he was a treacherous old bastard. He was right.

'No, I um … ' she gave an embarrassed smile. 'We rarely speak.'

Over the tea and shortbread Doyle did his best to satisfy her polite curiosity about his time on Skye and why he'd left while trying not to make it sound like a storyline from Eastenders. Eventually, the uncomfortable grilling – or what she obviously thought was innocent small talk – drew to a natural conclusion and she brushed away some crumbs from her skirt in a 'getting down to business' fashion. She picked up the notebook.

'Some of the lads at Uig came round a week ago and asked about George's gear. They were really very nervous but I told them not to be so daft. Sure, it's not doing anyone any good at the bottom of the sea now is it?'

Doyle understood. When the Morven II went aground it didn't have any of George's creel strings on board and she didn't appear to have been trailing any from her winch gear. Her hold had been breached but it had been assumed the crew had managed to service the pots and been on the way back with their catch when whatever happened happened. That would be thousands of pounds worth of lobster pots – part of the late George Macleod's estate if nothing else.

'They wondered if George's diary had been on board with him or … ' she ran her fingers round the edges of the notebook. 'Anyway, he kept it here and I let them have a look.'

Doyle wondered when he would get to have a look and what he was supposed to be looking for.

'It was Willie Macdonald … you know Willie?'

Doyle shook his head.

'He skippers The Lady Margaret. Anyway, it was Willie who spotted it.'

'What?'

'The problem with where the Morven II was found.'

Moira Macleod still smiled but there was a fixed, sort of forced look about it now. Doyle noticed a slight tremble to her head.

'May I?' he asked. She noticed she was still holding the notebook.

'Oh, I'm sorry,' she handed it over. 'Silly. What am I like?'

It was a diary after all – a diary of 1998 as it happened, but it could've been any year for it was just a template. It wasn't filled with entries about what he'd had for dinner or who he'd met. In fact, whole weeks were simply blocked out, arrows and cross-hatching referencing entries above or below. Those entries were locations – names and grid references. This was a creeler's diary – the record every skipper keeps of where he fishes and when. Each has their own favourite sites. Through the years – and some of this information can be passed down through generations of creelers – they build up a picture of where the best catches of lobster, crab, prawn, whatever are to be had at certain times of the year. There will be an element of overlap with other boats, of course; the restrictions imposed by, say, the breeding season for lobsters, will mean boats fishing for other species are sometimes in pretty close proximity to each other. But, even then, the skippers learn to keep a respectful distance from each other.

Doyle flicked through the well-thumbed pages and saw George Macleod's working life before him; his routes around the north of the island and out into The Minch, the notes on weather, time and tide, logs of what and how much had been caught where as well as his reminders of regular maintenance checks, even when he had to submit his paperwork and accounts to various forms of officialdom. His annual pattern over almost 250 square miles of ocean was, of course, subject to change. Fishing grounds for crustaceans ebbed and flowed but, Doyle guessed from what he read, much less than was the case for fish. Any changes to his routine George would be careful to log with the appropriate date. It was clear that he gave up his favourite spots only reluctantly and after many return visits.

'I don't understand,' he said. 'If they were looking for his creels to salvage surely the floats would tell them where they were. They just go to where George had been fishing that day.'

'Oh, no. It's not that,' Moira Macleod still smiled but now while twisting a tissue in her hand. 'They found the gear. Just not where they expected.'

Doyle frowned and looked back at the diary. He checked for that week in August. The assistant harbour master at Uig had told him that George Macleod had been fishing for prawn and crab and the diary certainly confirmed that that is what he was usually doing at that time of the year. The diary also confirmed that for the past 15 years without fail George Macleod fished that month to the south of the Ascrib Islands where his catch was always among the best of the season.

The problem was that the Ascribs are 20 miles and the other side of The Minch from the Shiant Islands where the Morven II was found breaking up on the rocks.

He would've gone back to the B&B to write the tea pot piece on his laptop but not only was it still daylight, there was stuff he wanted to check online and Mrs MacBeth, his landlady, had answered his enquiry about wi-fi when he moved in by pointing proudly at a 40-year-old 'music centre' in the lounge. It was past 5 o'clock by the time he got back to the office but Holly was still there, scanning the on-screen thumbnails of the pictures she'd taken that morning. Bob, she said, had gone to his GP and then the chemists with a repeat prescription.

'How did it go?' she asked.

Doyle decided on nothing less than full disclosure. Five minutes later he was about to summarise the entire interview for her benefit once more, complete with the make of shortbread, when she held up a hand.

'Couldn't it have just drifted?'

'No. It would've been spotted – The Minch is pretty busy, you know. Besides, I'm almost certain the currents don't run that way. I'm going to double check that.'

'So, what does it mean?'

Doyle shrugged, 'Search me. I'm sure this Willie Macdonald character will have told the police and coastguard but I'm also pretty sure they'll have worked this out before now but not thought it important enough to bring to anyone's attention. I mean, at the end of the day, Macleod could have sailed anywhere he liked for any number of reasons. It's not as if the Shiant Islands are beyond his usual range.'

'But still, worth a story?'

'Absolutely. Moira's a wee bit upset by it all but only because she's still waiting for the bodies to be found. I'll put in the calls, get a few quotes and see what we come up with.'

She seemed satisfied with that and returned to her screen. Doyle left a message on the number he'd been given for Willie Macdonald but decided to wait until morning before calling either the coastguard or police.

He'd just begun going over his shorthand notes on the Lytton interview when Holly spoke again.

'Did you see your father?'

'Eh, no,' Doyle was caught slightly off guard. 'No, I didn't.'

'Do you plan to?'

'No.' Doyle kept his head in his notebook.

'You really hate him, don't you?'

He put down his pen and scratched a non-existent itch on the side of his head. 'Hate? My only problem with that word is they say there's only a fine line between it and love. That does not apply in this case.'

'But you came back to Skye nevertheless.' Holly spoke softly but clearly determined to get to some point or other. Doyle also noted she was confident that he already knew that she knew about his background. Either she assumed Bob would have told him or, much more likely, Bob had simply told her that he'd told Doyle that he'd told her. Doyle's eyes goggled just trying to keep track of Bob's lack of discretion.

'Yes. I did come back. Your old man and the job he could offer me were here.'

'Still ... seems a thin reason to overcome half a lifetime's aversion to Skye.'

'Not from my – ,'

'And I understand it was you who called my Dad, not the other way round.'

'Well, yes. I asked him if he had anything to offer. I wasn't exactly getting swamped by other career opportunities.'

Holly got up from her seat and ran her fingers round the bottom of her thin sweater as it followed the curves of her hips. She crossed to where Doyle sat and slowly, carefully perched herself on his desk, the denim-clad thigh of her right leg covering his notepad. She pulled the scrunchy from her hair and shook those red ringlets loose like a model in a shampoo advert. Putting one hand on the desk, she leaned over him and smiled. Her scent filled his nostrils and he had a flash back to the floor of bog in the Isles Inn. He did not expect good news.

'Dan, I don't mind you not trusting me but please don't take me for an idiot. I bet you probably did sign a confidentiality agreement. But that's it; you signed away your ability to spill the beans … for a price. And I'm guessing, in this case, quite a big price. You don't need the money – certainly not enough to go desperately searching for the first low-paid, temporary post in a small town news agency you could find. This isn't even back to square one for you, is it? You started off on a daily and ended up Mr Big Shot in Fleet Street.'

Doyle shifted in his seat and made to speak but Holly hushed him and put a finger – actually put her finger – to his lips. He felt his body go rigid like he'd just been injected with concrete.

'Shush now. We both know you don't need to be here – you want to be. And it's got something to do with Geoffrey Lytton. He's the reason you came back to Skye. Now then …' She took her finger away and patted his cheek before sitting up straight and folding her arms with another warm smile.

'You either tell me why him and why here or I kick you out of this office and you do your super sleuth routine on your own time.'

It had been a foul March day in London. Just the previous week, Doyle had been having lunch at a pavement café in the West End, the clement conditions so early in the year still a joy to a boy from the Hebrides. Now, however, winter was enjoying an encore and a bitter north easterly wind was whipping up from the Thames estuary, blowing through the plane trees along Embankment and driving in rain drops cold enough to sting the skin. Dick Collins was waiting for him at the coffee kiosk in the shadow of St Thomas Hospital. In a Marks & Spencers anorak with a Tesco carrier bag at his feet (Doyle knew it would contain a shop bought sandwich and a copy of the Metro taken from his bus into town that morning) he stood under an awning beside one of the tall tubular metal tables. As ever, he'd applied so much gel to what little hair he had left that it had clumped together in just a few thick bands swept back over his head. It looked like a cycle helmet on a bald man. Like everything else associated with *The Sunday News*, Collins was cheap.

He handed Doyle a huge latté, the cardboard sleave of which had been further reinforced by a deftly folded sheet of A4. They stood in silence for a while, staring out over to Westminster across the river, shifting their feet in the cold and blowing into their buckets of lava.

'Don't know why you're interested, mate,' Collins said at last. 'She's not my idea of A-list.'

Collins was such a sleezeball. An ex Securicor guard who'd developed a certain level of expertise with the gizmos and gadgetry of electronic surveilance, he saw himself as an authority on just about everything. The cops were all bent – apart from his few, trusted contacts – journalists were naive fools who needed to be told what was and what wasn't real news, and the general populous were sheep to be led or fleeced depending on what the situation demanded. Apparently, only he and other fat greasers who drank in Chelsea pubs talking shite to anyone who would listen knew 'what was really going on'.

Doyle stood for a bit and listened to Collins's latest expletive-heavy, half-baked diatribe against the fourth estate and how they should stop paying him to do stuff and start paying him to tell them what to do. He listened just long enough to make sure he could wring maximum pleasure from the only thing he'd come to say. He raised a hand just as Collins was about to expound further.

'Dick ... Dick, Dick, Dick,' he said, suddenly liking the sound of the man's name. 'I'm afraid I'll have to stop you there.'

'You in a rush mate?'

'You know, I sort of am. Here's the thing,' Doyle managed a sip of the milky crap. 'As you know, the paper's been feeling the heat lately on this. Certain previously, ah ... reliable relationships at the Met are no longer quite so steadfast, shall we say. Seems like a few folk have had a sudden attack of scruples. Yes, you can look that up later. Anyhoo, our time is up. I suppose all great life-sapping, immoral and corrupting relationships must come to an end sooner or later. We've had our moment, old boy, but I'm afraid the gutter is just going to have to get by without us.'

Collins scowl was slowly clearing as he put the big words aside and understood what was going on. He immediately clicked into defiant, 'Who cares? I don't need you anyway' mode.

'No sweat, don't worry about me.'

'I won't.'

'But you're still gonna pay.'

'For this?' Doyle tapped the paper still wrapped round the latté. 'Of course. Your account is being reinforced even as we speak.'

'So that's it?'

'Yup,' Doyle managed one more mouthful before he slipped the sheet into his pocket and chucked the carton in the nearest bin. 'It's been a blast, Dick. Mostly from your arse. Goodbye.'

Doyle walked back towards Westminster Bridge. He didn't expect the list to reveal anything (he could tell from Collins' description on the phone that he hadn't understood most of what had been said – any business transaction more complicated than a pint and a packet of pork scratchings would be beyond him). But just the fact Doyle had used the scam at least once for something other than trying to make headlines out of some poor sod's love life made him feel ... well, a little less grubby.

With the rain seemingly set in for the day, he was almost at Waterloo Station by the time he managed to hail a taxi. After the usual north bank/south bank debate with the driver, he sat back in the seat and pulled the sheet from his pocket. Collins, as was customary, had typed it up in a spread sheet; numbers Chloe Carew had received calls from on the left, the date and time in the middle, and the text of the messages on the right. It looked like maybe a couple of dozen over the week. The vast majority were acknowledgements of missed calls or meaningless out of context messages about the day to day stuff of business – meetings re-scheduled, confirmation of deliveries, updates on contract re-drafts and the like. There were a couple of messages from unknown friends referring to themselves only by first names – a Maddy and a Felicity – apologising for running late for a lunch or some other trifle. And that was it. Doyle was folding the sheet up about to stick it back in his pocket when something caught his eye and he did a double take. Slowly, he flattened the sheet out again.

His breath caught in his throat and he heard his pulse suddenly thrumming in his ears. He licked his lips and traced with his finger from the phone number across the page to the message. It was the one about the safe delivery of some unmentioned item. It read:

'Hello Chloe. Just to say the latest delivery has arrived safe and sound. Here whenever you'd like. Take care and maybe see you soon.'

When the taxi pulled up outside the offices of *The Sunday News* 15 minutes later, Doyle was still staring at the message.

Doyle had been pacing up and down the cramped newsroom, Holly was still sitting on the edge of his desk and, about half way through his story, Bob had returned. He was now on the small couch, gradually working out what was going on.

'And?' asked Holly. 'That was it?'

'That was the message, yes.'

'I don't get it.'

Doyle walked back to the desk and picked up his bag by the side of the chair. From a zipped inside pocket he produced the sheet of A4 and showed it to Holly. The details of the message were underlined across the page.

'Look at the number,' he said.

'01470 592230 ... but that's a local number – that's somewhere on Skye!' she said.

'Not just somewhere,' said Doyle. 'I had one lifeline growing up in Halistra – one means of contacting my friends, anyone in the outside world. I will never forget the number of that phone box.'

Doyle told them about how he'd been staking out the phone as often as he could since he'd been back on the island. The call to Carew had been on a Saturday just after 6am and, even if he couldn't manage any other time, he'd made sure he did that one each week – just in case it was some kind of regular arrangement. Last weekend, he said, Lytton had driven over from the Geary road and put in a short call from the payphone at roughly that time. He'd followed him back to Knott House.

Holly was now walking back and forth and, there being no room for two people to do that, Doyle sat back at the desk. She ruffled her hair a few times and made some faces.

'OK ... OK, I get all that. But why the suspicion in the first place? Why Chloe Carew?'

Doyle looked over to the couch.

'Perhaps I should answer that,' said Bob.

13

The room was stunned into silence. For long seconds all that could be heard was the tick of the clock on the wall and the faint echoes of someone walking down a corridor in another part of the building. It couldn't last, but while it did, Chloe experienced a rush like none she'd ever felt before. The inevitable sniggering brought it to an end. Sister Benedict stepped to the front of the class to restore order past a still visibly stunned Archbishop Marchetti, while Chloe sat composed, straight-faced. And, inside, more alive than she'd ever felt before.

'Chloe Carew!' Sister Benedict turned her fire on her once the rest of the class had been threatened with excommunication if they uttered another word. 'I have never heard the like ... You apologise to His Grace this instant.'

'But, Sister – ,'

'This instant!'

If she'd meant it there was no way she would've apologised. Not on a matter of such apparent deep, personal principle. But, of course, she hadn't. She wanted to be rich when she grew up, not, as she'd just informed the archbishop, the first ordained female priest in the Roman Catholic Church. Besides, the best bit was over – no need to make matters worse for herself unnecessarily.

'Sorry, Your Grace,' she mumbled.

And so it was that in 1967, as the rest of Britain discovered peace, love and tie dye shirts, the ten-year-old Chloe Carew discovered the thrill of discord and controversy, of being the scandalous centre of attention – of confounding expectations. It had been said on impulse, yet Chloe was unsurprised by it. Something had taken hold of her, but something she had already felt growing inside her as she grew – a wickedness that, in years to come, others would forgive and condone as mere cheekiness or mischief. They were wrong, they could not (or chose not to) see that Chloe's naughtiness as a child, manipulative streak as a teenager, her single-mindedness in adulthood were all just the visible manifestations of something that ran much deeper, much darker beneath the surface.

She hadn't laughed with the other girls in the class, nor in the playground after she'd recovered from the battering she'd received once the archbishop had left. Her classmates noticed this and, though still giggly themselves with the audacity of it, they felt the first faint chill of that emotion Chloe, small dumpy Chloe, would somehow manage to trigger in so many others in years to come: fear.

And she did become rich. Her hard working, decent lower middle class parents in the Ealing semi that they could never quite afford to move up from, were pleased her high achievement at school and university was not being wasted. OK, if they were honest, it would've been nice if she'd made her money from something that at least appeared to be a bit more worthy, a profession of some sort. Much easier to get instant approval and kudos at the tennis club by saying 'barrister' or 'doctor' to any new acquaintances enquiring about their only daughter. Having to explain and enlarge upon 'business' or even 'property' was, if they were honest, a bit of a chore and slightly disappointing. After all, Brian himself was 'in business': what else would you call being senior sales manager at Wealdstone Pumps and Filters? But Chloe had always done what she wanted and they'd trusted her judgement. At least, that's what they'd said every time they'd caved in to her demands – dressing up submission as a lesson in responsibility. Because, if they were honest, they too were afraid of Chloe.

From modern history at the only fee-paying convent school in London her parents could afford to social psychology at the London School of Economics, Chloe took her studies seriously while having absolutely no intention of making a living from anything she studied. Not directly anyway. In any case, that living was already being made long before she graduated. With a gift of a large chunk of her parents' savings (which her father insisted, against all the evidence, was a loan) she'd bought her first flat – a single bedroom basement in Hammersmith with battleship grey walls to hide the damp and an ancient Baby Belling two-ring cooker in the chipboard kitchen. She rented it out to five cousins from Uganda who promised to come and go in ones and twos and keep the noise down. Between the rental income and her grant, she could afford the luxuries the wealthier students could. She shopped at Liberty and Laura Ashley instead of C&A and British Home Stores. She drank in wine bars rather than the students' union. She even bought a second-hand Austin Allegro and gave her new friends lifts to her other new friends' houses in Hampshire and Surrey for weekend parties. She never had them back to Ealing.

Was it the money that also made her more attractive? It was a question asked by many on the periphery of her increasingly well-defined circle since she seemed to have no problems in getting laid. Chloe had stopped growing upwards at the age of 15 but not in other directions. She was bubbly and engaging enough company when she wanted to be but no amount of drink at her expense was going to have you confusing her with Debbie Harry. Yet, there was no mystery to her success and certainly no element of financial coercion. For students at the LSE it was ironic they couldn't see what Chloe could – a simple case of supply and demand; she had a voracious sexual appetite and boys of a certain age – at least most of them – would shag anything with lipstick and a pulse given half a chance. It was true that in later life, as it became clear she was not the marrying sort and her drinking and smoking was robbing her of what little physical charm she'd ever had in the first place, she did deploy some of that wealth in the business of keeping her sexual frustrations at bay. But she had no problem with a transaction she saw as a damn sight more cost effective than her girl friends' expenditure on spa treatments. Relieve tension? Hot stones and a facial? For the money she could get her brains fucked out and still have change for a packet of fags.

By the time she graduated and launched herself at the property market, Margaret Thatcher was launching herself at Britain's post war political consensus. It wasn't long before Chloe's personal agenda of self advancement was chiming perfectly with that of her new heroine at No.10. And, just as Thatcher suffered no fools and took no prisoners, Chloe's business style became known as singularly robust. With a real bank loan taken out on the equity now in the Hammersmith flat, she began expanding her portfolio. She liked student flats (no problems in getting rid of bad payers plus a fresh intake of potential customers every year) and, of course, your basic slum for immigrants who didn't know and probably hadn't known anything better. When Thatcher's 'home owning democracy' got into full swing and local authorities were eventually cowed into selling off their housing stock, Carew was perfectly placed to take advantage of the resultant boom in the buy-to-let market. From a rental portfolio soon measured in hundreds across west and south London it was a small step into property development. This was a business that demanded economies of scale and Chloe lost no time in expanding her reach from individual flats to whole building redevelopments and, eventually, new builds.

Meanwhile, the City of London was booming and speculation and risk were paying off handsomely. Chloe was not above a dabble on the stock market but, while young men and women, some of whom she'd studied with, got champagne drunk on their success, she never lost her focus on property. When the state sell offs started and the nation scrambled for shares in British Gas and BT, Chloe demurred. As she liked to say at the time, you win Monopoly by owning property – not Marylebone Station and the water works.

Her speciality was off market dealing – securing plum sites before most people even knew they were for sale. The legitimate way to make money thus is through hard graft following development trends, spotting the growth areas before the crowd, knowing the best placed lawyers and estate agents who can point you in the right direction. Eventually you become a driver of economic development as much as its follower, a bellwether of trends and capital flows. In the right market, you make things happen just by showing an interest. Chloe achieved that status in London in the late '80s and early '90s. But her years in dealing with the rougher end of the building trade, with cowboys, scammers and hired muscle had taught her the advantages to be gained in taking short cuts. She made things happen alright, but a little more directly than normal business etiquette would recommend. Perhaps a reluctant owner suddenly saw the attraction in moving out when Chloe's associates explained their options. Maybe new and costly regulations (often, as chance would have it, ones from Europe concerning environmental or health and safety concerns) would turn out to have been unnecessary after all. And then again, it was always possible that like-minded officials in certain boroughs could be persuaded of the merits of speed over such unnecessary bureaucracy – especially after they'd seen trickle down economics work so instantaneously in their favour.

Did that mean she had a low profile, kept herself in those shadows from where she engineered most of her profits? No. The little girl who'd rendered an archbishop speechless still liked to mix it in public. The more Thatcherism was contested, the more Chloe Carew became one of its most outspoken supporters. She was a rent-a-quote for the *London Evening Standard*, for radio and, eventually, television. Her motivation was the same as it had been back in that classroom; to cause a stir, to shock and provoke. But it was also strategic; it was the magician's misdirection. She mouthed off like a columnist in *The Sun*, almost a pantomime dame of the hard right, and the largely right wing press took their cue. She was routinely quoted, her *bona fides* always simply taken for granted.

Chloe rode out the recession of the early 90s by diversifying, spreading her risk into everything from sandwich bars to servicing the new NHS trusts that were springing up all over the country. But her property businesses she kept afloat, even if some ran at a loss. When Gordon Brown's 'gaun yersel' approach to the banks in the early noughties put mortgages within reach of anyone who could write their own name, the boom years returned and Chloe was perfectly placed to take immediate advantage. By 2003, the various investment, construction and management companies under the umbrella of Carew Holdings Ltd constituted one of the biggest integrated property businesses in the UK. By now requiring an executive structure way beyond Chloe and her trusted inner circle to run, the vast majority of its business was of necessity entirely legitimate.

Every now and then, however, a project would present a 'challenge' Chloe could not resist and she would take personal charge …

Since the 13th century, the rivers Avon and Frome had been gated, dammed, redirected and press ganged into work as the main port for Bristol and the south west. After 20th century contructions of deep water anchorages at Avonmouth and Portbury, however, the writing was on the quayside for a facility not able to cope with supertankers and massive bulk carriers. With the local authority and development agency at the helm, a regeneration scheme was launched, the plan to visit upon Bristol Dock that miracle of post industrialisation: making a profit out of flats, museums and open air dining. Though not the favoured, main developer, Chloe's investment arm entered a joint venture scheme to build a shops and office block on one of the prime sites.

Meanwhile, just outside the regeneration project's boundary, a three-acre disused marine paint works was bought by a compamy called St Johns Developments. Having specialised in copper-based anti-fouling paint, the works' buildings were contaminated with, among other things, lead, arsenic, barium, chromium and the aforementioned copper. It had solvents in huge sunken tanks, benzene, toluene and acetone ingrained in the brick and woodwork and, just to round things off, asbestos lagging the pipes that criss-crossed the entire site. The price was based on a promise by the seller, a local builder-turned-speculator, to pay for the clean up. Half way through that process, however, the guy went bust and St Johns was left with a £3 million site (paid for) and most of a £750,000 clean-up operation (not paid for) yet to do. New contractors were brought in and the decontamination was completed, the buildings demolished and the site made good for development. Or was it?

The seller, now trying to reinvent himself once again and trading under a new name, approached the *County Post* with an interesting story – for sale, of course. The completion of the clean-up, he averred, had been too quick to have tackled everything that he'd left undone. He provided paperwork to back up his story and a list of all the work he knew had still to be done on site. The paper's chief reporter checked this against submissions to the Environment Protection Agency, got a stonewall answer from St Johns and went to press with the classic 'toxic time bomb' front page splash.

Within hours of the paper hitting the news stands, however, the previously shy St Johns Developments – or rather, its army of lawyers – descended on the *County Post* like a swarm of hornets. Far from being the villains of the piece, they contested, they were the victims. Signed statements and contracts appeared out of thin air proving false claims on behalf of the seller. The EPA, which was now investigating, commended St Johns for its transparency and co-operation while commenting tartly on the seller's lengthy rap sheet of previous misdemeanours. And, just to complete the seige, the seller himself backtracked and claimed everything from misquotation to not having his expenses paid.

With their own lawyers now panicking, the paper was forced into a humiliating climbdown and retraction. But that wasn't going to get them off the hook. Legal fees and the cost of having to now complete the decontamination work meant St Johns Developments was substantially out of pocket. Between that and the reputational damage it said the story had wrought, its lawyers assured the *County Post* it could demand enough reparation to close it down. Good relations with the local press, however, were important to the company which saw the old paint works as just the first of many investments in the area. Court action wouldn't be necessary, they said, if the paper demonstrated a commitment to the highest possible journalistic standards ...

Bob Miller wasn't told by his ashen-faced editor that day that his sacking had been demanded by St Johns Developments. He didn't have to be.

'I'd asked Dan to find out what he could about the company long before then,' said Bob, slumping back on the couch, tired from telling his story. He motioned for Doyle to pick up the baton.

'St Johns Developments was a shell company registered for a few bucks through an incorporation agent in Antigua,' said Doyle. 'Normally, you start running after one of those, you end up with a sore face from all the brick walls you hit.'

'But you didn't,' said Holly, now perched on the edge of her own desk.

'No. Well, I did to begin with but, before newspapers decided the minutiae of celebrities' lives was of vital national importance, they used investigators for all sorts of things. *The Sunday News*, where I'd just started, didn't just use Dick Collins. It had a whole listings page full of spooks and peepers for different types of job. I went to this corporate investigation service – asset recovery, offshore audit trails, that sort of thing. Anyway, long story short, St Johns' paper trail led all the way back to Carew Holdings.'

Holly wrinkled her nose in a way Doyle was beginning to find annoyingly attractive. 'But I thought they already had a development nearby and, besides, why assume Chloe Carew herself was behind all this?'

Doyle looked at Bob, but he just waved him on.

'I spoke to a friend of mine on the *FT* – former convenor of the Glasgow University Socialist Workers' Party, as it happens, now writing articles to make our masters of the universe feel all warm and fuzzy about themselves. Anyway, his soul's still reasonably intact. He'd started nosing about Carew a few years earlier and was getting some real dirt but nothing he could back up. Any time anyone said anything juicy it was always off the record. Former associates, even people she'd crossed – they were all, he reckoned, still shit scared of her.'

'Scared? Of Chloe Carew?' Holly almost snorted.

Doyle ignored her and pressed on. 'Two things he told me about Carew fitted what happened to Bob perfectly. First was her habit of approaching things from multiple angles – you know, like a general deploying a pincer movement. She'd have an upfront, possibly perfectly legit interest in something – a development project or a company she wanted to buy out – but also something in the background, a safety net or, if I may throw in one last metaphor, like having her cake and eating it. She'd maybe have an interest in a competitor without the competitor even knowing about it, or she'd already own a neighbouring piece of land that was vital for the success of some development, that sort of thing. Being part of a joint venture at Bristol Dock and owning land right next door was classic Carew.'

'Go on,' Holly was non-committal.

'The other thing was that she takes certain things personally – I mean Goodfellas personally. She's a thug, real old school: all knuckdusters and piano wire. If Bob's story had cost her a penny she'd have gone after him. As it happens, he cost her tens of thousands. My mate was surprised Bob hadn't lost his testicles along with his career.'

Holly turned to her father. 'So, that's how you ended up here?'

'Eventually, yes,' said Bob. 'I tried for other jobs but I was pushing 50 and, frankly, no-one believed I'd left the *Post* of my own free will – well, except for you and your mother. Sorry. Anyway, I heard about Skye News being up for sale and reckoned that, if no-one else would, I'd just have to employ myself.' He gave a wry smile. 'Despite Dan here telling me the place was a shithole, I came up and the rest, as they say ...'

Holly simply shook her head slowly and stared at the wall in front of her. There was silence for the first time in what felt like ages. Doyle looked out the window and saw that dusk had fallen, street lights were flickering on to that deep red colour before warming up to orange. The road was quiet, Portree's version of a rush hour already long gone.

Holly got up again and paced some more. 'Right,' she said, stopping to look at Bob. 'So you screwed up a story with some sloppy reporting, got the sack, couldn't find work anywhere else and came up here because you had no other options, yeah?'

'Well, in a nutshell ... ,'

'And you, ' she turned to Doyle. 'You figure Chloe Carew, far from being a five foot nothing middle aged TV personality and celebrity business woman – a national treasure, I think the *Daily Mail* called her – is in fact a hoodlum who likes to break peoples' fingers and throw poor old widows out onto the street. This you conclude on the back of unsubstantiated hearsay, guesswork and the fruits of the very illegal so-called journalistic practices you yourself were sacked for.'

Doyle drew breath to speak but Holly now had her back to him and kept talking. 'At my father's request ...?'

Bob shook his head and gave an 'I knew nothing about it – honest' look.

' ... OK then, in a desperate attempt to just salve your conscience and do your old pal a favour at the same time, you decided to illegally hack into the phone messages of this dangerous criminal and came up with what? A Skye phone number and a perfectly innocent message. You investigate and finally unmask her partner in crime as none other than Geoffrey Lytton, the teapot magnate. He is clearly up to no good because, as you have so keenly observed, he's got a new microwave and is having his roof fixed.'

Doyle met her stare and pursed his lips for a bit. She liked to play devil's advocate – that much had been proved already. But he saw something else in her hostility: an isolation; yet again she had been excluded. He realised that half the time he'd been with her, Holly was on the receiving end of information people had been keeping from her. Slightly amazed at his own sensitivity in spotting this, Doyle was still trying to think of something equally sensitive to say about it when Bob spoke up.

'I think we both owe you an apology,' he said.

'Damn right,' she said with feeling.

'Sorry, love. I just couldn't bring myself ... you know? Pride, I suppose. And, well, after all these years I didn't see any need to unburden myself.'

'You unburden yourself with everything else, for God's sake,' she said.

Doyle clamped his mouth shut to stop from laughing but it came out his nose instead. As he grabbed for his handkerchief, Bob burst into huge guffaws and Holly, after a second or two's valiant struggle, cracked into a wide grin and joined in. Only through the release of their laughter did Doyle realise just how much tension had built up in the room over the last hour or so. It was some time before they settled down again, dabbing their eyes with the heels of their palms.

'And what about you,' Holly turned the last of her smile into another quizzical look at Doyle. 'Anything else you'd like to reveal? You break any other laws I should know about? Got even more family up here – a wife and kids tucked away in Broadford, perhaps?'

'No, that's the lot. I promise.' (Interesting second question, he thought). 'Like you say, it's a house of cards at the moment. I know that. That's why I didn't tell you or Bob anything about it.'

'So what's your next move?'

'Go through Lytton's accounts, I suppose. See if they throw up anything.'

Holly looked at Doyle for a while. 'You used your own name with Lytton when you didn't need to. Carew knows about you, doesn't she?'

'Probably.'

'Are you trying to provoke her?'

'It's not the reason I get up in the morning but I don't go out of my way to avoid it.'

'And yet if she's as ruthless and vindictive as you say she could ruin you.'

Doyle opened his arms out. 'With all due respect,' he said. 'What's left to ruin?'

14

… The Devil soon reached Waternish, still singing. Here he met the wolf, an old ally of his. The wolf had just successfully accomplished a little bit of business for him and had come to report. The Devil, feeling happy, praised him for his skill and cunning and the wolf, encouraged by this unusual geniality, ventured to inquire what had so pleased him.

'God has given me a plant,' cried the triumphant Devil.

'What plant?' asked the interested wolf. The Devil stopped short as he was about to answer.

'You have put it out of my head with your silly chatter,' he said angrily. The wolf, rather alarmed, looked round hastily for some plant to suggest.

'Was it heather?' he inquired.

'Oh, no, nothing so common.'

'Was it rushes?'

'No indeed. You know they are holy.'

'It must have been thistle then,' growled the wolf, being no botanist and seeing nothing else growing near that he could suggest.

'Yes. Yes. Perhaps it was …' said the Devil doubtfully. 'But I did feel it was better than that. Still, it's a plant.'

Ever since, the Devil has busied himself spreading his thistles over the earth.

(**The Inner Hebrides and Their Legends** by Otta F Swire.)

It was a bone yard. A vast and ugly bone yard. And the moon didn't help.

Doyle tramped up the path to the west of the low hill of Maol nan Gillean and once again struggled to remember what it had been like all those years ago. The path was actually a forestry track – or had been – and led to a network of others criss-crossing the plantations of Lodgepole Pine and Sitka Spruce covering much of eastern Waternish. In his boyhood, this had been a favourite haunt. He'd prided himself in knowing these hillsides like they were his own back garden. Even in the piney gloom there was always something about the lay of the land, the echo of the sea on the shore, the angle of daylight shafting through the canopy that would tell him exactly where he was. But, in the years since, these woods had been sold by the Forestry Commission and much of it had matured and been harvested – like the hillside to his immediate left. All that remained now were thousands of bleached white stumps amid a vicious tangle of razor sharp broken branches and unearthed roots. And beneath it all, a fresh crop of thistles.

After perhaps quarter of a mile, Doyle passed an old quarry to his right and took the first path off to the left beyond it. Over the shoulder of Maol nan Gillean he walked, the way as easily defined by the full moon and a gazillion stars as it would've been in broad daylight. Ahead, he could see the edge of the harvested acres, dead and dying trees flattened as if by a giant hand or leaning like pale, exhausted skeletons against the dark green wall of the dense living forest beyond. On the high ground, past another old quarry, a wooden sign leads the walker north onto a zig zag track over the boggy hilltop of Cnoc Breac. Doyle ignored this and kept his bearing due east. Ten minutes later, he was enveloped by the dark stillness of the woods. Before long the track he was on made a sharp turn to the south and at this point, Doyle stepped off to the left, jumped the ditch and delved into almost total darkness.

He stood for a moment to let his eyes adjust; he carried a torch but he'd rather not use it. Gradually, black faded to shades of grey and he could make out the evenly spaced trunks and the route he must take in between them. Not a lot can grow on the floor of dense conifer plantations so his only concern from now on was the uneven ground – that, and the one major obstacle he knew lay just a couple of hundred yards ahead.

Old Nick's pal wasn't the only wolf in these parts – Waternish was indeed their last stronghold on Skye and the outlines of the traps dug by locals more than 300 years ago to capture and kill them can be found by those who know what they're looking for. A 12-year-old Doyle and his friends had come across one in here and spent the best part of a week that summer re-excavating it to its former, lethal glory. (Well … it seemed like a good idea at the time.) He looked down on it now, a black void at the base of a rocky outcrop not far from the eastern edge of the forest. He'd seen it since in better light and knew that, aside from a few small branches and a mulch of pine needles at the bottom, it was still as worryingly deep and sheer as when it was the scene for endless games of dare and double dare. Doyle skirted around it and continued on his way, heading straight for the sound and smell of the sea. Less than quarter of a mile further on, he emerged from the treeline. He took five more steps and then stopped. The bright moon and starlight almost dazzled him and he knew this was not the place to be treading unwarily. After a moment, he found the faint deer track, took a further step beyond it and peered over the edge of a 300ft cliff. This was the spectacular Beinn an Sguirr.

Below was not the sea but a shelf of land about a square mile in extent. Roughly triangular in shape, it consisted of more harvested spruce plantations, some dark, lush stands not yet felled, flanks of fern and heather close to the cliff and beyond, and a further 300ft below, the shoreline of Loch Snizort – six miles north of where it slapped against the stone jetty outside Knott House. Doyle took the track to the south east, the cliff edge only a few feet to his left. Carefully, he made his way past a couple of treacherously overgrown gullies before he reached a point where, just below the top of the cliff, a promintory of rocks hung out over the scene below. He scrambled down, shrugged off the small backpack he carried and settled into the grassy hollow he'd been in the night before and the night before that.

Like anyone else hurtling through their 30s at Mach 3, Doyle felt himself getting older by the hour. He ached in the morning for no apparent reason, he could remember when R&B meant R&B and the lack of an adequate pension plan was becoming a worry. He also found himself talking about 'in my day' as if it had already been and gone. But it was true – in his day, doing too many things at the one time - and none of them particularly well - was not considered smart. Now the world positively recommended it, now it was called multi-tasking. Without wishing it on himself, Doyle realised he had several plates spinning at the one time.

His engagement with Skye News – always supposed to be half-hearted and very temporary – was turning into rather a lengthy secondment. Yes, he was getting time off the diary to pursue … whatever the hell it was he was pursuing, but he did also have to justify his wage; Bob was simply not up to much these days and Holly couldn't cover all of the day-to-day tasks herself. And so he was doing his fair share of cheque presentations and council committees in between trying to make sense of everything else …

Not for the first time, Doyle found himself comparing the swirl of theories and conspiracies in his head to what he'd been told of the currents in the Minch. With in-flows from the Sea of the Hebrides and Irish Sea to the south, and the Atlantic through the Sound of Harris to the west and over the Butt of Lewis to the north, it was one complicated stretch of water. The net movement of currents varied according to depth, season, tide and weather conditions and mapping and predicting them was, in the words of one official at the government's Fisheries Research Services in Aberdeen, 'a total bugger'.

Willie Macdonald had told him that while he and many others in Uig thought it highly unlikely the Morven II could have drifted north to the Shiant Islands where she was found, there had been a stiff southerly wind that day and anything was possible. Between that and the probability that Macleod had simply gone there for some reason after servicing his creels at the Ascrib Islands, the authorities were not reading too much into the discrepancy. Doyle had written a story to that effect merely as a pot boiler for any paper or broadcaster still interested. He did not get many takers.

Though Moe and Curly had dropped off the radar, Doyle could not afford to believe they weren't capable of popping up at any moment. Scanning his surroundings for a couple of ugly Croats had become a habit over the last month, one he saw no reason to break. He remained convinced they were at the very least mules in some sort of smuggling operation and that they hadn't been on the island to climb mountains and buy fudge. It was a racing certainty that Sandy would come back with a 'thanks but no thanks' from his colleagues. But Doyle had dealt with cops plenty of times in the past. He would find some way of engineering a meeting with the right one, one who would turn a blind eye to the absence of any actual evidence (Norrie would have undoubtedly toked that within days) but would listen to Doyle's story and think it worth checking out. With Bob still wading through his first cycle of chemo, Doyle could well still be around for the conclusion of even a lengthy investigation.

The question that no-one, Doyle included, seemed brave enough to ask was could there be a connection between that speculative shot in the dark and the Carew/Lytton speculative shot in the dark?

Despite the lack of anything a court of law would even generously consider hard evidence, Doyle was convinced Carew was up to something. He also accepted that, for the moment at least, it was a conviction he had all to himself. Holly, after recovering from her fit of pique, could still muster nothing more than open-mindedness as to the possibility that this well-known national figure could be so villainous behind the scenes. Bob knew from first hand experience what a spiteful bitch Carew could be. But actually criminal? He'd need a lot more than Doyle had to believe it.

As Holly speculated, however, it was almost certain Carew had known about Doyle for some time. Collins was the kind of guy who operated in a world of his own invention, a flipside where notions of, for example, right and wrong, smart and stupid, had a different meaning from out here in normality. Of course *The Sunday News* had made him sign a confidentiality agreement before giving him a handsome pay off. But expecting vermin like Collins to be hidebound by legalities – or even a reasonably functioning sense of self-preservation – was like expecting insect repellant to stop midges biting. Knowing what he knew of Collins, Doyle was absolutely certain he would've tried to make money out of Carew. While he might not have understood what most of Carew's phone messages had been about, Collins knew that Doyle had been interested enough in her activities to ask for them. He would have thought it at least possible they contained something Carew would rather remained out of the public domain. Once Doyle had been given his jotters Collins no doubt 'reasoned' he was covered; any leak could be blamed on the ex-employee.

As for establishing his credentials with Carew, what better way than for Collins to reveal every detail of his dealings with *The Sunday News* – including the name of his contact. Would she have been interested enough to go looking for him? Possibly. If so, would she have been able to track him to Skye? Possibly not … until, that is, he'd called Geoffrey Lytton last week on the phone and said, 'Hi, my name's Dan Doyle.'

Lytton's accounts had been at once uninformative and revealing. On paper, the Suladale Estate was not doing very well at all. The addition of the new fish farm during the last financial year had taken its toll. Interest payments on the bank loan were penal and, so far at least, the thing was making no profit whatsoever – just soaking up more money for fitting out, stocking and maintenance. Equally, there was no mention of any new injection of cash from another source, no great upturn in profits from other activities, no new income stream to compensate for the losses. The Inland Revenue was being told that the estate was leveraged to the limit – betting the farm (literally) on the ultimate success of Lytton's decision to expand. Yet Holly and Doyle knew that was not the case. There was money to spend. Was Lytton merely up to the oldest trick in the cooked book – massaging the figures to make out he was poorer than he was to reduce his tax bill? It was possible of course but, despite Holly's enthusiasm for that theory, Doyle was sure he knew different.

Confirmation of the Chloe Carew connection was something else that enlightened and obfuscated in equal measure. She and Lytton obviously knew each other socially, but the very banality, the studied lack of detail in the message he left that morning had Doyle convinced it was no social call.

'Hello Chloe. Just to say the latest delivery has arrived safe and sound. Here whenever you'd like. Take care and maybe see you soon.'

Delivery of what? And why to Skye? 'Safe and sound' – why shouldn't it be?

Whatever it was, Doyle knew one thing: it had arrived via Lytton's new fish farm.

Its lights twinkled offshore, half a mile and some 600ft below where Doyle sat in the rocks, a newly bought North

Face jacket wrapped tight around him. To the north and beyond Beinn an Sguirr were the few lights of the crofting hamlets of Gillen and Geary, and eight miles away across the sea loch, the lights of townships along the western flank of Trotternish. Directly below him, the old loggers road, a spur from the road through Gillen, had been upgraded to service the fish farm. Nothing fancy, just a fresh layer of aggregate to allow the trucks and tractors to wend their way through the old plantations to the shore where a quay – out of sight from where Doyle sat – would give access to the cages out in the sea loch via the small service vessel.

Doyle took another recent purchase from the back pack, a pair of Bushnell night vision binoculars, and trained them on the farm, a collection of eight rectangular net pens arranged in two rows of four. Gangways connected the pens to each other and to a central spine which ran up to the docking area – a platform perhaps 50 yards square. On this was a old prefab shed and, around it, sundry piles of ropes, boxes and the other miscellany of fish farming. It was quiet and dark apart from the odd low energy lamp over a gantry and the weak glow from underwater lighting in the pens. To the uninitiated it looked normal and harmless. But Doyle was losing count of the number of things he didn't like about this fish farm.

He didn't like the fact that it was at the end of a road that led right back to Halistra and his old phone box. He didn't like the fact it was anywhere in Loch Snizort in the first place. Having worked on a few for summer jobs or providing free labour for his old man, he knew the rudiments of the industry well enough. Rule number one, he seemed to remember, is that you locate your fish farm in sheltered waters. This was the only fish farm he knew in Skye that was exposed to the prevailing westerlies.

The thing also didn't actually look like any other fish farm he knew. It's a basic enough business: big cages filled with salmon or trout or whatever, the means of putting them in, feeding and managing them and access for the barge or service vessel to come alongside and harvest. What this one needed with so much decking and a building the size of your average public lavatory, he had no idea. But he didn't like it.

And, partly because he had no idea why the coincidence should bother him so much, he didn't like the fact that just two miles away and visible in the moonlight, were the Ascrib Islands where the Morven II should have been the day it disappeared.

As Doyle lowered the binoculars, a movement below caught his eye. He raised them again and focussed on what turned out to be a dark-coloured truck bumping along the loggers road. He checked his watch. As far as he knew, there was never any reason to be heading to a fish farm at 3.46 in the morning. Something else he didn't like.

15

Doyle's eyrie had been chosen carefully. From a vantage point this far distant he could observe the road below, the fish farm and all possible approaches to it by sea. Moreover, if it was indeed being used for smuggling or some other illegal activity, it was a fair bet it would guarded, perhaps with lookouts posted on a perimeter. Already in Moe and Curly's bad books and having left his calling card with Lytton, Doyle had no desire to risk an encounter with any more of what Holly, no doubt ironically, still called the bad guys. Then again, should the occasion demand a closer look, he knew a short cut.

As the truck approached the southern end of the road, its brake lights came on and it turned to dip down towards the shoreline and out of sight. Doyle bit his bottom lip for a second, muttered a 'What the fuck,' to himself and jumped up. Ramming the binoculars back in the bag as he went, he scrambled back up onto the deer path and headed east. Fifty yards on he came to another overgrown gully and immediately ducked below its overhanging branches of rowan and ash. He waded through fern for a few paces and found the burn as it spilled over and around a narrow gash of exposed rock. Within a couple of yards of where he stood, it disappeared over a sheer drop. Hoping he'd remembered the right gully after all, Doyle walked to the edge, turned his back to the drop and lowered himself, left leg first. He found the foothold, took his weight on that and his hands and gingerly brought his right leg over and down below his left. That too, found a ledge. On he went, left leg then right, left then right, never having less than three points of contact with the rockface at any one time, the burn either splashing directly in front of his face or falling through a channel behind the rocks he clambered down. If he was honest, it was easier than he thought it would've been. The gaps between the hand and footholds that had been a stretch for his childhood self, were now much easier to negotiate.

Doyle reached the bottom within minutes, soaked but thankfully in one piece. He was on relatively open, sloping ground now, the road some 200yds in front of him. He set off on a loping run, swerving round rocks and ditches, thankful that the harvested forest and its assault course of stumps and branches was, at this point, on the other side of the road. As he stepped onto the course aggregate surface, he was acutely aware of how exposed he now was. Clouds were building to the south west but, for the moment, the moon and stars still had the landscape lit like the set of a cheap horror movie. Doyle stepped back off the road and crouched into the soggy ditch by the side. Rolling up the sleeves of his jacket, he took two handfuls of muddy peat and rubbed it over his face and hands. It smelled of stagnant water and as it dried it itched and made him feel like there were insects crawling all over his face. Maybe there were. Despite still being hot and panting slightly from the scramble and run, he took a black woollen beanie from his pocket and slipped it over his sandy coloured hair. With the rest of his clothing either dark grey or black, he could do no more to make himself invisible. He set off again.

Suddenly there was the unmistakable thrum of a marine diesel engine starting up. He approached the bend at the crest of the descent down to the shore in a sort of low jog, his shoulders slumped, his gait becoming more and more chimp-like. Some heather on a hillock to the left offered cover and he moved off the road and crawled up to peer over the top. The road turned into a rough track that wound down a steep slope with couple of hairpin bends before opening out onto a tight turning circle at the bottom maybe 30yds square. Some pallets were stacked to the side and in front of a large galvanised steel, open-sided shed. The truck – he could now see it was a long wheel-base Volvo, painted a dull, matt green – had been turned tail on to a t-shaped jetty thrusting out some 20yds offshore. What looked like an hydraulic hand pallet truck was left at one end of this, the end from where a reasonably small, maybe eight-metre boat was now leaving a silver trail in the water as it headed towards the fish farm. This had a cabin in the bows, doors port and starboard, and an open deck with a winch a-stern. Doyle took out the binoculars again but the deck was in shadow and he could make nothing out, just the silhouettes of two men under the weak overhead light of the cabin. He watched as it sailed due north, approaching the farm from the right hand side. When it was maybe 500yds out, Doyle got to his feet and, still sticking to the edge of the road and what cover there was from heather and scrub, carefully made his way down the hill.

Mindful of the possibility of someone left onshore, Doyle quartered around the open area and approached via the back of the lean-to. There was a small path but no-one there, nor by the pallet stack at the side. He stood for a minute, the shed on his left shoulder, the shore and jetty to his right. There was no movement. No sound other than the fading hum of the fast disappearing boat. From this angle, Doyle could see that one of the truck's rear doors had been left lying open. He walked over and looked inside. Several paces short of the truck he caught a powerful whiff of something deeply unpleasant and he instinctively slowed, apprehensive about what might produce such a stench.

The floor of the cargo space was at about chest height but he could see well enough into the darkened interior. It was empty. But what the hell was that stink? Chemical? Yes, but not like any he'd encountered before. There was an earthy, fetid quality to it, a staleness verging on the rotten. The longer he stood there, in fact, the more elements to the stench he could detect. It was like some foul pot pouri. He checked behind him and saw the boat now rounding the nets and heading for the large docking area on the far side of the farm. He took out his torch and, keeping the beam hooded under his hand, risked a quick scan of the inside. On all three sides of the load bay stanchions trailed various belts and ropes used for securing cargo and the lower four feet or so were covered with plywood boards bolted in place. These and the corrugated bare metal floor were streaked and scored with all manner of stains and scratches. There were some empty cartons right at the back and Doyle stuck the torch in his mouth and prepared to jump up … when the truck moved.

Doyle froze, one hand on the edge of the unopen door, his foot already resting on the rear bumper. Had he done that? Was he imagining it? No, there it goes again – a shake from side to side. Then he heard heavy footfalls on the ground and the slam of one of the doors at the front. What an idiot – he'd checked for a third man everywhere but inside the vehicle itself!

The new arrival groaned as he stretched then farted loudly. He took out his cigarettes and lit one as he walked to the back of the truck. Tutting as he saw the open door, he slammed it shut, leaned against it and drew on his fag. This Doyle heard more than he observed since he was at ankle height, having tip toed to the opposite side and rolled underneath. The tinny echo of music reached Doyle's ears and he realised the guy was plugged into his MP3 player. From the heavy beat, it sounded like some kind of rap crap and Doyle decided to take a chance. He rolled back out again and walked to the front of the truck. He stood on tiptoes and peered inside in the cab. In between frequent glances to check on the driver, he saw the usual detritus of long haul driving: newspapers, maps, empty sandwich packets and juice cartons. He wanted a closer look and, just then, he was given his opportunity. The driver, a young, thickset looking guy now singing tunelessly along to some misogynist pish about slapping his 'bitch', had pushed off from the back door and was walking down to the jetty. Doyle clicked open the passenger door, stepped up into the cab and closed it behind him.

Van and truck drivers all do the same thing – they use the shelf above the dashboard as a dumping ground for just about everything. Doyle waded through the remains of umpteen fast food meals but found no incriminating paperwork. Nor in the glove compartment or door pockets. He sat back and looked again at everything round about him: the rubbish, the newspaper, the road atlas … He had an idea and leaned over to lower the driver's visor. In the sleeve set into the back of it there was a plastic card about the size of a credit card. In the gloom he couldn't make out what, if anything was written on it and he was about to risk a quick flash with his torch when a faint but growing background hum reached the point where he became aware of it. He shot a glance in one wing mirror. Nothing. Leaned across and looked in the other. Shit. The boat was nearing the jetty. One of the men on board was at the prow and preparing to throw a mooring rope to the van driver.

He had to move fast. Pocketing the card, he checked both mirrors again and decided the passenger side offered the best angle of cover. He slid over, opened the door slowly and stepped down. He clicked the door shut again and backed off, keeping the truck between him and the activity on the jetty. Clouds had now reached the moon and, like a lamp being switched off, everything suddenly went black. Doyle sighed with relief and, reaching the corner of the lean-to shed, turned to find a suitable hiding place in some bushes. And then the last view he'd had of the vehicle in bright moonlight flashed again through his mind and he looked back. The visor was still down in front of the driver's seat!

He stood in frozen indecision for what seemed like an age. Would the guy notice? Of course he would. They'd just driven through the night – how could he account for his visor suddenly being down?

Cursing himself, Doyle retraced his steps, reached the cab and opened the door. Immediately, the boat's engine was cut and the silence that descended on the scene was shocking. Suddenly every move, every squeak of hinges or creak of the suspension would be heard from yards away. Gingerly, Doyle stretched up and, leaning on the dashboard, pushed the visor back up. Slowly, he stepped back down onto the gravel. Muttered voices from the jetty were getting louder, they were only yards away. No time to make it back to the bushes but no possibility either of dodging around the side – they would be using both doors. Doyle lowered himself onto all fours in preparation for going back under when moonlight once more shone through a gap in the clouds. To his horror, he could see that the high clearance of the wheels and the low approach from the jetty was giving the three men walking up a clear view of everything beneath the van. Sooner or later one of them was going to lift his gaze from his footsteps and see that inexplicable shadow. Doyle, still on all fours, took a long step backwards, then another and managed to put the entire length of the van between them. He crouched now below the grill near the front left wheel and prayed they'd have no need to do anything other than lock up the back, get in the cab and drive off.

'You left one of the doors open.'

'So what. At least it gets some air in there.'

'S'pose.'

Doyle heard the squeal of the rear doors being opened again and something thrown in the back, something big enough to make a noise but not heavy enough to affect the settle of the truck on its springs.

'Anything coming back this time?'

'Fucking hope not. Right, is that us finished for the night?'

'You see anything else needing done? 'Course that's us finished. I'll drop you two off then hole up as usual.'

Doyle slunk lower and lower as they approached. The rear doors were slammed shut again and locked. When the two front doors were opened, he grabbed the bumper and tried to swing under the front. But it had a spoiler he hadn't seen and, with his back pack on, he only managed to wedge himself tight against the road. The diesel engine started up and Doyle felt the vibrations rattle through him as he struggled, his chest rammed against the underside of the big, plastic bumper, his head in line with the number plate. As soon as that thing moved it was going to snap his neck back like dead-heading a matchstick.

He had no choice but to pull himself back out. He hauled with all his strength and shot out several feel in front of the truck. For an instant he saw all three men through the windscreen above him lit by the courtesy light the driver was using to check something on his mobile phone. The one on the end was trying to find his seat belt, the one in the middle yawning.

Doyle lay still, partly in the faint hope he wouldn't be seen, partly in shock. A cloud switched off the moon once more and Doyle was thrown into shadow. The courtesy light went out and he heard the crunch of the gear box. As the truck slowly edged forward, the air brakes hissed in release and the heads above him disappeared from view, he rolled himself on his side and, in the same movement, shrugged off one strap of his back pack. With no time to change direction, Doyle kept rolling and threw himself face down on the gravel. He felt the front right wheel roll over the pack still held by one strap to his shoulder and he heard the crunch of expensive night vision binocular lenses being broken. But the truck carried on. It straightened up and the rear axle passed over the back of Doyle's head. He had no choice but to lay still, even though one glance in a mirror and he was sure to be spotted. His face pressed into the gravel, his breath wheezing through gritted teeth, he remained immobile until he guessed from the engine note that the truck had reached the first sharp bend in the track that led back up to the logger's road.

Now he moved. He scrambled to his feet, grabbed the bag and covered the ten yards or so to the shed in three seconds. Sliding under it's overhanging roof he looked up and saw the vehicle turned side on and climbing, the driver automatically glancing sideways at the now empty parking area below. Doyle sank to his knees, turned and sat against the shed, his heart pounding inside his heaving chest.

Like the imprint of a bright light after shutting your eyes against the glare, an image still flashed and replayed in Doyle's mind. It was the three men in the front of the van.

He'd recognised two of them.

They were not the two he might've expected.

16

It was a long walk back up the road to Gillen then on, up the hill to Bun Sgoil A'Chnuic Bhric, his old primary school, outside which he'd parked. But Doyle took it easy, taking time out to wash the mud off his face and hands in the Aros Burn as he crossed it below the township. Not only did he have plenty to think about, he was keen to allow the truck time to get away, drop off its passengers and then 'hole up' wherever that was. The moon was now gone for good behind a thickening blanket of cloud while a wind off the Minch was building steadily. As the adrenaline slowly drained from him, he was introduced to a series of aches, sprains, cuts and bruises. He limped through the crofts, one dog offering no more than a perfunctory woof as he passed. It was after five o'clock by the time he reached his car and threw his bag and jacket in the back. For a long time, he sat behind the wheel, far too distracted to drive, certainly too wired to think about sleep. He looked at the old school building now sporting a rack of solar panels covering most of its roof. Another refuge, he remembered. Another place other than home.

And another reminder of why he'd stayed away. For as long as he could remember he'd lived in the present and the future. To hell with the past. When Leslie Poles Hartley came away with that line about the past being 'a foreign country: they do things differently there', he was living in a post war world where travel was still a big deal, easily able to conjure up notions of other, distant worlds. Well, 'foreign' was not nearly alien enough to describe Doyle's past – his was another life in another universe as far as he'd been concerned. That is until he'd set foot back on Skye when it came roaring back at him like some demented old adversary with a bone to pick. And there was no escape. Every view, every glen, loch, mountain and street corner was a memory waiting to leap out and mug him. And what do they demand, these memories? Answers.

If only he had them.

Perhaps the most shocking thing about seeing his father in the front of that truck was that, almost immediately, it wasn't really all that shocking. Somebody's up to no good in Waternish? That'll involve Gerry Doyle then.

His father was many things: a bully and a thief; a vicious, self-serving bastard whose interests extended as far as the end of his nose and/or dick. But Doyle also knew there were limits ... at least there had been in the past. His old man's voice hadn't been one of those he'd heard as he crouched behind the truck and it was him who'd been crammed into the middle seat in the front. As ever, it looked like he was the willing help – the 'ask no questions, do anything for a roll of 20s' idiot that every self-respecting criminal gang needed. He wasn't the mastermind, he probably didn't even know who the mastermind was or what was actually going on. He was cheap local hired help who could be trusted with nothing beyond doing what he was told and keeping his mouth shut. It was almost shaming.

Eventually the heat from his exertions left his body and Doyle shivered in the pre-dawn chill. He fired up the engine, put the heater on and pulled away without really knowing where he was about to go except back towards Halistra and on to the road to Portree. There was no light on in his father's croft as he passed a few minutes later. He'd have had a swift Teachers (his appreciation of uisge beatha began and ended with price) and gone to bed, dreaming of some pathetically mean ambition for whatever money he was earning from this latest racket.

Shortly after 6am, Doyle parked in the big free car park by the bus station in Portree, astonishingly not the first vehicle there; morning people always amazed him. He climbed the steps to Bridge Road and walked through what was now a grey, drizzly early morning to the office. He had a key and let himself in. He sniffed at the milk in the fridge, put on the kettle then clicked on one of the anglepoise lamps and fished out the card he'd taken from the visor of the truck.

Thicker than a credit card, it had a small indentation on an edge and arrows down one side showing which way it should be inserted or swiped. It was light grey and completely unmarked apart from the word 'Impasse' in a blue logo on one bottom corner. He switched on one of the huge monitors and made a coffee while it warmed up. When he eventually got through to Google, he found that Impasse was a company specialising in electronic access systems – 'offering security solutions for your business' – and that this thing was probably the pass for a car park. If he knew which businesses in Carew's empire used Impasse (hopefully not all of them) then that might help.

Doyle sat back and nursed his coffee. This sort of thing was just a small detail but of the kind that could be vital. It dawned on him that if he was really going to be able to pin something on Carew, not just stick a spanner in the works, he would need to know a lot more about her and her businesses. Sooner or later he was going to have to produce some hard evidence that could not be traced back, even indirectly, to that tap on her mobile phone. Anything less than that and she would walk, Scot free. He looked at the Google homepage in front of him. Well, this heap of junk was up and running. No time like the present.

When Holly walked in an hour and a half later she found Doyle asleep on his mouse pad. He woke to her touch with such a start she squealed in alarm.

'What!? Sorry … ,' he rubbed his face with his hands. 'What time is it?'

'Eight. What the hell happened to you?'

'Long night.'

'You back at that fish farm again?'

'Yes.'

'Looks like you fell in it.'

'I had a close encounter you might say.' And, in the new spirit of openess and inclusion, Doyle told her everything that had happened. When he'd done, she clearly didn't know whether to be alarmed, angry or sympathetic.

'You could've been killed,' was what she eventually chose to say. (Which was nice).

'Tell me about it,' he said, gingerly moving a shoulder that had stiffened up painfully.

'And you're sure it was your father?'

Doyle simply looked at her.

'OK, sorry. 'Course you are,' she said. 'You said you recognised one of the others.'

'Yeah. Don't know who he is but I bumped into him in a pub … actually shortly after we first met – remember that?' Doyle sat back and smiled at the ceiling. 'Happy days.'

'He was at the Isles Inn?'

'No, it was McNabs. He'd been in A&E with me and Scooby. Looked like he'd been in a fight. The mean and moody sort, I seem to recall.'

Holly was sitting, lost in thought, on the edge of the desk, coat still on, bag and keys clutched in her hand. Then she seemed to realise where she was and snapped out of her reverie. She got up and began bustling about the room.

'Well, we've a lot on this morning,' she said. It was her familiar business-like tone though perhaps this time with just a trace of apology. 'We need to be down at that planning inquiry site visit in Armadale by ten remember.'

Doyle nodded his understanding. Whatever else was going on – or not – Skye News had to keep working. She gave him her tacit approval to rummage around looking for whatever skeletons he saw lurking in Carew and Lytton's cupboards – just so long as it didn't impact on the agency's 'proper' work. He had his priorities and she had hers.

Doyle got up in instalments and walked stiffly to the window. His left hand was on his right shoulder as he moved it around, wincing every time it reached the sore bit. Looking out at Portree scuttling about in the rain, heading for schools, shops and offices, he suddenly felt exhausted. It was like he'd just flown in long distance and was at the end of a tiring, trying day only to find himself at the start of everyone else's.

It was agreed for safety's sake that Holly would drive. After he had a quick wash and change of clothing, she picked him up outside the B&B in her small red Alfa Romeo, the one that looks like a surprised budgie. He needn't have bothered with the colder than usual water in the shower; Holly's driving was enough to keep anyone wide awake. Portree to Armadale is an hour for the non-suicidal. They did it in a little over half that time. Holly pulled into the car park by the ferry terminal like Starsky and Hutch arriving at the scene of a crime. Doyle slowly released his grip on the door handle as she switched off the engine.

'I can't see how you could've hit a pothole that day up at Uig,' he said. 'Your tyres would need to be in contact with the road for that to happen.'

She grinned back at him. 'Hey, I was taking it easy. Thought you might want a nap on the way.'

The site visit was part of an effort to resolve a dispute over plans to build more houses along the shore at Armadale – a conflict featuring the usual combatants: a pro-development council and anti-development local residents (the irony of the latter having benefited from exactly this sort of development in the past clearly lost on them). Doyle hadn't been to this corner of the island since he'd been back. It had changed. Once Armadale had been the principal point of entry to Skye, being the other end of the ferry link to Mallaig, itself the end of the west highland railway line down to Glasgow. Like Kyleakin, however, it had seen a dramatic drop off in traffic once the bridge was opened in 1995 (and even more so when the larcenous toll was abolished in 2004). Again, like Kyleakin, however, this had only served to boost its growth. Armadale and neighbouring Ardvasar were now destinations in their own right, not just the names of places people sped past seconds after bumping off a Calmac car deck. They were still only small villages but Doyle looked at the variety of modern houses and holiday lodges dotted around and tried to remember the desolate place he'd known – little more than a road ending at a pier, a scene that always looked incomplete when the ferry, bow doors open, wasn't at the end of it.

He did his best to stay awake through the meeting, held in a clearing by some birch woods on the shore, the scar of Mallaig's 'Easterhouse-by-the-Sea' council housing clearly visible across the Sound of Sleat. Afterwards, while Holly roamed around taking shots, he interviewed the main players and got the usual hollow quotes (even community councillors are media-savvy these days). Then he sat in Holly's car and managed to wring 600 words out of the story on his laptop. There was no rush for the copy but Doyle feared any delay and he'd forget the whole damned thing.

'What's next?' he asked through a yawn when he'd finished.

'Lunch?'

'Sure. I'm starved. Anywhere good round here nowadays?'

Holly smiled and revved the engine.

The Eilean Iarmain Hotel nestles behind the island of Ornsay with its picture postcard lighthouse and a backdrop of the brooding mountains of Knoydart on the mainland. The rain, which had mercifully abated during the site visit, returned with a vengeance as Holly scraped to a halt on the gravel forecourt. They ran in through the turret-like door to the hotel bar and straight into Visit Scotland's next TV advert.

The snug wood-panelled room was nearly full, a crackling wood and coal fire to the right, the bar to the left. Like the Isles Inn, this was neither a tourist trap nor a laager of miserable, taciturn locals. There were crofters and estate workers, yachtsmen and hillwalkers, men in suits and women in yellow wellies. There was warmth and laughter, the guilty pleasure of a midday dram and the delicious smell of cullen skink and good old fish and chips. An un-plugged two-piece of guitar and fiddle in the far corner were playing a strathspey, loud enough to listen to if you wanted, quiet enough to allow easy conversation if you didn't.

Holly nodded Doyle's attention to a couple with their credit card on a table full of empty plates and glasses by the fire. But even as she approached to hover with intent, they simply stood and gestured for her and Doyle to take their seats. The waiter was over inside a minute to clear the table and, waiving the offer of a menu, they both opted to share a bowl of moules marinieres with crusty bread and, in Doyle's case, a healthy glass of house white. He sat back in something of a daze.

'What's wrong?' asked Holly.

'Nothing. I mean ... ' he looked around. 'This sort of thing doesn't happen to me. I'm lucky if I get the wobbly table with the draught in the café that serves yesterday's sandwiches and last week's soup.'

Holly laughed. 'You should come with me more often.'

They both smiled then busied themselves with taking off their coats to pretend one of them hadn't said that and the other hadn't heard it. After a few minutes more of vacant, 'isn't this nice' smiling, Holly leaned in.

'You said the truck was stinking. Any idea what with?'

Through the pleasant haze of the bar's atmosphere and his tiredness, Doyle took a reluctant while to drag himself back to the events of earlier that morning.

'No. It was … well, it was like nothing I'd ever smelled before.'

'Something to disguise drugs?'

He grinned. 'I like your reasoning young Thompson but no, I don't think so in this case. That's really a ploy for traffickers using freight routes liable to inspection through ports and the like. If they are moving drugs through the fish farm and their vans then they wouldn't need to bother about sniffer dogs at border controls.'

Doyle's wine arrived with the usual soda water and lime for Holly. He took an uncharacteristically small sip; the stomach was still empty and he was already knackered.

Holly put her own glass down. 'I've never been to one but fish farms must be pretty smelly. It could be just the things they use there – feed and, I don't know, just fishy stuff.'

He shook his head. 'I've worked on a few and they're not bad at all. If what they say about smell being the best trigger for memory then I can tell you there was nothing there that reminded me of summer jobs 20 years ago.'

'Any idea where the truck had come from, then? You said it wasn't local.'

'No. It had London plates and the driver was English.'

'That doesn't really prove anything though, does it?'

Doyle yawned again. 'Sorry. No it doesn't. But my guess is it did come up from somewhere in England. I wouldn't want to bet my life on this but there was enough junk from motorway service burger bars for that length of journey, the newspaper on the dashboard was *The Sun* – not the Scottish edition – and the road map was opened at south Yorkshire.'

'Any connections with Carew there?'

'I don't know but I think he was just passing through – I mean, you don't need a map for roads you're familiar with, do you? It was the page with the fiddly bit where the A1(M) and M1 get all complicated around Leeds. I think he came from further south, needed to plot his way through that lot then, when he was safely on the road to Scotland, he didn't need to bother again.'

'Why not just use a sat nav like everyone else?'

'Good question. I dunno, do these things have memories? Maybe they wouldn't want people like me simply looking up where they've come from.'

Holly looked at him.

'I know, I know,' he said. 'It's all a stretch. I've still got a lot of homework to do.'

Holly sipped her drink. 'I hate to say it. But you're not really much further forward are you?'

'No I'm not. There's nothing illegal about moving stuff around at night on your own property. Nor, though there really should be a law against it, hiring my old man.'

A huge steaming bowl of mussels arrived and they tucked in, quickly falling into a steady rhythm of shelling, eating and discarding with occasional breaks for lapping up the creamy sauce underneath. Maybe it was the tiredness, the comfort of his seat by the fire or just the fine food and wine, but Doyle found it easy to imagine this as a pretty good first date kind of meal. There was an intimacy about their sharing of the bowl. He looked across and wondered again about Holly Thompson.

Once more she was in 'snapper' attire – jeans, boots and what on anybody else would be described as an unflattering baggy jumper. Not on her. Frankly, the woman could make a Rangers top look good. Sparky, often unnecessarily bossy (although she'd toned that down a bit of late), she also had a real flair for pointing out holes in theories, asking questions she knew you didn't have the answers to. And yet, as with just a minute ago, he couldn't honestly say it was done with any ill will. In fact, she often seemed more disappointed by his lack of progress than he was. Then again, as he was often guilty of forgetting, there was more going on in other people's lives than Dan Doyle's Heroic Quest to Feel Slightly Better About Himself. Holly's father was fighting cancer, she suddenly had his business to run and then there was that failed marriage … Doyle began drafting clever, not as innocent as they seem questions in his head when, not for the first time, Holly just spoke up and got in there first.

'Why do you sound like a … eh, is it 'Weegie'?'

'That is the correct anthropological term, yes. Well, let me see … my dad's Glasgwegian and sounds the same today as when he left the Garangad 40 years ago. My mum only had one sister and she was an alcoholic lesbian who drove a bin lorry in Aberdeen and never visited so the only extended family I ever knew – and that wasn't much as they all hated my dad – came from Glasgow. The telly and radio up here was either from London or Glasgow and I spent four years in the city at university.'

Holly's expression said: 'And?'

'And … ' Doyle theatrically conceded. 'I deliberately put it on because I was fed up with people calling me Donald and asking where my troosers were.'

Holly laughed so much she almost choked on a mussel. After a few minutes of similar light-hearted banter, Doyle, unbeknownst to him, decided it was time to bring the pleasantries to a grinding halt.

'Your ex husband,' he said out of nowhere. 'Is he a journalist too?'

Holly pulled up as if given a sharp tug on a leash. The smile on her lips flickered and all but died, then flared back into renewed, defiant life.

'Ex fiancée. We were never married,' she said.

Ouch. The engagement ring must've been on for years to leave that kind of mark, he thought. He also noted her use of the word 'never'. Right, bawheid – where do you go from here, he was asking himself when she spoke again.

'And no, he isn't a journalist. He's a businessman. Owns a software company in Cardiff.'

'Difficult to do engaged from such a distance, I suppose.'

'I thought so. He didn't.'

It was a statement that meant either she'd ended it against his wishes or she'd wanted them to finally wed, he'd preferred more endless engagement and she'd pulled the plug. To find out which it was would be to take the prying just a tad too far.

'I'm sorry it didn't work out,' he said.

'Don't be,' she smiled challengingly. 'I'm not.'

They finished their lunch and Doyle settled back with a second glass of wine. Sod it, he only had some routine press release stuff to do that afternoon. Over his shoulder, the guitar and fiddle were finishing off a lament that had lulled the bar into a pleasant, post prandial repose. After a ripple of applause they kicked off again with a lively reel. At a table near the front, a young French couple –

honeymooners, Doyle guessed – suddenly got up to dance. And how. Urged on by the band, they spun and jigged, twirled and swung each other expertly in the tight little space. They were tall, handsome and obviously in love. They swayed cheek to cheek then threw each other to arms length and held on through a dizzying spin before pulling in tight to another intense pirouette. On and on they danced, staring into each other's eyes, oblivious to the bar and everyone in it.

Doyle looked around and smiled. The women sat mesmerised, a wistful expression belying their fixed grins. The men, on the other hand, were clearly not enjoying being shown up by this unselfconscious Gallic romantic.

'Why don't you ever dance with me like that?' the women silently asked their menfolk.

'Why can't you just sit on your arse like any normal person?' the men silently asked the dancing beau.

Doyle turned to crack a joke with Holly but stopped.

She too was captivated by the couple. She smiled, but her eyes shone with tears that had not yet fallen.

17

The laughter dissolved, quickly like Alka-Seltzer, into bubbles of murmured merriment.

The Carlton Club doesn't do laughter – not for any great length of time at least. Not the done thing.

'He's such a chump,' said Charles, putting the magazine back on the table. 'Don't you think, Chloe?'

'What? Yes, oh yes ... a, eh ... chump.'

The initial shock over with, she was now getting used to the idea. And the more she did so, the more she actually liked it.

'Still, harmless enough, eh?' said Sir Julian.

Only Chloe seemed to think long and hard before agreeing to that one.

As Erik called over a waiter for another round of pre-lunch drinks, Chloe's new Blackberry went off in her handbag (more difficult to hack into than her old model, she'd been told). This occasioned much good-natured rolling of eyes from her companions, far less generous reactions from members elsewhere in what is known as Cad's Corner.

The Carlton Club doesn't do mobile phones. However, should they be absolutely necessary, then, as every member knew – or should know – they are restricted for use in the bedrooms, the computer room and the study between the first and second floors. If you forget to switch yours off, you do so immediately the thing rings. That was the form.

'Hello.' Chloe didn't even bother to look apologetic. 'Yes. I've just seen it in fact … I think so, yes. Keep me informed.' She clicked it off, caught a fatherly expression from Sir Julian and, with an 'Oh, alright,' switched it to mute, her ultimate concession.

It was exactly the sort of 'incident', as it would later be termed in whispered conversations over the leather Chesterfields, that the club had been warned about if it changed.

The Carlton Club doesn't do change.

It does lots of other things and some of them very well indeed. It's pretty good at Georgian architecture, Victorian portraiture and haughty subservience. Also, the steak and kidney pudding is enough to make old Etonians go all misty-eyed. But change? No. And one wouldn't expect it of an institution that has set its face against such dangerous nonsense since it first opened its doors (cautiously, with a 'Ye-es, can I help you?') in 1832 to like-minded souls opposed to the scandalous notion of extending the democratic franchise to one in six of the adult male population – a folly from which, of course, the country has never recovered.

Yet even this place, the heart and soul of the Conservative Party, has had to give at least a nod to the realities of its existence in the 21st century. Since 2008, it has allowed women as full members (even Margaret Thatcher as a Conservative prime minister could previously only be granted honorary membership) and has put a brave face on it (stiff upper lip, no chin) ever since. Tensions, nevertheless, continue to exercise not a few of the members from time to time. There are, among this new breed of intake, some who, despite impeccable Tory credentials in all other regards, still just don't seem to fit in with the general ethos of the place, what?

Chloe smiled sweetly in response to a couple of florid scowls aimed in her direction as her party were escorted from Cad's Corner, a reception area, into the Churchill Room for their meal.

The Churchill, members like to think, plays host to what might be called lunches of consequence most days of the week. Minor royalty, major aristocracy, even some elected members of the ruling class – they can all be seen sticking their patrician noses in the silver trough here beneath the empire crystal chandeliers and the Winterhalter and Von Angeli portraits of Victorian politicians and their wild facial hair. Chloe and her associates had planned to be entertaining the new secretary of state at the Department for Environment, Food and Rural Affairs this day but the ungrateful bugger had called off at the last minute. T'was ever thus: you got front bench spokesmen crawling all over you when they were in opposition, only for them to disappear like a fart in a fan factory the moment they got into government. They were saddled instead with Rufus Smith, a junior minister and ludicrously young fogey on the first rung of what he clearly hoped would be a distinguished career and who was determined not to fuck it up before it'd even begun. To that end, he was sticking to the letter of his brief from his superiors: agree to nothing.

'More bread sauce, Rufus?'

'Mmm ... well, not right at this moment.'

By the time they got to the coffee and mints, the exasperation around the table was palpable. Enough, indeed, for the normally elliptical Erik Vandepear, a man who made the average Whitehall mandarin seem blunt, speak in the most direct of terms.

'Rufus, we are seeking nothing more than the honouring of commitments made in the course of the election campaign. It is, as the party recognises, time for the 2004 Act to be reconsidered. The anti-hunt lobby cannot complain that we have been unreasonable. We have done everything that has been asked of us yet the situation in our countryside remains deplorable.'

The self-styled rising star at DEFRA dabbed his chin with his napkin even though it had been almost half an hour since he'd actually eaten anything. 'I can only repeat what I said earlier. It will be for cabinet to decide on the balance of priorities for this particular legislative programme. You have no idea what a mess we've inherited from the last lot. We certainly didn't, I can tell you.'

He shot his eyebrows up and cast an invitation for sympathy around the table. Only Sir Julian gave him the comfort of a smile in return.

What made the frustration all the more galling was that Erik, Chloe, Sir Julian Le Sueur and Charles Greer, as almost the entire executive council of the Country Matters Foundation, represented one of the most formidable lobby groups this novice was ever likely to encounter in his entire career. He was just too wet to recognise it. The foundation was not – in spite of having Chloe in its ranks – one of the more high profile players on the rural scene. But with an annual sub in five figures and a strictly controlled system of 'electing' office bearers, it remained the preserve of only the atrociously wealthy and the immoderately influential. If your wage, bonus and stock options amounted to less than half a billion, if your landholdings would fit on the Isle of Wight with room to spare, then there were plenty of other campaign groups for you to join.

Erik shot his Jermyn Street cuffs, sat back and looked at his associates, his eyes an open invitation for anyone else to try their luck.

'Do I look like a criminal to you?' asked Chloe.

'Sorry?' Rufus swung round, startled.

'I asked if you thought I looked like a criminal.'

It was fair bet that he did not. In fact, it looked like it had taken most of the lunch for Rufus to get over being just a little star struck at sharing a table with Chloe Carew. As he spluttered and broke into a sweat, Chloe carried on.

'I only ask, you see, because right now, under this … this appalling legislation, I could be committing a crime every time I ride to hounds.'

'Well, no Miss Ca – ah, eh, Chloe. We recognise there are potential – ,'

'There is no potential about it, Rufus.' Chloe had turned it up to about 50 per cent – more than enough for the Churchill Room and certainly enough to have her victim reaching for his napkin again like a toddler grabbing teddy.

'Just as the metropolitan meatheads cannot forever go on denying nature – man's nature as a hunter – so I cannot hope to deny the nature of my dogs. One of these days, Rufus, one of these days I will not be on the spot soon enough and the pack will do what nature will compel it to do. It will dispatch the fox and then, through no fault of my own, I will be deemed to have broken the law. I, Rufus, ' she raised her voice just a smidgen, 'will be carted down to the police station like a common criminal and charged with an offence.'

'We all share a distaste for the shortcomings of the Act – ,' began Rufus.

'But we don't all share the means to do anything about it,' interrupted Chloe. 'Is the government happy to have Britain a land were perfectly honest, law-abiding citizens can be criminalised? I don't recall your boss saying as much when we all lunched – frequently – these past months.'

'As I said, there are priorities for any new government.'

'And none more pressing than relieving its citizens – it's own constituents, may I remind you – of the burden of iniquitous laws.'

Rufus was quiet for a while. Slowly, he assumed the look of a man about to confess a fondness for wearing his wife's pants.

'I agree it is an unsustainable state of affairs,' he said at last, each word a painful extraction.

'Then we can count on you to use your influence with the secretary of state?'

'Well, I will of course be reporting back the strength of feeling – ,'

'Because I think we all are grateful for the expressions of support you have given us today,' Chloe was all smiles again. 'And an ally, someone batting on our behalf right at the heart of government would be wonderful.'

If Rufus detected the change of tack, he was too slow to react. Chloe's colleagues, however, took the cue. Before Rufus could think of some phrase to water down what was clearly being re-written as his enthusiastic commitment to their cause, Sir Julian coughed gently. 'Your seat,' he said simply.

'My ... my seat?' Rufus actually grabbed the edge of his Regency dining chair.

'What constituency do you represent?' asked Sir Julian with a patient smile.

'Oh, ah Easthampton Mid. It's in Berkshire,' he said with a mixture of pride and caution.

Sir Julian looked around the table. Chloe and Erik gave the faintest shake of their heads but Charles leaned in to top up his coffee from the pot on the table.

'Ah yes, a lovely corner of the country,' he said. 'And with a chance of becoming an ever more prosperous one, I understand. You must be hoping for a favourable decision on the new semi-conductor plant.'

Rufus's proud smile broadened again. 'Well, our enterprise zone offers every incentive for such a project and, as it happens, I have been in close contact with Mr Ishiba from the Kawamura Company for some months. I don't think I am being presumptuous when I say we have an understanding.'

He didn't actually tap the side of his nose but he might as well have.

'That does sound encouraging, I must say,' said Charles, feigning polite interest. 'You will give my regards to Mr Ishiba the next time you meet, won't you?'

The smile remained on Rufus's face but suddenly looked a little rictus round the edges. 'Oh. You know him?'

Charles finally got to the end of pouring himself a coffee and stirring in some sugar. His tone was perfectly pitched for a casual afterthought to the exchange. 'No, but he knows me – or at least my private equity firm. It owns 40 per cent of his company.'

Chloe was at the window lost in thought when Sir Julian approached.

'He'll go far that boy,' he said.

She smiled. 'Well, he learns fast. That's always a good sign.'

'Now, as for that chump Geoffrey …' he held up the copy of *Swanky* again.

Chloe glanced around quickly to check no-one was in earshot but lowered her voice nevertheless. 'I just wished he'd OK'd it with us, don't you think?'

'Yes, I agree. But, you know, it is just him and his blasted teapots. In a way, we wouldn't want the estate to disappear off the map entirely. This sort of thing helps to preserve a sense of normality, no?'

'I suppose. Still, I think a word in his ear … '

'Leave it to me.' He patted her on the arm and drained the last of his brandy. 'Well, must dash. You want this?'

Chloe took the magazine and received Sir Julian's peck on the cheek as he departed with another reassurance. She walked to the window and pulled aside the heavy, navy blue drapes. She was entirely unconcerned about the article; Sir Julian wasn't to know it had been the by-line that had caused a shock. But now she smiled. There was something freeing about knowing this Doyle character was definitely planning to take her on – no other explanation for him being anywhere near Knott House. How far his nosing about had got him was neither here nor there.

Chloe looked unseeingly at the passers by enjoying the warm sunshine on St James's Street.

No, the only important thing was knowing – finally – exactly where he was.

***

Doyle enjoyed the warm sunshine on St James's Street as he walked past the Carlton Club, crossed the road and turned right down King Street. The change in direction took him into cool shadow, the difference in temperature a clue to the season. Otherwise (and certainly compared to where he'd spent the last few months) he could be forgiven for thinking it was a summer's day.

A week since his adventures at the fish farm and he was taking advantage of Bob's return to more active duty. With his first programme of chemo over with and now waiting for the result of his latest scan, the old chap assured them he felt better than he looked and was in the office every day making a big play about 'doing his fair share'. Sandy had disappeared off the island somewhere and Doyle, unwilling to risk bumping into his father and his new friends again, had decided to leave the fish farm alone for the moment and concentrate on delving a little deeper into Chloe Carew's business empire. Jake, his pal on the *FT*, was now on the Eurozone beat and no longer plugged into the world of Carew and her sort. But he did recall his most useful contact on the story – a former non-executive director of one of her companies who'd been ousted in a boardroom coup. Having checked the guy was still all nicely bitter and twisted, Jake put the two of them in touch. It sounded like Doyle couldn't have wished for a better source; he'd made it his business to keep a close eye on Carew's business. But he was reluctant to email or talk on the phone.

Doyle walked on through the expensive corner of the Monopoly board – Piccadilly and Mayfair were just up to his left, Pall Mall parallel to his right. Everywhere it was members' clubs and auction rooms, private banks and Gulf state embassies. Through the narrow street, made more so by nose to tail UPS trucks and delivery vans at the kerb, he eventually reached St James's Square. He turned left past the London Library, crossed over and entered the small park at the square's centre. He was early so he found an empty bench near the middle, sat back with his arms out stretched and, lifting his face to the sun, closed his eyes.

The racket of London going about its day filled the air. The whacky races of buses, vans, taxis and motorcycle couriers could be heard throughout St James's above the indistinct drone of exactly the same thing going on for mile after square mile across the city. It had been ever-present in his former life and now he found it at once familiar, melancholy and, he was interested to note, a little irritating.

'Ahem.'

Doyle opened his eyes with a start and found himself about to share a bench with a tall, immaculately tailored city gent. From his sparkling brogues and tan leather gloves to a Venetian twill covert coat and club tie that looked like it was strangling him under a crisp, starched collar, he looked like he'd just walked off an Ealing Studios set in the 1950s. Suddenly, the world seemed futuristic and discordant around him; there should be nannies walking by pushing huge Silver Cross prams to the chuff and whistle of steam trains, not a parade of people on mobile phones to a soundtrack of whining, snarling motorbikes.

He perched himself on the edge of the seat, those gloved hands resting on a completely unnecessary umbrella. 'You'll be Dan Doyle.'

Doyle sat up and tapped the copy of *Private Eye* on the seat beside him, the one he'd been asked to bring along. 'That's me. Bernard Sommerville?' he said, offering his hand.

Sommerville gave a half-hearted, still gloved handshake. 'I will take your word that this is not being recorded – or filmed,' he looked around sharply.

Doyle laughed. 'Filmed? No, I can assure you it's just you and me. Here – frisk me if you'd like.' And he opened his jacket.

Sommerville didn't look amused. 'That won't be necessary. I just want to restate the conditions for this meeting. If and when you eventually broadcast, I and my lawyers will be watching very closely.'

'Broadcast?' Then Doyle twigged. 'Ah-h. Look, Bernard – can I call you Bernard ... ? Right. Mr Sommerville. Look, I think you're mistaken ...' And then he stopped himself.

Clearly the guy was only going to speak as far from the record as he could get. This conversation, he would probably say at the end of it, never took place. So what was the harm in letting him believe he'd had it with a reporter from Sky (without an 'e') News?

' ... Mistaken about our practices. All we're looking for at the moment is deep background,' – suddenly scenes from All the President's Men popped into his head – 'We'll keep your name out of it, I promise.'

Sommerville settled back. 'OK,' he said. 'So tell me what you know.'

'Eh ... is that not my line?'

'You tell me what you know and I'll confirm it or otherwise.'

Great. Deep Throat.

The problem was that Doyle knew bugger all. And he wasn't about to start faking it. He guessed Sommerville carried a big enough grudge against Carew to still want to stick it to her. He also guessed the guy was simply interested in getting some new dirt himself.

'I'm afraid it doesn't work that way, Mr Sommerville. For us to be sure you know what you're talking about, you have to provide information yourself. I could say anything and someone who knows nothing about Carew could agree with it. That doesn't constitute a corroborating source.'

He looked unhappy but he didn't get up and walk away.

'Well, let's put it this way,' he said at length. 'What precisely is your area of interest and what has prompted it?'

'I – we'd like to know how her various businesses are structured and what possible threats they might be facing,' Doyle took out his notepad and flipped it open. 'We think she may be tempted to take some, shall we say – extreme measures. We just don't know if that's her being greedy or needy.'

'I strongly suspect it is the latter.'

'Go on.'

'She is, as I understand it, in danger of a covenant breach on her loan facility. It's cross-guaranteed on her majority shareholding in an ISTC which is staying afloat but my information is they're sailing awfully close to the wind.'

'Ri-ight ... '

'There's a "look forward" test, you see and with the scrapping of the PCTs her procurement contracts will all be up for grabs again. As I'm sure you can guess, maintaining healthy three-monthly cash flow forecasts in those circumstances will be tricky to say the least.'

Doyle stopped taking notes.

'She really shouldn't have got involved in the MBO of Olive Grove at the peak of the market for an EBITDA multiple of ten – ,' he shot an incredulous look at Doyle who simply stared back blankly. ' – But then you might as easily ask why Assured Equity backed her at all. It's one thing raising mezzanine debt with an 18 per cent PIK note on a business model – ,'

Doyle held up his hand. 'Mr Sommerville.' He tried to smile through his annoyance. 'I would very much like to learn more about Carew, and you, I think, would like a light shone into whatever murky depths there are to her business practices. That's why we are both here. But it really will be a waste of both our time if I haven't a clue what you're talking about. You're going to have to speak English.'

Sommerville looked for a moment as if he'd just eaten something disagreeable but eventually he sighed. 'As you wish,' he said, placing his brolly on the bench and slipping off his gloves. 'Let's start with her property portfolio … '

Chloe Carew, it seemed, had been as exposed to the vagaries of the post crash economy as anyone else. With the housing boom well and truly over and commercial developments put on ice all over the country, her property empire was all but moribund. Yet the habit of diversification, begun in the last recession in the 1990s, had stuck with her and she was now the queen bee of a hive that ranged from delicatessens to on-line clothing suppliers, from a chain of pre-school nurseries to private healthcare facilities. But bad luck – or bad management –

had dogged her steps in recent years. Local government funding cuts forced Carew to raise money for the nurseries through a sale and leaseback of the properties on onerous terms. Serious quality problems with clothes from its Shenzen suppliers forced the on-line business to take a substantial stock write off and find alternative suppliers in Taiwan, causing a massive drop in yearly profits. The short term solution was to consolidate everything under an enlarged Carew Holdings Ltd but the extra drag was soon causing problems for the entire group – the cornerstone of which was now Danbury Healthcare.

Danbury ran a number of independent sector treatment centres (ISCTs) across the east midlands. Offering day surgery procedures (varicose veins, cataracts etc.), it was underpinned by a 'take or pay' minimum volume NHS contract with the upside coming from private sector referals. The general trend towards back door privatisation of the NHS by governments of whatever hue only served to bolster Danbury's business case. That was until the last one announced the scrapping of the primary care trusts to be replaced by GP fundholders – a move the new government was unlikely to reverse. The result? All Danbury's procurement contracts with their 'take or pay' guarantees would have to be renegotiated. Without them Danbury's business model falls apart. And if Danbury goes …

'You serious?' asked Doyle. 'You mean everything she has is being held up by just one company?'

'Effectively, yes. She's only surviving because of the facility agreement she has with Assured Equity which is cross-guaranteed on Danbury. They are, if you like, her bankers. And the way the deal is structured it all depends on the continuing health (if you'll pardon the pun) of

Danbury Healthcare. Assured will have someone on the board of Carew Holdings scrutinising the cash flow figures and three-month projections. At the first sign of Danbury dipping into the red, they can and probably will pull the plug.

'Jenga.'

'I beg your pardon.'

'It's like a game of Jenga. She has her entire business empire resting on just one wooden block.'

'I haven't the foggiest what you're talking about but I think you catch my drift.'

Doyle leaned forward and stared at his shoes for a while. 'What does she need to do then to ensure Danbury stays in the black?'

'It's very simple. She must balance the books. She must avoid new and potentially ruinous costs or increase efficiency or find new ways of generating income.'

'Or earn money from something else entirely and launder the profits through Danbury's books?'

'It's possible. If she's artificially keeping Danbury alive through injections of cash from elsewhere, I suggest you find out where from.'

'Or, or …' Doyle smiled. 'As you might say, Follow the money. Eh?'

'What?'

'Follow the money. That's what Deep Throat said in … ach, never mind.'

18

Doyle stood in the doorway of an empty estate agent's shop in Balham High Road and looked across at his flat, two floors above a dry cleaners on the other side. The more he thought about it, the more he was convinced Carew knew he was in Skye. Besides, he reasoned, a cash-strapped operation desperate to keep its books in the black was hardly likely to have stretched to almost three months of round the clock surveilance. But he still stood there for ten minutes, casually flicking through the *Private Eye* and watching the street and everyone in it. Eventually he reached the tipping point between caution and just being a crap bag and walked over the road. A few moments later he swept aside a small wave of junk mail with the inside of his front door and stepped into the hall. He stood for a moment, feeling himself the ringmaster at the centre of a whirl of cavorting emotions: nervousness, sentimentality, self pity, anger ...

The click of the outside door as it had closed behind him and the sound of his footsteps on the stairwell, his own front door's familiar look and now the smells, sights and sounds of his flat were all dragging him back through time. Indeed time, he'd recently found, was becoming a bit of an obsession. This time last month, he'd think, six months ago, this time last year ... constantly he caught himself trying to put the upheaval in his life in context – as if a certain passage of time meant things like breaking the law, or losing your job, or conducting a one-man crusade against a national celebrity as yet entirely beyond reproach could all be made somehow normal.

Doyle walked slowly into the kitchen-diner and ran his hands along the back of chairs, the table top. The life he'd lived from here: going to work for a national newspaper, his friends and his routines – his nights out in the pub, in jazz clubs, the odd game at Upton Park – it all seemed like he'd lived it yesterday. But yesterday in a parallel universe. It didn't take too much effort to imagine the last few months hadn't happened. Then again, he was kidding himself if he thought everything before then had been all sweetness and light; working for that bunch of unreconstructed misanthropes and yahoos had required a daily wrestle with his temper as well as his conscience. His life in the newsroom hadn't been helped by usually being conducted through the veil of a hangover – the consequence, of course, of an evening spent neutralising the previous day ... spent in a hangover. If he was nostalgic, then, for this life he had to admit it was for a version now many years in the past.

And yet he did feel something had been taken from him. It might have been a shit life, but it had been his shit life. Doyle looked at his furniture, his books, CDs and vinyl collection, the snaps of holiday larks with pals pinned to a board in his kitchen along with old concert ticket stubs, mini cab business cards and the like. He'd persuaded his landlord to let him redecorate the previous year and looked at his handiwork now, remembering what he'd been listening to when he'd papered that wall, painted that door, tackled that tricky bit of tiling under the kitchen's wall units ... just there behind the small stack of cookery books that always hid the cigarette burn on the laminate work top a party guest had left one night.

The mark he could now inexplicably see.

Doyle frowned and walked forward. Yes, the books were where they'd always been, but turned lengthways now against the side of the microwave, the very alignment he never put them in. He felt his pulse in his neck and heard it through his inner ear as he looked again at the scene round about him. The cork kitchen notice board had everything there, but was it really in the same place, in the right order? Now that he thought about it, why would a postcard from last summer be wedged in front of a council notice about bin collections he'd only received in January? Doyle retraced his steps and looked around the lounge area with its flat screen TV, it's book cases and its pair of Habitat sofas. He didn't live like a slob but, if he wasn't Oscar from The Odd Couple, he was no Felix either ... he was certainly no plumper of cushions. Doyle walked back out to the pile of mail behind the door and slowly, carefully, began removing the top layers. Eventually he found an envelope with what, by now, he'd expected: a footprint.

In that moment, London lost yet another coat of gloss for him. Suddenly, he did not want to spend a minute longer than absolutely necessary revisiting a past that now held the promise of a decidedly uncertain future. He threw the few items he'd come to collect in his shoulder bag, stepped over the mail and closed the door behind him. As he walked down the stairs, his musings on when – if – he'd ever be back came to a sudden halt on reaching the first floor landing when he saw, by the shaft of light under the outside door, the shadow of someone standing, waiting, in the street. The logic of Carew's employees having long-since ended their interest in his flat still applied – but on balance he decided illogical paranoia was a much safer bet. He unlatched the landing window, slid the sash up, stepped out onto the ledge and dropped down to the roof of the boiler room at the back of the dry cleaners below.

Four hours later, Doyle retrieved his car from the short stay car park at Inverness Airport. An hour after that, he had crawled through the early evening traffic in the city centre and was on the A82 heading south west, the gloaming settling over the Great Glen as he made his way down the western shore of Loch Ness. By the time he was on the A87 down broad Glensheil and past The Cluanie Inn it was pitch dark and he was bombing it, the few on-coming vehicles giving miles of notice with their headlamps. Through the evening he drove, Hank Mobley's Workout on the car stereo keeping his mood and his thoughts focused. Skirting Kintail to the south, he sped along Loch Duich and past floodlit Eilean Donan (the most photographed castle on the planet) to Loch Alsh and the first hints of the open sea beyond. The Cuillins loomed now on the horizon, black even against the night sky, as he passed through Kyle of Lochalsh, swung up over the bridge, hung a right at Kyleakin and started the long road up the island to Portree.

When he pulled up outside Mrs MacBeth's B&B it was just after 9 o'clock. He was hungry again after eating nothing but the tiny portion he'd been offered on the plane, but too tired to do anything about it. Instead, he sat for a long while, listening to the tinking of his engine cooling down, reviewing the events of the day and persuading himself that progress had been made, clarity achieved. After months of unanswered questions, of chasing shadows, at last he had a clear idea of what was going on. Dangers may lie ahead but at least he could concentrate now on firming up his story with some hard evidence. No more mysteries and weird surprises.

'Aye, a big cat with antennae and wearing mascara.'

'And false eyelashes.'

'Is that not the same thing?'

'Oh, George,' the woman laughed and made a 'Men, eh?' face at Holly.

Holly flicked a smile and continued with her note-taking.

'Anyway, it barked.'

'Sorry,' said Holly. 'I thought you said it was a cat.'

'Aye, it were. But it still barked. You know, like a dog, like.'

'Ri-ight.' Holly made a note.

The Yorkshire-sounding couple in matching fleeces and woolly hats had been sitting at Holly's desk when Doyle finally got himself into the office at ten o'clock the following morning. He'd nodded an enquiry at Bob but only got a quick roll of the eyes in return. Still dozy from a long but troubled sleep and over the noise of the boiling kettle as he made coffee, Doyle was only catching snatches of the interview that seemed to range from pot-holing to cartoon creatures. He shook his head and decided to just tune it out.

Taking his mug over to the desk, he sat and began a trawl through Google to confirm as best he could the information from Sommerville in London. As he'd predicted, there were no apocalyptic reports on Carew's financial vulnerability, but he found enough commentaries on business and market-watch websites to back up the guy's accounts of the challenges facing independent sector treatment centres, the local government cutbacks hitting nurseries and other privately run services, even sector-wide quality control issues at previously reliable Chinese suppliers. One other check was easy to make. He called the Danbury Healthcare main switchboard.

'Good morning. Could you put me through to your service manager please ... Hello. Yes, this won't take a moment of your time. I'm calling from the British Security Industry Association. Just a quick question for a member's survey - can you tell us which company you use for your access control systems? ... Lovely, thanks. Have a nice day.'

Doyle put the phone down and found himself the object of curious looks from all corners of the office. He aimed a beaming smile at the visitors.

'PR contract. Skye News offers a full range of media and marketing services tailored to meet your needs. Would you like one of our brochures?'

They smiled nervously and declined. Both turned back to face Holly. As they did so, Doyle spotted something on the side of the man's face – a distinctive, triple scratch to his left cheek.

Suddenly, Doyle had filing to do. He got up and went to the cabinet beside Holly's desk.

' … well, no. We didn't really want to hang about after that,' the woman was saying.

'And you didn't see it again?' asked Holly.

'To be honest, we weren't really looking, were we George?'

'No. Besides I, eh … I were a bit shaken as you can imagine.'

'Apart from the police, then, have you spoken to anyone else about this?'

'We had t' tell the, eh … the hospital like, and ………
Why is that man looking at me?'

Doyle realised he was leaning over the cabinet at an inexplicable angle. He straightened up as Holly said reassuringly, 'Pay no attention to him, Mr Hardwick. He's on a work placement,' before mouthing, 'care in the community'.

'May I ask how you came about your injuries?' asked Doyle, also noticing a bandaged right hand.

'No you may not, Dan,' said Holly. 'Mr and Mrs Hardwick have given us enough of their time already without having to repeat everything for your benefit.' She flared her eyes at him pleadingly.

'It's all righ' with me, luv. I'm quite – '

'No, I insist,' said Holly with a set smile. 'I have it all here in my notes. My colleague can read them later.'

'It were a big cat,' said Mr Hardwick, ignoring her and turning to Doyle. 'Out at Tungadale Souterrain. Y' know it, son?'

'I do indeed, carry on,' said Doyle, settling down on the edge of Holly's desk.

George and Carol Hardwick, recently retired post office workers from Harrogate, were a pair of self-styled 'Megaheads'. Standing stones, burial cists, souterrains –

anything big, made of stone and very old, that was their thing. They travelled the country ticking off slabs of vaguely rectangular sandstone as determinedly as any Munro bagger. The previous day, the pair had hiked out to the Tungadale Souterrain, a bronze age underground passage in as remote a spot as it's possible to get on Skye. Although notoriously difficult to locate in a wooded hillside, they got lucky and found the distinctive terraced entrance and went in to explore. At least George did. But he only got a few yards inside when he heard a noise ahead of him. He was just raising his hand to switch on the lamp he had strapped to his hat when something barked loudly and launched itself at him. He caught a blow to his face and fell backwards as the thing jumped over him. He barely caught a glimpse – it was Carol who got a full eyeful of the creature as it paused briefly at the mouth of the passage before shooting off into the trees.

'And you said it looked like,' Doyle turned Holly's notes round and read, 'a big cat with antennae and mascara.'

'That's it. Right strange it were.'

'How big?'

Carol held her arms out as far as they could go. 'At least this big from nose to tail.'

'I have a full description,' said Holly tartly.

'Definitely not a wildcat?'

'Not a chance,' said Carol firmly. 'It were nowt like anything I've ever seen.'

Holly shoved Doyle from her desk as she took over the interview again, eventually ushering the Hardwicks from the building with promises to meet them later that morning at a suitably rural location to take shots of George's injuries to go with their 'incredible' story. Doyle was lost in thought when she got back into the office and looked bemused at the black look she gave him from the door.

'What?'

'I'll tell you what. I was ready to fob that pair off and now I'm committed to writing the whole bloody thing out complete with pictures. You've got them thinking they'll be on the BBC news this time tomorrow.'

'Oh, so you don't believe them?'

'No-o I don't believe them! There've been three or four 'we saw a big beastie' stories on Skye this summer and every single one of them have come from either drunks – remember those pished golfers at Skeabost? – or nutters like the Hardwicks there.'

'Holly's right,' said Bob. 'The police think it's just a wind up and I know the *Free Press* have long since stopped taking it seriously. The only animal they think's involved is a copy cat. That's why that pair ended up here. No one else would listen to them.'

'If we start the whole thing up again we're going to have everyone from the cops to hoteliers associations on our back,' said Holly. 'Anyway, why are you so interested all of a sudden?'

Doyle was pulling out a map of the island from a desk drawer. "You remember that guy I mentioned was with my old man at the fish farm? When I'd seen him at MacNabs a couple of months ago he was just out of A&E and he had had exactly the same injuries as George there. Right now … you said there were a number of sightings. Can you remember where?'

Bob and Holly looked at each other and irritably counted them off. 'Skeabost, Roskhill and … yes, Colbost. And now at Tungadale.'

Doyle put a cross on each location. They formed about three quarters of a rough circle about ten miles in diameter. With Holly and Bob watching, Doyle completed the circle at it's northern end. The line passed directly over Knott House.

19

The afternoon was steely grey as Doyle's car turned off the A863 at Coillore, rumbled over a cattle grid and made its way up the rough single track road by the southern bank of the Amar River. As rivers go, it isn't the longest – barely quarter of a mile – and soon the Saab reached the point where several burns converged and created that single flow down to Loch Beag. After reversing into a parking space carved out of solid rock (another old quarry perhaps) the engine was cut. Doyle and Holly sat for a moment in a silence that was almost deafening after the bumps, scrapes and scrambling of the tyres up the track. Ahead along the bottom of a low hill dotted with sheep was a motley collection of farm buildings, some derelict. There were crumbling drystane walls, buckled corrugated iron roofs to broken down sheds and everywhere the tangle of rusted wire fencing.

'Nice,' said Holly.

'Yeah. If you listen carefully you'll hear duelling banjos. Come on.'

They got out and put on boots and gators, stuffed cameras and spare waterproofs into back packs and set off up Glen Bracadale.

The going was easy enough for the first mile on a tractor track and they passed more stone and wire enclosures, shielings and holding pens. At one point Doyle thought they might have company up ahead, a white pick-up was parked by the side of the trail. But it turned out to be long-since abandoned and just gently rusting away on its burst tyres.

Eventually, the gentle climb afforded a brief view back the way to the distinctive flat-topped mountains of Macleod's Tables, ten miles distant in Duirnish. Ahead, however, was still the same featureless roll of heathland, the Glen Bracadale Burn cutting a low gash a dozen yards or so to their right. They were on heavily grazed ground, the grass as short as on any lawn and everywhere the scatterings of sheep shit. It was not a pretty landscape, the grey of the day was turning ever more dark and threatening and their destination – somewhere beyond that conifer plantation, itself a dark mark against a hill in the distance – never seemed to be getting any closer.

With the path now just a narrow track weaving this way and that along the flank of a hill rising to their left, it called for walking in single file and what little conversation there had been between them – he had updated her on his trip south – petered out. Once again, Doyle felt himself cast as the gullible fantasiser chasing improbable theories with Holly playing Scully to his Mulder. She hadn't exactly sneered at this latest twist in his pursuit of Carew's alleged criminality but, since he was just as clueless as to the connection between that and weird creatures attacking retired postal workers from Yorkshire, she didn't have to. With the clarity he'd had from his trip to London so immediately fogged up, not to mention the sinister edge to the return to his flat still preying on his mind, Doyle's mood was darkening with the sky. Not even the view he had of Holly's peachy rear end a few yards in front was cheering him up.

Gradually, the track became less and less distinct. It branched into several options from time to time, Holly carefully choosing the best way around a stretch of boggy ground or over an outcrop of rocks. By and by they found themselves looking down on the head of a small loch, the plantation now just a half mile away on the far shore. They debated the best way forward for a while and ended up climbing down to the shore. On reaching the point at which the Glen Bracadale Burn flowed from the lochan, however, it was clear it was too treacherous with deep channels of fast flowing water in between banks of sand and gravel. Despite the route having been a joint decision, Doyle got the distinct impression, as they clambered back up the way they had come, that Holly was granting him full ownership of it. The only option now was to back track some way up the burn to find a narrow enough fording point.

After a half hour of winding back and forth, once or twice sinking up to their knees in mud, they eventually found a place to jump the burn and head back down to the loch. There, they pushed in under a wire fence and began the walk up the southern shore. Down at the water's edge the landscape seemed to close in on them and it dawned on Doyle what had been so strange about the trek so far; there was no view of the sea. Only in its absence did he realise how normally ever-present the island's coastline was in its scenery. Not only that, but the rising ground to the south was blocking any view of the Cuillins. A corner of Skye that could've been anywhere in the northern half of the United Kingdom … very strange.

Progress now was even slower. The path wound around and over the rocky shore, there were numerous inlets to jump or detour around. And all the while the day grew darker. Doyle checked his watch. It had taken two hours to get this far and he reckoned there was perhaps only three left of daylight. He would certainly want to be back on the main path down to the car before dusk …

'Aieee!'

At Holly's scream Doyle looked up in time to see a truly massive bird launch itself directly over their heads from a fence post not 30 feet in front of them. One beat of its enormous wings – seven, eight feet from tip to tip? – and he could feel the downdraft as it swept overhead. Low over the loch's still waters it glided before two more wing beats had it rising in time to make the far shore.

'What the bloody hell is that?' asked Holly, clutching her chest and hanging onto a rock.

'Sea eagle, I think. Big innit?'

'God, I didn't think we had stuff that size in this country. That thing could pick up my car!'

'Did you see what was strapped to its back?'

'Yeah. Was that a transmitter?'

Doyle nodded unhappily. 'Must be part of the re-introduction programme. I just wonder … that was a pretty big aerial … do you think there's any chance the Hardwick's beast with antennae is also being tracked?'

Holly stopped hyperventilating in an instant and stared at him hard. 'Well, this is a bloody good time to be reassessing your theory! You mean I'm covered in cuts, bruises and mud in the middle of nowhere and we could've sorted this out with a call to Scottish Natural Heritage?'

'I'm just saying … y'know, what if it was a wild cat or something else and it's part of some scientific study …'

'Aarrrgghh,' Holly turned her back to him and resumed the scramble along the shore. 'We've gone this far,' she said over her shoulder. 'Let's get to where we're going so I can take some really interesting shots of a hole in the ground and it will all have been worth it.'

And on they went. Around the next bend, another fence had to be negotiated. As Doyle lifted over his trailing leg something caught his eye a few yards up the hillside in the trees. He jumped down and led Holly to a small clearing. It was a feasting ground, the leftovers of everything from rabbits to lambs lying all around. Doyle bent down to examine.

'Oh, of course,' said Holly, her voice heavy with sarcasm. 'So, tell me Tonto, what killed this lot and when? The nearest half hour will do.'

Doyle ignored her and carefully picked his way around the remains. After a few seconds he stood and faced Holly with a grin. 'Big beastie story back on track,' he said.

'Oh, come off it. From Sherlock to Indian tracker?'

'Who this Sherlock, Ke-mo Sah-bee?'

'Seriously, Dan. What gives?'

'Well, for a kick off, sea eagles don't take packed lunches into the woods – and certainly not to the same place time after time, at least I shouldn't think so. And there are too many bones in the small mammal remains. Birds of prey just swallow bits of animal whole, don't bother to pick out the bones – they get excreted in pellets along with the fur and other indigestible stuff. Plus there are some seriously big teeth marks – look.'

Doyle picked up the bottom half of a rabbit leg by its foot and stuck it under Holly's nose. She tutted and backed off but held his arm and focused on the leg.

'OK, that does look like the work of some large incisors but who's to say it wasn't a dog?'

'Out here? The only dogs are sheep dogs. You think maybe a collie went over to the dark side?'

Holly simply frowned.

'Come on,' said Doyle. 'We can't be far now.'

They weren't. Fifteen minutes later, they reached the eastern end of the loch and the corner fence post George and Carol had told them to find. But that wasn't the end of the quest. Their instructions told them to head up the slope away from the loch. The souterrain was only a few hundred yards up there, they were told, somewhere in the trees.

'I wish they'd stuck a bloody flag on top of it,' said Holly 20 minutes later. 'This is impossible!'

She had a point. Although the plantation thinned out in sparse stands of mainly young trees towards the shore of the loch, it still covered a large flank of hillside – and that hillside was a treacherous jumble of moss and grass-covered boulders, ankle-breaking gaps hidden between them with, from time to time, the sound of an underground stream rushing underneath. Doyle anxiously checked his watch once more.

'We don't have the time for this,' he said. 'It'll take us –
'

'There it is!'

Doyle followed the line of Holly's point over his shoulder and, sure enough, there through the trees was a long, low ridge, far too regular in shape to be natural. Before they reached it, the entrance itself could be seen – a small, square opening beneath a squat lintel of stone. Holly took another step forward but Doyle put a hand out to stop her.

'Hold on there, Sparky,' he said in a fierce whisper. 'Remember, the supposition is there's a bloody big pussy cat in there.'

She sighed. 'OK, then. What do you suggest – Here kitty kitty? … Dan? … What is it? … Dan?'

Behind Holly and about two yards to the left, a grass-covered boulder had just stood up. And it had a gun.

***

Chloe took the call on her way to the airport.

'We have Doyle,' said the heavily accented voice on the other end.

'Big deal. He's been right under your nose for months,' she said. 'Any information from him yet?'

'No. He is claiming innocent so we, ah, encourage him to search conscience a little more.'

'See that you do. Anything else?'

'Mr Lytton is … is not happy.'

'Good. He has every right not to be happy. I will deal with him myself.' She hung up and turned to Adam beside her in the car. 'Any word yet on the shipment?'

'Arrived on schedule.'

'Mmm.' Chloe frowned even as she nodded. Everything sounded reassuring. Everything was still going according to plan. And yet … She stared out at the late afternoon traffic on the M4 edging, with them, west along the flyover south of Gunnersby Park, and tried to regain her usual equanimity, her confidence in herself.

All but the biggest A-listers have an arc, like a firework. They burn brightly as they climb, hit their peak with a spectacular display when, like the biggest rocket, they seem to be the only thing in the sky, before they inevitably fade from view. She knew she was approaching her peak. The second series of Chloe Carew, Business Angel would air in the spring after the runaway success of the first, she was a regular on chat shows and her book was now out in time for the Christmas market and selling well. More than that her scheme to keep Danbury Healthcare – and the rest of her businesses – afloat was working like a dream. And she knew it was just a temporary measure, an adjustment that allowed her time to put some bad breaks behind her and push on to a new phase of commercial success – now backed with a much healthier public profile. So what was the problem?

Doubt and indecision did not come naturally to Chloe Carew: they were like foreign bodies infecting her own – and right now this felt like the flu. She had crossed a line, but only the same one she'd been crossing again and again her entire career. Ever since her first expansion into the London property market all those years ago she'd seen the advantage of breaking the law and regularly given thanks for the squeamishness of her competitors. Financial short cuts, regulation dodging had quickly morphed into more direct, violent means of 'effecting commercial outcomes'. This, too, she had absolutely no problem with – just so long as it could be conducted at more than arm's length. She had a stomach strong enough for it, quite liked life in the rough house, in fact – business was a ruthless, dog-eat-dog world and she saw little distinction between metaphorically and literally ripping the shirt from a man's back. But of course her public image and who and what she really was needed to be world's apart. To achieve and maintain that distance she had always chosen her associates very carefully and delegated appropriately. No one who could rat on her would ever do so because she ensured the very real and present danger that would involve for them always outweighed any possible threat to herself. Anyone thinking of taking the risk merely had to look at the odds.

But this arrangement – of necessity – involved more than her usual closed circle. She was having to take other people's word, rely on someone else's assurances and that never sat well with the Carew constitution. Throw in the loose cannon that is Geoffrey Lytton, useful idiot though he may be, and this Doyle character's unhealthy interest in her affairs and it all added up to the nearest she'd ever gotten to being out on a limb. The sooner she could take direct control, the better. And first order of business was some plumbing.

'We may at last be about to plug some leaks,' she said, still staring out the window.

'If I may … ' Adam shifted a little in his seat. 'Why lift the father first? Dan Doyle must surely be easy enough to find now.'

Chloe didn't like being second guessed – even by Adam – but she kept her voice level. 'This is a containment exercise. You start from the inside and work your way out. Only that way can you be sure you don't overlook anything. First, we deal with Geoffrey – he knows he's in for a rollicking – then we find out just exactly what Doyle senior knows and what he passed on to his brat. Then we deal with Dan Doyle and anyone he's working with. We follow the possible flow of information in one direction. And we do it quickly.'

***

Maybe it was the blood draining from Doyle's face that alerted Holly to the fact that he wasn't playing the old 'look behind you' prank. Whatever it was, she stopped protesting and turned. Then she gave a little yelp and stepped next to Doyle, grabbing him by the arm.

The man was enormous. His battle fatigues were covered in netting which, in turn, was plastered in mud and peat with moss, grass and heather attached all over to create a carapace of foliage. Even the rifle he held was camouflaged and, when he lifted his head under a helmet similarly adourned, his face was streaked with green and brown paint.

Doyle let out his breath. 'Aw, for fuck's sake! I need new underwear, ya bastard.'

'Sorry … no, wait a minute. Why am I apologising? You've just screwed up my entire day. I've been lying there for hours. What the hell are you doing here?'

'Same as you, I suspect. Looking for big beasties.'

'Ahem!' said Holly pointedly.

'What?'

'Who is this?'

'You've not met? He's your inside man with the cops.'

'He's a … ,' she turned. 'You're a policeman?'

'Sgt Sandy McNair. You must be Holly, Bob's daughter.'

'Yes, that's – ,' she stopped herself and straightened her back. 'Look, what's going on here? You nearly gave me a heart attack.'

'Well, the point of camouflage is that you don't get spotted. I can't help it if I'm just really good at it.' A silly big white grin appeared in the middle of all the greens and browns.

'Respect, big man,' said Doyle. 'That is one helluva fancy dress.'

'Good isn't it? I went on a course. The army – ,'

'If I can interrupt once more,' said Holly. 'You mean to say you're out here looking for the Hardwick's big cat? I thought the police had given up on that.'

'Some have. Some of us have more of a roving brief, not to mention a wee bit more imagination.'

'But the sightings have all come from drunks and drop outs, the cops said it themselves.'

'And if you dismissed all those on Skye, you wouldn't have much left, would you?'

'Fair point,' said Doyle. 'So, any signs of it?'

'Signs, yes. It's definitely been holing up in the souterrain. I've got some fur samples and there are scent marks and scratches on that tree trunk there.'

Holly asked, 'And you don't think it's just a wildcat?'

'No chance. It's way bigger than that. And a different colour. Quite apart from the fact that wildcats don't bark.'

'That's right, I'd forgotten about that,' said Doyle. 'A cat that barks – what the hell is it?'

'It could be a number of things but definitely nothing from round these parts.'

'Scotland?' asked Holly.

'Europe,' said Sandy. 'Whatever it is, it's been brought here from a very long way away – and illegally.'

As Holly continued questioning Sandy, Doyle walked over to the entrance to the souterrain. He knelt down, pushed back the over-hanging grass and fern and crept inside.

Souterrains, he'd read, are found all over the world. In Europe, most date from the Iron Age although this one is thought to have been built in the earlier Bronze Age. But built for what? It was a question for which no one had yet come up with a definitive answer. Too small to have been dwellings, too well finished with stone or sometimes timber cladding inside to be used for burials, the best guess was they were either food stores or refuges when settlements came under attack.

Doyle preferred to let his eyes become accustomed to the gloom rather than switch on the torch he carried. A small hole in the ceiling a few yards ahead afforded a little light and it wasn't long before he could make out the dimensions. He was crouched in a passageway that ran, with a few kinks and turns, to his left and right. It was, he soon discovered, about nine yards long and only a few feet high, making it impossible to do anything more than crawl on hands and knees. It was damp and, strangely, just a little bit warm. Towards the far end on his right, the passageway took a turn and immediately around the corner there were the obvious signs of flattened earth where something large had made its bed.

With every one of his senses on full alert Doyle knew there was a chance wires were getting crossed, false memories created, that he was just imagining it. So he turned and sat down, closed his eyes and breathed as easily as he could through his nose. It had been stronger at the entrance to the souterrain but it lingered here too. It was a smell that was at once distinctive yet faint. It was having to fight its way through a confusion of other scents, some from here and now, others remembrances of those that had obscured it before. But the longer Doyle sat there, the more he trusted his recollection of the back of the truck at Lytton's fish farm.

20

Sandy's stake-out having been so comprehensively ruined, he decided to call it a day and walk back with Holly and Doyle. He had actually approached the souterrain from the south east – 'down wind,' he said pointedly – a much longer route skirting the hill of Roineval and through the Tungadale forest. His car was parked several miles down the road towards Sligachan and Doyle agreed to give him a lift. After pausing at the clearing with the animal remains long enough to let Sandy pick up some more samples, they pushed on, keen to reach Doyle's car before darkness. With Holly once again striding out in front, Doyle fell into step with Sandy.

'Any joy with those names I gave you at Kyleakin?'

'Oh, aye. Well, I've got some results for you but I suspect not ones that'll give you much joy. Let me see now … Mahmoud left the island years ago and hasn't been heard of since. Our old mate Scanlon is currently enjoying Her Majesty's hospitality at Peterhead having finally tested the patience of the procurator fiscal to breaking point with flogging stolen mobiles and hot-wiring his electricity meter.'

'And Vic Robertson?'

'Still here and still in his heart I'm sure a very naughty boy. But I can assure you, Dan, he isn't smuggling drugs.'

'How so?'

'He's out on licence. He got done some years back for breaking into holiday cottages and nicking tellys. Anyway, prison overcrowding and all that – he's back home now but watched like a hawk.'

'What, 24/7?'

'Not quite. But seriously, Dan, his conditions are pretty strict. His probation officer even gets reports on things like going to hospital.'

Doyle stopped. 'Can I guess that he did indeed attend hospital?'

'Aye. Like I said.'

'Can I also guess that it was Portree A&E, it was in August and he was treated for cuts, bruises and a facial injury?'

'I don't know what he was treated for but it was in Portree and in August,' said Sandy, now eyeing Doyle carefully.

'He's in work, isn't he?'

'Ye-es.'

'And, finally – for the one million pound jackpot,' said Doyle in corny gameshow host voice. 'His employer is … the Suladale estate?'

Sandy pushed up the front of his camouflaged helmet and stared at Doyle. 'Correct. Something you want to share with us, Dan?'

'I hope so.'

At Sandy's distrustful expression, Doyle went on, 'That is to say I hope I will be able to share it with you just as soon as I'm sure what it is I would be sharing. If you see what I mean.'

Sandy shook his head and began walking again. 'You know there are people who can do that sort of thing for you. They're called the CID.'

'Who're far too busy I'm sure to be chasing wild geese hither and yon.'

'Or other wild animals,' said Sandy with some heat. 'Speaking of which, I can see Skye News churning out another few hundred words on the Hardwick's story. I can just about see a reason for a photographer coming out to take some new pictures. But why are you here? Don't tell me you think there's some connection between Tigger and your drug smugglers.'

'No, no, no.'

Doyle was forceful in his dismissal, partly to put Sandy off the scent – the last thing he needed was someone else telling him he was Walter Mitty – and partly to see if it convinced himself. Hearing Sandy articulate it was almost shocking; drugs, Carew's activities and a big cat scaring the shit out of tourists all being part of the same story – how could that possibly be? From mysterious through absurd, this whole thing could easily get downright embarrassing.

'So?' asked Sandy after a minute of walking in silence.

'What?'

'Why did you come out here with … ' and he gestured ahead to Holly. ' … Oh, I get it.' Sandy's voice came over all suggestive. He looked again at Holly and nodded with the face of an appreciative connoisseur.

'Nothing wrong with your taste, Dan. But d'you not think that's punching a wee bit above your weight?'

'Ach … not interested.'

'Right. 'Cos, of course, if you were she'd already be dancing on the end of your – ,'

'Keep it down, will you?' said Doyle, grabbing his sleeve.

'You're the one who needs to keep it down. Phnarr, phnarr! Anyway, what difference does it make? I thought you weren't interested.'

Doyle took a while to say, 'I … might change my mind.'

'Aye. You let me know how that works out for you.'

'How what works out?' Holly had slowed to pick her way across a burn flowing into the loch.

'Nothing. Just … stuff.'

'Oh, stuff. Yeah, tricky that,' she said, deadly serious.

The path on the other side of the burn climbed onto a shoulder and exposed them to the weather now pushing down Glen Bracadale. The wind had picked up and was straight into their faces. Doyle felt the first spits and spots of rain from clouds that looked like they'd had enough of lugging that amount of water about and were eyeing Skye as the ideal place to dump it. He zipped up his jacket and tried not to think of the long walk they had ahead of them in what was now going to be driving rain. He stuck his hands in his pockets and trudged on, looking at nothing but the yard or so of ground between him and Sandy's heels ahead. Which is how he came to walk right into his back when Sandy suddenly stopped.

'Oof! Hoi, what's the – ,' Sandy turned and clamped a huge hand over Doyle's mouth. Holly, too, had stopped.

They had reached the edge of the forest close to where Doyle and Holly had jumped the Glen Bracadale Burn. Doyle slowly took Sandy's hand away and peered ahead. It was perhaps 300yds away, straight in front of them and coming their way across open ground. Doyle could make out it was fairly large and sandy-coloured. It held something black in its mouth, possibly a crow, and was moving in short bursts, pausing every now and then to raise it's head and look this way and that.

'Well spotted,' whispered Doyle as all three lowered themselves behind a rocky bend in the path.

'It wasn't me,' said Sandy.

Holly's smile was brief. 'If it's heading for it's usual restaurant it's going to be here any minute,' she said, worriedly. 'What do we do?'

Sandy unshouldered his rifle and clicked off what Doyle presumed was a safety catch. 'No time like the present,' he said.

'Tranquiliser?' asked Doyle.

'No, depleted uranium. I'm gonna blow the mother' into next week. Of course, it's a tranquiliser, ya eejit.'

Doyle gave Holly a sheepish grin as Sandy edged his way back up to the brow of the rocks in front of them. Staring at each other for a moment, they then simultaneously made the decision not to miss the action and crawled up to join Sandy.

The animal was moving fast, like them possibly fearing a soaking, and was now barely 150yds away. Doyle didn't get long to focus on the thing before it finished another low trot and raised itself up for a quick scan of the horizon, at which point Sandy fired. Immediately, the animal recoiled and dropped its kill. And then it ran – boy did it run. Sandy jumped to his feet and gave chase. Doyle did likewise and it wasn't long before he was overtaking the lumbering big man.

'Keep it in sight,' gasped Sandy. 'Don't … let it drown.'

On Doyle ran, desperately shifting his gaze back and forth from the disappearing creature to his next footfall, convinced a broken ankle was only seconds away. And yet even in those frantic moments Doyle registered that whatever he was chasing was indeed a cat, but the strangest looking one he'd ever seen.

Doyle was still on the western side of the burn, scrub and trees to his left. The animal was on the other side, only open hillside beyond. Knowing something was on its tail, it suddenly lurched off at right angles, naturally enough heading for the cover of the trees. Unfortunately that meant crossing the burn and the swampy ground all around it. Even as it made its turn, however, Doyle could see it was flagging. The bright red fletch of the dart could be seen on its front left shoulder, a good shot from Sandy.

Two more bounds and the thing was in trouble. It struggled through mud that was almost up to its neck but then reached some more solid ground close to the burn. It took a moment to hunker down before launching a doomed leap to try to make the far side. Doyle saw its hind quarters buckle just as they tried to provide a springboard for the jump. It landed in the burn with a muddy splash. One or two more pathetic attempts to move and then it finally collapsed. It looked like it was only in shallow water but limp, helpless and, just as Sandy had feared, now in real danger of drowning.

Doyle, without stopping to think why he should be so desperate to save the thing, accelerated over the last 100yds and then threw himself into the burn. The water was much deeper than it looked – and freezing. The cat was being dragged downstream, rolling and flopping in the current, and Doyle had to wade after it, slipping on the rocks below. He got within range and made a grab … tripped as he did so and ended up dragging the creature down with him as he plunged headlong into the stream. He managed to get up onto his knees and get a grip of the animal under its front legs. Lifting it clear of the water, however, only increased its weight and Doyle keeled over again. It took all his strength to lift it clear of the water once more and then, using one hand to help haul himself, he dragged it to the side.

Doyle collapsed on the bank, gasping for air, the big cat sprawled over his chest, one paw either side of his neck, its head resting on his shoulder. Holly was the first to arrive and her expression of concern soon gave way to barely disguised amusement. Sandy, on the other hand, didn't even try to contain himself.

'Get a room,' he managed to say after trying to catch his breath and laugh at the same time.

'It's a what?' asked Holly some minutes later, as she moved around taking shots of the prone beast.

'Caracal,' repeated Sandy. 'It's from Africa mostly, but also found in the Middle East and Asia.'

He was bending over the animal, checking for injuries and making sure it hadn't taken on board too much water. 'It's a 'she' and, thanks to Crocodile Dundee there, she seems OK.'

Doyle was sitting on a rock rubbing the worst of what felt like dozens of minor injuries and trying to fight an involuntary shiver, soaked as he was to the skin. He looked at the animal as the rain finally began to pour with a vengeance. About the size of a labrador, it was uniformally a light, almost pinkish tan in colour save for a black nose, black-rimmed eyes and the most remarkable ears – also black but with outlandish tufts of hair growing from their tips – the Hardwick's antennae without doubt. It's eyes were open and it was breathing heavily after its exertions but thankfully completely comatose.

'Any idea what it's doing here?' asked Holly, quickly stowing her camera out of the rain.

'Well, like I said, it's not here by choice and I'm pretty sure it's not an exotic pet that somehow escaped,' said Sandy.

'How do you know?'

'Mostly because there is no way we wouldn't have heard about it by now. Unless it came over the bridge or sneaked onto the ferry at Mallaig, this thing escaped or was released here on Skye, not the mainland. If it had spent any time here at all we would've heard. You don't keep an animal this size and with this diet in a but'n'ben. And speaking of diet, it's clearly pretty good at hunting. No, this isn't a pet and my bet is it's not been here for very long.'

'She's beautiful, isn't she?' said Holly. 'Y'know, in a weird kind of way.'

'Aye, it's a helluva animal. I saw one in a zoo when I was on a hiking holiday in Pakistan years ago, remember reading all about them. Come to think of it … yeah, I think they're almost impossible to domesticate – another reason for it not being a pet. They're great hunters, bloody quick over short distances but the big thing about them is they can jump. From a standing start it can get several metres in the air. That's how they catch a lot of their prey, wildfowl and such.'

Holly looked at Doyle. 'You OK?'

Doyle was staring at the caracal, rain dripping from the end of his nose, a frown ploughing a furrow across his brow. But he said nothing.

'Och, he's fine,' said Sandy. 'But we better get him moving again before he catches his death.'

'What about the caracal – are we taking it with us?' asked Holly.

Sandy managed to keep his smile just the right side of condescending. 'No. That sedative won't last long enough for us to get to somewhere we can secure it. Besides, I don't think Dan and I would appreciate having to lug it all the way back to the car. I think it's time for a little assistance.'

And with that he pulled out a satellite phone and began dialling.

'What's the date?' asked Doyle suddenly.

'Eh?'

'The date. Or rather, what date is tomorrow?'

'This is the 15th,' said Sandy still punching in numbers. 'And, as tradition has it, tomorrow is the 16th. Of October, in case that was your next question.'

'Interesting …'

'Aye, calendars are just the best aren't they?' Sandy rolled his eyes at Holly and put the phone to his ear. 'Hello, Karen? Aye, Sandy here. Look, I'm going to need the coastguard helicopter – ,'

'Hang up!' said Doyle, jumping to his feet.

'What?'

'Hang up. Now - please.'

'Sorry Karen, just a minute.' Sandy clicked the mute button. He said nothing to Doyle, just waved an invitation to explain himself.

'Any chance you can delay all this for 24 hours?'

'What?' said Holly.

'Nope,' said Sandy.

'OK … ah, any chance you can get it out of here without using the coastguard or anyone else. I'll carry it – happy to.'

'Do you think he hit his head?' Holly asked Sandy.

'Dan. That's not going to happen. It's dangerous for the animal as well as us.'

'Right, right, of course. Is there … any way you can keep a lid on this. Get the thing out of here but not make a song and dance of it. You know, big cat caught on moor, mystery surrounds blah, blah. Just … just not tell anyone.'

'You've got the exclusive, don't worry,' said Sandy. 'I mean, who else is going to be able to write what you can?'

'It's not that.'

'It isn't?' asked Holly.

'No.'

There was silence for a moment as three people stared at each other in total incomprehension.

Sandy clicked off mute and put the phone to his ear again. He looked at Doyle. Doyle did his best puppy dog impression.

'Karen? Hi, sorry about that. Give me a minute. I'll call you back.'

'Thanks,' said Doyle.

Sandy stuck his hands in his pockets. 'You have the floor Mr Doyle. This better be good,' he looked up at the thunderous sky, ' – and quick.'

Doyle opened his mouth several times but nothing came out.

'I definitely think he hit his head,' said Holly.

'Come on, Dan,' said Sandy. 'What is it?'

What is was was a piece of a jigsaw. Maybe not the final piece but a significant one. It hadn't looked as if it should fit, but it did. And once in place it suddenly made a lot of other pieces look as if they too could be connected. Doyle's mind was racing. Was it the cold that was now making his head bob up and down and his teeth chatter? Was it the adrenaline from the chase still coursing through his veins? Or was it just the rush from seeing things for what they were? Things he'd read and things he'd seen, things he'd smelled and things he'd heard ... a swirl of images and a soundtrack of quotes – the same ones over and over.

'How about you get the chopper in but just say it's for a walker – one of us, if you like – with a twisted ankle. You load up the cat and take it back to ... wherever you would be taking it.'

'The SSPCA animal rescue centre at Inverness probably. And no, I can't order in the coastguard on false pretences.'

'OK, fair point. But let's say you're not that specific on the blower. Get the guys in, take it to Inverness and, you know, just ... sort of ... look after it for a bit. Request a temporary media blackout for ... "operational reasons". That possible?'

'It is. But why would I do that?'

'I can't tell you.'

At Sandy's reaction, Doyle went on, 'Seriously Sandy, I can't. Believe me, you'll understand when the time comes.'

Sandy groaned in exasperation but closed his eyes and flapped his arms against his sides.

'24 hours?' he said after while. 'I suppose that's not such a problem. The animal will need to be checked out, there'll be paperwork and I'll probably have to stay behind in Inverness anyway. So, yeah, I could do it.'

'Brilliant, big man. Cheers.'

'But I think you might have some problems closer to home.' And Sandy nodded over at a deeply scowling Holly.

A little under an hour later, Doyle and Holly made it back to his car at the head of the Amar River, the rain still driving into their faces. About halfway along the track they had heard rather than seen the Sikorsky from Stornoway as it clattered low over the hills to the north on its way to Sandy's location. After that it had presumably headed east towards the mainland and Inverness.

Doyle reached the car first – he had set a fast pace with Holly struggling to keep up – and quickly threw his backpack into the boot. He knelt down and with trembling useless fingers began picking and pulling at the mud-caked laces of his boots. Finally, he pulled them off, opened the rear door, threw them in and began stripping off his sodden clothes. By the time Holly had put her own waterproof and camera gear in the boot and climbed into the passenger seat beside him, the engine and heater were on and he was hugging himself wearing only boxers and a t-shirt.

'G-gies a cuddle,' he said.

Holly leaned forward but only to shrug off her fleece. She put it over his shoulders and turned the fan up full. 'You'll survive,' she said.

'Heartless. Th-that's what you are.' But the fleece was warm and soon his shivering subsided. He looked over and saw Holly staring levelly at him.

'Sandy may be prepared to play along with this, but I don't have to. This is the biggest exclusive Skye News has had … probably ever. Have you got one good reason why I shouldn't file it as soon as we get back to the office?

'No.' Doyle put the car in gear and moved off. 'I've got seven.'

21

The day dawned dry, sunny and unseasonably warm. At least, everyone else seemed to think so. Doyle, on the other hand, was pulling the tags from a just-bought combat-style jacket he wore over a heavy sweater. Black jeans and a pair of old Doc Marten boots completed the outfit. He was sitting against the front wing of his car parked in one of the bays in the middle of Somerled Square in Portree. At just after 9.30, Holly's red Alfa pulled up beside him and she jumped out. She was back in one of her linen trouser suits.

'I don't remember Suladale being that far north,' she said, looking him up and down.

Doyle sneezed and pulled out a handkerchief. 'I caught a chill. You got the gear?'

Holly walked round and opened the hatch back. From her camera bag in the back, she pulled out a Canon handheld video camera and passed it to him.

'You've used one of these before, I assume.'

'Long time ago. Bit heavy, isn't it?'

'It's not the latest model, no. But then, we don't run to state of the art at Skye News. Don't worry, it works fine and it's got a great focal length zoom range: x10 optical and x100 digital.'

'Good. I think I might need that. All charged up and ready to go?'

'Did it this morning. I still wish I was coming with you.'

He didn't know why but Doyle felt almost embarrassed by the sentiment. 'I appreciate that but, as you said, you can't.'

The Skye News diary for the day was choked with commitments and Bob was due back at hospital in Broadford.

'All the same, if you're right about this – and frankly, the more I think about it, the more absurd it gets – ,'

'Gee, thanks.'

'But if you are right, that isn't going to be a tea party you're gatecrashing.'

'I'm not planning on gatecrashing anything.'

'You know what I mean.'

'Yes, I know. I'll look after myself.'

'Sod you. Look after the camera.'

Doyle grinned and checked his watch. He had allowed plenty of time but was still anxious to get into position.

'And we're cool on the deadline? You hold fire until at least 1 o'clock.'

Holly looked like she'd just been reminded of last night's drunken visit to a tattoo parlour. 'Fine. But, remember – the first whiff of this story from anywhere else and I'm hitting the 'send' button.'

'Fair enough. Right, I'm off to catch the bad guys,' and he sneezed violently. 'If I don't catch pneumonia first.'

Doyle pulled out of Somerled Square and took the usual route north out of the town on the Dunvegan road. It was familiar enough for half his mind at least to soon drift off and wonder at how he'd arrived at the end game so suddenly. Way sooner than he'd anticipated – and over a matter that had come charging out of left field (with its daft pointy ears) – he was about to bring the curtain down on both his months-long pursuit of Carew and, hopefully of course, her career. It wasn't the denouement he had thought or hoped it would be – but then, Al Capone got done for dodging his taxes. For the umpteenth time in the last 18 hours, Doyle ran through his reasoning, concluded, yet again, that he was right, worked out the unavoidable consequences for Carew … and wondered – yet again – why he wasn't more happy.

The perfect conditions looked set for several hours at least when Doyle reached the high ground around Borve and could see a panorama of the north western sky all the way to the Outer Hebrides and beyond. If anything was on its way to spoil the day it would be coming from there but it was clear blue to the horizon. On balance this had to be good – a better chance of clearer pictures from a further distance and he wouldn't be in for another soaking. Or so he thought.

Not long afterwards, Doyle drove past the unobtrusive entrance to Knott House at some speed – he didn't expect Lytton to be at the road end but there was no point in taking any chances. About half a mile further on there was a parking bay on the opposite side of the road. He drove past this, used the driveway to a house to turn around then returned and parked in the bay facing back towards Knott

House. Should he have to leave the scene in a hurry, he preferred the idea of driving 'innocently' on the other side of the road while any pursuers were tearing along in the opposite direction. To his right across the road now the land rose quickly onto the moors, peat bogs and low hills that constitute the vast dreary interior to the north of the island. Across a low ditch on his left was the fenced edge of the birchwood that fringed the conifer plantations that in turn extended in an arc to the shores of Loch Snizort and around Knott House. Doyle put Holly's camera in his backpack, slung it over his shoulder and, making sure there was no-one on the road to see him, jumped the ditch and then the fence.

It was like going back in time. This day may be sunny and dry but the woods retained all the sodden chill of the previous day and night, like an imprint caught on film. The moment Doyle stepped into the coppery light he saw his breath plume out in front of him. He sneezed repeatedly and felt the cold from the day before return to his bones. Every branch and trunk was wet to the touch, every disturbance brought a fresh shower of drips on his head and everywhere there were puddles and treacherous hollows of slippery moss and mud. The going was slow. The air was filled with the pungent scents of soggy autumn – damp wood, bracken and thorn bushes on the turn, stagnant water. Doyle wasn't banking on his blocked up and so recently broken nose giving him either directions or an early warning of an approach – he was no bloodhound. But the memory of the smell in back of the truck and at the souterrain was strong and, if he was right about all this, he should be getting another reminder of it before long.

What he expected sooner than that, however, was some noise. Voices at least, the sound of vehicles being moved.

Half an hour into his slow, careful traverse of the woods, however, and all was still deathly quiet, just the occasional distant swish of a car going along the 850 behind him. Further and further into the woods he went until the birch gave way to sitka and lodgepole pine. Now he really was getting close, or at least he should be. He stopped more frequently to listen keenly. But still nothing. Had he been spotted already? Was the unnatural quiet the result of collective breaths being held as they moved in on his position? Doyle's stops now featured slow, careful 360 degree turns as he scrutinised every tree and bush as a possible hiding place. And then he reached the sea.

'Shit,' he said to himself in a low whisper.

Doyle stood on a high bank before it ran down to the shore of what was at this point the opening to Loch Snizort Beag and looked across at the western flank of Trotternish. From the craggy tops of Beinn Bheag and Creag na Cuthaige on the horizon he could work out exactly where he was in relation to Knott House, guess how far he'd walked through the woods and calculate the chances of having missed what he was looking for. The chances were zero. He hadn't missed it; it wasn't there.

***

She watched him search. She knew it was in vain and slowly, reluctantly, he realised it was too. As he waved off the last, packed car, she could see him make an almost physical effort to hide his disappointment, raise his chin and walk smiling towards her dark grey Land Rover Defender. Adam sat behind the wheel, a pile of bags and other gear that could easily have been put in the boot occupied the front passenger seat leaving just the one beside Chloe free. Of all the seats in all the vehicles she had ensured it was always going to be the only one free. Lytton climbed in.

They did not have far to go so Chloe got right to the point. Cutting across Lytton's umpteenth paean to the glorious weather that morning, she said, 'You've been avoiding me, Geoffrey.'

'I ... ah, no. I ... ah.'

'Exactly.'

Lytton nodded significantly at Adam in the front seat.

'Adam is my right hand,' she said impatiently. 'Now, what have you got to say for yourself?'

A little defiance at that flared in his aristocratic features. With reflexes bred through generations of looking down aquiline noses, Lytton's neck extended and his head rose. 'I've said all I am going to say to Julian.'

'With all due respect to Julian and his clients, he is not repairing your roof, is he? He hasn't put this estate back on its feet and put money in your pocket, has he?'

Lytton's haughtiness became a little fixed, determined.

'And may I remind you that Julian also does not know the full extent of our business here and therefore the full extent of our potential exposure. What might seem like a relatively harmless lapse in judgement to him looks like bloody recklessness to me.'

More defiance. 'But why? No one has yet explained to me exactly why I shouldn't have spoken to a local news agency about my collection. These people live and work on Skye. Local people, Chloe, covering our quotidian, dull little local lives.'

Chloe smiled. 'Would it interest you to know that Dan Doyle, until recently, worked for *The Sunday News*?'

Lytton's left eye twitched.

'That in ten years on national newspapers of one sort or another he won three investigative journalism awards and has covered town hall graft, organised crime and all points in between? That just over six months ago he asked for my mobile phone to be hacked into and was given transcripts of messages left on my voicemail? And that one of those messages, dear Geoffrey, was from you?'

Lytton's mouth had fallen open.

'Would it also interest you to know that you employ – sorry, employed – his father?'

'I … what …?' Lytton whined.

'Precisely. Why is it, Geoffrey, that I seem to know more about how you run this place than you do?'

He said nothing but sat in abject misery, his earlier resistence just a preposterous memory. Chloe wrung the maximum from the rebuke. It was only after a long pause that she spoke again.

'When they were in the house, did you ever leave them alone?'

'Wha – no … ' Lytton answered absent-mindedly, staring out the window. 'Well, only when he used the bathroom.'

'Pay attention man!' Chloe snapped. 'Did you accompany him, did you see him go in and come out, how long was he gone?'

'He, eh … he went on his own. I was with the photographer,' yet another pained expression creased his face. 'I suppose he … he was gone rather a long time.'

Chloe caught Adam's glance in the rear view mirror.

Moments later they had arrived, pulling up behind the car in front. Lytton turned to unclick his seat belt when Chloe put a hand on his arm.

'No, Geoffrey. Not this time.'

***

Doyle kept himself just inside the treeline and made his way south east along the lochside. It wasn't long before a turn around a small promontory afforded him his first view of Knott House. Even from about a quarter of a mile away it looked deserted. Nevertheless, he cut further into the trees and slowed his approach all the more, every step a carefully taken one. It was a route that took him back out of the conifers and once again into the older wood. Here the birches were mixed with alder and gnarly Atlantic oak, rhododendron thriving in the half light below. There were glades of open ground, fallen trees left to rot, their trunks infested with weird fungi bulging in the cool, sodden air.

As Doyle caught his first glimpse of the house's western gable through the trees something else registered on the periphery of his vision. He stopped and turned to his right. He could see nothing. Turning back he took another step and yet again something made him look to his right. This time he saw it – an odd regularity in the undergrowth at the far end of his view, maybe 400 yards through the trees, a pattern that only his movement showed up. He changed direction and headed straight for it. Half way there, Doyle knew that it was a cage.

It was big, maybe 30ft square around the base and 20ft high. The walls, like the enclosed top, were made of high tensile deer fencing tightened over metal scaffolding, itself anchored by guy ropes. The ground around it had been cleared and although well-worn only at the end where a simple hinged and padlocked door had been built in, the rest of the periphery still showed the faint signs of men at work. Doyle inspected the cut marks to the scrub that had been cleared and looked at the raw earth where the vertical poles had been dug in. Close to ground, he caught that now familiar musky smell, but not as pure as before – like it was an ingredient in some olfactory cocktail. The space inside the cage was empty save for two features: a small, almost scratched bare and therefore indeterminate tree, and a rough shelter in one corner made from three wooden pallets nailed together, heather lining the bottom.

He took some snaps of the cage with his mobile phone then began filming. After a walk round the extent of it he set off for Knott House, the camera still recording. There was no path as such from the cage but the way ahead was as clear as one. The well-trodden route came out on the far edge of the back courtyard he and Holly had driven into. Doyle made sure the camera caught the distinctive features of the house before switching off. He paused for a long time in the shadows of the trees to look and listen. Again, nothing. He walked out and stood in the middle of the muddy yard now a Jackson Pollock painting of criss-crossing tyre tracks and footprints. He checked his watch and knew that while he had been right about the what and when, he was wrong about the where.

He had one last chance. News of the big cat's capture would be making the TV and radio bulletins that evening, irrespective of when Holly sent out Skye News's exclusive take on the story. Long before it was in the morning's newspapers, he fully predicted Carew and Lytton's entire operation on Skye (and he still didn't know what that was) to be shut down, every last scrap of evidence cleaned up, carted off or dumped. But if he presented this film to the police in Portree as soon as possible, got them to check with Sandy in Inverness and at least send someone to see the cage for themselves …

Doyle began jogging up the approach road. Half way along, he guessed where the layby was he'd parked in and took a shortcut right, back through the trees. It didn't take him long to curse his stupidity; it might have been a more direct route but his progress slowed over the uneven, slippery forest floor. When he eventually climbed over the fence again at his car, he called Holly and got a gratifyingly warm response to the discovery and filming of the cage. She would carry on as before and wait for him to update her on progress by lunchtime.

Doyle threw his pack on the back seat and set off, accelerating hard in the direction of Portree. Moments later he drove past the turn-off for Knott House where he saw the muddy tyre tracks emerge and turn off both left and right along the road. He drove on. The tiny settlements of Treaslane and then Bernisdale unfolded to his left: the crofts and the farmsteads, the gardens, the tracks down to the shores of the sea loch, the holiday cottages, the B&Bs ... He looked to his right: nothing. He drove on. Cars heading in the opposite direction flashed by as he picked up speed. He paid them no heed.

It was a long straight and he pushed harder and faster, eyes now fixed on the road, mind set on the job in hand. Or was it? Well, not entirely. The hum of his wheels on the road couldn't quite cover the sound of a small yet insistent voice at the back of his head. It was very particular that he'd seen something significant – a damn sight less so about exactly what that was. Doyle shook his head in irritation. He didn't need this just now – he had to get to Portree as soon as possible. But the voice wouldn't be still. It told him to pay attention, to think. He told it to sod off and he drove on.

Just short of the Skeabost Hotel Doyle came to a cluster of buildings by the roadside, a turn off to the right and a sign pointing the way to Glen Bernisdale. He was no more than 100 yards from it when the voice came again, only this time it was his, it was out loud and it said, 'That's it!'

He stamped on the brakes and squealed to a halt. He'd been going so fast there was nothing on his tail that could've objected. In fact the road on both sides was empty and he sat there for a long moment, his foot still on the brake, a double streak of rubber on the road behind.

The cage had told him he'd been right – but unlucky. Dare he chance his luck again? He checked his watch once more, thrummed his hands on the wheel. It was time to stick or twist. A van appeared in his rear view mirror … and he decided to twist.

Doyle yanked the wheel round and made the turn onto a single track road that climbed and then weaved around a string of houses and crofts. After less than a mile the road came to a boggy end, a sea of black mud with a dilapidated barn like an island in the middle. There were black plastic covered hay bales, piping, buckets, old troughs all lying around in a yard beside the corrugated iron building. Just beyond a five-bar steel gate led to a track that headed up the northern side of a wood.

Doyle parked up by the gate, switched off the ignition and got out, almost slipping in the mud. He looked to the right at the terrain as it led up from the track by the wood all the way to the flat top of modest Ben Roishader. It looked easy but he knew it would be nothing of the sort. Ignoring his shivers, he took off his jacket and jumper. He put the back pack on, locked the car and set off at a steady jog. He sprung himself over the gate and took the track by the wood. It wasn't long before he warmed up but he knew this was just the start. A quarter of mile on, he saw what he thought would be his best bet for firm ground and headed off the track and onto the southern flank of the ben.

It was hell. Ground like sponge covered in grasses – some with razor sharp blades – and dotted here and there with outcrops of rocks and heather made Doyle pant and swear and curse as he ran, stumbled and clambered up the hillside. Glancing up only enough to check his bearings, not enough to get discouraged by his lack of progress, he ploughed on – sometimes literally – through peat bogs and marshes. By the time he reached the stony top, his lungs felt too swollen for his chest, his throat rasped and his legs were barely following orders. He struggled out of the straps to the pack and collapsed into a grassy hollow, rolled onto his back and saw stars in a bright blue day. Eventually, his breaths came less painfully and he could no longer hear his pulse pounding in his ears. He rolled back up onto his knees, then his feet, and looked out on almost 40 square miles of bugger all.

Bordered to the north and east by the A850, to the west by the A863 Sligachan to Dunvegan road, and to the south by the single track B885 that links Portree on the east side of the island directly with Struan on the west coast, there is an interior to the north of Skye that features nothing but peat bog, moor and forest. There are no townships or crofts, nor ruins of any note. There are no roads, just a few rough tracks and footpaths, yet no-one consulting any walking or climbing guide to the island would be directed anywhere near them for the simple reason there is nothing worth walking to or climbing up in the whole, miserable landscape.

If you lived in Knott House and wanted to engage in fairly large scale illegal activity in broad daylight, would you risk it in your own relatively small back yard ... or come here? The tyre tracks at the end of the house's driveway had been that elusive 'something significant' Doyle had seen. Assuming – as he did – that everyone there that morning would be involved, would they have gone off in different directions? Yes, if they wanted to avoid drawing too much attention to themselves by driving in convoy. Better to reconvene later having approached the rendezvous by different routes.

Doyle took one last long restorative breath, sank back down to his knees and pulled the pack towards him. First out was the OS Landranger 1:50,000 scale map of north Skye. This he flattened out on the ground, aligned, as best as he could, with the reality in front of him. Next he took out the second bloody pair of binoculars he'd had to buy since he'd arrived on the island (the first night vision ones having been crushed under the fish farm truck).

From the foot of the hill he was on to the horizon was, he guessed about three or four miles – although that varied according to the topography – while, from south west to north east, he reckoned to be seeing a span of perhaps ten miles at best. Doyle began at the bottom left corner of his view, the reedy shores of what the map told him was Loch Niarsco, and tracked slowly west to east until he reached the stretch of the 850 he'd just driven down and, a little beyond, Loch Snizort Beag. Moving up a degree or two, he then swept back the way, east to west. He searched slowly and carefully – their choice of location and dispersal tactics were not the only precaution they had taken against being seen.

There were three large plantations in the landscape and he paid particular attention to those. About half way along this second sweep he came to the forest around the base of Cruachan-Glen Vic Askill, the craggy high point of the entire view. The sun was off his left shoulder and gave him perfect light and definition. He picked up the northern-most corner of the plantation and panned ever more slowly to his left. In a direct line with the top of the hill he saw a flash and he had them. Two vehicles, a Land Rover and another 4x4 were lined up by the treeline facing away from each other. Neither of them sported light or metallic finishes but the sun was glinting off something shiny, a windscreen perhaps, or wing mirror. He sank to the ground and steadied his elbows on a rock. There were two figures by each vehicle. They were either waiting, watching or both.

Doyle jumped up again and crammed the gear back in his pack and took a few seconds to pick a route. Once down on the relatively flat ground he could see there would be two low hills he could keep between him and the forest edge if he approached from the south and west. He checked his watch and his bearings once more then set off down the ben. Not having to climb a gradient was something of a mixed blessing – less punishing on the lungs, but it afforded far too many opportunities for achieving what would be, in that terrain, a reckless rate of knots. Doyle forced himself to concentrate on nothing but his next step, to trust his directions and just keep battling on over moor, burn and bog.

He reached the treeline, he guessed about half a mile south of the two off-roaders, in just under 50 minutes. He was exhausted, covered in mud and bruised and cut from numerous falls and collisions with hidden rock. But his heart pounded with excitement and he was in no mood to stop for a breather. For the second time that day he set off into woods, the bad guys to catch red-handed.

It was a mature stand of sitka spruce of the old 'regiments of foreign invaders marching across the highlands' variety: planted in plumb straight lines. Doyle chose a line heading in roughly the direction he wanted and simply walked along a dark, pine needle-coated roadway to his destination. And this time he did hear it before he got there. Voices, the rattle of metal on metal, and dogs. Doyle saw the fence ahead and dropped to a low crouch. He covered the last few hundred yards in short bursts, moving from tree to tree. He reached the last one by the fence and sat with his back to the broad trunk, breathing heavily. Taking the camera from the pack he switched it on and swivelled the LCD monitor to face him. Slowly, very slowly, Doyle eased it out from behind the tree trunk. And almost immediately, it felt like his arm had been caught in a light shower. He grimaced.

That was not what he'd meant by red-handed.

22

It had been a fleeting, split second image on the LCD monitor – a tug of war between two dogs only feet from where sat. And it had ended with the 'rope' bursting and then snapping in two. Doyle somehow managed to keep the camera steady and watched the dogs (lurchers or greyhounds, he didn't know which) gnawing at their respective halves of what had been a hare, then tossing them in the air in apparent triumph. It was a celebration obviously shared. Off to Doyle's left, unseen from his position behind the tree, a chorus of baying, whistling and applause accompanied the dogs' success.

Slowly, Doyle retracted the camera and remained motionless behind the tree. The last thing he needed was to attract any canine attention. Moments later he heard handlers approach the scene and control the dogs. From the voices and yelping growing more faint he guessed when it was safe to move. He slid down the trunk from his sitting position until he was flat on the ground and then rolled over, wiping the blood from his hand and arm in the process. The slightly raised ground around the tree gave Doyle enough clearance, even at worm height, to see almost the full extent of what looked like at least three acres of open ground. It was formed by a bend in the forest marked out by a high – unusually high – deer fence. This pocket of open ground was then closed over a distance of about 100yds by a line of tall, glavanzied steel temporary fence panels, half a dozen vehicles parked behind to lend extra resistance. All but one of the vehicles was a Ranger Rover or equivalent, the other was the truck from Lytton's fish farm. They were dark in colour, most with a matt finish. Tail gates were open, hampers were in evidence and of the 20-odd people Doyle could see, a be-tweeded dozen were clearly the clientele, the others paid hands.

As the dogs were returned to one of a number of plastic portable kennels and the assembled 'sportsmen and women' engaged in a raucous round of smug back slapping, Doyle swapped the binoculars he had been using for the camera once more. He wiped the lense clean and focused on the far left corner were the party were gathered. Using the optical zoom to the max – but avoiding any distortion with the digital – he could easily spot Carew, small and dumpy in her ludicrously tailored hunting jacket and breeches, Sir Julian Le Sueur, merchant banker and Tory grandee, one or two other vaguely familiar faces and four or five aristocratic European types – Italian perhaps – immaculate in herring bone and plaid.

Nothing much happened for some time. Doyle stopped recording to conserve the battery and worried that he'd arrived just too late. Then Sir Jullian addressed the others. He had his back to Doyle and his words were lost. But it was clearly something along the lines of saving the best 'til last. To another round of whistles and some curious-sounding calls of encouragement, a cage was pulled from the back of the truck. A cacophony of barking got up as it was hauled by two green-wellied workers, one of them Vic Roberston, to a gap in the temporary fencing. Without a pause, a latch was sprung and out bolted – now that was a surprise – not a caracal.

It was a small, horned deer, roughly the same colour as the caracal on top but with white undersides and a black flash down the side. It looked all wrong, out of place – which, of course it was. About 3,500 miles out of place. Doyle had seen them on African wildlife programmes before and knew it to be a Thomson's gazelle. After darting clear of the cage it covered 40, 50 yards in the blink of an eye. Then it stopped dead and looked about, no doubt wondering where the hell it was. Doyle heard a low growl and moved the camera in time to catch two fresh dogs being slipped from their double leash. The chase was on.

To ever more boistrous whooping and whistles from the on-lookers, the two dogs sped side by side towards the Thomson's which took one look at them and shot off. It headed for the trees but, seeing the fence at the last split second, dived left and began an anti-clockwise circuit around the enclosure. The dogs, huge and muscular by comparison to their prey, matched the turn and tracked its progress, replicating every dart or tiny change in pace or direction almost as if they were connected by some invisible tether. Less than a minute into the chase and it was obvious this was a grotesque miss-match; the dogs were nowhere.

Given a big enough head start, a Thomson's gazelle can outrun a cheetah – the fastest land animal on the planet. The two greyhounds, fast though they were, lost ground so quickly the gazelle's biggest danger was lapping them and being caught in the process of overtaking. Doyle almost laughed. He was sure if running backwards while sticking two fingers up was in the gazelle's repertoire it would be doing it by now. But then he realised the wee fella's triumph would be short lived. As he understood the so-called traditions of hare coursing – before it was made illegal – any animal that managed to outrun the dogs (and many did) was released. Such a reprieve was not going to be granted here. The only reason a caracal had been free to roam around the island was that it had escaped (Doyle guessed before the deer fencing had been extended upwards) – not because it had been congratulated on a splendid show and given the equivalent of Caesar's thumbs up. The Thomson's gazelle was going to die one way or the other.

In only two minutes, the dogs tired and slowed to a trot before wilting to a disinterested mooch about the middle of the enclosure. It was all jolly bad sport. Luckily, one of the foreign Johnnies was on hand to even things up. Doyle heard the shot before he saw what the guy had done. He flashed the camera left to see a puff of smoke and the rifle being lowered then right again to see the gazelle take off … as best it could with three legs.

The end, 20 seconds later, was little different to that of the hare's, though perhaps the dogs enjoyed their fresh meat all the more with a little spice of revenge for having had the piss taken out of them.

Doyle had seen enough. He checked the recording on the screen, packed the camera back in the bag and carefully stood inside the shadow cast by the tree trunk. Once the dogs had been pulled from what was left of the gazelle and dragged to the kennels, the focus was all away from

Doyle's position and he felt safe to start walking back the way he'd come. He was shocked, revolted and angry. He was also thinking seriously about jumping in the air and clicking his heels. If this film didn't nail Carew nothing would. His mind swirling, Doyle retraced his steps to the edge of the plantation and, seeing the two vehicles and their drivers were no longer in sight, struck out for the southern flank of Ben Roishader.

His pace was slower now but still far from a casual ramble on the moors. He had solid gold in his back pack and was anxious to share it with the world. Different scenarios for how to break the story and how Carew would be snared played out in his head as he trotted over the open ground. Perhaps it was that preoccupation that was to blame.

Doyle was about half an hour into his walk when he heard a distant engine noise from off his right shoulder. He turned just too late; by the time he'd focused on the off roader coming round the southern edge of the forest, the driver had already altered course, gunned the engine and begun heading straight for him. He'd failed to identify the vehicles and their drivers he'd seen on the edge of the forest as look-outs – movable ones that, sooner or later, were always going to reappear.

The stretch of open ground between the forest and the end of the track down the side of Ben Roishader that would take him back to his car was a little shy of two miles. He had almost half of that as a head start. But he was wiped; he could feel his energy levels, already low from whatever bug he'd picked up the day before, further drained from the climb and subsequent yomp over to the plantation. He stood looking around for a few seconds calculating his options. There was absolutely no cover.

Plenty of bog to hide in – covered in mud and all but submerged in some peaty water he could almost disappear. But he knew there were two in the vehicle, one driving and one doing nothing but making sure he never lost sight of Doyle's exact position. It was too risky. He had to run.

Relegating the risk of a broken leg to the least of his concerns, he set off across the moor as fast as he could. He leapt from the raised hillocks of grass to rocky outcrops. He dived headlong into the boggy mud. And all the while he heard the whine and roar of the low gear ratio vehicle grow ever closer. On some of the terrain he knew his two legs were more efficient than four-wheel drive, but on firmer ground his pursuers were able to make up hundreds of yards on him within seconds. He didn't turn. There was no point – he was already going as fast as he could. But he could hear the thing getting closer and closer.

And then it stopped. There was a loud shunt before the silence. Doyle turned at that and saw only the rear end of the vehicle sticking up at an implausible angle. He was by now level with the shores of Loch Niarsco and it was maybe 500yds further back. After a few seconds he heard the engine start again and the wheels spin. But it was useless. The doors opened and two figures got out and shrugged off their jackets. Doyle groaned. He'd didn't recognise them but they were young and they looked fit. That was all he needed to see. He turned again and willed his legs back into action.

It was two against one again. It was a miss-match again. But this time it was the quarry that was hopelessly outclassed. The two pairs of fresh legs gained ground on Doyle yard by yard. They didn't shout taunts or threats – and that silent, remorseless intent was all the more frightening. Before long he heard their panted breaths, then their footfalls. They were gaining fast. Doyle's chest felt like it might explode, his legs had long been on automatic – their instinctive negotiation of the ground as seemingly remote from his intent as if they belonged to someone else. But they were flagging and he had no means to spur them onto to yet more effort and speed.

Doyle crested a small rise and there it was – the edge of the wood by the farm and the end of the track that would lead him back to his car. The sight gave him hope and, from somewhere, a last reserve of energy. He risked a quick glance back and almost shouted in relief. One of the men had fallen badly and the other had stopped to help before being waved impatiently on. With an extra few yards advantage Doyle pushed on for the end of the track, reached it and pounded down the slope towards the farm.

But better ground for him became, within seconds, better ground for his pursuer. Doyle reached the five bar gate, picked a launch point in front and attempted a jump with push up from the top bar to clear it. But his legs had absolutely no bounce left and he simply collided with it and fell to the muddy ground. The guy stopped a few yards back and just stared at him, hands on his legs, panting hard. Doyle scrambled to his feet and almost had to hold onto the gate to keep himself up, so utterly exhausted was he.

If it were a western both would be hovering over their holsters waiting for someone to draw first. He was in his twenties, lean but not classically built – there was no breadth to his shoulders, his legs looked too long, his headed jutted forwards on a neck that didn't go straight up. A guy you could easily picture in his old age. He didn't look like the brightest fairy light on the tree either. Maybe the one who'd fallen behind was the brains of the team.

Keeping his eyes straight ahead, Doyle fumbled for the sprung bolt to open the gate. The guy didn't like that, you could tell. But he didn't seem to know what to do about it. Doyle found the bolt and pulled it back with that fingernails on a blackboard noise they always make. It seemed to rouse the guy from his stupor and he lunged, throwing out two long arms. Before they reached him, however, Doyle's boot reached his crotch and he doubled up in pain. Doyle swung the gate open and made a dash for his car. When he got there, however, he couldn't stop on the downslope and almost ankle deep mud. He was about five yards further on than he wanted to be before he slid to a halt. He threw off the back pack, pulled the car keys from a zipped pocket and tried making his way back up the incline to the car ... where his attacker was now waiting for him.

'Oi! What's all this then?'

Doyle swung round to see a man in blue overalls and wellingtons emerge from the corrugated iron shed. In that instant the young guy dived at the pack. Doyle's grip held but both of them went flying into the mud.

They rolled and they slid, they threw punches that mostly didn't land and they pulled and shoved at the pack. The farmer was shouting and Doyle was vaguely aware of losing a hold of his keys. But he held on to the bag for all he was worth. That is until the farmer waded in and, while trying to pull the two of them apart, stood on Doyle wrist. His grip sprung open and the bag was gone.

'No-o!' roared Doyle as he scrambled after it. But the faster and more urgent the motion in that quagmire the less effective it became. The farmer seemed content the two of them were no longer wrestling in his mud and actually held Doyle back as the other slithered away and managed to get to his feet.

'Stop him!' screamed Doyle, too weak to fight the man off. 'That's my bag he's got.'

The farmer looked from Doyle to the young guy who smiled now – a show of bad teeth in an entirely black, mud-encrusted face – and, sticking up his middle finger, turned back for the gate. Perhaps realising his mistake, the farmer shouted after him but it was too late. He reached the gate, checked over his shoulder and loped off back up the track where his companion could be seen limping into view. Doyle squirmed out of the farmer's grip and scrambled and splashed his way to gate to give chase. By the time he got onto the track the two had met up just on the horizon of a rise some few hundred yards ahead.

They didn't move. Doyle began staggering towards them, telling himself he could take them both on. And then a car roof appeared on the brow of the hill. It was the second 4x4 and Doyle knew he was beaten. He stopped and watched the two guys climb on board and then it just sat there, as if those inside were toying with the idea of coming after Doyle once more. Eventually it turned around and went back the way it had come.

It took the farmer an hour and the loan of a metal detector from his neighbour to find Doyle's car keys.

***

They had insisted on flying in and out. Chloe would have much preferred they hadn't but pressing the point too much would have had Sir Julian wondering what all the fuss was about. And after all, a well-heeled shooting party landing their hired twin prop at Skye's modest aerodrome at Ardnish was not that unlikely or unusual an occurrence. Still, she was relieved to be seeing the back of them.

The lunch at Knott House had been Geoffrey's usual mixture of public school stodge and what he imagined trendy metropolitan types might like. Today it had been a mish mash of cured meats and salads followed by spotted dick. Beyond a few amused comments behind his back, their guests had raised no objection. Chloe guessed they actually liked a touch of old world eccentricity as part of the experience. Certainly, Sir Julian seemed delighted with how the day had gone. He ushered the last of his guests to the waiting Piper Seneca on the tarmac and turned to give Chloe a fairwell kiss.

'Splendid show as ever Chloe,' he said. 'And, you know, I don't think our finalé wasn't so bad. I rather think Stefan enjoyed, ah, getting involved.'

Chloe shared his laugh before assuming a more serious air. 'Yes, but it was as well the matter was taken in hand one way or the other. Can't have our showstoppers roaming around Skye can we?'

'Absolutely. No, your diligence in that regard is exemplary, my dear. But let's keep working for the day when we won't have to skulk about in the undergrowth like common poachers in the first place, eh?'

He took his leave and Chloe stepped back towards Adam and the Land Rover parked by the Nissan hut and collection of sheds that constitute the airport's infrastructure. The already turning rotor blades whined ever louder and the plane taxied to the north end of the runway. Moments later it climbed above a backdrop of Kintail and distant Torridon, their hills already turning orange in the late afternoon sun, and set a course south east for Edinburgh.

Chloe had every reason to feel satisfied. Another event had gone off with nary a hitch, soon that irritant Doyle would be dealt with and, as Adam explained on the drive back north to Knott House, his morning with Geoffrey had revealed no causes for concern.

'He took me through the interview minute by minute. There was nothing either on or off the record that could've been a problem,' he said, keeping carefully to the 40mph speed limit through the outskirts of Broadford. 'I'm sure he stuck to the script.'

'And the house? He said Doyle had been gone from his sight for some time.'

'Well, we know there's nothing obvious lying about, certainly in the public rooms. We went up to his office and not only is there, again, nothing with any direct reference to our business, Geoffrey remembered that while Doyle had been gone, presumably in the bathroom, he had gone to his office himself to check details of a recent purchase. It is, as you have seen, little more than a small attic so it's pretty safe to assume he didn't miss Doyle standing there.'

'Well, it's of little consequence as we're about to lance that particular boil once and for all.' Chloe smiled. 'Looks like we may be back on track.'

She was still smiling half an hour later when they pulled into the back court of Knott House and found Lytton in animated conversation with a man covered from head to toe in dried mud.

23

Doyle's mobile had not been in the backpack. It contained pictures of a big cage in a forest. As pieces of conclusive evidence go, it lacked a little something. In desperation, he'd taken it to Portree nick as soon as he got back into town. But the desk sergeant took one look at this mud-covered lunatic talking about big cats on the loose and offered him a choice between the door and a charge of wasting police time. Sandy wasn't back on duty until the morning. Doyle had attached the pictures to a text message. So far, he'd received no reply.

Bob looked at it and handed the phone to Holly who passed it back to Doyle. It was shortly before 7pm and they were sitting in Bob's front room with a spread of pizza boxes on the dinner table and carpet between them. It had started out as something of a celebration but Doyle was successfully pooping the party.

Bob's scan results were encouraging – the tumours were already in full retreat and he was going onto a lighter dose of chemo straight away. Between that and Skye News having sold its big cat story to practically every broadcaster and newspaper in the country once Sandy had set the ball rolling earlier in the day, Holly had been in good spirits – good enough to let Doyle away with a tut and roll of the eyes for losing her camera. The full gory details of Doyle's story, however, quickly punctured the happy mood.

As for him, apart from feeling like a lump of tenderised steak from his batterings on the moor, he had spent the afternoon coming to uncomfortable conclusions. The shortcut to nailing Carew having proven too good to be true, he was forced to reassess everything he knew about her operation. What, when connected to what else, made sense – and what was it about his assumptions that didn't? Somewhere behind the dots – the fish farm, the financial imperative, the hare coursing, the truck – even, he was reluctant to admit, the fate of the Morven II and her crew – there was a pattern, a purpose. Eventually, he found himself left with only one explanation that seemed to fit. After checking certain elements with contacts, including Jake on the *FT* and Sommerville, Carew's ex non-exec director, it still fitted. Unfortunately.

Back at Bob's, mein host was struggling to catch up. 'I'm sorry, I'm obviously missing something,' he said, pulling himself up a bit in his chair. 'How did we get here, again? I understand what you're saying about what happened out there today but how … I mean, why were you there in the first place?'

As quickly as he could, because it already felt a bit after the Lord Mayor's show, Doyle ran through six of the reasons he'd given Holly the day before for believing illegal hare coursing – with a twist – was going on at Knott House.

First, of course, there was Lytton's original message on Carew's phone referring to a package having arrived 'safe and well'. Then there was their visit to do the teapot interview. The sound of the dogs barking as they'd got out his car had bothered Doyle. The only reasons for having working dogs on Skye – and thousands had – was for sheep. Having grown up in a crofting community he knew exactly what a border collie sounded like, and those dogs didn't. In Lytton's office, the first oddity were the entries in the diary for meeting this person or that – but then other entries that said simply 'meet'. They weren't, as he'd first thought, just absent-minded references to meetings with unidentified individuals – they were the dates for 'meets' of the so-called sporting variety. But not ones worthy of any further identification and, curiously for occasions that would normally be social as well as sporting, always on a weekday. Doyle had remembered there was one such entry for today.

Also in the office were the photographs – Carew, Lytton and their pals all enjoying days of sport. But what sport? Pictures of these occasions are like the game itself, the object of the hunt, trophies to display. Yet those pictures had been strangely diffident. There were no guns in their hands, or dogs at their feet. There were no fishing rods or horses or dead pheasants or grouse or salmon or anything else on show. Just a relatively close shot composition of figures in tweeds in front of some trees and deer fencing.

Then there were the coincidences – the similar injuries to Vic Robertson, as seen by Doyle in Macnabs Bar that night, and George Hardwick, and that musky, wild animal smell that linked the souterrain to the truck at Lytton's fish farm.

'The seventh reason is Carew herself,' said Doyle. 'She's not just your average huntin' shootin' fishin' type. She's hardcore. If you Google Chloe Carew and Waterloo Cup you'll see what I mean.'

'What's the Waterloo Cup?' asked Holly.

'Was. It used to be the premier meet for hare coursing in England before the thing was made illegal in 2005. Anyway, Carew was rent-a-quote on that at the time, how it was a scandalous infringement of their inalienable rights, nanny state intervention on a Soviet scale blah, blah, blah. She contents herself nowadays with being on the board of the Country Matters Foundation – along with the aforementioned Sir Julian Le Sueur I might add – but she's really just a blood-thirsty wee bitch.'

'Well, we can't argue with that after this morning,' said Bob. Silence fell on the room before he spoke again. 'Are we in any danger?'

'What?' said Holly.

Doyle stood up and, before he realised what he was doing, flicked the curtain to have a look at the street outside. 'Don't know. Depends on how threatened she feels.'

'I say again – what?'

'Think about it Holly,' said Bob. 'If Dan's right about Carew – and, let's be honest, he has been up to now – then she's not going to take kindly to him sticking his and Skye News's nose in her business.'

Holly looked from one to the other, some real concern in her eyes. 'Come on, guys. You can't be serious. She's the little bossy woman from the telly – not the Godfather.'

'You're right, you're right,' said Doyle, walking past her so she couldn't see him flare his eyes at Bob. 'Nah, she'll just shut the whole thing down – probably has done already – get the hell off the island and lie low.'

'Exactly,' said Holly. 'She was lucky – her hired muscle got your evidence and roughed you up in the process. I can't see that she's got anywhere else to go with this now, or a good reason to. It's over.'

Holly looked around for assenting gestures or comments and got plenty of both.

'Of course,' said Bob with a shrug. 'She'll know he either hasn't involved the police or persuaded them to investigate – otherwise he wouldn't have been sneaking about on his own with a video camera.'

Doyle said, 'By now the enclosure out on the moor, Knott House, the fish farm, everything will be getting wiped clean of anything that could either point to what they've been up to or especially any association with Carew.'

'So if Dan did manage to get anyone else interested in his story – even the police,' said Bob. 'It's not going to get him anywhere. Carew will know that.'

Holly stood up and stretched, 'And what would be the point in drawing attention to herself by going after you and/or Skye News? Honestly, you two watch far too much bad telly.' She laughed through a yawn. 'Right, I'm turning in early; I think we may just be a little bit busy tomorrow. You need a lift?'

Doyle found an unclaimed slice of pepperoni and took a bite. 'No thanks,' he said, munching. 'I think if I don't walk a little this evening I'll just seize up.'

Holly gave her father a kiss goodnight – it was obvious from the awkwardness that this was not normal procedure – and let herself out the house. Doyle went to the window and watched her car reverse out of the driveway and head down towards the main road. Nothing followed.

'Do you think she bought it?' asked Bob.

'I don't bloody know – she's your daughter,' said Doyle in some exasperation. 'What do you think?'

'No idea. She's like her mother. I never had a clue what was going on inside that woman's head.' He got up and poured himself another glass of coke from the oversized bottle the take away place had insisted turned a pizza into a 'meal'. 'So, what exactly are we talking about here?'

'It's hard to say. A lot of what we just spun for Holly is quite true.'

'But?'

'But we both know Carew's not the forgive and forget type. She might not know how much I know – or those I associate with,' Doyle waved graciously at Bob, 'But I don't think she's likely to take the risk.'

'On the other hand,' said Bob. 'Holly is right. She'd be mad to draw attention to herself just now.'

'She doesn't need to. All the rumours I've heard about her strong arm tactics: the coercion, the bribery, the blackmail are just that – rumours. And that's because she doesn't do it in broad daylight.'

The two men made their way back to the easy chairs either side of the fire and sat in silence for a while. A logical case for any reasonable eventuality could be made but what would be the point? Carew was hardly a model of reason and logic, easy to predict. And talking themselves into a false sense of security would maybe help them get to sleep that night. But then what?

'Well, at least you've managed to call a halt to her activities,' said Bob as brightly as he could. 'That has to count for something.'

Doyle stopped staring at the fire for a moment and gave Bob a puzzled look. 'I've stopped nothing.'

'Come on, Dan. Camera crews are already pouring onto the island. Every North Briton correspondent in the country will be here within the next 12 hours. You won't be able to buy a pint of milk tomorrow without someone sticking a microphone or notepad under your nose and asking about 'big beasties'. Then there'll be the Sundays and magazine treatments. Between that and nervousness about how much you – we – know about it all, I can't see Carew and Lytton putting out so much as a mousetrap for a long while.'

'You are assuming this is all about illegal hunting.'

'It's not?'

'No, Bob. It's not.'

***

The log fire was lit and the curtains drawn against a cold, cloudless evening that had brought the first hint of the winter that was to come. Out of the glare of direct sunlight through those massive windows and with a judicious lamp here and there, the drawing room of Knott House lost it's slightly shop-soiled, threadbare edge. In the soft focus glow of the fire, shadows dancing in the corners, the old place had a country house hotel look about it, could almost pass for chic.

Chloe, however, was oblivious to its charms. She was working on her pulse. It was getting better – the ludicrous amount of gin in her hand had helped – but she could still hear it in her head, stoking her anger. That, and the sound of her teeth grinding.

The first thing she'd been told about on their return from the aerodrome was the snooper with the camera at the coursing event. She had no doubt it was Doyle. But if that wasn't bad enough, Lytton then confessed that several months ago they'd 'lost' one of their imports. Having been told that the capture of a wild caracal on Skye – the first ever live confirmation of any 'big cat' story in Britain – was all over the radio and television news, he knew he had to come clean. Chloe had kept her anger under some control at the time – making arrangements for the total sanitation of Knott House, the fish farm, everywhere was an obvious and immediate priority. But now she was in the mood to vent.

'And you didn't think I needed to be told?'

Lytton was standing by the fire. It was, she suspected, the standing that he was intent on, not the fire: it at least gave him the advantage of altitude – the only one he had.

'As I said, we thought it was injured. One of our chaps swore blind he'd winged it. We thought it wouldn't last long.'

'We thought, we thought,' said Chloe with relish, like she was enjoying some silly piece of nonsense poetry. 'And did you also think that shortly after breathing its last it would disappear in a puff of smoke? Or maybe you thought no-one would bat an eyelid at a dead caracal lying about the place.'

Lytton was spared another steaming load of sarcasm being shovelled on his head by a tap at the door and one of his men inching into the room. They had been doing so periodically all evening.

'Sorry Mr Lytton, ma'am,' said the guy holding a tweed cap in his hand. 'Just to say that's the cage down. Do you want the ground lit tonight? It might draw a bit of attention.'

Lytton only needed to see Chloe's expression from his peripheral vision. 'Yes, tonight, George. Quick as you can.'

'Are they annoying me in the misguided belief it shows you to be in some sort of command?' asked Chloe as the door closed over. 'Or are they really that lacking in resource and nous?'

'You said you wanted this place exorcised – your word, Chloe. That takes some doing. I would have thought you would appreciate the attention to detail.'

'The attention to detail I would've appreciated would've been not allowing a fucking caracal to walk out the front door in the first place – then deciding I didn't need to know about it.'

Lytton merely stiffened his shoulders and stood with his back to the fire, staring straight ahead. He was old fashioned enough that it was entirely possible at least part of his offence was at the use of the 'f' word. Chloe took another slug from the enormous G&T. Actually, it was getting a bit heavy to hold onto so she put it on the occasional table by side of the sofa.

'Honestly, Geoffrey. I don't know what I'm going to do with you. I – ,'

'S'cuse me,' said a voice from the door which was creeping open again. The mud-caked man, now washed and changed, stepped in. 'The dogs, Mr Lytton. We're short of places for them to go.'

As Chloe swooned back in her seat theatrically, Lytton asked, 'How many short?'

'There's two we cannae house.'

Lytton screwed up his face and looked at Chloe. She gave him a look that said 'please don't ask me to state the bleedin' obvious'.

Lytton turned to face the fire and put his hands on the mantlepiece. His shoulders slumped. 'Do whatever you have to do, Johnnie. They can't be here tomorrow morning.'

'Aye, but, like I said – ,'

Lytton turned a fierce look on him. 'Whatever you have to do!'

The man called Johnnie looked puzzled for a while before his face cleared. 'Oh … right. Got ye.'

She nearly felt sorry for Lytton then. After all, she had gotten to know the old buffoon quite well over the last few years.

It had been his brother's introduction. Nick Lytton was a partner in a City law firm, five years Geoffrey's junior, a damned-sight more dynamic and a member of the Country Matters Foundation. Chloe had thus shared tables with Geoffrey at society functions and they had been once or twice removed from each other at a number of shoots. The relative of a friend / friend of a relative gap was one Chloe had initially no desire to bridge; Geoffrey was such a fusty old sort and, besides, his land was on Skye – who the hell would want to go there? But then her problem arose – and the potential solution. Suddenly, knowing someone with an estate on the north west coast of an island off the north west coast of a country off the north west coast of Europe was actually quite lucky. Her initial attempts at ingratiating herself with him were, in retrospect, far too presumptuous and ill-thought out. She could rely on her public profile – even before the TV series really took off – with most people. But it meant little to a man who lived in the middle of nowhere and only listened to Radio 4 when he wasn't worrying about his roof. But they shared interests, a common view on the realities of rural life, a fury (quiet in his case) at what was being lost without a fight. She changed her tack and won his confidence. It was a short walk from there to his day-to-day concerns, to his exact financial situation, and to his weaknesses.

'It's necessary, Geoffrey,' she said. 'You do know that, don't you?'

'For whom I wonder,' he said, still staring at the fire. 'Do you know what is going on here – I mean everything?'

'Clearly not,' said Chloe, instantly irritated again. But also puzzled.

Lytton, staring moodily at the flames, offered nothing more.

'Is there something else you'd like to get off your chest?' she prompted.

But before he could answer the door opened once more.

'Oh, for crying out loud!' shouted Chloe as a man walked in and straightaway opened his jacket appreciatively to the warmth of the fire. But there was something different about this guy. He didn't linger at the door; he strolled in like he owned the place, went up to the fire and warmed his hands.

'And who the hell are you?' asked Chloe.

The man smiled. 'Dan Doyle. And you are?'

24

Yesterday in Glasgow some magistrate ruled
feudal rights prevail. Crofter reform turns out
a cruel joke. You pay and pay and own nothing.
Wouldn't we welcome them back this minute,
Those clowning men from Kilmuir?
They were crazy like dolphins. When Gilleasbuig Aotram,
most dolphin of all, met a real crazy
raving in chains, headed for the asylum, he said:
"Had you the right madness bread would be secure."
Have the right madness. This land has always passed on
and, like you, it is still here.

The Semi-Lunatics of Kilmuir by Richard Hugo.

He guessed she would've liked to sit back in the couch –
the better to play the suave villain, all insouciance and
lurking menace. But if she did her legs wouldn't reach the

floor. She was tiny and not even hair and stilettos as high as those could hide it. She remained perched on the end of the seat like Ronnie Corbett in drag next to what looked like a G&T of heroic proportions. Lytton had turned, mouth open, the moment he'd walked in the room. And, as Doyle had advanced on the fire, he'd backed off and was now almost behind Chloe's sofa. Notwithstanding that this was actually his house he said nothing, accepting immediately his role as a bit player in this vignette.

Doyle shivered and rubbed his hands before the fire. 'Cold as a witch's tit out there,' he said. 'Wouldn't fancy spending all night on a fish farm with the marigolds on, would you?'

Carew had been stony-faced, her eyes fixed on Doyle. He could almost hear the frenzied processing going on behind her lack of expression. Now she smiled and reached for her flagon of gin.

'So, you've managed to surprise me at last,' she said, then sipped. 'I must say you've been awfully predictable 'til now.'

Doyle chuckled. 'Yes, that's why you were watching my flat in London for two months while I was at the other end of the country. That's why you hired my old man without knowing it. That's why, even after this afternoon, you have no idea how much I know.'

She watched herself slowly put the glass down on the table. 'Whatever it is, Mr Doyle, it's not enough, is it? Why else, I have to ask myself, are you here?'

At that, a man walked into the drawing room, came up short on seeing Doyle and turned immediately to Carew for a steer. Doyle did not like the look of this guy at all. Maybe the same height but he was probably about five years younger and a lot sharper round the edges. His face wasn't the right colour or texture – he'd overdone something or other in his youth – and while his pink, cutaway collar and cuff-linked shirt said 'toff', his detached, almost drugged stare and thin mouth said 'thug'.

'Adam. Perfect timing as ever,' said Chloe, instantly relaxing. 'This is the famous Mr Doyle.'

The man called Adam started at that.

'As you can see, he has kindly saved us the bother,' continued Carew. 'Would you do the honours?'

Adam advanced on Doyle at a pace that was neither casual nor rushed. But before he'd crossed half the distance between them Doyle had raised his hands.

'OK, OK,' he said and, opening one of the breast pockets to his combat jacket, carefully removed his dictaphone by his finger tips. 'It was worth a go, eh?'

He clicked the off button and tossed the device onto the sofa. It didn't stop Adam from frisking him thoroughly and none too gently.

'Enjoy that?' Doyle asked him when he'd finished.

Adam didn't so much as make eye contact. Leaving Doyle with his wallet and keys, he took his mobile, said, 'Clean,' to Carew and took up position half sitting, half perched on the arm of the opposite sofa to his boss. When he folded his arms Doyle could see several hours a week in the gym through his shirt.

'I will confess to some curiosity,' said Carew, glancing almost subliminally at Adam. 'How did you get in here, and why? Please don't tell me your clumsy attempt at a fishing exercise was all you had in mind. After such a promising start that would be so disappointing.'

Doyle shrugged. 'The how is I walked in the door while everyone was busy doing something other than watching who was walking in the door. I knew this place would be going like a fair tonight. The why is I'm here to offer you some advice.'

Carew made great play of swallowing her mouthful of drink. 'You? Offering me advice? Wonderful, simply wonderful. Please,' she waved her hand, 'dispense your kindly words of wisdom.'

'My advice is you should quit while you're … well, let's put it this way – not so far behind.'

Carew just smiled at that and waved him on.

'You're going down, Chloe. At the moment just for breaking the law governing field sports which, I know, sounds a bit naff – but bad enough, eh? I can't see many commissioning editors for the BBC beating a path to your door after this breaks. Then again, we both know your unnatural proclivity for killing small furry animals is the least of it.'

Carew shook her head sorrowfully. 'Such a shame. I understand you grew up in the country – here on Skye, in fact. But it appears you've lived in the city far too long. 'Unnatural'? You've forgotten the meaning of the word.'

'Mmm. I'm still pretty sure being carted half way round the world to be torn to bits by big dogs is reasonably unnatural.'

'Life and death, Mr Doyle. It is the noble reality of the countryside – as you have clearly lost sight of. You should go on a refresher course, our Country Matters Foundation would be the ideal starting point you know.'

Doyle seemed to consider that for a moment. 'What conditions do you need for sowing winter barley?' he asked.

Carew frowned over her sardonic smile.

'What's the EU subsidy for a purebred hill flock of sheep and how is it calculated?'

'I'm not sure what – ,'

'Name me three truly indigenous British trees – I bet you get at least one wrong. What causes potato blight?'

Whether or not Carew knew the point of this game, she decided not to play. Suddenly her manicure needed inspecting.

'How much feed does the average beef herd need per head per week in winter?' Doyle paced back and forth. 'If you ate a liberty cap mushroom would it make you giggle or kill you? Woolly willow – animal or vegetable? List the harmful ingredients in sheep dip. ... no? Can't help me with any of that? Strange. See, that's what we would call country matters. The kind of stuff that helps you make a living, not get killed, that kind of thing.'

Carew's jawline hardened beneath the make up and the fat. 'I see we have a new rural radical among us.'

'No, Chloe. Just someone who knows his arse from a PR campaign for vicious in-breds.'

The room flinched. Adam stood up but Carew waved him down again.

'We shall agree to disagree on what does or does not constitute issues of concern in our countryside. I take it there is a more pertinent point you'd like to make. I suggest you do so quickly.'

He'd gambled and won. That was not the response of a person in complete control who knew exactly – entirely – what was going on. Such a person wouldn't sit there and take that sort of abuse. It was she who was doing the fishing. All well and good but, while he was prepared to tell her everything he knew (or thought he knew), one of the points of this exercise was to get her talking, not him.

'Well, let's start with dispensing with all the smoke and mirrors, who-knows-what crap eh? We know the fish farm in Loch Snizort's a phoney, or at least a front. It's real purpose is as a staging point for your import business ...' Chloe's hand moved again towards her glass, ' ... and your export business.'

The hand didn't so much pause as jerk. Doyle had hit pay dirt again. Carew finally reached her drink and took a long draw, turned back to Doyle and simply inclined her head.

'It was the truck – yes, I know about the truck. I've been in it. Very unusual smell. That and the Thomson's gazelle that gave you away. If all you're doing is bringing in weird animals to get your jollies killing, then why use something that size – and from one of your companies in England? In particular, why use a vehicle with a barrier pass for Danbury Healthcare?'

Chloe was a study in mild interest.

'And a caracal – now that could come from just about anywhere from Malawi to Mumbai, but a Thomson's? No, that has to come from Africa. So your shipments are running from Africa to Scotland. Much easier – and closer – locations for sourcing, say drugs, than Africa and, frankly, not a lot else of value to be had from there worth the risk. So, the movement of goods has to be going in the opposite direction.'

Doyle was conscious he had everyone's undivided attention. It wasn't quite rabbits in headlights – he suspected Carew at least was still confident of being able to deal with this later. But there was something hypnotic for them to be hearing someone else talk openly about that which they'd worked so hard to keep secret for so long. Doyle walked to the opposite end of the sofa from Carew, talking as he did so.

'But, of course, it's not exactly goods we're talking about here, is it?' He sat down. 'It's shite.'

Chloe almost smiled. To be fair to the old girl, it was obvious she could at least see the irony in the situation. 'Among other things, yes,' she said.

'It must be galling, eh Chloe? To be so tantalisingly close to staying in the black. And that's all you need to do, just stay in profit – because the moment Danbury so much as looks like having a bad month Assured Equity will call in its loan. Then, all that you've worked for 30 years to build up will head for the u-bend. Which brings us back to the jobbies.'

Doyle could see Lytton shift uncomfortably. 'Chloe, really,' he said. 'Must we listen to all this?'

'Yes, Geoffrey. We must.' She took advantage of Doyle being seated to stand herself and take her turn by the fire. 'What was it Mr Micawber said?' she asked. '"Annual income twenty pounds, annual expenditure nineteen nineteen six, result happiness. Annual income twenty pounds, annual expenditure twenty pounds ought and six, result misery."'

Doyle said, 'There are two ways you can ensure Danbury Healthcare remains just the right side of profitable, two sides of the balance sheet to tackle. You've decided to reduce costs. I imagine clinical waste is a bugger to deal with.'

'Oh, you have no idea,' she said. 'About £400 a tonne. Then there's the admin: the local authority regulations, the NHS guidelines and, not forgetting of course, our friends in Brussels and their yard of red tape.'

'It costs the NHS nearly £100 million a year to dispose of clinical waste safely,' said Doyle. 'Your treatment centres don't deal with the big stuff but still produces enough to be expensive, I'll bet. It'll be the low volume high toxicity stuff you're dumping?'

'Needles and syringes,' Chloe nodded. 'Old isotopes from radiotherapy, human tissue, swabs, nappies and the afore-mentioned attendant waste products. And it all has to be categorised – hazardous, offensive, pharmaceutical, sharps, hazardous sharps – and all disposed of in different ways with different middlemen leeching off our profits at every turn.'

'So you've been skimming some of this scum off the top, lugging it up here and then shipping it out to dump on someone else's backyard. Thomson's gazelles don't do jungles so I'm guessing east Africa. Tanzania?'

'Mozambique. Nice and remote.'

'Not remote from the people who live there though, is it? The poor sods who're wading about in your infectious, lethal crap.'

'How touching that you should care about them, and, again, how boringly predictable.'

'No, Chloe. It's you who's being predictable. We've been taking shit from people like you for centuries. Remote?' Doyle shook his head. 'That'll be Skye, the highlands, Africa, the colonies – anywhere far enough away from your own definition of what and where matters. But somewhere you nevertheless seem to think you own the right to exploit or ruin. I know you didn't inherit your feudal attitude. You just bought it.'

'It appears I was wrong,' said Chloe sorrowfully. 'You don't have anything new to say after all. Certainly nothing that is going to leave this room.' And she looked at her assistant.

Adam stood like a retriever who'd heard his special command but just as he took a step forwards Doyle slouched back in the sofa and put his hands behind his head. Adam hesitated.

'One more piece of advice, Chloe,' said Doyle, stretching luxuriously and staring at the ceiling. 'Ask Geoffrey here what you asked him before, you know, just as I came in. Only this time make sure he gives you an answer.'

It was like a small but dark cloud passing before the sun on a blazing summer's day. She dimmed. She also stared at Doyle for a long time before finally, and with obvious reluctance, looking up at Lytton skulking about in the shadows behind the sofa.

He flustered under her gaze. 'I am not sure it would be appropriate – ,'

'You were saying …' she said pointedly.

'Chloe. It's not … ' Lytton tailed off into anguished silence. Two minutes of badgering from Carew later and the silence was almost catatonic.

Carew took a deep breath then drained what was left of her drink. She composed herself and looked at Adam. 'I'm going to ask Mr Doyle here to provide chapter and verse on whatever it is he knows, or thinks he knows, that I don't. At the first sign of prevarication or just being the smug little nobody he's been since he arrived, you have my permission to break a bone of your choice.' Adam's mouth split into an unpleasant smile, like a fresh cut on lean meat. Without pausing a beat Carew turned to Doyle, 'Start talking.'

'Ah, yes. So, where was I … ?' he said, shuffling up into a less vulnerable position on the sofa. 'Now, I don't want you taking this the wrong way, Chloe, but I've always thought of you as a deeply unpleasant person.'

Adam took a step forward but Doyle raised his hand. 'Steady, Igor. Hear me out.' He turned again to Carew, 'Let me see if I can put this another way … eh, no, that's it I'm afraid. You're a scuzzball. But – ,' again he held a hand against an advancing Adam, ' – either for moral reasons (which I doubt) or, more likely, through simple calculation you're no killer.'

'I'm no … what?' said Carew.

'Murderer, Chloe. One thing to hunt and kill anything that moves on four legs, but you've shown admirable restraint when it comes to actually bumping off your human adversaries. You've ruined careers and wrecked lives but, as far as I can tell you draw the line at murder.'

'Well, thank you for that touching testimonial.'

'So you need to ask yourself why have people died?'

'Died? Who's died?'

Adam returned to the arm of the opposite sofa and Doyle looked over at Lytton now seated by the window and examining the curtains.

'George Macleod and Kevin Patterson.'

'George – , look, I've never heard of these people. What are you talking about?'

'I'm talking about you, Chloe. You and your presumption that all you need to do is click your fingers and what you want – and only what you want – will happen. A lifetime of being a spoiled little only child who always gets her way. It breeds arrogance, Chloe – the kind of arrogance that thinks it can control anyone. The kind of arrogance that costs lives.'

Doyle stood but kept his distance from Carew and Adam. 'A property magnate, even an unscrupulous one like yourself, doesn't have the wherewithal to start shipping stuff in and out of the country behind HM government's back. For that you need the expertise of those who do it for a dishonest living. You need drug traffickers.'

'Ex drug traffickers,' said Chloe.

'Oh, grow up. They may have been technically 'ex' when you hired them but they sure ain't any more. Let me take another wild stab in the dark – Croatians?'

Chloe's lack of response was confirmation enough. She was a hard bitch with an inflated ego amply covered by a skin as thick as a rhino's. But it was clear even she was wilting under the barrage of revelations about stuff she'd either failed to keep secret or didn't even know about in the first place.

'Probably thanks to you and your money, they are now firmly back in business,' said Doyle. 'And these guys, dear Chloe, don't play by anyone's rules, not even yours.'

Chloe looked at Lytton, still preoccupied by the soft furnishings, but addressed her question to Doyle. 'Are you telling me there have been more security breaches up here, that people have been … no, that's impossible.'

'Security breaches? If by that you mean have more poor unfortunates stumbled across your stupendously inept operation then the answer is yes. George Macleod and Kevin Patterson – I suggest you commit the names to memory, they'll be taking up residence on your conscience – were the crew of a creel boat called the Morven II. Late one evening back in August they were still working out on Loch Snizort when, I'm guessing, they happened upon your associates' vessel. Maybe it was just a zodiac or somesuch from the main boat still out in the Minch somewhere, it could've been on the way in or out – either way they didn't expect company in those waters so late. And maybe George and Kevin took just too keen an interest in this vessel for their own good. The result was that the Morven II was found smashed up on rocks 20 miles away and the bodies of George and Kevin have never been found.'

Carew was moving her hands unconsciously, picking at her nails, pulling at her hair behind her ear. 'There's a lot of guesswork in there, Mr Doyle.'

'Fair enough. Let's see,' Doyle turned to Lytton. 'How'd I do Geoffrey?'

'They're uncontrollable, Chloe,' he burst out. 'You have no idea. I can't … I have no …' and he was off on another tortured silence.

'Don't blame them, Chloe,' said Doyle. 'They're only doing what's in their nature. You're familiar with that concept, I understand. If it's good enough for dogs, it's good enough for drug dealers. You paid them to set up a route from the Hebrides to Africa to ship your hazardous waste out and, just as a wee treat for yourself and your equally deviant chums, bring in something interesting from time to time to spice up your day's sport. Actually, let me guess – that was their idea, right?'

Chloe nodded glumly.

'Yeah. International wildlife crime – second in value only to drugs and more often than not conducted by the same people. You think you're running a nice wee safe waste disposal business. In actual fact, whether you like it or not, Chloe, you're an international drug trafficker. And an accessory to murder.'

Doyle adopted Adam's position, perched on the opposite sofa's arm, and returned his level stare. For a long while all that could be heard was the hiss and crack of the logs burning in the grate. Chloe walked over to a sideboard and poured herself another drink. It looked like it was just for something to do; the measurement was certainly a more modest one.

'It appears I have more work to do here than I'd thought,' she said, returning to the fireplace. 'But be in no doubt, Mr Doyle, this situation will be contained. Any ideas you and your colleagues may have for exposing any of this had ... better ... you seem amused.'

Doyle was laughing. 'My colleagues? You do know it's Skye – with an 'e' – News, don't you? They wouldn't know a story if it started with 'Once upon a time',' he continued chuckling. 'No, they know nothing about this and they certainly won't be exposing anything. This is my unfinished business from *The Sunday News*, remember?'

'And it will remain unfinished. Your input has been valuable. But only to me. Without any evidence, you've still got nothing. I intend to keep it that way. In the meantime,' she nodded at Adam. 'I think I'll have you where I can keep an eye on you.'

Adam walked over to the door, taking a mobile from his back pocket as he went. He hit a quick dial button. 'Vic? In the house. Soon as.' It was the first time Doyle had heard more than a single word from him. The voice was just a little too high, too thin. The accent pure estuary. Adam closed the door over and leaned against it. Moments later he opened it again to a tap from the other side and Vic Robertson walked in. If he recognised Doyle from their brief encounter in Macnabs two months previously, he didn't show it. Carew had been lost in thought, now she looked at Adam.

'The cellar door locks I seem to remember. No rough stuff. Just keep him secure for the moment.'

Adam nodded then, looking at Doyle, jerked his head towards the door.

'Bad move, Chloe,' said Doyle. 'My last piece of advice? Stop this now. Come clean and plead ignorance to everything the Croatians have been up to. You have no choice.'

She just turned her back on him and looked at the fire. Adam walked over and made to grab Doyle by the sleeve. He pulled away.

'Just ask, cupcake. Just ask.'

Doyle walked out of the room, Robertson ahead, Adam behind. He tried dawdling but Adam shoved him on so they formed a tight little convoy, no chance for a quick dash left or right. Robertson led them back down the passageway towards the kitchen and scullery but half way along took a right turn into an alcove. He opened an old four panelled door, the ancient and chipped light blue paint worn shiny and black around the wooden door knob. Doyle saw the top of some stone steps. He saw Roberston reach for an old brown Bakelite light switch just past the door frame and heard him begin a warning about the steepness of …

And then nothing.

25

He knew he had been no saint when he was alive so ending up in hell, while a total bummer, was not entirely unexpected. Neither, of course, was the excruciating pain. Pain so intense it had its own sound in his head. What was mildly surprising was that theologians who, like Dante, had postulated hell as a uniquely personal experience had been on the money. Eternal damnation, it appeared, was tailored to the individual. Like Room 101 with bells on.

Doyle was claustrophobic so – naturally – he was completely encased in something, held close and suffocatingly tight. Panic was only seconds away. He was having difficulty breathing – or whatever the equivalent was in the afterlife. His mouth was stuck shut forcing him to use his nose which, given the stench down here in Hades, would not have been his first choice. To add to the sensation of growing nausea, he was aware of a slight movement, a swell with exactly the same degree of swimminess that had kept Doyle off boats whenever he could help it when he'd been alive. Any minute now, he thought, the reggae music will start.

'Dan?'

Perfect, thought Doyle. Now my hell is indeed complete.

'Dan? Can you hear me?' Yes, he could hear his father but was powerless to acknowledge the fact or tell him to shut up.

He felt hands on him somewhere but not directly, as if through a thick cocoon he was wrapped up in. He was spun round and then he heard a cutting and a tearing. It reached all the way up to over his head and suddenly the stench became almost overpowering. He felt his eyes water and he was struggling not to gag – with his mouth sealed shut, that would choke him to death.

Wait a minute. Was he not already dead?

Fingers on the side of this face and then – *rip* – whatever had been over his mouth was torn off.

'Dan – it is you innit?'

'Yes, but …' He checked by opening and closing his eyes deliberately, there was definitely nothing left covering his head or face and yet he couldn't see a damned thing.

'I – I'm blind,' he croaked.

'Naw, it's just dark, son. Really dark.'

Doyle was rolled back onto his side and he felt a knife cut at more tape he now realised was binding his arms behind him and his ankles together. Gradually he felt blood flowing again through his limbs. As the numbness abated, however, only freezing coldness took its place.

'Where is this?' and even as he asked, he knew.

'We're on the fish farm. I think they're gonnae kill us.'

'Aye, well. We'll see about that.'

Doyle fumbled his way to the metal wall of the hut and pulled himself up to stand. That move did not go down well with his body. Gingerly he put his hand to the back of his head, where it felt like he'd grown his own golf ball, and waited for the new intensity of throbbing to ease. Eventually, he began inching his way along to the right. After only a couple of steps he stood in something so revolting he could hear it squelch and feel its oozing, slippery consistency even through his boots. He decided to shuffle his feet from then on. As he made his way along, his father explained how, after he'd been beaten up and interrogated by 'a foreigner' he'd never seen before he was bound and gagged as Doyle had been, stuck in what looked like some old mailbags sewn together and brought out here. They'd only checked his pockets so they missed the fisherman's knife he had down the heel of his boot. After several hours struggling with his binds, he'd been able to reach it.

Doyle shook his head in the dark, remembering his old man's tendency towards the melodramatic and his hair-raising tales of growing up in The Garngad where, if he was to be believed, assault with intent to rob lurked behind every corner. It explained his lifelong habit of always carrying a 'chib'. Well, hooray for that now. When he'd heard the boat returning, his father had put the tape back over his mouth, slipped inside the sacking and kept his hands behind his back. The quick check they made on him as they'd dumped Doyle in the hut wasn't thorough enough to spot he was no longer actually bound. He had intended, he said, to pick his moment to jump them and make his escape but they were in and out too quickly for him.

Such hesitation, such doubt didn't sound like the father Doyle had known. And he couldn't help but notice he spoke quickly and with an anxiety he'd never heard before. Though he'd hated his domineering, bullying confidence when he'd been growing up, it was unnerving to hear it had deserted the old bastard now.

On the second wall Doyle reached what felt like the door. But the seam between the jamb and the actual door was incredibly tight, almost hermetic, and it was covered by a fixed strip of thick rubber. It explained the total lack of light and was probably designed to keep the stink from in here wafting out on warm days and reaching either passing boats or even the shore. Doyle completed his trip around the hut and, remembering his view of it through the night vision binoculars, concluded it was about the size of a couple of shipping containers stuck together. It was certainly not built on the platform – it was far too old for that. Given that the farm was never intended to be properly operational (and Doyle had to guess Carew's money was being used to keep the thing off the authorities' radar) the hut was undoubtedly a prefab bought on the cheap from some farm or scrapyard and just plonked on the floating framework. He could feel it was badly rusted but otherwise inside it was entirely without detail – no ledges or frames, not even any riveted joints.

'I take it you've tried the knife on the door,' he said into the darkness.

'Aye.' His father coughed. 'I cut a bit of the rubber off but the blade's too thick for the gap. I can't get it in at all. Anyway, there's three padlocked bolts on the outside. I don't why I was even bothering.'

'I've just been round the walls. Have you been all over the space – ,' the fetid air caught at the back of his throat and made it difficult to speak. ' – is there anything else in here with us?'

'Well, there's the last load on pallets near the back. I remember it. No' big but fuckin' honkin'.'

'You mean it's not just the stuff swilling about our feet that smells?'

'Naw, that's just left overs. The main event's in plastic buckets, boxes and cartons on the pallets. And it was leaking like fuck when we moved it in here a week ago.'

This was very bad news indeed. Not only was the short term risk to their health even greater, but it meant that they would be coming back that night; either a pick-up was already scheduled or they had other plans for dumping this consignment. There was no way they were going to risk it still being here should a combination of the big cat find and Doyle's accusations actually prompt even a cursory investigation by the police.

Doyle pulled the collar of his jacket over his nose and mouth. 'We've got to get out of here. Right now. Anything else in here?'

'There's this …'

Doyle heard his father move and then knock into something. It rattled like a cage. Which, of course, it was.

Doyle followed the sound of his father's voice and found himself running his hands over something he guessed was no bigger than a veal crate. It was metal and apparently very solidly built. He searched for the door and found it. It was closed by means of a heavy spring-loaded bolt. It felt smooth, un-rusted – galvanised steel.

'Give me the knife.'

Only after he'd said it, did Doyle realise he'd just given his old man an order. There was silence for a moment before he felt an unsure hand on his arm and then the knife was carefully handed over.

It was a good one – the blade was not long, perhaps four inches, but thick, strong and sharp. Doyle knelt and found the retaining pin for the spring return. Thankfully, it was not welded and a few blows with the point of the knife (positioning was tricky in pitch darkness) and the pin dropped and the spring shot off. No problem: it was the bolt he was after. He had just put his hand on this ... when something moved in the cage.

'What – ,' Doyle froze in fear.

'Dan?'

Doyle swallowed hard. 'Eh, stupid question. This cage is empty, yeah?'

''Course. They don't keep the animals long in here.'

'But – ,' And then Doyle felt a scuttling over the backs of his legs. He scrambled to his feet. 'What the hell is that?'

'Oh, right. Rats.'

'You're joking.'

'Naw. Sometimes the stuff's infested before it gets here. Fuck knows where they store it first.'

Distinct from the noise of the sea lapping beneath the platform, Doyle could now hear the sounds of one, probably many more, rats splashing somewhere around his feet. He shivered.

'Only a matter of time before they start going for us. Then who knows what'll kill us first, a bullet or the plague.'

Doyle slid the bolt from the bracket and hefted it in his hand. He would've liked it to be heavier – a lot heavier – but it was all he had.

'You gonnae go for them when they come back?' asked his father after he'd explained what he'd done.

'Nope.'

Doyle shuffled his way to the wall and retraced his route. Somewhere close to the back wall he found what he was looking for. It was a depression in the floor of the hut with a puddle of God knows what on top. All around the hut the floor had felt at least as rusted as the walls. At this spot, he hoped, it would be at it's oldest and thinnest. From the sagging, it at least felt as if there was clear air beneath it … he just hoped it wasn't a few inches before the solid floor of the platform.

The first line of attack was a jump. He put a hand on the wall to give himself some orientation, bent his knees as far as he could and sprang up. He landed with a splash of stinking, greasy liquid – and a howling, searing flash of pain through his head.

'A-ahhh, fucking, fucking, fuckity FU-UCK!'

'What is it? You a' right son?'

'What's it sound like? Jesus, my head nearly came off!'

Doyle staggered back against the wall and held his head. It was a long time before he felt able to move again. With a bit of fumbling awkwardness and pushing and shoving, he got his father onto the same spot and told him to do the jumping. The old guy couldn't get very high and his forbearance of the tactic ran thin after he stumbled and fell into the puddle. Next, Doyle got on his knees and tried smashing the bolt down as hard as he could. But the water was deep, and he knew he was acheiving nothing but showering them both in liquid crap.

He was about to get up when he had an idea. Summoning his courage and ignoring the distinct possibility of encountering a rat or, just as bad, cutting himself on the metal, he plunged his hand into the puddle and ran it along the join between wall and floor. It felt badly corroded and, though there was clearly a reinforcing corner plate on the outside, he decided that was now the weakest spot.

'We need the cage,' he said.

Ten minutes of splashing, banging, heaving and swearing later, they had managed to half lift, half drag the cage around the offensive pallets (Doyle was by now picturing something from an Hieronymus Bosch painting) and over to the back wall. They caught their breath, which was hardly a respite in there, and lifted it to shoulder height. With an aim that was more guesswork than anything else, and on the count of three, they threw it – they hoped – at the corner between wall and floor.

The clatter was ear-splitting and reverberated for what seemed like minutes. When Doyle finally took his hands away from his ears he heard it. Pouring water.

'We did it!' he shouted.

He dragged the cage aside, went onto his knees again and felt the tear now opened up along the join. It was only a few inches wide and so far was still submerged as the liquid gushed out. But it was there and, if nothing else, it would soon be providing some fresh air. Doyle took the bolt from his jacket pocket, inserted it into the gap and levered. It was like opening an old, very big tin can. The rusted metal came away easily along the welded seam and the flow of crap briefly became a torrent, then subsided. The rush of fresh, salty sea air that followed and filled his lungs was, Doyle decided there and then, the best physical experience he'd had in his life. Ever.

'Aw man,' said his father. 'I'd forgotten what fresh air smelled like.'

Taking turns with the bolt and knife to chip away at either end of the gap, it didn't take them long to open up a man-sized hole. Doyle lay down on his front and slid his head and shoulders out into the starlit night. The hut stradled four struts with nothing but the sea a few feet below. He twisted round and was about to explain what he was seeing when he heard his father exclaim in disgust. A split second later a rat ran over Doyle's chest and face and leapt for the nearest gangway – then another, then ... Doyle fought through what felt like a dozen of the squirmy bastards to claw his way back inside the hut. He sat against the wall panting. That, he concluded, was quite possibly the worst physical experience he'd had in his life.

'Off to find a nice clean sewer, I suppose ...' he shivered. 'Right, I think we'll be alright, but I can't guarantee we won't get wet.'

Doyle lay on his back and hauled himself out until only his waist and legs, held by his father, were still inside. By turning to his left and grabbing the nearest supporting strut, he could leverage out the rest of his body – but only, as he'd feared, by allowing his legs to momentarily drop and splash into the icy water below. By the time he was able to pull himself onto the platform his bottom half was soaked through. His father followed, Doyle anchoring himself on the corner of the hut and leaning over to hold him by the arm, but he too received a dunking in the sea before being able to scramble onto the platform. They stood shivering for a moment, scanning the walkways and cages.

Health and safety regs say there should always be a liferaft or dinghy tethered to a fish farm – but would that apply to this sham? He set off along the central gangway looking left and right but found nothing by the time he got to the end.

'Here!' he heard his father call from the other side of the hut. He ran back, his legs already beginning to go numb in the cold. At the end of the large decking area his father stood by a handrail. 'It's no' much but it'll dae, eh?'

It was an old wooden rowboat with an empty catering-size baked beans tin, presumably for baling out, floating in several inches of water in the bottom. But it looked otherwise perfectly sound, the oars were there and soon they were pulling away from the platform, Doyle rowing, his old man on the bean can.

The night was clear and still. It was good for sea conditions and made the rowing that bit easier. But bad, very bad for their prospects if they stayed out here too long. The cold would be a silent killer tonight. Although working as hard as he could at the oars, Doyle could already feel it like an infection creeping into his body, numbing as it went, gnawing at his movements, his thoughts. He had to steel himself. He had to make the right choices – and one of them was not to head for the nearest landfall, the jetty where the service vessel was tied up. There was no point, he told himself, in the false comfort of dry land if it was still miles from help and, worse, held the threat of running into those who would kill them quicker than the cold. Instead, he took them north west towards the dark conical peak of Stac a'Bhothain on its spit of land jutting out into the sea loch. It was the right thing to do, he told himself. And the decision made, Doyle settled into a steady stroke and concentrated on nothing but his rowing.

How long it took them, therefore, to round the stac and turn into tiny Loch Losait, he had no idea. All he knew was the prow of the dinghy suddenly ran up on a shingle beach and he could row no more. He sat for a while, catching his breath with his arms like jelly by his sides. He had been staring past the hunched figure of his father for the entire journey but now he focussed on him and realised something was badly wrong.

'Dad ... Dad!' Doyle leaned forward and shook him. His father felt tense and iron hard beneath his jacket, when he reacted to Doyle's touch he did so in a kind of spasm. He tried to talk but it came out slurry, like he was drunk. Hypothermia.

'Shit!' Doyle slapped the thighs of this own legs to try to get some feeling into them then half jumped, half fell into the shallows – and another shock of freezing water. He grabbed the boat and tried to haul it up the beach as much as he could but he managed only another few feet. He waded back to his father and dragged him from the boat. By the time he had them both on dry land they were all but soaked to the skin from the neck down. And there was a breeze. It wasn't strong, would barely be noticable in other circumstances, but it was enough to chill their sodden clothes still further. His father's steps were uncoordinated at best, non-existent the rest of the time. Holding his arm around his neck with one hand and hoisting him by the waist with his other, Doyle set off up the beach towards the one or two pin points of light from the township of Gillen a few hundred yards up the hill.

After somehow negotiating a burn and a stile over a wire fence, they made their way up an enclosed strip of grazing to the nearest building, sheep sulkily getting out of their path as they went. It was a small prefab holiday cottage – obvious from the neatness of the paintwork and lack of crofting junk lying about the place – and all the lights were out. After banging on the door with no success, Doyle left his father slumped there and jogged round the house, banging on windows as he went. Still nothing. Not that that was going to stop him. Now shivering violently himself, he picked up a rock and tapped in one of the small panes of the half glazed panelled door.

From the collection of boots and walking sticks he tripped over just inside it was obvious the place was currently rented. Doyle called out but got no response from holidaymakers presumably still out for the evening so he flicked on the light and pulled his father inside. He seemed to remember reading somewhere that a hot shower or bath wasn't the best idea for hypothermia sufferers – something about providing too much of a shock to the system. So he took him into the twin bedroom, stripped off his outer, soaked clothes and, laying him on a bed, carefully wrapped him in the duvet and blankets from both beds. Then he went looking for the phone. The cottage consisted of that bedroom, a bathroom and an open plan living/diner – if you could call 20ft square 'open plan'. It didn't therefore take Doyle long to realise this was one of those basic 'get away from it all' cottages. There was no phone.

Doyle was now shuddering so much he couldn't even swear at his bad luck without risking biting his tongue off. He felt cold right to his core. If he had a pilot light, it was out. He went to the front windows and stood, shaking like an alky on day three of an ill-advised de-tox, and checked the road. The nearest neighbour, at least one he could see with a light on, was about a quarter of a mile away down the road towards Geary. Every instinct he had demanded he ignore his condition, open the door and get to a phone. But the detatchment that allowed him to make that call was also registering the fact he could hardly stand, his limbs were convulsing and his head bobbed uncontrollably. It also noted that this indecison wasn't helping. He went back to the bedroom to check on his father. Remarkably in just a few minutes his breathing and pulse had picked up from the worryingly slow rate it had fallen to, his skin felt warmer to the touch – or maybe it was just that anything felt warmer than Doyle at that moment. He made his decision.

Doyle all but fell into the bathroom. He pulled the power cord for the shower and set the water to as luke warm a setting as he could face then set about getting his clothes off. Between the shakes and the sodden, brine-hardened, shit-encrusted state his clothes had gotten into it took forever to strip and get under the jet of water. He was two phone conversations away from the end of all this – one to get an ambulance, the other to get the police. He had a witness, and more besides. If that wasn't reason enough to hurry, he still felt chilled to his very core. But he may be suffering from mild hypothermia himself. He had to wait. Doyle stood in water that was barely room temperature for several minutes before he slowly, only very slowly, he began to turn up the temperature of the water.

Fully half an hour later and feeling almost human again, Doyle stepped from a roasting hot shower and viewed the prospects of putting on his cold, wet, smelly clothes with distaste. His old man was mumbling in his sleep when he got back to the bedroom – which he took to be a good sign – while the wardrobe revealed even more good news: some decent men's clothing about Doyle's size. He dressed in a blue Ralph Lauren shirt over a pair of chinos and had just pulled on his own boots over a pair of fresh socks when something in the shadows at the foot of the wardrobe caught his eye.

At that very moment, he heard the sound of a car turn into the gravel driveway. The light from its headlamps flashed across the room and lit the back of the wardrobe … where Doyle could see two pairs of matching pristine white Reebok trainers, matching blue Hilfiger windcheaters hanging on the rail above.

26

He expected Moe and Curly to be wary; the lights were on
and there was a hole in their front door. But he didn't
expect it to be the wee baldy one who came in first.

There was no call, just a lapse of about two minutes
between the sound of car doors being closed behind them
and the first sign of movement. It was the top of the guy's
head bobbing up in the bottom left corner of the living
room window through the thin curtain. The front door
eased back and Doyle heard slow careful footsteps in the
small hallway. He sat in an armchair, now with one of
Moe's jackets on, hands in pockets, and smiled a welcome
as the big ugly head on narrow shoulders oosed round the
edge of the open door.

'Come in. Make yourself at home,' he said brightly.

'You!'

The swimmy eyes at first cautious, frowned and then
creased in the corners as a frog-like grin smeared across his
face. He walked into the middle of the room then stopped

abruptly as Doyle produced something else he'd found in the wardrobe. It had been a long time since he'd done that series on Albanian gangster families in London and their weapons of choice, but he still remembered the Glock pistol that had been waved under his nose for a laugh – and how it had been loaded and cocked for an even bigger one.

Doyle flicked off the safety catch and pulled the top of the barrel back to chamber a round. 'Don't make the mistake of thinking I don't know what I'm doing,' he said pointing it vaguely in his direction.

If he was honest, his show of bravura didn't have nearly the humbling effect Doyle had hoped for. And he soon found out why. Moe walked in and was, if anything, even less impressed that Doyle was holding a gun. No doubt that had something to do with the fact he had one of his own. And it's barrel was rammed into the underside of Holly's jaw.

'Ah, right. Fair enough.' Doyle turned the Glock towards the ceiling then laid it carefully on the carpet beside the chair. As Curly bustled over and picked it up, Doyle and Holly exchanged looks that conveyed a thousand things, and none. She was dressed as before – the thin linen suit now a forlorn reminder that, a long long time ago, it had once been a warm day. Now, it was hard to tell whether it was the cold or fear that was making her visibly shake.

'Up,' said Curly.

When Doyle stood he towered over him and he backed off. Moe looked Doyle up and down and scowled. He spat out something in his own language and Curly translated. 'Why you … his clothes?'

'Hey, the man's a style icon. I'm getting the pudding bowl haircut next week.'

Curly didn't understand but clearly decided something wasn't right and left the room to investigate. Moe took the gun from Holly's neck and threw her onto the couch under the window. Then he moved further into the room, gestured Doyle to join her and took up a position where he could easily cover them both. It was all the time it took for Curly to come back and begin a long and intense conversation with his colleague which no doubt featured the Serbo Croat words for 'shower', 'stink' and 'there's an old man in your bed'.

Doyle felt Holly's hand move to his on the couch and he returned her fierce squeeze with what he hoped was a reassuring amount of pressure. They both kept staring straight ahead at the guns, one of which throughout the animated exchange, always still seemed to be pointing in their direction. At one point, Curly took out his mobile phone but was clearly not getting a signal. Doyle had a thought. And the more he thought it, the less he liked it.

'What kind of car did you come in?' he whispered.

'I don't know,' she replied, trying not to move her lips. 'Why?'

'Small silver hatchback?'

'I think so, yes.'

'Shit.'

Moe and Curly had a problem – and Doyle did not like their options for solving it.

He had to assume they were back on the island to oversee the latest exchange of waste for drugs and, who knows, perhaps another playmate for Lytton's dogs. They would have been informed of the day's events – by Adam no doubt (Doyle could feel the back of his head still throbbing) – and decided it was time for their usual belt and braces approach, to hell with what Carew thought was necessary. In hindsight, Doyle's attempt at a misdirect in Knott House's drawing room earlier in the evening had always been doomed. Carew may or may not have bought his 'lone crusader' routine but, even if Moe and Curly had been there, they wouldn't have; Holly was already in their sights. Doyle's old man undoubtedly told them, with or without persuasion, that she had been with him when they'd first called at his house, and Lytton would have told them she was at Knott House to take the pictures for the magazine piece. In fact, Holly had probably already been lifted even as Doyle was talking.

What now? Their original plan would have been to make sure Holly was involved in the exchange at the fish farm before presumably legging it over the Skye Bridge with their own consignment in the car's fuel tank or head rests as usual. Doyle's efforts had still only produced the possibility of exposure; Carew's lock down of Knott House and, after the night's shipment, the fish farm, was still only precautionary. And Moe and Curly had a good thing going here, earning money every which way up. If the thing had been definitely going down the toilet, the Croats would be pulling out for good – and a damned sight less bothered about leaving dead bodies lying around a holiday cottage. No, they would want to employ the tried and tested method of doing the messy stuff far out at sea. But with just a hatchback at their disposal and three people to deal with …

The debate ended and the pair nodded at each other in silent agreement. Moe made to leave the room and Doyle stood up.

'Sit!' shouted Curly.

'No. You can't – ,'

'I am saying down!' he raised the gun to level with Doyle's forehead.

'Shoot, ya wee bastard. Go on, fucking shoot me!' Doyle took a step forward.

Moe paused at the door and his face cracked open to show his tombstone teeth in a monstrous grin.

'Dan!' Holly screamed at his back. 'What is it – what's going on?'

Doyle turned his head and said, 'They're going to – ,'

***

'He what?'

'Fell.'

The sitting room at Knott House had an end of party feel about it. The fading fire was losing the battle against the chill of the night, drink had long since morphed from fortifying refresher to sticky-mouthed duller of the senses, and everyone was more tired than they were willing to admit.

Adam's tone had run the boundaries of respectful pretty close for as long as Chloe had employed him. Now he had at least one foot in insolent. She calmed herself and played along.

'How? Where?'

'On the stairs down to the cellar. He's out cold.'

The embers of the last big pine log of the night were glowing ever weaker but Chloe moved them around with the poker nonetheless.

'And he's safely tucked up in the recovery position, of course.'

'Of course.'

Chloe put the poker down and turned to face the room. 'Geoffrey. It's very late and you've had a long day.'

Lytton, who'd barely moved from his seat by the window in two hours, didn't need a second bidding. He mumbled a goodnight and left without so much as a glance at the other two in the room. Chloe sat and motioned for Adam to do likewise.

'I know you don't think me a fool, Adam, so I can only guess there is some point to this charade. Please tell me there is and I haven't been employing a complete idiot these past three years.'

Adam tilted his head sort of diagonally. It was neither a nod nor a gesture of defiance. 'I take care of business, Chloe. That's what you hired me to do. I have taken the view for some time that there are aspects of that business you don't want or need to know about.' He crossed his legs. A normal enough thing to do in most circumstances. Not these.

'I see.' She pinched the top of her nose. It had indeed been a long day. She was tired, a little woozy from the gin and didn't doubt her make up wasn't at its sharpest nor her hair exactly as she would've liked. She was not feeling at her imperious best. But, then, she didn't need to.

'It's my fault, I know,' she said quietly. 'I suppose I've been too distracted by the filming and publicity over the last year or so. You've taken on more of a burden and I've not appreciated that.'

'It's not the burden, Chloe. It's the method. You require security, certainty – and yet you choose not to sanction the one guarantor of that. Curious.'

She didn't need to yawn but she made herself do so anyway. 'Do you believe in magic?' she asked, smacking her lips at the finish.

He didn't answer, just knitted his brow.

'No, I didn't think you would. Card tricks, illusions. It's not magic, is it? It's sleight of hand, misdirection. The magician can get on with the serious business of palming cards or hiding rabbits because his audience's attention is elsewhere, following a hand gesture perhaps or looking at the tart in the sequined bathing suit.'

Chloe's voice dropped even further. 'I'm a magician, Adam. I have created the illusion of, if I may misquote, the acceptable face of capitalism. I make money from property and delicatessens and all points in between. I have my face on the TV and write books about how to make your first million for cretins who would struggle to make the minimum wage. And all the while I am busy behind the misdirection securing even greater commercial advantage, making even more money. Why do you suppose I can do that? What's the trick?'

Adam's veneer was looking a little lacquered. His continued lack of expression could almost be imagined as a means of ensuring nothing cracked. He also continued to say nothing.

'It's all to do with the quality of the misdirection,' she answered her own question. 'It's about show over reality, image over substance. We both know how I go about my business. I have always taken a, ah, purest approach to competition and market forces. But I can only do that while everyone is looking the other way. One more question,' – still soft – 'what do you suppose would be most likely to cause people to question what they were seeing? What would ruin the illusion?'

This time she left it hanging in the air. Adam, no doubt concerned his continued silence would only appear weak, opened his mouth to speak – but only got as far as an intake of breath.

'A dead fucking body!' Chloe spat.

She stood again and Adam uncrossed his legs.

'Dan Doyle was right – I am not a killer. Why? Because people are picky that way – nothing gets their attention like bodies or even the lack of them.' She raised her voice still further. 'The mafia kill because they can afford to because they don't have a legitimate corporate facade to maintain. I do.'

'I –,'

'You? Who the fuck are you? I'll tell you, Adam, since you seem to have forgotten: you're my employee. I don't kill people because I don't have to – I control them. Do you think I don't control my employees – you? I know about your cosy relationship with the Croatians because I know about your cocaine habit. I know who you screwed to get far enough up Erik Vandepear's organisation to catch my eye, I know about the boyfriend in Chelsea and the joint savings account you have in Banque de Montagrier in Basle. I know in which nursing home in Enfield you dumped your invalid yet perfectly sentient mother. Adam, I know the home telephone number of your GP. So don't sit there and presume to tell me what I should or should not do or how I should run my affairs.'

Adam sat motionless save for a bead of sweat that made it's way down his temple, under his chin and, running onto the collar of his shirt, stained it dark.

'Now, let us hope for all our sakes your presumption hasn't cost us,' Chloe walked towards the door. 'Make damn sure Doyle's body – and that of anyone else you and your Balkan pals have slaughtered are quietly, cleanly and permanently put out of reach. And I want everything spotless by the time I get up. So get the men together and ready to deal with the fish farm as soon as that consignment goes tonight. Oh, and Adam,'

He turned to look at her at the door.

'You're on a warning.'

27

It was the cattle grid that roused him. He came to in a jostling, bumpy world, his head swaying loosely on his shoulders, nausea once more rising in his craw. Something was soft and warm to his right, something cold and unyielding on the left. Doyle blinked hard a few times and painfully lifted his head from his chest. The first thing he saw was Moe's gaping maw just inches from his face.

He was leaning over from the front seat, gun in hand, and was clearly having a whale of a time. The hard thing on the left was the side of the car, the soft thing, Holly. Even in the half light she looked bloody awful – strain was pulling at her, dragging and stretching her skin into a distorted version of her face, her eyes fierce and fearful beneath her brow. He had to guess from the way she looked at him he wasn't doing any better.

'Are you OK?' she asked.

His tongue felt fat and furry in his mouth and it took him a while to work up enough spit to talk. 'My dad. Have you seen my dad?'

Holly looked confused for a moment and then her face sagged as it seemed she connected Doyle's question to his behaviour in the cottage. She looked at Moe and her horrified expression was all the answer Doyle needed. Holly hadn't known his father was in the other room nor, therefore, that Moe had gone in there to kill him. There would have been no gunshot because he was just a frail old comatose man in a bed, his head resting on what no doubt became the means of his death.

Doyle turned away from Holly and Moe's gloating gurn and stared out the window. It was an occasion, he knew, to feel something and, for a moment, he tried. He tried sorrow, guilt, remorse at never having patched things up. But none of those fitted. Anger did. But even that would have to wait because right now he was noticing two important things: neither he nor Holly was bound in any way – presumably they simply didn't have any rope or tape to hand – and they were not heading for the jetty. Their headlights were off and Curly was carefully picking his way along a forest track, avoiding the bigger rocks and pot holes in their path. Doyle swivelled his head around but couldn't see anything distinctive, just blocks of conifers, some open patches of felled wood.

Once again, Doyle put himself in their place and worked out their options. They couldn't contact anyone at Knott House and the fish farm, they now knew, wasn't secure. Holly, Doyle and his father's body would still be going on a short sea voyage, he was certain of that, but it seemed the Croats were determined to make sure of their total co-operation before even setting foot on the jetty. They were heading for a killing ground.

After perhaps half a mile, Curly put the lights on and it narrowed the field of vision. Now everything but the fan of light over the track in front was black and invisible. He took a left turn and moved deeper into the forest. There was a short exchange between them and he swung the car round to face the wall of trees and stopped. He did not cut the engine – they were not going to muck about. Curly got out and pushed the seat forward to let Holly out, the Glock already in his hand.

There had been just one pistol in the wardrobe and Doyle now guessed it had been the only one in the cottage. Why else would they have assumed he was no longer armed at all – why else had they not bothered to frisk him? As Doyle adjusted his position on the back seat he felt his father's knife in the jacket pocket. Moe was now also out of the car and pulling the seat forward in front of Doyle. Holly leaned into him and tried to wrap her arm through his. He could feel her shaking violently.

'Sshh, now,' he whispered in her ear. 'It's going to be alright. Trust me.'

Both gunmen were now shouting at them to get out of the car, Curly shining a torch in Holly's ghostly white face. Gently Doyle took her arm from his. 'All I need you to do is stay exactly where you are.'

Curly pulled the driver's seat forward and screamed all the louder at her, but she wedged her feet and took a firm grip of the armrest.

Doyle gave her an encouraging smile and had just managed to get his right hand to the jacket pocket when Moe reached in, grabbed him and pulled him forcefully from the seat. Holly screamed as Doyle left her but he called out, 'Just stay put Holly. Do not move.'

In that instant, Doyle got some purchase with his left foot on the ground, stopped resisting the pull and launched himself at Moe, at the same time pulling the knife from his pocket. His head hit the big guy's chest as he swung his arm over and stabbed as hard he could. With barely a grunt in discomfort, Moe staggered back and fell, the knife buried up to the hilt in his left shoulder. For a moment that felt like an eternity, Doyle was aware of everything round about him: Curly and Holly screaming at each other on the far side of the car, Moe lying in the beam from the headlamps juggling with his gun while trying to pull the knife from his shoulder ... and Doyle standing there with no weapon doing nothing at all.

Even with a knife in him and on the deck, Moe represented a bigger threat that Curly. So Doyle turned and rolled himself over the bonnet to land on his feet on the other side of the car. Now there was just the door between him and the wee guy who was in a tug of war with a snarling Holly wedged in the back seat. Doyle kicked the door which slammed into Curly, knocking him off balance. He ran round and grabbed him round the shoulders, pinning his arms to his side. But he should've known it wasn't going to be that easy. Thick set with a low centre of gravity, Curly was no push over – literally. The two of them became locked in a strange, silent, dance. Doyle managed to wheel him away from the door and at that moment a shot exploded in the night.

It was the noise that was most shocking. Doyle's ears whined and he wondered if he'd been hit but just hadn't registered it yet. Then he felt Curly sag in his grip. In the next second he was too heavy to hold and Doyle let him fall to the ground. Blinded by the headlights, Moe could only have seen Doyle's taller silhouette beyond them.

Doyle heard Moe scramble to get back on his feet and he shouted for Holly to get out of the car. He ducked and picked up the torch but there was no sign of the gun. Had Curly fallen on it, was it under the car? They did not have the seconds it would take to find out

'The trees – go!' he shouted and clicked off the torch.

Holly ran from the car, leapt the ditch and sprinted into the gloom of the forest, Doyle right on her tail. Another shot rang out and a tree trunk beside Doyle's head burst apart and sent bark and wood spinning off into the darkness. A few yards on, Holly paused to kick off the heels she was wearing and then took off at an impressive rate on bare feet over the pine needle-covered forest floor.

'Weave!' shouted Doyle.

Holly began darting left and right, moving like a slalom skier between gates. Doyle tried to plot her pattern and make the opposite moves. He could hear Moe give chase. He had no idea how far behind he was but wasn't going to turn round to find out and risk sprinting headlong into a tree trunk.

After a few hundred yards they burst out onto another track through the forest. Holly skidded to a painful halt on the gravel and, dancing on her skinned feet, she turned a wild, questioning stare at Doyle. He stopped beside her and turned a full 360 degrees, looking at the sky, the tree tops and the road.

'Jesus, Dan! Does it matter?' she panted.

'This way,' and he led her on a diagonal across the road, over a ditch and back into the trees. No sooner had they passed the first tree trunk than another shot split the air and Holly cried out in pain.

'Holly!'

She was hopping to a halt. 'It's my foot … he got my foot.'

He could see nothing in the darkness. 'How bad?'

She put her foot down and winced. 'I think he nicked it. I'll try.'

And she did but her limp was nowhere near fast enough.

'On my back – quick!'

Holly jumped on Doyle's back and he set off on a lumbering run even as he could hear Moe's footsteps on the gravel behind them. Holly gripped tightly around his neck as he ran. She was light enough but this was still taking a toll – and Moe would be gaining with every step. Only a few hundred yards further on, he fell heavily to his knees. As he tried to pull himself back up against a tree Holly slid off his back.

'Let me try again,' she said.

'No,' Doyle was gasping for air. 'This … way.' He took her hand and led her limping around in a semi-circle until they reached two particularly broad trunks. He leant her against one and, a few paces to the right, placed himself behind the other.

'But – ,' she stopped as Doyle raised his hand. They heard crashing footfalls frighteningly close and then they stopped dead. All Doyle could hear was his panting breath. Holly could obviously hear it too and he saw her wave at him to shut up. Then the footsteps began again, only this time they were walking, not running.

Doyle took one deep breath and stepped out from behind the tree. Even in the half light he could see Moe's shoulders heaving – one of them, astonishingly, still with the knife sticking out of it.

'Dan!' Holly hissed. 'What the hell are you doing?'

'Stay there,' he said, lifting his arm out to the side and looking straight ahead. Holly peered round the side of the tree. Moe was walking ever closer, now maybe only 30 paces away. Doyle saw him drop the gun on the ground, reach up and pull the knife from his shoulder with no expression of pain whatsoever. He hefted it in his hand and nodded approvingly, clearly relishing the damage he was about to inflict with it.

Doyle stood and waited. When Moe had covered almost half the ground between them, he took Curly's torch from his pocket and switched on. He trained the beam straight at Moe who stopped, dazzled. Then, squinting into the light and grinning that grotesque grin of his, he resumed his steady walk towards them. And then he disappeared.

Doyle heard a bone break and this time there was a cry of pain.

'What ... what just happened?' asked Holly.

'I'll show you.' Doyle took her hand again and walked her over to the edge of his old wolf trap. He shone the torch on Moe writhing in agony at the bottom. Somehow he managed to get to his feet but that was when his problem became apparent.

'Oh dear, that doesn't look right, does it?' said Doyle casually.

'Eech,' said Holly. 'I bet that smarts.'

Moe's right arm – the previously 'good' one – was flopping around uselessly and at an entirely unnatural angle from the elbow down. Round and round the base of the pit like a wounded, captured animal he stumbled, a stream of Serbo-Croat expletives pouring from his slavering mouth.

Doyle tutted. 'Language.'

He turned to Holly. 'I want to check something. It's not far.'

Taking Holly's arm around his shoulder, he led her the few paces to the edge of the trees overlooking the Beinn an Sguirr. The fish farm's lights could be seen far below. It was impossible to be certain from such a distance and in the dark, but Doyle thought he could see at least one vessel tied up at the large decking area, perhaps fumes or smoke coming from the hut. He looked at what turned out to be an empty wrist.

'Huh. Some bastard's nicked my watch. What time is it?'

Holly squinted at her's. 'After four ... quarter past.'

'How long was I out for back there?'

'An hour maybe. The small one kept watch on us while the other guy packed stuff up and loaded ... ' she tailed off.

'What?'

'I didn't know what it was at the time, Dan. I'm sorry. It – he – was all wrapped up in maybe a blanket, bin liners. I ... I think he was burying your father's body.'

'He went off in the car?'

'Yes.'

'No, he wasn't burying him. He was going to the jetty. That's Lytton's phoney fish farm you see out there and that's where we were all supposed to be going – dead or alive.'

They doubled back to the wolf trap where Moe was still pacing round and round in a tight, demented circle. Doyle stared at him blank faced then walked back to where the gun had been dropped. He pulled his hand inside the sleeve of the jacket, picked it up and went back to the pit, the gun held at his side. Moe stopped and they stared at each other for a long moment.

'Dan?' said Holly, nervously.

Doyle raised the pistol and the torch in unison and pointed both straight at Moe's head.

'Dan!'

Anger and pain turned to panic in Moe's face as he glanced left and right in a hopeless search for cover. He dashed to the other side of the pit and Doyle stepped around the edge to keep him in his sights. He cowered and Doyle lowered the gun's barrel to follow. Doyle was tired. He was more tired than he'd ever been in his life, than he ever thought it was possible to be. And he was empty, spent. The two lives he'd led had come to an end that night. Whatever tomorrow had to offer it was never going to be a continuation of today, of yesterday or any day before that. It would be … different. Only with his father's death did Doyle realise how ever-present he'd been in his life. The ogre of memories, the electric charge in his drive to succeed, now the old man was a hole in his future. There was a void in Moira MacLeod's future too, and that of Kevin Patterson's family. All the work of this man now at his mercy.

A voice. Holly's voice. It was soft, beseeching.

'Dan. Don't.'

Doyle blinked and peered through the fog of his exhaustion. He raised his aim to the side of the pit just above Moe's head and squeezed the trigger. And kept on squeezing – he emptied the magazine, 12 bullets slamming into the mud with Moe cowering beneath them. After the last shot, Moe raised his head. And Doyle caught him between the eyes with the empty gun.

He drew a deep breath. 'Right,' he said, turning to Holly. 'That's that done. Shall we?'

After bandaging Holly's heel with a strip torn off his – Moe's – shirt, they set off back the way they had come. Their progress was slow. Sometimes Holly was on Doyle's back, sometimes limping by his side, he holding her up by the waist. Eventually they could see the headlamps through the trees then hear the car engine still running.

Holly got herself into the front passenger seat as Doyle rolled Curly's body off into the ditch. He decided to leave the other gun where it was. He pushed the driver's seat back and got in beside her. Using the courtesy light, they examined her foot. It did not look good – a wound from her heel along the sole. It was bleeding badly and was caked in dirt.

'That's going to get seriously infected,' said Doyle. 'I can stop at the phone box next to my old man's croft and call an ambulance if you want but it will be quicker if we get you to hospital in Portree ourselves.'

'OK,' Holly was clearly in some pain. 'But what about the police?'

'We've got all the evidence we need and besides, we'll only manage a 999 call. Can you imagine how long it would take trying to explain this lot to some night shift numpty on the switchboard in Inverness? No, there's time enough for that. Let's get you fixed up first.'

Doyle turned the car around and headed down the track, his desire for speed having to be compromised by the need not to break the thing's fragile suspension on the boulder-strewn, pot-holed surface. At length, he rumbled back over the cattle grid on the edge of the township of Gillen and swung up to the left past his old school once more. He made good progress on the single track road after Halistra and Hallin with nothing coming in the opposite direction at that time of night but once on the main road to Portree, the little car's lack of speed was apparent. Holly had stopped responding to Doyle's attempt at distracting conversation and was now curled in a ball on the seat beside him. Among the things he'd taken from his own clothes in the cottage was his car keys ... and their route was going to take them past where he'd left it – the same layby as before just down the road from Knott House.

He screeched to a halt and used the remote to unlock it even before jumping from the VW. He opened both front passenger doors then picked up Holly. He was half way back to his own car when he became aware of movement through the trees. A man emerged from the shadows and walked onto the banking beside the layby. Then another and another. In a few seconds they were surrounded.

28

The first blueing of the darkness was underway in the eastern sky as Doyle and Holly were escorted down to the muddy back door of Knott House. Funny, he thought to himself, I never get to go in the front of this bloody place. They went in via the kitchen as usual, down the corridor, past the door to the cellar he never made it to, and eventually back into the drawing room. It was cold and smelled of ash.

Holly had just been put on one of the sofas when Carew came bustling in, a clearly over-wrought Lytton at her elbow. They were in dressing gowns – his exactly the kind of sturdy, old fashioned type you'd expect a man of his age living in a house with these draughts to wear, hers an incongruously soft pink affair. Between that and the lack of war paint she looked almost grandmotherly.

'But, but … ' Lytton was saying.

'Oh, shush Geoffrey for pity's sake!' snapped Carew. When she saw Doyle her face actually flushed with something like pleasure then, glancing around at the others – Holly and three big burly guys in boots and heavy jackets – her face clouded again.

'Not sure we need quite so much protection. Can I suggest at least two of these oafs have something more profitable to be doing?'

'Chloe,' said Lytton nervously, 'I don't think – ,'

'Alright, alright. So,' she turned brightly to Doyle. "We meet again' I think is the appropriate line.'

Doyle smiled back. 'Either that or 'Any last requests?'.'

'Oh, don't be so melodramatic. Your fate won't be that terminal despite,' she nodded a concession, 'some unfortunate recent incidents.'

'You misunderstand, Chloe. You're the one getting a last request.'

Carew had enough experience of Doyle by now for that to hit home. But it was just a flicker of doubt, a subliminal, fleeting hesitation. She drew herself up to her full 5ft in slippers, walked to the nearest sofa and sat.

'You really are entertaining,' she said. 'I may even miss you when you're out of my hair for good.'

'Chloe, I really must – ,'

'No you mustn't Geoffrey.'

The door was pushed a little further open and Adam walked in, still wearing his clothes from last night.

'Excellent,' said Chloe. 'As you … can … see …'

She tailed off, her mouth open, her eyes staring at Adam's wrists. They were handcuffed in front of him. A second behind him, an unfeasibly large, ginger hairy man walked in and, as usual with him, instantly made the room look smaller.

'Who … ,' she stood again. 'What is the meaning of this?'

She was good, thought Doyle. Despite the considerable shock she must have just had that question actually carried a little authority.

'Sergeant Sandy McNair. And this is an arrest,' the big guy paused. 'Several probably.'

Carew swung round the room. She looked at the men she must now be realising she hadn't actually seen before, the injured girl on the sofa, a smiling Doyle and an almost hysterical Lytton.

'These are not my men,' he whined. 'I've been trying to tell you, Chloe. I don't know who they are.'

She paused a beat and then said icily, 'They're police officers, Geoffrey. Am I right, sergeant?'

'Quite correct,' said Sandy.

Carew's face was already paling. Within seconds, she looked positively dead above the pink towelling.

'One mystery solved but another as yet unanswered.' Out of habit, perhaps, she walked to the fireplace despite the fact it was as cold there as anywhere else in the room. 'Why, I must ask, are they here? Arrest? Who and on what charge? Most importantly, of course, based on what–,'

'… *isotopes from radiotherapy, human tissue, swabs, nappies and the afore-mentioned attendant waste products,*' Carew was interrupted by her own recorded voice. '*And it all has to be categorised – hazardous, offensive, pharmacutical, sharps, hazardous sharps – and all disposed of in different ways with different middlemen leeching off our profits at every turn – .*'

Doyle clicked off the dictaphone he held in his hand.

It was the final straw. Carew's incomprehension, her final, total and complete loss of any semblance of control was as devastating as it was unprecedented, and it showed.

'There was always a chance you would manage to sterilise this place in time and, who knows, even the fish farm,' Doyle said. 'No doubt your lawyers would've had a stab at distancing you from your Balkan associates – one sadly no longer with us I'm afraid – and, if push came to shove, I'm sure you'd even find it in yourself to hang old Geoffrey here out to dry. But there's nothing like your own words to do the dirty on you, eh?'

'But you … '

'Switched it on when you thought I was switching it off. I'd poked the wee red LED out and it's a digital device – no whirring tapes to give the game away. It was on the sofa next to you and I just picked it up again when you weren't looking. Simples.'

Doyle's smug grin got little response from the rest of the room which suddenly seemed busy with it's own affairs. Sandy swiped the dictaphone from his hand as other cops manhandled Lytton and Carew while reading out their rights, Adam was sulking furiously and Holly was wrapping herself in a blanket and trying to lift her injured foot onto the arm of the couch. Doyle's face fell for a moment before he beamed again to himself.

'Well, I thought it was brilliant,' he said to no-one in particular.

EPILOGUE

Sandy had gotten back to Skye that night and tried to call Doyle to talk about the picture he'd sent. When he got no reply he spoke to Bob and was told he'd left much earlier in the evening. Doyle's landlady hadn't seen him since that afternoon and he was getting no reply from a number Bob had given him for Holly either. Since they'd left Bob's house seperately and at least half an hour apart he had to assume they weren't out somewhere together.

Suspecting Doyle was just the type to take matters into his own hands, Sandy drove out to Knott House. There he found Doyle's car in the layby and, led by the smell of burnt paraffin, the scorched earth around where the cage had stood – the holes for the wooden uprights a dead give away. It was also clear from the movement of men and vehicles around the place that something major was going down there and then. He called it in to his boss, persuaded him they had enough probable cause and within two hours, every spare hairy-arsed cop in the north west Highlands was piling up the road in unmarked vans.

News of the extraordinary goings on was broken the following day by the instantly renowned Skye News of

Sraid a' Bhanca, Portree – an agency which had just 24 hours earlier scooped its rivals with exclusive reports and photographs of a wild African big cat captured on the island. To the frustration of the wider media, however, many of the details, thought to be in Skye News's possession, had to remain unreported until the conclusion of legal proceedings as charges had been formally laid. Certain facts were, however, released by the authorities and provided enough material for endlessly repetitious reporting on rolling news channels such as BBC News 24 which, for once, had a rapt audience in The Isles Inn.

At Knott House, Waternish, Skye, home of Geoffrey Lytton (65), ex guards and owner of the 10,000 acre Suladale Estate, officers found 15 kilos of cocaine with a street value of around £6 million, plus small amounts of assorted uppers, downers and chill-outers. They were in a rather revolting Burberry sports bag belonging to one Adam Sturridge (32) of Walham Green London. The bag was in the boot of a Land Rover Discovery resgistered to Carew Holdings Ltd. This was something of a major issue for Mr Sturridge but an almost infinitesimally small matter for Chloe Carew considering what else she had on her plate.

The shock arrest of the diminutive national treasure was, of course, the headline news. The fact that a police spokesman would only confirm she had been detained and charged with offences under the Wildlife and Countryside Act (1981) as amended by the Nature Conservation (Scotland) Act 2004 did nothing to dampen the feverish speculation. Nor did the fact the spokesman admitted further charges could not be ruled out – those relating to ongoing investigations surrounding activities at Knott

House, a Skye fish farm, several Danbury Healthcare facilities in the East Midlands – oh, and Mozambique.

In other developments the police admitted were probably connected to the 'evolving' situation, a Volvo truck, also registered to Danbury Healthcare, was found torched behind a builder's yard in an industrial estate on the outskirts of Portree while a hut on the aforementioned fish farm in Loch Snizort was also just a charred shell.

The coastguard and Royal Navy confirmed they had been alerted by police in the early hours of the morning and, four hours after the arrests on Skye, a South African-registered freighter was boarded in the Irish Sea and its five-man crew of Nigerians and Kosovans taken into custody. On board was a cargo of highly toxic medical waste in unmarked containers. Coastguard and naval vessels were continuing to search for the body of Gerard Doyle (72) of Halistra, Waternish, Skye, who, it is alleged, was murdered by Drazan Vučemilović, a known drug traffiker Interpol had been trying to trace for some years.

As it turned out, he was found in a big hole in the ground in forest near Beinn an Sguirr. Police, acting on information received, attended said big hole and found Vučemilović suffering from dehydration, a knife wound and associated severe loss of blood, a shattered elbow and concussion. It still took six officers to rescue, restrain and arrest him. The body of a second man believed to be of Croatian origin was also found nearby. Unconfirmed reports suggest he had been killed with a gun found in the hole with Mr Vučemilović.

The police also added that they were re-opening the investigation into the sinking of the Morven II, a creel boat out of Uig, and the loss of its two-man crew.

A day later and in response to an unprecedented public response to the story, a spokesman for the Northern Constabulary said yes, the big pussy cat was doing fine, thank you.

***

'And you managed to keep the hacked voicemail out of it?' asked Bob.

'In my official statement, yeah,' said Doyle. 'Sandy took me aside at one point and placed a fist next to my chin. So obviously he knows now – off the record. But they're uncovering more stuff every day and he's pretty sure everything will stick without needing to dig too deeply into my end of things.'

Bob checked his watch. 'Looks like she's not going to make it after all, I'm sorry Dan. She's been acting a bit strange lately.'

'Lately?'

Bob laughed and finished his diet coke. Doyle tried to pay for the lunches but Fat Murdo, in an unnerving display of amiability wouldn't hear of it. They emerged from The Isles Inn to another cold but clear October day, the sun noticeably low in the sky, the melted ground frost giving the pavements a slick, just rained look.

It was a week later. Bob was well enough to resume at least part time work at Skye News and Doyle wanted no debate about his long term plans. He was back in his Hugo Boss suit and heading back to London.

'The new dosage is going OK, is it?' he asked as they walked to his car.

'Nyah … good and bad,' said Bob. 'I'm going for a piss five times a night – but my dick glows in the dark now so I don't need to put the light on.'

Doyle laughed and beeped his car doors open. 'It'll all be worth it. You let me know how you get on, alright?'

'Course.' Bob held the driver's door as Doyle slid off his suit jacket and hung it up behind the driver's seat. 'Dan. You sure this is what you want to do?'

'I'm sure.'

Bob nodded glumly. 'But … any time, eh? You know where we are and, well, with your old man gone you're a landowner up here now.'

Doyle smiled, 'Thanks, Bob. For everything.' The handshake that followed turned into a hug and then he was in the car and gone.

On the southern edge of town the road straightens out as it runs along the western shore of Loch Portree. Between the water's edge and the road is a long layby. At the far end of this sat a small red Alpha Romeo, a woman leaning against its bonnet. The sun caught her red curls and made them flicker and flame in the wind off the loch. She was digging her hands deep into the pockets of a heavy, dark green coat and shrugging down behind its upturned collar.

'Flat tyre, hen?' asked Doyle throwing on his jacket again and walking the few yards from where he'd pulled over.

Holly smiled briefly. 'I'm fine.'

He looked at her bandaged foot covered in a thick ski sock. 'I'm surprised they let you drive with that.'

'They don't. Apparently.'

She seemed content for a while to just look out over the loch to the slopes of Ben Tianavaig rising beyond it. Doyle did the same.

'Look, um, I'm sorry,' she said, still looking over the water. 'The job in Broadford ran on. I would only have just made the tail end of lunch.'

'And?'

She she drew a deep breath. 'And I know dad would have been trying to talk you into staying.'

'Only a little bit. Don't worry – as you can see, I'm still heading home.'

She turned and looked at him. 'Home?'

Doyle frowned, 'You know. Sort of. London.'

He had no idea what to expect from this encounter but her sudden look of sympathy was still a surprise – almost as much as her holding out her hand to take his.

'I can't tell you what you should do, Dan. But I think you would want me to be honest?'

'Fire away.'

'Skye News is too important to me. My father is and so is – now – this island. I just can't see how … I mean, it's not that … ,' She ran aground, lost for words.

Doyle smiled. 'It's OK, Holly, I know. All this Chloe Carew fuss will die down and you'll be back to recreation sub committees and the quayside price of fish – and that's exactly as it should be. I don't do that stuff.'

'No.'

'And you wouldn't be much use at it either if you were spending all your time in the office fighting the normal sexual urges of any red-blooded woman.'

Dropping his hand with a laugh, she glanced again out over the loch, before turning back almost shyly. 'So, are we OK?'

'We're fine. I wish you good luck, Holly. You deserve it.'

Her eyes reddened. She reached over and held him tightly. Then she whispered 'Thank you Dan Doyle,' in his ear, kissed him on the cheek and got into her car.

It took a shoulder to his front door before he could open it against the snagging of the junk mail behind it.

After an uncomfortable overnight with relatives in Glasgow (having to explain how his father had died and sleep on a burst couch) the second leg of his drive down the motorways of England had been as dreary as it ever was. He hadn't taken much with him to Skye and since Mrs Macbeth at the B&B had kindly washed and ironed anything he wasn't wearing, it didn't take him long to unpack. It was early evening, dark outside and, he was noticing, hellish noisy. He looked out the window, craning left and right but could see no particular disturbance or traffic incident. This was normal.

Music might help. Doyle liked to ration listening to his favourites, fearful of them growing stale. And the album he had to ration more than any other, of course, was Kind of Blue by Miles Davis. But right now, he decided, was definitely a Kind of Blue moment. He flicked the CD into the player, poured himself a large Talisker and settled down on his black leather sofa just as Davis's horn picked up the chords on 'So What' and did its best over the sound of London.

Home, he thought.

'So what,' he said out loud.

Printed in Great Britain
by Amazon